PAS DE DEUX

a dance for two

D1520158

LYNN TURNER

Cover art by Lynn Turner, with help from Nina St. Peter of Arisa Creative, Inc.

Edited by Alex Benkast and Vicki Mack.

IT'S SAID THE artist is born of a damaged soul…

Wilhelmina Allende is a prima ballerina. When tragedy turns her beloved Paris into a gilded cage, she jumps at the chance to work with one of the most prolific choreographers she's ever seen. But Zack's style is *way* out of her comfort zone. So is his teaching method. And his humor. And his everything. He's a charming little *connard*. It's hard not to like him. *Merde.* What has she gotten herself into?

Zachary Coen's first musical is opening on Broadway. Much like his life, it's anything but conventional, so hiring Mina is simply out of the question. She's too…classical. Too perfect. She's all wrong for the role. Then he meets her in person and sees her cracks. Her broken pieces. How unique and beautiful each one is. And he can't help but notice how her edges seem to fit his…perfectly.

Just when teaming up seems to be working, the monsters they've kept hidden threaten to rip it all apart.

Dedicated to every soul,
and to the art that reminds us all we have one.

"A pas de deux is a dialogue of love.
How can there be conversation
if one partner is dumb?"

                        -Rudolf Nureyev

CHAPTER ONE

Paris

PERSPIRATION COVERED WILHELMINA in layers. It was hot and sticky, slow-dripping down her spine, tightening her skin as she moved. Her sweatband was soaked, but still held up somehow. Rehearsal was in its sixth hour. Her feet screamed in pain and her pointe shoes were *ruined*, but her body was conditioned for this. She powered through it, because *Giselle* was the role of a lifetime. A ballerina could go her entire career and never get to play the coveted part. It was both theater and dance, a story of love, betrayal, vengeance, and forgiveness.

She and the other *Danseurs Étoiles* and the entire corps de ballet had just finished a run-through of Act Two on stage. It needed to be flawless. There would be no quirkiness in tomorrow night's performance because Madame Durand would not allow it.

Earlier that morning, in rehearsal of Act One, Madame obsessed over the acting and pantomime. In Act Two, she was critical of technique. Mina's stomach was pulled taut, sucked into her spine, her back arched, shoulders back.

"Take care to hold your pose *and* your expression,

Mina," Madame coached. She formed an effortless arabesque, her face stoic. "Tomorrow night, I want to see the same peace in your face as you land that I see when you're in the air."

Mina nodded and mirrored her body language.

"Beautiful," said Madame. "Sophie, watch those arms. Take your time when you bring them down. Giselle is already dead, my dear." And then louder. "*Again.*"

Sophie instantly became Myrtha, queen of the young ghost brides, moving like her muscles were made of water to summon Giselle from the grave. Then Mina was airborne in a lightning-quick series of jumps…

"*Ya-ta-ta, ya-ta-ta, ya-ta-ta!*" Madame fired off, clapping out the time.

Mina's right leg kicked out high and to the side with each jump, her body moving into an arabesque in mid-air on the final landing.

"*Yes!* You've got a *lovely* light jump. Let's use it more."

Mina stood center stage, hands on her hips, the sound of labored breathing echoing off the walls. Even after weeks of touring the world, *Giselle* continued to be more complex, more physically and emotionally demanding than any role she'd done before. Her body cried out for a chance to collapse, but if Madame commanded, she would charge up again.

"Take five."

Mina shuddered with relief.

"Where is Albrecht?" asked Madame.

Anton, the tall, lean soloist with dimples and eyes like whiskey seemed to materialize out of thin air.

"There you are. Prepare for the pas de deux with Giselle. The rest of you, *again!*"

Mina waited for the other dancers to clear the wings and then sat on the floor to gingerly untie the pointe shoe on her left foot.

"Oh, those are wrecked," Sophie said between quick puffs of air.

"I was hoping…they'd hold up until…tomorrow so I wouldn't have to…break in another pair…so soon." Mina worked to get her breathing under control.

"Your shoes have the shortest shelf life I've ever seen. Ballerinas. So… many…steps…" Sophie teased, doing little jetés between each word. She was too exhausted for anything else.

"Principal, Sophie," Mina said. "Same as you."

"*Not* the same. You're the only Ballerina here and everyone knows it. The rest of us are just 'ballet dancers.'"

Sophie was right. The hierarchy of the Paris Opera Ballet didn't include "prima ballerina" like the rest of the world, but the roles Mina landed spoke for themselves. There was no point in playing coy. She gently peeled the shoe and toe pad from her foot, wincing at her angry red toes. She felt a blister forming between her big and second toe, and her calluses would be tougher by morning.

"I almost miss dancing with the Willis." Mina sprayed Ambesol on her toes. "I was so desperate to be Giselle, do you remember? Two years in a row before I finally got to be the Queen. Last year, I started to think it would never happen." Replacing the toe pad, she slipped the shoe back on, securing the ribbon around her ankle.

"And now I'm Queen and *you*," Sophie said, handing Mina a coconut water, "are my bitch."

Madame Durand's voice cut through the air. "Giselle, Albrecht, *pas de deux!*"

❧

New York

The sights and smells and humanity of the city were what Zachary Coen missed most during his year away. It vibrated with energy that never died down. As if the city read his thoughts, a persistent rattling on the street below ripped his attention away from the television. He glanced at the fourth-story guest room clock and watched the minute hand creep past midnight, quietly ushering Wednesday morning in.

Sighing, he moved to shut the window against the obnoxious sound but stopped as the culprit came into view. A homeless man pushed a shopping cart down the street, the big black trash bag inside of it bursting with every material belonging he owned. The café at the corner was still open, and the humidity of late June carried the smell of coffee and day-old croissants with it through the open window. Zack pulled the cash from his wallet on the tv stand, balled it into a wad, and sent it out of the window just as footsteps sounded at the top of the stairs.

Reaching for the remote, he paused the audition footage he was half-heartedly watching and turned to greet the man who'd inspired his entire career.

"Why are you still working at this time of night?" Alex Verenich set a cup of hot tea down on the night stand. "You're conventionally attractive, relatively young, virile, etcetera. It's New York! When you aren't sleeping, you should be out charming the dress off some beautiful, eager young lady."

Zack grinned. "No time for debauchery, Alex. History wasn't made under a pretty lady's dress."

"Appropriately dramatic, if a little untrue. This is obviously your calling—May I?" Alex gestured at the reupholstered chair in the corner.

"You know you don't need to ask."

At sixty, Alex was wiry, the powerful muscles of his youth long shrunk, but he still moved with the grace of his glory days. Sitting down and crossing his long legs, he glanced at the television. "Still searching for your Camille?"

Zack nodded, sitting at the edge of the bed. "Every time I think I've narrowed it down, I change my mind again. I don't know…" He rubbed the back of his neck in irritation. "They're all beautiful. Perfect technique, incredible stamina…but something's missing. Something I can't seem to figure out-"

"A certain je ne sais quoi." Alex smiled. "I find it endlessly amusing that something so profound as to leave us tongue-tied is defined simply as, 'I don't know.'" He considered the image frozen on the television. "Céline Depardieu," he acknowledged appreciatively. "Quick feet, despite her height. She'd be able to keep up with that neoclassical stuff you've been doing in San Francisco that's got the world off its axis."

"Yeah, but we're a bad match for the pas de deux. We wouldn't fit together well, and the lifts-"

"Mmm." Alex folded his arms over his chest.

"I had high hopes for Anastasia Romanov—her technique is flawless. Her voice…is not." Zack pressed a button to rewind the footage. "What about Ruby Bertrand?"

"Fine, fine. She's lovely. She'll suit just fine."

Fine. A double-edged sword, and Zack knew the end Alex assigned to the word was blunt and without shine. "Don't string me along!" he said. "Who've you got?"

"A firebird. Brightest of them all. Constantly recreating herself, rising from the ashes. She's the jewel of the Palais Garnier."

Zack knew instantly who Alex had in mind. And no *way* was she right for this. "Absolutely not."

"Zachary! She's-"

"Willful. High-maintenance. Egocentric."

"Determined. Strong-minded. Reserved. Compelling actress. Physically, she's perfect. She'll fit you like a jigsaw. Stir the hearts of men…" He grinned. "*And* women."

Zack's brows hiked in reluctant agreement. He'd never seen Wilhelmina Allende in person, but given her superstar status, there was no escaping that high brow, those delicate cheekbones, and dark eyes that shone from the glossy covers of magazines. *The jewel of the Palais Garnier, indeed.* She *was* beautiful…But so were the others.

"She's an *Étoile*," Zack reminded him. "I've toured there, Alex. It's a bloodbath. I'm sure she didn't scrap her way into the coveted seventeen just to lower herself to American theater."

"She's as American as you and I. Moved to Paris to live with her mother at just eight years old. Trained at the Paris Opera Ballet School where ninety percent of dancers don't make it into the company. But *she* did. A black woman." He frowned. "It pains me to say it, but very few people beat those kinds of odds."

Zack shook his head, still not convinced. "What about the rumors, Alex? Or the fact that I'd have to *untrain* the equivalent of a black ops prima ballerina in a matter of *weeks*? I'm not interested in working with some prima donna."

"I'm accustomed to the mild neurosis of passionate artists, but fatigue and pride are making you blind, my friend.

This weekend is the final performance of her tour as *Giselle*. If you're as quick as I know you are, you'll ask her about the rumors yourself." He held Zack's gaze for a scolding moment, then moved on. "You've listed the reasons she isn't right, but I will convince you why she is with just *one*. The only reason that matters."

The quiet storm that shook Alex's tone drew Zack's eyes to his in silent question.

"One of the most interesting things I've ever read was written by Dan Brown," Alex said. "'Angels and Demons.' Have you heard of it?"

Zack frowned. Alex loved to wax philosophical. It's what endeared the dance legend to his pupils throughout the years, but this sidebar was hard to follow. "Of course."

Alex dropped his arms and leaned forward, his elbows resting on his knees, the forefinger and thumb of one hand pinching together to hold a small, invisible object. "In it, a seemingly inconsequential number of subatomic particles is kept in a tiny, indestructible glass case and locked away underground. It is so powerful, so devastating, that if released, could incinerate a radius spanning miles and miles."

"Alex-"

"*That* is Wilhelmina Allende."

❧

Paris, 42 hours later

Zack watched Wilhelmina and her partner move into position from the darkened balcony of the Palais Garnier. The pianist sent the melody up into the hot air to blend with the echo of their feet hitting the wooden floor. The choreographer studied them with hawk eyes. She chimed in about a drooping arm here, a dragging pace there. They were a burst of flowing arms and lifting legs, flying limbs and tilted heads.

The distinct scent of sweat filled the space, drifting up to where Zack sat. His own memories of performing in venues like this one were quick flashes in his mind, over-shadowed by the exquisite mass of sinew and bone that was Wilhelmina Allende - "Mina," the choreographer called her.

She wasn't what he expected. Graceful and precise, but with a subdued energy at rest that ignited the instant she moved. She looked younger than her twenty-eight years without stage makeup and bright lights. Her vulnerability stirred a protective instinct within him, but there was also an unmistakable sensuality simmering beneath her glisten-ing brown skin. The combination made him lean forward, absurdly trying to get closer.

He wasn't surprised that she nailed the first act. She didn't pace herself at all, throwing herself into her move-ments, the music absorbed into her muscles. Moving with power and immense control, none of the effort showed in her expression. Her billowy jetés and high, drifting pirou-ettes drew appreciative sounds from the few other specta-tors in the theater, but his expression was unmoved. He hadn't hopped a red-eye and submitted to highway rob-bery for Paris's tiniest hotel room to see what he could catch in fifteen seconds of audition footage. He'd come to see Act Two.

It was difficult to imagine her as a spirit being—she was far too arresting a presence—but she quashed his expec-tations with a performance of haunting other-worldliness. She looked every bit the whimsy spirit floating through the air. Her arms came over her head to execute her flawless arabesque, holding it for several seconds before her partner drew her close from behind for their pas de deux. Her partner's long, nimble fingers gripped her rib cage, the muscles of his arms rippling as he plucked her from her feet and lifted her into the air.

The competitive jealousy of a dancer ripped through Zack like a commercial airplane landing in his gut. The hairs of his neck prickled like chicken skin and his jaw was nailed shut. Mina was tirelessly gentle and forgiving, rising in her partner's arms as if weightless, taking heartbreaking possession of Giselle's affliction. She was a figurine atop a music box come to life. Though she wore yards of white chiffon and a shimmering headpiece, Zack conjured her in red, her hair free and feet bare. He knew from the rigid set of his bones and the blood wailing through his body that he'd found her. She was Camille, and he had to have her.

CHAPTER TWO

STAGE FRIGHT WAS nothing new to Mina. She'd accepted it for what it was and willed the nervous energy to go where it was needed…in her muscles and in her soul. And all the while, the ghost of a beautiful dancer with blue eyes and black hair kept her company, entertaining her with one of her favorite conversations from when they were nineteen. His thick French accent and boyish face gave his words a poetic quality, and she adored everything he had to say.

"*You're so reserved and shy, bichette. Like a lotus flower, always opening and closing your petals,*" Étienne teased.

Mina smiled at the memory, vaguely aware of Sophie pecking her cheek before hurrying off to finish dressing.

"*I like that you open them for me, but why the hell does an introvert become a ballerina?*" he asked.

"*Passion, I think.*"

"*Ooh, something romantic!*" He brushed her cheek with the back of his fingers. "*So beautiful. If I was a choreographer, I'd cast you only in romance-none of this tragedy you like so much.*" He dropped his hand. "*Alors, what does passion mean to a romantic?*"

She sighed wistfully. Talking about herself always made

her feel naked. But she was safe with Étienne, had always been since they were fourteen.

"Need," she finally answered. "A need to be seen. I… can do things on stage that I wouldn't dare try in life."

"Bullshit! You don't leave yourself backstage when you dance. In some ways, being up there is the greatest truth." He took her chin in his hand. "Never be dishonest."

The orchestral introduction heated up quickly, snatching Étienne away and making Mina's heart hammer from her place in the wings. Every dancer not already on stage stood in silence, mentally counting, conserving their breaths.

The curtain went up and Anton swept across the stage on feet as light as a hare's. He was skilled in the art of seducing audiences, and this audience was no different. In fact, the air hummed with more energy than usual because this was the final night to see *these* ballet stars play their iconic roles.

And star Anton was, boyish and beautiful. Every movement of his muscles was visible as he led the pantomime about a nobleman, already betrothed, who fell in love with a beautiful peasant girl.

Mina was given her signal, but she didn't need it. She looked out and down at the stage floor, battered and scarred from the feet of the hundreds of dancers who had come before. "Entrée de Giselle" began to play.

Never be dishonest…

When she looked up again, she was Giselle.

Alex was right.

Something happened when Mina took to the stage—some kind of surreal phenomenon where she sucked the energy from the air in the opera house and stowed it deep within her.

It built as Giselle blew kisses to Albrecht with artful movements of her hands…and as they skimmed sideways arm-in-arm in a series of gliding steps…and as they sat on a bench center stage for a game of "He loves me, he loves me not" with the petals of daisies. Only minutes passed, but there was no question that they were hopelessly in love.

Zack knew this ballet well. He'd been Albrecht himself, years ago, and he knew exactly how the first act would end. Leaning forward in his orchestra seat, his body was unconsciously primed for the moment when all that energy would ignite.

Giselle learned the truth of Albrecht's identity, and the tone darkened, a hush falling over the space. The audience was still, as if holding their breaths en masse. Giselle's despair only magnified her beauty. It flushed her skin, widened her eyes and deepened their depths for several heartbreaking seconds…

And then, finally, the energy combusted, burning away at all that beauty and naiveté. Innocence was lost.

The woman next to Zack wept, and if he'd had the capacity to be aware of anyone else in the room, he would have understood. Because he was caught up himself. Suddenly the aura about Mina that had made her seem so out of reach dissipated. She touched him when she danced, and it felt like he could touch her. His fingers flexed then, and without even thinking, he reached out his hand to trace the outline of her silhouette.

The theater in all its gilded grandeur was nothing more than a red velvet music box for her to dance in. A light sheen of sweat collected on her skin, making her glow beneath the light of the stunning chandelier. Just as Zack lowered his hand again, her body went limp, and Giselle was no more.

He nursed his drink during intermission in the grand foyer. Enchanted tourists walked about with their heads tilted back to marvel at the expansive hallways and towering pillars, marble balconies and ornate ceilings. Not a single square inch was left untouched by nineteenth century splendor, but Zack only glanced at it, still the willing captive of a most compelling ballerina.

"Zacharyyy! *Darling*!"

A voice that sounded like it'd been smoking unfiltered Camels and slinging drinks in casinos for thirty years echoed in the great hall. Zack didn't need to look for the owner of the voice, because the lady *always* made an entrance.

She stood on the landing of the solid marble grand staircase, where it split into four directions that seemed to lead into heaven. Her silvering hair was piled high, and the deep lines of her face were made more pronounced by the heavy-handed makeup on her cheeks. She was preposterously overdressed for the occasion, with two young attendants scrambling to gather the long train of her ball gown as she descended the stairs. When she finally swept her way to Zack, she raised a veiny hand for a kiss.

A few tourists gawked at her, but most people familiar with fine performing arts knew she was a fixture at theaters around the world-and she was *loaded*.

"Vera," Zack said with a charming smile. He pressed a kiss to her bony knuckles and released her hand. "Not surprised to see you at all, but it's a pleasure just the same."

She thwacked him in the arm with her folding silk fan. "Had I known you were coming, I would have reserved your seat next to mine."

He grinned. "Had I known I was coming, I'd have sought you out first."

"*Rogue!*" She narrowed her heavily-lined eyes at him in curiosity. "Walk with me."

He quickly set his glass on a passing server's tray and offered her his arm.

"French noblemen brought their wives to the Opera on Monday nights, their daughters on Wednesday nights, to be shown off up there." She pointed to the marble balconies above them. "On Friday nights, they brought their mistresses!"

Zack looked up, as if truly seeing his surroundings for the first time. He envisioned The Phantom of the Opera stalking the halls, easily imagined Parisian high society on display in style here, and Vera keeping them all on their toes. She wasn't pretentious at all, just trapped in an era long gone. "And on Saturday nights?"

"On Saturday…" She released his arm to meet him face-to-face. "…they come alone. To think. Or not to think. Perhaps, to fall in love."

He saw the quick flash in her eyes, and then he knew. "Alex got to you."

"Oh poo," she snapped, taking his arm again. "There are only *two* reasons a man like you flies halfway around the world at a moment's notice. Money or a woman. And since I'm already backing your production, I can only assume that you have the lovely Mina tapped for your Lady in Red."

The title of his life's blood rolled easily off her tongue, making him smile. He was re-imagining *La Dame aux Camélias*, one of his favorite love stories, for a more contemporary audience. The importance of casting the right woman to be the most desirable courtesan in Paris weighed heavily on his shoulders, and in his heart. He was as much a part of the piece as the words and music.

"Some coincidence, you being in Paris this weekend when *Anastasia* is playing in Moscow," he teased.

"*Fine*," she spat. "Alex may have called me. But it was a hell of a first act, Zachary. She has charisma, that one. If she can sing, I think we may have a hit on our hands."

He nodded. "I expected her to be technically flawless, but I'll admit…she has a command of the audience I haven't seen a dancer achieve single-handedly in some time."

The warning was given for patrons to return to their seats. Vera stopped again, openly studying Zack's face. "I haven't seen that kind of stage presence since *you* were Albrecht. You brought the male principal out of the shadow of the ballerina, and then you retired."

"I didn't retire. I can make an *impact* as a choreographer, make dance—*all* of theater-exciting for everyone."

"Yes, yes." She waved away his impassioned speech. "I'm not oblivious to the success of *Hamilton*, darling. I see the potential in seducing a younger—and more colorful—audience. But I selfishly look forward to seeing you come out of the shadows again."

He nodded once in gratitude, kissing her hand again.

"Ta-ta, Zachary," she threw over her shoulder, and swished away.

"Vera."

There was more passion in Mina's pas de deux with Sophie that night than any other, Giselle's forgiving nature a stunning contrast to Myrtha's bitterness. When, at last, Giselle's ghost saved Albrecht from the sinister snare of the Willis, a faith in love was restored that, if they'd danced it well (and

Mina knew they had), the audience had not even realized they'd lost.

The curtain fell at the end of the second act, and the corps gathered in the wings. Mina patted her face with a clean towel just before Sophie tugged at her arm and dragged her to center stage. She stood between Sophie and Anton as the curtain rose again. It remained so for fifteen minutes, the audience applauding and cheering, and Madame Durand leading the parade of dancers to the stage with hundreds of flowers.

The cocktail party after the show was held in the magnificent foyer, where a small orchestra played on the landing of the grand staircase. Zack knew it was as much a spectator sport as a celebration, the dancers wearing provocative evening attire so guests could admire their impressive physiques as they mingled about the space.

He tracked Mina's movements with his eyes, even as he was engaged by old acquaintances and fans. Dutifully, he thanked them for their congratulations on his recent Emmy award for his choreography on a popular televised dance competition. Fielding probing questions about what he was up to now, his eyes kept searching for her. He couldn't help it, really. It was impossible *not* to look at her.

Her white lamé gown shimmered when the light hit her a certain way, intensifying the alluring contrast with her smooth brown skin. The halter neck was high, held up by thin straps that went over her defined collar bone and disappeared behind her. It was fitted to her lean form so thoroughly that he could see her abs move when she laughed, the outline of two small, pert breasts. And her legs…

He hadn't thought to mourn the absence of the traditional tutu during the performance. It was one of Zack's favorite things, seeing the well-formed legs of ballerinas as they moved. But Giselle had been so pure, so innocent in her flowing garments that his mind hadn't even gone there.

But Mina was not Giselle.

Her legs went on forever, like they disappeared right into her waist. Even her feet were interesting—slim, arched impossibly high, and long for her height, and wrapped in satiny blue heels that clicked to their own beat. She walked like she had all the time in the world to get where she was going, like time slowed down for her, while everyone else hurried for fear of losing it. Yet, she arrived the same time they did. When she joined Madame Durand for a toast, he got a peek of her perfectly round, gorgeous ass. Her eyes were striking, wide and smoky and full of sincerity when she spoke.

"I feel very content tonight. I thought I'd feel sad, or nostalgic, but I woke up with such a sense of…fulfillment. Because I danced with the greatest company in the world, dancers I adore," she said, and kisses were blown to her from dancers throughout the space.

Someone near Zack groaned, and he grinned sympathetically. As if the gods were not satisfied with Mina's tempting body and beautiful face, they saw fit to torture her fellow mortals with a subtle French accent that belied her composure with sexiness that sizzled.

"I cherished every second." Her eyes glistened with tears. "We watched each other grow up and achieve our dreams. For eleven years, I *lived* this with you, and I'll never forget it. I hope it has given you as much joy as it has given to me. I love you. *Merci.*"

There were cheers and whistles, more kisses and laughter, and he watched her make her way around the room, until her expression started to betray its fatigue from her constant smiling, and she graciously excused herself.

The loggia outside the opera house was less crowded. Some tourists posed for photos before moving along, and enamored party-goers kissed between pillars. Mina took a deep breath, relieved for some relative solitude. The humid air wrapped its arms around her as she gazed out into the night lit by street lamps and passing cars.

What now? her mind tortured her on a constant loop. *The Royal Ballet? New York? Could I live in Russia?*

She'd received offers for contracts with them all, and even spots in American short series, but more options just made the decision more difficult. She buried her face in her hands.

Dieu, I wish you were here, ma moitié.

As soon as the thought left her, she sensed a presence that comforted her immediately. It was so familiar and yet…so eerily strange. Her body shivered like a whisper had run through it. Her pulse picked up. Her heart slammed once, then sank to her toes.

"Étienne?" she whispered into the night.

"Not quite," a deep, gentle voice answered instead.

It filtered into her dreamlike state, beckoning her back to the world of the living.

She looked spooked when she whipped her head around, and Zack hurried to set her at ease. "Whoa, it's okay. I'm-"

"Zachary Coen." Her eyes were sharp now, clear of whatever haze had just gripped her. "I know who you are. I'm so honored that you came."

It took him a moment to recover from the sound of his

name on her lips. Her English was softly accented, naturally husky, making it sound as if she'd uttered his name in passion after a few glasses of wine. He blinked away the tempting imagery to study her face, marveling at her transformation.

In a single evening, he'd seen her embody so many personalities. She was a slip of a girl as Giselle on stage…a charismatic celebrity who moved like a lynx in her white dress in the foyer…a skittish, vulnerable woman just seconds ago…and now…

She was regal, out of reach once again to the likes of common men. A sneaking suspicion he was the cause of her latest character quick-change ate at him.

"The honor is mine. You're an incredible performer." He stared at her openly, knowing she was accustomed to people sizing her up, gaping at her body. "Even now, you're performing."

Her smile evaporated. "Excuse me?"

There was something about her eyes, an intensity that made her instantly mysterious and compelling—like one of the Willis, luring unassuming men to their untimely deaths. It was thrilling, being so close, recognizing the danger at the last second when it was too late.

His heart pumped ferociously, but he didn't back away. "There was a chink in your armor back there. Figured you needed some air."

"I-don't know what you mean." She looked at him less politely then, as if her subconscious was picking up on the energy he emitted, telling her to put her guard up.

Interesting.

"It's okay," he said. "I know what it's like, all those eyes. It's one thing when you're on stage, but it gets a little overwhelming when you're trying to be yourself."

A myriad of expressions flitted across her face, letting him know he'd read her right, seen through her pretty shell to her rich, yolky soul. Her body visibly tensed, poised to flee.

"*Enchanté.*" She moved quickly to go around him and back into the building.

But he was faster, and he reached for her hand without thinking. "Zack."

"I-What?"

Her hand was warm, heating his fingers until they curled tighter around her hand like a reflex. She was so close, he could make out the complexity of color in her eyes, like shades of earth and gold on a painter's palette, expertly coaxed to the richest brown with the swirl of a brush. The longer he stared at her in silence, the farther the heat from her body traveled through his.

It made his palms itch.

It made his heart constrict.

The prospect of controlling so much passion excited him to the point of sweating, and his voice was gruff when he spoke again. "I didn't get to introduce myself before. It's Zack. Just Zack."

"Zack," she whispered.

The sound was like a shock, and he didn't even realize it the moment he released her hand. He stared after her for several minutes, then turned and walked away from the grand monument and disappeared into a taxi.

CHAPTER THREE

UNSEEN HANDS MOVED over Mina's body. They lifted her, and then she was drifting…up and down, up and down…in a never-ending wave. Smoothing over sensitive places no one had touched in a while. Reaching inside her to unlock the space she'd cordoned off, where no one had been for even longer. The closer the hands got to the lock, the faster the pulse behind it pounded, and then a voice replaced the hands.

Baritone. Rich and soft, like the harmony in a tender duet. It whispered in her ear, raising the downy hairs of her neck, coaxing the other voice in the song to a higher note, making it moan the melody out loud—startling Mina awake. She sat up in bed, her earbuds yanking from her ears, the pillow trapped between her thighs flying to the floor.

"*Merde,*" she cursed, trying to regulate her breathing.

Her body hummed, and her fingers moved down to apply pressure where her body still bloomed with the aftermath of release. She trembled, her toes curling, riding the wave once more.

She'd fallen asleep to an audio featurette about an

explosive contemporary dancer-turned-prolific choreographer. And woke up alone, humping her damned pillow.

Zack.

He'd wanted her to call him that, practically begged her in that deep, commanding tone, and with those darkly lashed eyes. She still felt their intensity on her face, a stare the color of the Mediterranean where its crystal-blue waters turned green at the shore. She'd felt connected to him even after their hands had stopped touching. Even now.

It was such an unusual reaction to meeting someone, so it was natural to want to investigate him. Completely normal to download the featurette…to immerse herself in that velvet voice as it played on repeat throughout the night…

Cursing again, she climbed from her bed. She stretched like a cat, removed the dampened, solitary scrap of clothing she wore, and went to start her shower.

∽

1:00 am, New York

"I see we're making a habit of this," Alex groaned, sinking into the chair.

Zack felt remorse, but there was no way in hell he was going back to bed. Not when Mina's sumptuous voice haunted his dreams, repeating his name over and over as he groped around for her in the dark. He was thirty-six years old, too fucking old for wet dreams.

"Not enough hours in a day," he mumbled, pausing the tape again. Flipping to a clean sheet in his notebook, he scribbled down more notes, then gave Alex his attention.

Alex was looking at the screen, where a ballerina was frozen in a mid-air pose that defied the laws of physics. Her right leg extended straight out in front of her, level with her waist, and her left leg mirrored it behind her. Her back arched so deeply her head nearly touched her calf, and her arms stretched overhead and behind her until she could have clasped her ankle in her hands. "Even after decades of dancing and teaching new generations the art of movement, it still amazes me the way dancers contort themselves in ways the human body shouldn't be capable of." He turned from the television. "I assume, since you're taking her apart frame-by-frame, that Miss Allende has agreed to be Lady Camille?"

Zack wasn't about to admit to blowing almost three grand on a flight to Paris, a hotel room and last-minute tickets to the ballet without so much as *mentioning* the part to Mina. Not in a million years. "I didn't get a chance to extend her an offer in person. She was swarmed all night and I had an early flight back."

*And besides…*He studied her impeccable posture. *She's all wrong for this. Completely wrong… Mostly wrong.*

Fuck.

"I see—*Oh, dear God…*" Alex cringed. "That means you'll be contacting her manager…?"

"Already taken care of."

Alex's brow ticked in curiosity.

"I sent a friend," Zack said.

"A friend?"

Zack shrugged. "She was in the neighborhood."

"*Oh.*" Alex grimaced, finally catching on. "Dear God."

⋘

Mina stood on the large, continuous balcony of her mother's upscale apartment in central Paris, gently towel-dry-ing the soft, curling ends of her thick hair as she looked out at the garden below. It wasn't exactly the lap of luxury, although she and her mother could both afford it now. But the historic Saint-Germain neighborhood was quieter than the flats she typically rented during the season in the lively Eleventh Arrondissement.

It's not that she didn't appreciate the eclectic people and places, but navigating the social scene was terrifying without Étienne's hilarious running commentary and effortless charm. She'd thought it would comfort her to be surrounded by their favorite haunts, and people who wouldn't immediately recognize her, but lately she felt like a timid guppy thrown into a sprawling tropical aquarium. She was relieved her lease was up.

"Madame, *please*!" her mother's voice rang out. "It's early. I realize your seniority affords you certain privileges where you come from, but-"

"Oh, don't be silly," a distinctive voice carried throughout the apartment. "It's not my age that makes me bold. It's my *money.*"

Mina left the balcony to quickly finish dressing and wrestle with her hair. By the time she joined her mother and her uninvited guest in the dining room, Mirielle Allende's courteous tone was losing its luster.

"I'm due at Christie's in an hour," she tried again. "In the interest of time-"

"There you are!" Vera ignored Mirielle now that the person she'd come to see had finally emerged. "You must know who I am?"

Mina hid her amusement at the woman's metallic gold headscarf—*or was it a turban?* She wore a velvet brocade jacket, minuscule penciled brows, and harsh red lip. It was as if she couldn't decide which forties fashion trend to wear and donned them all. *Enfin,* the woman was heiress to her late father's multibillion-dollar media conglomerate. She could wear whatever she wanted.

"Of course, Madame Tetley." Mina kissed Vera's pale cheeks. "I hope you're enjoying your time in *Paris*."

Vera Tetley wasn't known for social calls, or mundane niceties. "Listen, doll. I'm not getting any younger. I'm ready to make my own mark on Tetley Media Group." Sipping her tea, she left bright red smudges on the edge of Mirielle's delicate china. "My sources tell me you haven't renewed your contract, which is interesting, since Forbes lists you as the fourth-highest paid ballerina this year-"

"Madame, if you please," Mirielle cut in. "This is between my client and I."

"Of course it is." Vera did not look away from Mina. "Which is why I've called on you here. You haven't renewed, or signed a new contract, because nothing's jumping out at you and grabbing you by that pretty little throat."

Mirielle sucked her teeth in distaste, but Mina looked at Vera with interest. "And you have something that will... grab me?"

Vera smiled for the first time since her arrival. "The industry is pissing all over itself to find the next *Hamilton*. It's too dense to understand that the next big thing won't *copy* Hamilton's model, it'll evolve from it."

If it were possible to *see* a headache take physical form, it would look like Mirielle's expression. "We love Broadway as much as anyone, Madame," she said, "but I don't see-"

"*Hamilton* is Adam," Vera continued. "The first of his kind. A new era of theater will spring from his loins, and I have every intention of making sure the show I'm backing will be Eve."

Mina took a seat. The woman really was draining. "So I'm…*Eve*?"

"No, sweet girl. I won the bid to be the sole financier of an upcoming production written and directed by Zachary Coen."

The bottom fell out of Mina's stomach. She was very glad to be sitting down.

"Good heavens, my dear! You look like you've seen a ghost!"

"*Pardon,* I think I just need to eat." Mina felt Mirielle's eyes on her and reached for a piece of fruit from the center of the table.

Vera stretched out her hand at the same time, selecting an apple and turning it in her hand. "Coen's production will be Eve, and *you* will be the apple."

Mina saw her distorted reflection in the apple's waxy red surface, subtly aware of the irony of an old woman tempting her with a succulent piece of fruit. Vera's voice kept going and Mina processed everything in pieces. Broadway. *New York!* Zachary Coen. *Zack.* A musical? She could dance, but his choreography was…radical. And…*nom de Dieu*…she was no Audra McDonald.

It was at once terrifying and incredibly enticing.

"What do I have to do?"

"Mina…" Mirielle cautioned.

"Sing something for me, darling."

❧

"*Ooohhhh my Goooood,*" Sophie groaned in French.

"*Mmmmmm,*" Mina moaned at the same time.

26

Fresh from the Hammam, they still wore their terry cloth robes, their skin supple and damp. Their eyes rolled shut and they practically melted into their spa seats, sinking their feet into the warm sea salt foot bath. A few other patrons of the spa stared at them with amused faces.

"I have waited for this." Sophie lifted her head to look at their long-time pedicurist. He was a miracle-worker, and never balked at the sight of their battered feet. "Sorry, Guillaume. They're in bad shape this time. I could walk on nails with these puppies."

Guillaume smiled. "Don't worry, *choupinettes.* I love it when you two come to see me."

"I can't wait to wear open-toed shoes again," Mina said wistfully.

"So you shall," Guillaume assured her. "Soak. I'll be back in a little while."

"Okay, I'm *dying*," Sophie pounced when he'd gone. "Did you sell your soul to Cruella de Vil or what?"

"*Sophie!*"

"What? She looks like she devours human souls." Sophie sat up in mock alarm. "*Oh mon Dieu*, are you okay? Let me see your eyes."

Mina swatted her arm. "Will you *stop?* She was a little… overbearing…but-"

Sophie scoffed.

"Fine. She was scary. You should have seen *maman.*" Mina grinned. "She didn't even scold me about my clothes."

"Sweats are *not* appropriate street attire," Sophie parroted in Mirielle's austere tone.

"She couldn't get a word in! But for once, I was grateful for it."

Sobering, Sophie peered at Mina. "It must have been

something, if it silenced Queen Mother," she joked softly. "What is it, *chère?*"

"Broadway."

Sophie gasped.

"A modern adaptation of *La Dame aux Camélias*…"

"*Oh mon Dieu!*"

"And I do mean *moderne*."

"Whoa." Sophie fell back in her seat. "That's *way* out of my comfort zone."

"Mine, too. But it's such a rare opportunity, and I've been looking for something to…something that's-"

"Away."

Mina nodded. "The musical is called *Lady in Red*. Choreographed by Zachary Coen."

Sophie shot forward. "*Putain de bordel de merde!*"

"*SOPHIE!*" Mina burned with embarrassment, every eye in the space now trained on her.

Sophie was oblivious. "*Sleep orgasm guy?!*"

"*S'il te plaît*, I'm begging you…" Mina wanted to crawl from her skin.

The scandalized brunette finally looked around at their riveted audience and lowered her voice. "*Désolé,*" she repented sheepishly. "But *oh mon Dieu, Mina!*"

"I know."

Sophie leaned back again with a sinful grin. "The way he moves, oohhh, I bet he's *good*."

Mina knew *exactly* what she meant.

Zachary Coen was a wonderfully expressive dancer— he used his entire body to tell a story, like the words were trapped in his atoms, and only movement could draw them out. His proportions shouldn't allow him to be so extraordinarily elastic and quick. But he was. He could make great leaps, then continue in a lazy stride, like he'd merely taken a little hop. Unlike the partners she was accustomed to, his poses weren't showy, but clever. It was completely rational to wonder what that kind of…skill…was like in other ways, was it not?

She turned to mush in her chair. "I miss sex. Everything about it. I miss the sounds, the smell, the sweat—the feel of someone strong and heavy moving between my thighs."

There wasn't a man in Paris who wanted to date a woman he'd never see, and with her recent fame, casual liaisons were out of the question now.

Sophie blew a sympathetic breath. "So… aren't you the least bit curious?"

"Of course I am."

"Scared?"

"Shitless." Mina wiggled her toes. "Étienne used to say that's how you know you have to do it."

Sophie reached for her hand and squeezed just as Guillaume returned. "A *musical.* Not my cup of tea, but I'd endure a two-hour singing telegram for you, *chère.*"

"Oh, *merci,*" Mina deadpanned.

Sophie looked thoughtful. "*Enfin,* the piano and violin may have been failures, but you should thank Queen Mother for making you get voice lessons. Have you heard Monsieur Coen sing?"

"*Oui.*" Mina smiled conspiratorially. "I found some off-Broadway stuff on YouTube. He sounds like…*chaipas*… like, Hugh Jackman and Luke Evans had a baby."

Guillaume whistled appreciatively.

"*Damn.*" Sophie bit her lip. "And Cruella? She said yes?"

"I don't know yet, but she made me sing."

"*Ahaha!*" Sophie cackled. "What did you sing?"

Mina blushed furiously and even Guillaume stopped to stare at her.

He snapped his fingers. "Out with it, *choupinette*."

"I was put on the spot, *okay*? It was the first thing to come to mind…from my favorite movie when I was little…"

"'*FIEVEL GOES WEST?!*'" Sophie howled.

"I was *eight!*" Mina snapped.

"Hush," Guillaume said to Sophie. "I want to hear."

Straightening her spine, Mina took a deep breath and sang the first verse of "Somewhere Out There."

❧

"What do you think?" Zack asked Mrs. Perez, the vocal coach they'd tapped for the cause.

She, Zack and Alex had just watched Mina perform her…interesting…song choice on a tablet device. Vera's breathing was audible over the speakerphone as they awaited Mrs. Perez's expert assessment.

"Well, she's not winning any Grammys for that little show," she said frankly, "but I think she's a lovely lyrical alto. Rich and full at the bottom, lighter at the top. Good resonance. But most importantly, she's *loud*. Impressive, considering the French have a natural huskiness in their tones."

Zack looked at Alex, trying to quell his mounting excitement.

"That kind of chest voice is perfect for Camille," she concluded.

"I agree," Alex said. "Naturally sultry. Not trying too hard."

"Good." Vera clapped once. "The invitation to open the Tony Awards this year means people are dying to see what's under our skirts. I say we give them a peek! We've got our shiny ballerina and your ballsy choreography, Zachary. So, whet their appetites with the bawdiest number, and they'll be drooling at the box office come opening night."

Alex looked toward heaven in exasperation and then cocked a brow at Zack. "Can we do it in a few weeks?"

Zack raked his fingers through his hair. Honestly, he wasn't entirely confident. The rest of the *Lady in Red* cast had been selected weeks ago during workshops. After returning from Paris, he devised a plan that was completely batshit, but just might work.

If he split the cast into groups to rehearse with dance captains he hand-picked, his evenings would be free to work one-on-one with Mina. They had six weeks to prepare for previews, and less than two weeks of previews before opening night on Broadway.

"It's risky." He rubbed the new growth on his chin. "Her schedule will be grueling. I'm gonna need the first few weeks just to teach her technique and prep for the Tonys. The remaining three weeks, she'll have to play catch-up in rehearsals with the rest of the cast. But…I have a good feeling about her."

"She's got something I can work with," said Mrs. Perez. "I'll need to see her a few times a week to iron out any pitch issues, and help her with stamina, so her voice isn't cracking halfway through a performance. After that, I'll see her once a week like everyone else."

"That's what I like to hear," Vera croaked. "When does she need to be there?"

"*Yesterday*," Zack and Alex said at the same time.

"I'll see what I can do."

❧

New York was loud. Loud in the morning, loud in the afternoon, even overnight. Outside Mina's hotel in Times Square, it was a symphony of honking horns, Euro beats, and the never-ending stream of people going about their everyday lives. Paris was busy, too, but she'd never describe it as noisy. The offbeat soundtrack of the city made her feel…*alive.* After a few days, jet lag was finally wearing off, and she was beginning to get a feel for her surroundings.

The dance theater was less than a mile away, an easy jog to get her body temperature up each morning so her ankles wouldn't snap during warm-up class. The metro ran twenty-four seven, she remembered from her last visit, as did a smorgasbord of every kind of food establishment she could imagine. She was grateful, because she'd awakened *ravenous* at four in the morning the last two days.

Eventually she'd need to find someplace that didn't offer a days' worth of calories in a single serving. Most urgently—she glared at yet *another café* chain sign over-head—a good, *strong* espresso. Just before she was reduced to scratching herself in withdrawal, a friendly native (who *loved* her accent, by the way, where was she from?) directed her to a cafe on West Thirty-Eighth.

Her cell chimed, and she answered without checking the caller ID. "*Allô?*"

"*Ça va,* Mina," Alex's upbeat voice came over the line. "How are you settling in?"

"Oh, Monsieur Verenich!" She was slightly breathless from rushing across the crosswalk. Pedestrians, it seemed, were moving targets here. "*Ça va bien, merci.* So kind of you to pay for my hotel."

"Think nothing of it. Sorry to treat you like a nomad, but it's a temporary arrangement. Hopefully we'll find something more suitable in the coming weeks."

"It's no bother," she said. "Dancers are like nomads, I think."

He chuckled. "They are, indeed. Listen, don't be a stranger. If you're not doing anything this evening, why don't you drop by the summer intensive course I'm teaching? They're kids, and they'd get a kick out of meeting a famous ballerina."

Alex Verenich just asked me to "drop by."

"Of course." She tried to sound casual, digging for a pen in her enormous Chanel bag. It was her baby, a rare splurge that fit her entire life in it easily. "What is the address, *s'il vous plaît*?"

Mina hadn't been to Harlem since her father had taken her when she was a child. They'd seen *Cats* on Broadway, and then taken the train to eat at Sylvia's after. It was the latest she'd ever stayed out and was still one of her fondest memories. Much had changed since then, but much was still the same: the towering brick and mortar, bodegas on almost every corner, and the virtually uninterrupted sea of brown faces, one of which smiled warmly at her and pointed her in the right direction.

The dance theater was rife with nervous excitement. It was like it was airborne, bouncing from person-to-person as soon as Mina walked through the storied doors. She didn't need to ask where to go because she was recognized instantly, escorted by the gushing receptionist to the introductory pas de deux class Alex was teaching that evening.

She slipped in as quietly as possible, just in time to see

Alex demonstrate to a young man the proper hold for his partner's échappé.

"The left hand holds." Alex moved the teen's hand to its proper position on the girl's abdomen. "And the right pushes, gently at her back, helping her with the turn…Good!"

A few whispers had already made it around the studio, and Alex looked to where Mina stood in the rear of the space.

"Mina!" He walked toward her with a warm smile. "What's it been, ten years?"

"Almost exactly." Leaning in, she exchanged cheek kisses. "I was seventeen when I joined the Paris Opera Ballet, and meeting you is still one of the most exciting things that has ever happened to me."

"Well bon-*jour*," someone said in a cheeky tone.

"*Damn*, she's fine," someone else piped in.

"She looks smaller in person."

"She's foreign, not deaf, stupid."

"Don't say *foreign,* it's *rude, stupid.*"

Alex clapped: two loud, swift raps of his palms, to silence the peanut gallery, and then turned to Mina again. "Are you up for a few autographs?"

She smiled. "Of course."

Fielding fifteen minutes of questions ranging from *exactly* what it was French ballerinas ate in a day, to what it was like being one of only a few black ballerinas in one of the world's most prestigious companies, Mina was pleasantly overwhelmed. There was such an array of skin tones and body types in the room, something she hardly ever saw in her world, and that profound feeling of being alive came over her again.

She was posing for a final photo for an adoring fourteen-year-old girl's camera phone, when an eerie whisper sent cold through her body like a brisk autumn breeze. Her skin reacted, prickling as if exposed to the invisible current, and the camera flashed at the exact moment her face froze with anticipation. It was a feeling she hadn't experienced in… *How many days had it been?*

Eight. Eight days…

Hushed squeals and excited whispers preceded the voice she knew would come, and then it seemed to fill the space, carrying on every floating dust particle in the air.

Alex didn't mention he'd be here…

"Sorry I'm late." Zack's grin didn't seem apologetic at all. "But I see they've met our star."

The warmth in his tone somehow made his voice richer, and Mina had to turn around before she started to look as unhinged as she felt. Her gaze drifted to his face, and her lips parted at the sheer *manliness* of him. The dimly lit night outside of the Palais Garnier after her show had softened the face that seemed to be made completely of angles now. Midnight eyes sharpened to striking green, narrowing as they skimmed her face.

He was dressed simply, in fitted jeans that hugged his hips and hinted at the strength of his thighs. His T-shirt screamed from the effort of covering his biceps, stretching over the impressive muscles of his chest that arrowed down to his narrow waist. He looked like he kicked a ball across a field for a living, but there wasn't a soccer player alive who could contort himself the way Zachary Coen could.

"*Non, s'il vous plaît,*" she protested softly. "I think time will be the judge of that."

"Even so." He stepped forward to take her hand. "Welcome to New York."

His long fingers grazed the bare skin of her wrist beneath the sleeve of her cardigan, and she flushed, hoping he didn't feel her pulse pick up there.

"Well, how about an impromptu demonstration?" Alex suggested. "What better way to learn the beautiful complexity of the pas de deux than to see it done by two of the best ballet dancers in the world?"

Excited chatter exploded around the room.

Mina gasped. "I-I wasn't prepared to…I'm not dressed properly…my shoes…"

"It's fine," Alex said. "We'll keep it simple. *Swan Lake.* The grand pas de deux from Act Three."

It was politely worded, cheerfully phrased, but with the firm resolve of a seasoned professor, and Mina didn't protest further. She lifted her eyes to Zack's, but they were guarded, giving nothing away. Turning away, she removed her cardigan and slipped off her loafers. She wore only a tank top and leggings, but the air in the room felt stifling. Her heart was in her throat now, and she swallowed to chase it back down.

The students seemed to float back, making hardly a sound, waiting for Zack and Mina to get into position.

"From the attitudes derrière," Alex instructed. "And… *five, six, seven, eight…*"

Mina was Odile to Zack's Siegfried, the beautiful maiden the prince met in the forest. He looked transfixed as she encircled him in a repeating sequence of steps, beckoning him with sensual, fluid movements of her wrists and arms. She executed her pique turns as well as she could without her pointe shoes, and Siegfried gazed lovingly at her. Then, finally, she bent provocatively backward, and a pin drop could be heard as he moved close and clasped her waist.

His touch was light but firm, and she wanted to lean into it more, to feel his fingers press harder against her body. There was no music, just Alex's voice providing the count to music that was branded in her DNA.

They moved again, and Zack was behind her, his hands fanning out above her hips. Her hair was up, and his warm, measured breaths tickled the hairs at her nape. Mina gave into it. After all, she was an accomplished dancer. Acting was part of the job. It was *expected*. Shutting her eyes, she controlled her breathing and let the room disappear.

There was no need to think. They moved from the pirouette into the lift, his hands at her back, and the room spun upside down before he set her on her feet again. It felt like they'd done this countless times, synchronizing the next step…and the next…and the next.

Mina held out Odile's hand for a kiss, freezing as Zack's eyes caught and held hers. *Merde,* she was supposed to withdraw it coyly at the last moment, but her *stupide* hand lingered. Grinning wide, he took her fingers in his and brushed a kiss against her knuckles. She winced at her mistake, but his eyes were calm. Sure.

Trust me, they telepathed.

She might have imagined the gentle squeeze to her fingers, but then they were moving again. Curving his arm about her waist, he tipped her, her back arching deeply over his forearm. He held onto her like she weighed nothing. A beat passed. Then two. And three. He helped her up again.

He was so close, she could taste him, a hint of his soap and everywhere he'd been that day settling on the back of her tongue. His breath was in her ear, more labored now but steady. His hands still clung to her ribcage, his thumbs brushing the soft skin of her back. Pulling her close, her back to his chest, the short hairs of Siegfried's chin gently scratched Odile's cheek. A beat. Then two. And three. The whisper of their breaths together, the rapid beating of their hearts…

The silent music built to a climax, and Odile turned away, performing a series of high arabesques travelling backwards, as Siegfried gazed in awe. Finally, she was still, and he knelt at her feet in adoration.

Alex had stopped counting time. The studio was silent but for Zack and Mina's breaths, still but for the remnants of energy still crackling between them. Then the students broke into raucous applause, whistles and more cheers.

Mina's eyes were riveted to Zack's, which unmistakably said, *Well done.*

Alex lifted both brows in silent praise for the pair, who quickly returned to upright positions…a full three feet apart. "Twin souls with one body," he told his students. "That is what you will learn to be this summer."

Chapter Four

THE ENTIRE CAST and crew of *Lady in Red* gathered in the studio the following evening for the mixer. *Well, almost everyone.* Zack skimmed the room.

The Lady herself hadn't arrived, and it occurred to him that she was probably still on Paris time when a small group of dancers huddled around a laptop started shushing everyone. They hooked it up to the TV mounted in a corner and cranked the volume up.

The interviewer was thin and blonde, her features pinched but not cold. She spoke in French, but the subtitles were easy to read.

"I'm here with Mina Allende, the ballerina who caused quite a stir in the ballet world this week when she announced she would no longer be dancing with the Paris Opera Ballet."

The camera panned out to bring Mina into the frame. She looked like a movie star with her hair styled bone straight, wearing a sleeveless dress that looked like she'd been sewn into it, and makeup that expertly played up her arresting features. Especially her eyes. Even from behind her media-ready mask, they were wide-open windows to her soul, lending a vulnerability to her sexy persona he instantly forgot when her lips parted into a smile.

Some of the dancers nudged each other, and Zack grinned.

"*You've quickly sparked comparisons to another dynamic dancer, Sylvie Guillem, who left Paris for the Royal Ballet at just twenty-five years old,*" the interviewer continued. "*She found classical ballet too confining, once describing the Paris Opera boarding school as a prison she wanted to escape, even calling the teachers witches.*" She eyed Mina with expert pointedness. "*Is that how you feel, too?*"

If Mina was uncomfortable, she didn't show it. Her expression remained stoic and her posture was impeccable, her hands settled primly in her lap. She took her time with her answer, wetting her lips when she was ready:

"*I admire Sylvie so much, and I felt a kind of heartbreak when I learned that she was retiring. She said something once that has stuck with me since I first heard it, that having limits to push against is how you find out what you can do…that frightening yourself is how you grow.*"

The interviewer's thin brow rose at Mina's attempt at evasion, but she was determined to pick her bone. "*And you don't feel that you can grow here any longer.*"

The ballerina's high forehead creased. Suddenly, the interviewer had manipulated the tone to sound distinctly like "us versus them," and Zack was keenly aware that he was the ring leader of "them." He tensed in expectation of Mina's answer, so riveted, he didn't notice her when she walked in.

Mina was good at going unnoticed when she wanted to. All it took was a shift in her psyche and she affected a posture that was less regal, a gait less assuming. It probably helped that her hair was swept up in its typical bun, her face unadorned except for kohl around her eyes. Her clothes were deceptively understated, a skill she'd learned from her mother. She'd showered after her pointe class and thrown on the cropped black slacks, cream silk camisole and sling-back heels in hopes of making a good impression.

But it looked like the effort had been unnecessary. Hugging the wall, she observed everyone observing *her* on screen, and felt…relief. Perhaps this days-old interview could satisfy whatever curiosity anyone might have about her, and she could bypass the anxiety of talking about herself too much.

"Even paradise can feel like a cage to a bird if you clip its wings," she heard herself say. "I'm frightened for the first time in a long while, and there is something freeing about it."

Mina had done so many interviews that day that she couldn't even remember saying those words, but they held such naked honesty that she felt completely exposed. Then, the question she'd pushed from memory hit her right in her chest.

"Does this sudden move have anything to do with the tragic death of your long-rumored…friend, principal dancer Étienne Lemaire?"

Mina gasped, and suddenly every eye in the studio held her in its gaze.

Merde.

"Shit! Turn it off!" someone said.

A couple of people scrambled to shut down the interview, and several others migrated to where she stood to introduce themselves. It was sort of a blur. There was the assistant stage manager, musical director, costume designer

41

and makeup artist, members of the chorus line and so many others…Mina was sure she'd get their names and faces down eventually.

A man who looked like he'd stepped out of GQ Magazine presented himself with a bow. An *actual* bow. Mina stifled a snicker. It was quite good, really. He bent from his trim waist, his thumbs hooked into his suspenders into a near-perfect ninety-degree angle. He looked up at her with grinning black eyes and then stood upright again.

For a split second, it seemed strange to her that he'd dress so formally for no apparent reason in the month of June. He even wore a bowtie, like a young Fred Astaire with deep umber skin. When he opened his mouth to speak, she instantly understood.

"Harper Holloway at your service, Little Bird." He made fluttering motions with his hands. "Composer extraordinaire and *very* happy to make your acquaintance."

Charisma dripped from every word, and Mina couldn't help but smile at his clever name for her. He was obviously making light of the interview, trying to make her feel comfortable. And it was working.

"*Enchanté,*" she offered her hand.

He took it and kissed it, to her further amusement, and then the hairs rose on the back of her neck…

"Good stuff, Harp." Zack came to stand beside him. "I think you've made your point, you're a smooth son of a bitch."

Mina gasped, looking at Harper for any sign of offense, but the younger man just laughed and embraced Zack enthusiastically.

"Watch how smooth." He winked and spun on his heel, crossing to the other side of the room where the laptop was set up.

Mina would have kept her eyes trained on Harper (she *was* curious about the expensive looking equipment he was setting up) but they were distracted by the way Zack was moving toward her…The way his eyes trailed her open neckline and down her body…The way they came right back up again, pausing at her exposed throat, like he could see her pulse beating triple time. When he lifted his eyes to hers, she knew that he would kiss her.

Merde.

It happened so fast. His warm hand touched her naked shoulder in greeting. The breadth of his chest grew wider as he loomed over her, occupying her space. His face was so close, she could trace his tawny eyebrows with her tongue.

A tiny gasp escaped her at the thought.

What the hell? her subconscious snapped. *Pull yourself together!*

Enfin, she would have pulled herself together just fine, except his cheek grazed hers, gently scratching, and she sucked air in through her lips again.

It was just *la bise,* a friendly little peck on the sensitive skin where her ear met her cheek. But her face heated anyway, the microscopic hairs of her cheek stretching out to prolong the contact.

When he pulled away, her eyes were glued to his bottom lip. She still felt its pressure against the tip of her ear lobe. He cleared his throat and her eyes flew up to meet his dancing gaze.

Dieu, he heard me!

He was so polite, greeting her in the French custom, trying to make her feel welcome, and here she was behaving like *une idiote*. It was kiss, not a *kiss*. And it was their third time meeting in-person, so some familiarity was to be expected, *non*?

Of course. Back home, there'd have been *two* cheek kisses. *Bon Dieu.*

The way she was hyperventilating, two kisses would have killed her.

Don't be ridiculous.

She was a grown woman, not some swooning schoolgirl.

It's fine. He probably didn't hear me.

He'd heard her.

That first little intake of breath hardly registered in his brain. She could have been overwhelmed with meeting so many people at once, and Harper wasn't exactly subtle. But when he brought his lips to her cheek, his ear was positioned just right to hear it a second time. Uneven and sharp. It was just a whisper of sound, but it was loud and clear to his libido.

Zack knew women. And this one wanted him.

He wasn't gonna to do shit about it, either...no matter how much he was enjoying the way her eyelashes did that fluttery thing before she took a deep breath and stepped two feet away from him. She really should stop staring at his mouth.

Don't start, his brain told the blood zinging to his extremities. *Eight years to get here. Don't fuck it up now.*

"Ladies and gents!" Harper interrupted Zack's thoughts mercifully, snapping his fingers and motioning with his arms for people to clear the floor. "We've come to the entertainment portion of the program, and today's your lucky day, because it's your first look at Zack's *crazy* choreo. —That's right, give it up..." He waited for the applause to subside. "Accompanied by a little something I've been working on, me and my homeboy Chopin. Hope y'all enjoy."

Mina's expression turned to sheer admiration, and Zack understood why. Two incredible bodies took their positions in the middle of the floor. They were nearly nude in flesh-colored dance briefs, the woman in a bra top to match. They looked like Olympic gymnasts…or gladiators. Their overt strength and definition was a stunning contrast to Mina's lithe frame. She was about to get a peek at her future here, and Zack couldn't *wait.*

The opening piano strokes were gentle, a meandering solo line that went on for fifteen seconds and always made him hold his breath. The dancers hadn't moved; they just stood there, him behind her, their chests rising and falling, the sound of a soft heartbeat coming through Harper's speakers.

The cello started, deep and soulful like the tender voice of a lover, and she began to touch herself. Her arms wound in a slow filigree, and she moved her hands up over her body, caressing her face and the hair that fell softly about her shoulders. Her partner rested his hands at her waist a few seconds as the heartbeat intensified, her arms rising above her head in invitation. His hand smoothed a path over her hip and down her thigh to grip her calf, his cheek to hers. They pantomimed breathless sighs with their open mouths.

Only twenty seconds passed, but the tension was nearly unbearable. Mina's breathing had become audibly labored. Zack listened and watched her with rapt interest, anticipating the moment the tension would be released.

A single keening note from a violin cut through, sharp and lingering. The woman's leg was pushed up high by her lover's hand, opening her up to him in a most sensual way. Ten agonizing seconds of breathing, heartbeats and longing ticked by before he slowly let her leg back down.

The rhythmic chords exploded, and he flung her into

the air by her waist, her legs flying apart into a side split. He caught her by her open thighs in the crooks of his arms, her toned derriere sitting on his chest as he spun them around. Facing forward again, his hands pressed down on her lower back to angle her body down, and her legs moved over his shoulders, his face nestled between her thighs.

She dropped down at startling speed, swung between his legs, her head dangerously close to the floor…and back up again. Down, and back up again, gaining momentum until he threw her into a lift over his head. Suspended there, her back arched exquisitely, her legs curving until her toes nearly touched her head.

Mina was practically panting now. Pure bass had replaced the heartbeat in the music and she looked like she was struggling to breathe. Zack licked his lips at the intensity on her face. Part of him simply desired to share his art with another exceptional artist…but there was something else inside him that was finding it increasingly satisfying to stun this pristine ballerina until she was hot and flushed.

Wait for it, he willed her silently.

The dancer's thighs returned to their position over her partner's shoulders, her legs extended behind him as he pushed her down again. This time, her hands trailed slowly down his thighs, her torso aligning perfectly with his. His hands held her in place by her ankles, and her arms hugged his waist, their heads nestled between each other's legs. They were posed in a perfect sixty-nine.

Audible reactions filled the studio. Mina's gasp was fullbody this time, forcing her chest forward, her eyes widened in shock.

Zack's ego soared. Working with her was going to be *fun.*

46

The music faded back to lyrical piano and persistent heartbeat, signaling the demo's finale. The male dancer pushed one of his partner's legs until they scissored apart into a split while she was still upside down. She clung to his waist as they pulled apart, and he leaned back as far as he could go. It was a stunning show of strength and flexibility. Gripping an ankle in one hand, he arched his back until their bodies formed a T.

Zack had to know. "What do you think?"

Mina shivered when Zack spoke. The room had fallen quiet as the dancers held their pose. She hadn't noticed that he'd moved so close. She couldn't look at him. His voice was *way* too deep and low, and given what she'd just watched, it felt like whispers between lovers. The imagery *that* traitorous thought drummed up...hot, naked bodies twisting and writhing together...made her blink like mad.

Bordel!

"Is... that what we will be doing?" She didn't mean to sound so panicked.

"Part of it."

She gasped.

Zack grinned. "It's a little suggestive."

"*Suggestive?*" she breathed, unable to stop herself from staring right into the deep-sea green of his eyes.

"No, you're right." He studied her face with unmistakable amusement. "It's pretty overt."

Loud whistles, clapping and cheers interrupted the words Mina couldn't manage to get out anyway, and Harper was already making his way over.

"My guy!" he congratulated Zack with a grin. "I think that pretty much spoke for itself, but I'll let you say a few words."

"Hey, shut up, will ya?" Zack said playfully at all the noise. When it died down, he cleared his throat. "Thank you to those phenomenal dancers, by the way. Now I remember why I hired you."

That brought good-natured jibes from the cast, and then the man who'd introduced himself as Pete Something-Or-Other (the dramatist who'd helped Zack write *Lady in Red*) handed him a glass of wine.

Zack shook his head. "And the *genius* that is Harper Holloway—I mean…come on, that was *amazing*."

The room erupted with more praise.

"Can we just take a second and appreciate that this guy deejays nightclubs in a suit and tie? People have no idea they're getting cultured by a Julliard grad. He's got them twerking to Mozart. Incredible."

More laughter.

"Holy hell." He rubbed his chin. "This is really happening. It took three years from the time the idea came to me, to write the first words…two years after that to write just *two* songs-"

"And by then I thought it might be time to move things along," Pete cracked, and more laughter ensued.

"It's true," Zack said. "But we're finally here, and I couldn't be more grateful. A few weeks from now, one of the best ballerinas in the world is gonna help us shut down the Tony Awards—No pressure, Mina."

He was obviously joking, but a tiny tornado of terror was brewing in her stomach. *What the hell did I get myself into?* She managed a small, embarrassed smile.

"I realize our rehearsal schedule is a little unprecedented," he continued, "but so are we, and so is *Lady in Red*. I know you're as invested as I am, and I know we're gonna kill it." He dragged his fingers through his magnificent hair. "Shit, I'm no good at speeches—and yes, I realize the irony, thank you very much, Pete."

Pete guffawed, and Zack wrapped things up. "Just… thank you, from the bottom of my heart. I'm one step closer to my dream, and I can't think of better people to bring along with me. Cheers."

"*Cheers!*"

᷍

First Rehearsal…3 Weeks Before the Tonys…6:27 pm

She was going to have to stop flinching every time he touched her.

A thin sheen of sweat covered her satiny brown skin, lending a slightly acidic note to her natural aroma. Years of grueling rehearsals made him accustomed to the smell of musk. It was unique to every partner, like a scent signature. It tended to be strong, which was why he detested dancing with partners who wore perfume.

Mina's musk was burning wood and cinnamon and flowers—and the distinct odor of sweat. His mouth and nose were millimeters from her long, graceful neck. With every inhale, he tasted her, and for the first time in his career, it felt deeply personal.

"Try and relax." His voice wasn't as steady as he'd intended, but his hand was, pressing gently against her lower back, encouraging her to arch more deeply. He felt her abs tighten in protest.

"It doesn't feel right," she panted, losing her balance despite his support, her leg dropping from its high position behind her.

The vein in his neck throbbed, as much from exasperation, as from the way her words blended together in that sweet French accent. He'd never had this much trouble staying focused before. Dancing required *everything*: every muscle, every breath, every thought. It was far too demanding—and frankly, *dangerous*—to be distracted by a partner.

A huffing, puffing, *sweaty* partner.

For fuck's sake.

It was more awareness than arousal. He was *aware* of her, of her breaths and movements, and the thoughts in her head. On some level, it was like this with every partner. He had to anticipate her next move, familiarize himself with her body. He knew women's bodies the way astronomers knew the sky. Years of partnering had made him aware of the pockets of space most people didn't think about, the hidden crevices beyond peaks and valleys most recognized and oft-traveled.

His favorite part was a woman's true ribs, those first seven bones extending from her underarm and down beneath her breast. There was something provocative about them, the way they were strong by design, fragile in his hands. He itched to hold Mina there, to nestle his fingers between those fine grooves, his thumbs brushing the smooth skin of her back; to be entrusted with her safety, to help her make the impossible look effortless. But he couldn't do any of that until her thoughts stopped screwing with her confidence. He needed to get into her head.

"It's not *going* to feel right," he said finally, in a soft tone. "Not until you *relax*."

Merde.

His voice was like velvet, so deep and soothing…and so *annoying*.

Her back ached, because he *insisted* she lean forward into the arabesque instead of keeping her spine straight. Her feet felt sticky…and cold. Dancing barefoot was more challenging than she thought. New callouses were forming in all the wrong places and her feet kept slipping. Toe splits were *not* fun. And his hands…

Dieu, his hands!

They were on her. All over her. All the time. Shockingly, he spoke more with his hands than his mouth, and it was driving her *insane*.

"I need to catch my breath," she huffed, feeling quite like she was at the end of her rope.

"You're fine." His timbre was even more soothing this time. "The best way to get used to the water is to just jump right in. So *jump.*"

She groaned inwardly, but positioned herself again, hugging the floor with her foot, extending her arms out wide for balance as she lifted her leg behind her again.

"Good." He adjusted his palm over her poor, overworked core muscles. "Go as far as you can."

She did. Flexibility wasn't her problem. Her arch could go as deep as a Chinese classical dancer's, and she could hug her leg to her face. So it was a shock to her psyche to feel her weight shift forward suddenly, to have to hobble on one foot to compensate. She winced, her toes splitting again.

"*Merde!*" she spat. "It's no use! If I cannot get this stupid move, the others will be impossible!"

"Whoa, hang on, *petite.*" He was obviously taken aback by her outburst. "Mind over matter."

"*Pardon, 'petite'?*"

He had the nerve to grin. "You're small. French. Seemed like a no-brainer."

Espèce d'idiot! The comeback in her head was too easy. She refused to voice it aloud.

Massaging his temples, he seemed disappointed at her lack of enthusiasm for his feckless wit. "Mind over matter, it's a saying."

"I know what it is," she snapped. "English is my first language."

"Splendid. Then you know it means you have to stop overthinking things. Stop analyzing. That's what I'm here for, okay?"

She blew a long, uneven breath. He was the teacher. She would *try* to trust him, though she knew quite well what she was and was not capable of, and the fact that he didn't was about to break her foot.

She needed her foot.

"*D'accord,*" she said skeptically, but moved into position again.

"Okay," he parroted her in English, returning his hands to her waist. "Again."

This time, she made it all the way into the arch, her arms ascending to the ceiling, her hands wrapping around her ankle. She concentrated so hard, she didn't notice it when he removed his hands…which is probably why it shocked her so when her precarious balance was lost again.

Leaning forward, she stumbled *hard.* Her leg swung down fast, providing the sinister momentum needed to twist her other leg just so, that her poor toes split…*again.*

He stepped forward swiftly to set her aright, but she swatted his hands away.

"*Non!*" Her eyes watered from the pain. "I don't understand. What *is* this? Balanchine? Graham? Lucifer? *Hades?*"

"Calm down," he said gently, visibly trying not to laugh

at her theatrics, which just further irritated her. "That was actually not ba-"

"Stop telling me to calm down!"

Turning away, she tried to collect herself. Her toes were still smarting, and she mumbled softly to herself in French, trying to get out of her own head.

"I'm not exactly fluent in French from my touring days," he offered unhelpfully, "but I think I caught enough to know you're trying to psyche yourself up."

"*I'm a ballerina…*" She tried to drown him out. "*From the Paris Opera Ballet.*"

"Yeah well, we all have to start somewhere."

She spun around, her eyes stinging. (Annoyingly, she was a crier. Especially when angry.)

Superbe.

Now would be the *perfect* time to cry. Right now, when she needed to look capable and competent and strong.

"*Fuck me…* You're not gonna cry, are you, *petite*?"

The room grew eerily quiet. Still, but for the sound of her breathing. Heavy and deep, as if she was slowly drawing the energy from the air into her body. The heat of anger roiled through her. She felt flush with it, suffocated by it. She wanted to crawl from her skin until it cooled, but since she wasn't a lizard, and he had to stand there with his stupid lock of hair falling over his forehead, staring at her like an insipid, crazy, fragile piece of glass…

Merde.

She broke.

A stream of French epithets slammed into him like a ship blown ashore in a tsunami. He recognized quite a few of the choice words (not that he needed a translator to understand she wasn't singing him a sonnet).

Finally, it was quiet again.

Oh, what's this?

It seemed he'd just witnessed his first nuclear melt-down from this tiny ball of fire. And damned if it wasn't the sexiest, most confusing shit he'd ever seen. The cloud of hyper focus evaporated, and desire hit him like an eigh-teen-wheeler. He trailed his eyes over her sweaty, seething frame with deliberate slowness. It was probably bad that he wanted to snatch her up and lick the pulse in her throat, to bite her pouty lower lip and suck her toxic little tongue into his mouth.

Definitely bad. He'd have to give his dick a stern talk-ing to later.

For now, he smiled inwardly, stowing this particular button away to push as needed. The passion was *clearly* there. He had three weeks to whip his volatile star into shape and he'd do it by any means necessary. Outwardly, his expression remained passive, and his voice was flat when he spoke again.

"Feel better?"

She gave him a curt nod.

"Good. *Again.*"

CHAPTER FIVE

IT WAS PROBABLY bad that he thought of her when he did this. Definitely bad. But no matter how hard he tried, he couldn't conjure a face that wasn't Mina's, hips that didn't swell softly from her short, trim waist, lips that weren't full and deliciously curved.

Unbidden, an image of her taking him into her mouth clouded his mind, her expression full of promise. He moaned and shut his eyes. Maybe, if he gave himself over to the fantasy, didn't let his mind take over, he could get off this way…

No, no, no…dammit! No!

He tried to re-focus his thoughts, change their course, but it was too late: Mina's rich brown irises faded to soulless, chalky blue. Her lips thinned and turned sinister, muttering threats instead of promises. Her hands aged and paled, holding him captive rather than willing. He cursed—at his lost erection, at his stupid, *stupid* vulnerability—and his lashes flew apart despite the hot water running over his face. It stung like hell, but at least it was real.

Blinking rapidly, he bent his head, letting the swirl of the water down the drain ground him to time and place.

He felt the sting of tears and swallowed against the nauseating shame that always came with those memories. The ones he could control if he stuck to what was safe.

Safe was Mina's legs, long and limber, hiked over his shoulders, her arms pinned above her head as his thrusts sent her breasts bouncing in a tantalizing rhythm.

Fuck yes. He sprung to life again in his hand. *That's it…*

He gasped, gripping himself harder, jerking himself faster, as if the rapid motion could propel him further from the pain.

It was working.

"Yes," he sighed with relief, hunching over.

Sultry brown eyes that had glared at him in annoyance just hours ago were glazed over in his fantasy now, and those angry French oaths softened to delirious moans in his ear.

His body convulsed with such force, his palm shot forward, planted against the tile for purchase as pleasure rippled through every limb. Squeezing his eyes shut, his ass clenched tight and his toes curled as evidence of his release joined the hot stream of water swirling down the drain. He had to blink several times to clear away the hazy darkness and tiny flashing bulbs. His heart beat out of control, his flaring nostrils sucking in hot water each time he breathed.

"Jesus."

It was a good thing the world wasn't crashing down around him, or he'd be *screwed.* He could hardly stand up straight, let alone run. The thought sent him into a fit of laughter that echoed off the shower walls.

He turned his face up directly into the spray.

Fucking hysteria.

Maybe, but the nightmare was forgotten.

᪥

Non.

She wasn't going to do it. She wouldn't give him the satisfaction.

Even as the warm pulse intensified until it felt like someone was beating a war drum in her clit. Even as that traitorous clit swelled until she was shoving her fist between her thighs and clamping them together in agony.

The hotel bed was cushy and big and inviting… and Mina tossed and turned across every centimeter. She dreamed of arrogant lips pressed against her inner thighs, and a tongue too busy circling her clit to annoy her with flippant remarks. When he moved his lips to murmur (probably something filthy), she snatched up handfuls of his glorious hair and pushed his face against her.

She woke up with her fists full of sheets, panting from throbbing so intense, simply turning onto her stomach was her undoing. Her breasts were crushed deliciously beneath her weight, her panties brushing her clit with enough friction to send her muscles fluttering uncontrollably. She buried her face in the pillows to muffle her frustrated scream, holding her hips still because she *refused* to give in and press herself into the bedding for the ultimate release.

When it was over, the emptiness felt bigger. Wider. She squirmed, yearning emanating from her abdomen to her core until she couldn't take it anymore. Sitting up in bed, she reached for her phone. The voice on the other end was soft and groggy.

"*Allô?*"

"I can't sleep."

"Mina?" Sofie asked. "What's wrong?"

"It's…I feel…" She couldn't think. How was she supposed to put her frustration into words? She couldn't understand it herself. Her sigh was shallow and shaken. "*Merde! I don't know!*"

"It's *four* in the morning here, Mina. I need you to try."

"It's hard."

"You knew it would be."

"*Oui*, but it's not just the choreography, it's…I don't think it's working out. We're so different. His teaching style…It's like he doesn't know how to use his *words*. Always touching me. Always saying these things…"

She broke off as Sophie's laughter pierced through the phone.

"Why are you laughing? I'm *serious*."

"Believe me, I know," Sophie said. "Why do you sound so raspy?"

"It's the singing," Mina explained. "I spend all day running lines and rehearsing with the other principals… and then I eat if there's time. Then, I change my clothes and go back to the studio to rehearse the death trap he calls 'choreography.' I had to see my voice coach tonight. So, I'm raspy."

"Sounds brutal. So what things is he saying?"

"I-what?"

"I just wonder how Sleep Orgasm Guy is able to say things without using his words. These things that have you not sleeping."

"*Will you stop calling him that?!* I didn't even want to… My body just does it all by itself.*"

"Wait a minute, are you abstaining in *defiance*?"

It was quiet on Mina's end, and Sophie snickered. "No wonder you're so uptight. It's not like he can *see* you, Mina…Now *what things?*"

"Stupid things, okay? Like *calm down,* petite*, you can do this,* petite*, it's okay* petite. *Petite this, petite that. Petite petite PETITE!*"

"You're right, he's a monster." Sophie audibly choked back another laugh. "And you *like* him."

"*WHAT?!* Are you even listening to me?"

"Mina, partners touch us all the time—some of the lifts we do are probably illegal in certain countries."

"*Oui,* I know this, but-"

"And his dance style is new to you, you need a lot of help."

"Yes, but he's such a…*connard*…and-"

"And he gives you sleep orgasms."

Mina cursed.

"*That's* what this is about," Sophie insisted. "He's touching you all day and he's giving you sleep orgasms and you're calling *me,* you horny little toad!"

"*Sophie!*"

"*Admit it!*"

"I-*FINE.* He's making me crazy, okay? I'm not even sure I can do these things…It feels like my body is twisting into pretzels all day. And then he's touching me, and I swear he's trying to provoke me…"

Sophie's snort-choke blew through the phone.

"I hope you sprain something from trying not to laugh at my misery," Mina snapped.

"If it's any consolation, I'm heartbroken for you. What happened?"

Mina groaned.

"Mina…"

"I got upset. I-might have lost my temper."

"*Mina!*"

59

"I know."

"He's your teacher."

"I *know,* okay? I'm so embarrassed. I don't know what got into me, but it can't happen again."

Sophie couldn't contain her laughter now.

"I shouldn't have called," Mina moped. "I'm going to sleep."

"I'll come. Okay? Next week, I'll come and stay with you. We'll wear little raspberry berets, you know, like the Prince song? We'll eat American fries and pretend to get lost, so we can seduce *stupide* unsuspecting men with our accents."

Mina's heart rate calmed at the idea. "You will?"

"*Mmhmm*, just do me a favor, okay?"

"What?"

"Get yourself off, get some sleep, and call me when you're not insane."

⤳

Zack felt *great.*

Breakfast was the same as always: over-easy eggs, turkey sausage, coffee, fresh-pressed orange juice—but the umami gods must have been smiling down on him because it tasted like Michelin greatness. His endorphins were through the roof after his morning workout, and he'd even caught Wilson, the scatting street performer he'd admired since he was a kid, doing a rock and roll cover on his guitar in the subway. The old man's voice was pure, gritty soul, and he'd let go his guitar every so often to pat rhythmically against his thighs, chest, or an upturned bucket—a one-man show. Wilson had always been good luck. Every time Zack saw him, he had a good day.

"Good to see you, man." Zack gripped Wilson's hand briefly.

"Back from the left coast, I see." Wilson gave a toothy grin. "I tol' you you'd be back. The whole world is in New York City. Can't get that nowhere else."

"You never lie." Zack tossed cash into the old man's battered guitar case. "Whenever you're ready to stop busking and make some real money for your brilliance, you know where to find me."

"Yeeaaahhh, man," Wilson intoned. "I know."

Zack practically strutted up the subway steps to the contemporary class he was teaching two days a week. His cell vibrated just as he walked through the dance theater's doors. Reading the caller ID, he smiled. "You ready, Coach?"

"I'm never not!" Alex said. "But this is *your* baby. I'm just here to feed it, burp it, and keep it from hurting itself."

Zack chuckled. "You have no idea."

"Hiccups already?"

"Little ones, but I expected them. Nerves. I think having you there today will help us out a lot."

"Why is today significant?"

Zack was walking past a warm-up class that very moment and spotted his compact ball of wire finishing her stretches on the studio floor. She moved slowly and carefully, working each muscle to insure against injury. "I'm introducing some floor work today," he said, watching through the door as Mina rose to take her place at the barre. "No one does floor work like you. We could use your expertise."

"Well, I look forward to it."

"Thanks, Coach. See you soon."

Zack sensed the tension in the studio even from outside its doors. Wilhelmina Allende was a superstar ballerina, but an outsider. This company had its own stars, and even the instructor seemed wary, waiting to see if the "Jewel of the Palais Garnier" was a diva, or if she'd respect the hierarchy of a company to which she did not belong.

To everyone's obvious surprise, including his own, Mina didn't take a place in the center. Instead, she smiled graciously and moved to the end of line, where she could better observe. And learn. The instructor's expression softened in approval.

You're full of surprises, aren't you, petite?

He was quickly losing count of her many facets, and as he continued to his own class, he decided he liked that about her. He liked that a lot.

౼

Second Rehearsal...3 Weeks Before the Tonys...7:45 pm

Zackary Coen was *slinging* Mina into the air...and then down between his legs...up and down, up and down...and her stomach dropped every time. She was *far* too stiff, she knew it, but she couldn't help it.

"*Stop!*" Alex barked, and they froze at his command.

Shooting her hands out in front of her, she gripped Zack's thighs for dear life, her head mere centimeters from the floor.

Alex sucked his teeth. "Mina, my dear, I'm having visions of your lovely head smashing like a melon on the studio floor."

"I'm not working up a sweat for nothing," Zack gritted. The room blurred as he twirled her at the waist in a mid-air cartwheel to set her upright again. "Your death grip wasn't necessary."

She glared at him over her shoulder, and he retaliated by holding her there for a second, letting her dangle a bit for good measure before setting her back on her feet. Alex moved between them, she suspected, to separate them like they were quarreling toddlers, forcing their attention to their coach.

"Your lines are gorgeous, Mina." He used the lightest touch of his fingers at each of her arms to nudge them into an arc above her head. "Your extension goes to the tips of your fingers and toes. But in *this* piece, when the two of you are together…" Stepping aside, he signaled for them to get back into position. Zack immediately took Alex's place behind her, carefully leaving space for her to extend her leg behind her. "…it's not about the line, but the *shape.*"

At Alex's cue, Zack plucked her from the floor by her waist and lifted her to his shoulders.

"There, now *reach,* Mina," Alex said.

Her back arched, and her abs pulled taut as a wire, her body contorting until the leg she'd lifted behind her formed a near-perfect circle with her arms.

"And *five…six…seven…*now bring her down, Zack—*slowly* this time…"

Zack did as instructed, but her stomach dropped again, and her arms flew out in an instinctive defense against the floor.

"Hold." Alex stepped forward.

Zack hugged her in sixty-nine, her head between his legs, their torsos bent over the floor. Her muscles ached with tension, but thankfully Alex moved quickly to correct her arms, drawing them behind her.

"Your hands should be grabbing that ankle." Alex

stepped back again, nodding when Mina adjusted. "And up again."

Zack swept her back onto his shoulders and repeated the motion, but her arms went right back to the floor again.

Merde.

"Stop." Alex folded his arms across his chest, waiting as Zack set her on her feet again.

Struggling to catch her breath, fresh sweat collecting on her skin and seeping through her clothes, she looked anywhere but at Zack.

"There is a disconnect." Alex cut his eyes between them. "Consequently, this move *looks* as dangerous as it is. It should look daring, but *effortless.* Otherwise, its impact is lost. Mina, when you bring your arms down like that, your body language screams distrust. If *you* don't trust him to hold you, the audience won't either."

Zack scoffed. "Oh, she trusts me."

Mina looked at him in disbelief.

"You knew who I was when we met, and the kind of work that I do," he continued. "You wouldn't have signed on for this if I'd spent my career dropping my partners. I could keep tossing you in the air and catching you for two *more* hours and you would still be afraid. Because you don't trust *yourself.*"

Her body went stiff and her gaze shot back up to his. The same uncanny familiarity that had come over her the night they'd met returned, like a breath blowing through her. It had been irrational at the time—absolutely *insane*— to think it could have been Étienne there with her outside the opera house. His presence had felt so *strong.*

It had been there when she and Zack danced for Alex's class. Now here it was again. His tone was eerily similar, too. Almost painfully direct, but with a softness in its intent that reminded her of Étienne. And *Dieu*, those *words*. The second they left Zack's mouth, a fourteen-year-old memory flooded her brain…the first time she'd met Étienne Lemaire:

"*The barre is for balance, Mina. It's not life support,*" *Madame said brusquely.* "*Start on both legs…You must get your legs* higher."

Madame snatched Mina's leg up higher, and Mina tried not to wince. She tried not to react at all, which would have been insolent. But no matter how hard she tried, Mina couldn't seem to please her.

"*Stop leaning back, Mina…Why are your arms so perky? What is that,* gymnastics? *You're not taking this seriously.*"

Mina's face burned with humiliation. She wanted to cry. This was Third Section, after all, where true rivalry was born, where the rivalry would continue each year, as only two-to-four of the best moved up. It was a machine that crushed the weak, and right now, Mina felt very much like a weak link.

"*You have to trust yourself,*" *a boy's voice came from behind her, his breath tickling her neck. But she did not dare turn around. Whoever he was, he risked his* own *neck for talking during class, even in his hushed tone.* "*You made it to this lovely little hell, didn't you, you witch?*" *he teased.* "*So…you can do* anything.*"

The memory dissipated, replaced by two very real bemused expressions.

"Do you need to take five?" Alex asked.

Merde, he thinks I'm insane.

"*Non,* I'm fine," she said, shaking her head. "I was just…remembering something."

Zack stared at her, obviously wondering what sort of memory made someone disappear from the planet for several seconds.

"I suggest we try some trust-building exercises." Alex gave Zack a strange look.

"That's not necessary," Mina quickly objected. "Really, I can go again."

"No, he's right," Zack said. "The lifts you're used to aren't this risky. We have to get you comfortable before we can move on."

"What are we going to do?" she asked skeptically, crossing her arms over her chest. "Trust falls?"

Alex cleared his throat, sounding suspiciously like he was stifling laughter. "Oh, my dear, you're about to be introduced to the Coen method of breaking in new dancers." He lifted his hands. "Godspeed."

Zack's eyes locked on Mina's confused ones. "I'm gonna throw you."

"Throw me what?"

Something was obviously clawing at Alex's throat, because the man was coughing uncontrollably now. Mina frowned at him, then at Zack. His obnoxious grin was all she needed to finally comprehend what he'd said.

"You can't be *serious!*" she gasped, stepping back instinctively.

"You'll be fine." He spoke carefully, stepping toward her. He stalked her like that until they'd reached the far end of the space. He was a foot in front of her. There was nowhere left for her to run. Casting a pointed look at her feet, he grinned into her face. "I'm sure those…foot underwear you're wearing will perform just fine."

"You can't intimidate me into this!" she spat, deliberately looking past him at Alex. "Per your suggestion, I train my upper body every morning. I see a physical therapist every afternoon. So, you see, this is really not necessary."

"Those are for pussies, *petite*," Zack whispered, insulting her protective footwear again. "It's like cheating…in little baby toe thongs."

He was baiting her, manipulating her so she'd give him what he wanted. Fine. Let him. If she died from the ordeal, she'd haunt him the rest of his arrogant days. Straightening her spine, her eyes blew flames into his. "Throw me."

"Now, remember," Alex said. "In classical ballet, we strive to be light and airy, but in parts of this piece, we will deliberately use gravity to our advantage."

Zack's fingers flexed at Mina's sides in silent encouragement, but the increased pressure only heightened her awareness of him and she stiffened again.

"Relax," he said softly.

She'd been so preoccupied with trying to stay alive during their lifts earlier that his proximity hadn't distracted her overmuch, but now her nerve endings buzzed with its effect…and with the urge to release her tongue from her teeth and lash him with it.

"Once you're in the air," Alex was saying, "do what feels natural. Form any shape you like. Your goal is simply to *land*…" He angled his head. "Or fall, tastefully. And…go."

She took a deep breath.

"On three," Zack said. "One…two…"

He flung her into the air with a powerful lift-shove, propelling her about a quarter of the way across the studio. It was such a shock, the only thing that crossed her mind was the fact that he'd *tricked* her, the *connard*. And then she was falling…*way* too fast.

"*Merde!*" she cried out angrily, her right side taking most of the impact.

Alex brought his hand to his mouth, clearly questioning the wisdom of this activity for the first time. Mina imagined smoke coming from her nostrils. She could take a sip of kerosene and incinerate Zack with a well-aimed huff. He lifted a brow at her in challenge.

"Again," she said through clenched teeth.

"Eyes open, Mina." Alex waited for them to get into position again. "There is no fear of the unexpected. The floor is where you begin, and it is where you will end. *You* decide how."

She nodded, and Zack threw her again. This time, her butt cushioned her fall.

"Don't worry about momentum, Mina. He's giving you that. You just *move*. Again."

There was hardly any time to think before Zack tossed her again. So, she followed her instincts, bending her body into a bow pointing left, stretching her sore right side. Her arms were lifted above her head, her hands grabbing her wrists, her legs stretched into a perfect line all the way to the tips of her toes. Landing on her feet this time, she couldn't hide her triumphant smile.

"*Yes!*" Alex cried. "Stunning lines but relax more. You don't need to point those toes."

"Better," Zack murmured in her ear with pride. "But this time, think less, okay?"

"Sure, I'll just beat my chest and yell like a cave ma-*ooh!*"

She was in the air again before she could finish her thought. Half her time was wasted in shock, so all she could manage before a less-than-graceful landing was a quick split.

"Don't stand there preening, Zack," Alex said. "And don't just *chuck* her like a used cigarette. I want her to *fly.*"

So, she did. Over, and over, and over, and over again.

"Okay, *petite*," Zack said as she turned her back to him

for the dozenth time. They were both sweaty and breathing like marathon runners. "Let's kick this up a notch."

Bending into a lunge, he used his legs like springs for more momentum into the launch. That's exactly what she felt like, a little rocket being sent straight up into the atmosphere. She was grateful she'd breathed into it this time, because all her energy was focused on her position as soon as she was in the air.

The height made her breathless. She couldn't worry about her landing *and* choreograph a single, mid-air movement at the same time. It was *impossible*. In a millisecond, her body responded to her mind's command, and she was spinning. One…two complete turns with her arms hugged close in front of her. Her legs bent for the landing and her arms whipped out, her palms up, her head back.

It was silent when she stood upright again. Her nostrils worked overtime to accommodate her breaths, and she licked her moisture-deprived lips. Alex was frozen in disbelief, almost like a caricature. When she looked at Zack, she knew she'd nailed it, and heat filled her face with her smile.

"Did you just…was that a double tour?" he asked, hoarse with shock.

"What?" She was still catching her breath. "You said, 'kick it up,' *oui*?"

Zack shook his head, his mouth still slack as he and Alex stared at each other.

Alex found his voice first. "Take five. I think we're ready for some floor work."

After four more repetitions of the lift, Zack felt things were finally starting to take shape. The choreography looked daring and effortless. Alex's face muscles were doing a poor job of hiding his victory celebration. It was a small victory, though. They still had work to do.

"Okay," said Alex. "Now that it's technically sound, let's dress it up."

He signaled for them to get back into position, with Mina's leg lifted behind her, and Zack's hands at her waist.

"And, *five…six…seven…*bring her down…and *stop.*"

Zack brought Mina halfway down from the lift, her face at his abdomen, her…treasures…in his face. *Not my most brilliant choreography,* he groaned inwardly. He drew her musky scent into his nose and throat with every deep and frequent breath. *Jesus Christ.*

"This pas de deux is the most significant in the entire production," Alex said. "You must show how hopelessly in love you are, against all that is good and proper. Because you are, Mina, after all, a courtesan. And so, you have a unique set of skills…" Taking Mina's hands, he brought them to Zack's thighs, then stepped out of the way. "… As you come down, maybe caress here. Bring her down, Zack…yes, *slowly…*"

Mina ran her hands along his taut thighs slowly, before reaching up and back to clasp her ankle, her head between his legs.

"*Yes!*" Alex clapped. "Dear God, e*xcellent,* you two! *That's* what the audience should see on your faces. Should *feel.* That urgency, that raw, desperate desire. And… *up…* Work with the natural tension of your movements…good. And *hold…*six…"

Zack couldn't see Mina's face, since they were posing in that cursed sixty-nine, hugging each other tightly, but it was a safe bet, since Alex hadn't commanded them to do the move again, they were both convincing enough. Now they were stuck breathing each other in for the most *awkward* three counts they'd ever endured until Alex finally got to…

"…eight…and *split*…nice and slow. Good, Zack. Push her legs apart gently, caress that leg…and five…six… seven…"

Their bodies formed the T, holding the pose until their muscles cried out.

"*Breathe* through it," Alex instructed. "I need to *see* every breath. Use it to paint the picture. No need to be subtle… good…and transition for the plank, nice and smooth…"

Zack moved upright again slowly, allowing Mina to lift her leg back up. They were perfectly aligned now, and with a quick twist of his arm around her waist, he spun her around so she faced forward, her legs hooked over his shoulders.

"Hold his hips here, Mina. It'll support you and add that sensuality. Good…and down…"

Holding Mina's knees, Zack bent to a sitting position on the floor. Her body curved with him, until he was lying flat on his back with her sitting on his stomach.

"Lovely, but it's dragging a bit," Alex said. "It should be smooth, but fast. Again."

It was torture, but they did it once more, until Zack lay flat again, with Mina on his stomach.

"Good. Come up now, Mina."

She stood, her feet on either side of his face, and bent at the waist sensually, bringing her face to Zack's for a count.

"And five…use your hands, Mina."

Dragging her hands up her body, she pantomimed the moment she flipped her flowing hair.

"And *hold*. Keep breathing. I want to see those chests rise and fall…Good."

Zack wished he'd hurry up. From his vantage point, all

he could see was leg…miles and miles of flawless leg…and the place where legs meet…

"Mina, breathe into it. Hug his head with your legs-"

Zack coughed.

"Don't *kill* him, Mina…"

She shifted her stance a bit and Zack gulped for air.

"Better…No need for nerves. His body is there to support you. Arms, Zack."

Zack lifted his arms in front of her, one hand gripping his wrist for reinforcement, the other flat against her tummy.

"*Carefully* now…and, *down…*"

Their muscles were locked, every inch of their bodies tense and vibrating. Breathing felt most difficult of all, because they needed to keep their bodies perfectly straight. Mina leaned forward, Zack's hand stiff against her abdomen. Her legs hugged his head, anchoring her on her slow descent, until the soles of her feet began to leave the floor…

"Arms, Mina."

She brought her arms down to her sides, and Zack felt her trembling with the loss of her extended arms to help her balance. He was demanding the most challenging show of strength she'd ever been tasked to do, but he knew she could do it. Every muscle was engaged, and she had to appear as though trapped in a slow free-fall. The more she leaned forward, the more level she was with the floor, suspended just inches above it.

Zack's back arched deeper into a bow the more Mina's body became parallel with the floor. His face was red between her legs, his muscles burning as he worked to keep his shoulders, butt and calves flat on the floor. With each millimeter, his arms lowered, and his hands moved lower on her abdomen. The force of her body dragged his forward some millimeters, but they were almost in a perfect plank.

"Good. Keep compensating, Zack. Don't lose her center of—*Shit!*"

It happened so fast. The last thing Zack remembered was adjusting his arms and hands to Mina's new center of gravity before they fell apart. She'd collapsed to the floor in a gasping heap, and then, lightning fast, one hundred and five pounds of solid prima ballerina muscle powered the slap that sent his head reeling. Sitting up, he blinked hard several times, holding his stinging cheek, flexing his jaw left and right.

"Dear God," Alex said over and over, visibly cringing as a slew of shrill French epithets echoed off the walls.

"Mina." Zack tried to get through to her, but his head was still ringing. "It's not what you thi—I didn't know my hand would end up there…*Goddamn it, will you calm down*?!"

Immediately, the studio fell quiet. Shaking as she was, he thought she might take another go at him.

"Apologies, Mina." Alex wrung his hands. "These things are…unpredictable. I should have considered that outcome."

"No, I'm sorry." Zack stood to his feet. "It's not unusual that I'll have to hold you pretty intimately." He massaged just beneath his left eye until the room was no longer blurry. "But maybe we *should* have done a few trust falls until we were more comfortable with each other."

Mina looked horrified, like she'd turn to vapor and get sucked through the vents. "I-I'm sorry."

Frankly, Zack was impressed she'd lasted so long before she flipped. Choreographers talked amongst themselves, and when he'd inquired about Mina, the consensus was, she's brilliant, if a little...impassioned. Now here she was, exhausted, and he was pushing her to the brink of her comfort zone, then pushing her some more.

"I think that's enough for today."

The words had barely left Alex's mouth before Mina crossed to the other side of the studio, hefted her gym bag over her shoulder, and fled the building.

Zack blew a long, exasperated breath, then glared at Alex. "'Twin souls with one body,' huh?"

"Oh, don't give me that!" Alex snapped in a rare outward show of annoyance. "I needed to inspire my students! My very *young*, impressionable students. And what you two did? It was-"

"Inspired," Zack said dryly, massaging his aching jaw.

"Yes. And so is what you did today." Alex gripped Zack's shoulder briefly. "Let our firebird cool down. Tomorrow's another day."

Zack nodded.

Firebird.

Indeed.

CHAPTER SIX

Sunday, 3 July

MINA'S DREAM OF having pretty feet someday sprouted wings and flew from her delusional subconscious, out through her ears, and into the muggy New York air. Sophie Danis had dragged her to Greenwich Village in four-inch heels (*expensive* four-inch heels) to look at Carrie Bradshaw's apartment. After squealing around the place like schoolgirls, Mina navigated them back to the Upper West Side to view listings that were within the realm of possibility.

"You said reliving Sex and the City would be *fun*." Mina collapsed onto a bench in Riverside Park. Letting her shopping bags fall to the ground, she laid out as if she'd fainted, leaving Sophie precious little room to sit.

"Will you quit being so dramatic?" Sophie complained, nudging Mina to sit up. "You're making a scene."

Mina cut her eyes at the elderly couple grinning at her as they passed by. "I can't feel my toes."

"You've danced with tendinitis, stress fractures, sprained ankles…A little Louboutin won't kill you."

"I can't believe you made me buy six hundred-dollar shoes."

"Isn't it wonderful? So empowering!"

"Buying *shoes*?"

"The shoes, the clothes, the air," Sophie crooned. "We work our asses off. We should cover them in pretty things. Besides, it was either Carrie Bradshaw's apartment or these shoes."

Mina giggled, feeling her body relax a little. Her ass would indeed be covered in brand new pretty things. Lacy things. Satin things. Things with tiny bows that no one was going to see anyway, because she lived in leotards and sweat pants. She would wear them on her days off with a conspiratorial smile, content that her derrière knew the finer things in life.

She took a deep breath, the sweet warmth of summer filling her lungs. "I like it here. It's less crowded than Central Park. Reminds me of home."

Mina couldn't hide the melancholy in her tone. She had been stifling it all morning, because Sophie was trying so hard to keep her distracted, but what bothered Mina was beyond the help of a shopping spree in fabulous, strappy heels.

Seeming to sense her mood, Sophie bent forward and lifted a small box from one of her bags. "I know his birthday isn't until tomorrow, but I brought you something, *chère*."

Recognizing the pastry box from the famously gay-owned bakery she and Étienne had loved for its phallic breads and sweets, Mina reached for a naughty baguette.

"It's not *tartes*," Sophie said apologetically, "but I couldn't risk getting fruit everywhere and having to explain to the stewardess why I was traveling with a box of dicks."

Mina laughed despite her tears, which made her nose run. She didn't care, because the sight of the soft, chewy bread nestled in a box she hadn't seen in a year was already trapping her in a memory…

Étienne sat irreverently on top of Mina's vanity in the oth-erwise-empty dressing room, playing with her makeup brushes.

"You know that drives me mad," she complained, slapping the brushes from his hand and replacing them in their case. But she left a small pastry box in front of him in return.

"So this is why you lured me here so early," he quipped, lifting a brow with dramatic flair. "You want to fatten me up so I can't fit into my tights. Make me look ridiculous. You know it's the only way to upstage me!"

He shot his hand out to tickle her ribs, grinning as she twisted away from him with a squeal.

"So you'll buy new tights." She shrugged. "No one could steal your shine. Now open the box, you fool."

He complied, but his face lost all trace of amusement when he saw the fruit tartes shaped like pretty little cocks peeking up at him. There was a candle stuck in one of them, and he swallowed the sudden lump in his throat.

"Happy seventeenth birthday, ma moitié," she whispered. Removing the tarte with the candle in it, she lit it with a match. "I love you."

He didn't say anything yet. Didn't move. He just watched the flame dance for a moment, sheltered by her cupped fingers, as her gesture sank in. When he looked up at her again, there were tears in his eyes. "How long have you known?"

She smiled. "You live in my heart, so as long as you have, I think. And you never tried to hit on me," she joked with a shrug.

"Maybe you're just not my type."

"I'm everyone's type."

He grinned, watching the flame again. She knew him, knew that feeling vulnerable was hard for him, so she

understood why he couldn't meet her eyes for his next question.
"And you don't care?"

"Do you care that I'm straight?"

He frowned up at her. "Of course not. What kind of ques-
tion is-"

"A stupide *one. And so is yours," she said with conviction,*
lifting her free hand to cup his face. "Now blow out the candle
before we set this place on fire."

"Mina," Sophie's soft voice grounded Mina back to their
bench. To the present.

Swiping her tears away, Mina glanced around them to
make sure she hadn't made a spectacle of herself. "I'm sorry. I
don't know why this keeps happening. It's like he's haunting
me. Or I'm hallucinating or-"

"You're not crazy, okay?" Sophie took the pastry box
from Mina's lap. "It's his first birthday after he…" She didn't
say the word. Instead, she dug a candle and matchbook from
her bag. Sticking the candle into one of the pastries, she lit it
and handed it to Mina. "Here, *chère*. Make a wish."

Mina took a deep breath and looked out across the park.
Closure. I just want closure. She shut her eyes. *So you can rest,*
ma moitié…and I can live…in peace. "Okay."

Sophie squeezed her hand, and Mina blew the flame away.

&

Zack was the last to leave the studio after his students had
gone, wearing old sweats and warm-up clothes, his gym bag
slung over his shoulder. He checked his watch.

4:07 PM—seven minutes late.

Well, technically, he allowed himself a ten-minute
window for his meals. Also, technically, this was a snack,

and he still had a few more minutes before he missed the all-important window, so he didn't need to be such a lunatic about it. Cursing, he dug into his bag for a banana.

"Oh good, I haven't missed you!" a voice rang out from some distance behind him.

He turned to see one of the company's senior contemporary choreographers hasten her small steps to catch up to him.

"Christine." He took a bite, reducing the banana by half. "Impeccable timing, as always."

"Very funny," she said when she was close enough to lower her voice. "You may have quicker feet than me, but I've got *stamina*."

"Fair enough." Grinning, he consumed the rest of the banana in another bite. Tossing the peel in the waste bin just outside the studio doors, he dusted his hands on his sweats. "How can I be of service?"

"Well, thanks to your ballerina, I have all the help I need." She was oblivious to his bemused frown as she reached into her gym bag. Removing a pair of slightly-worn ballet slippers, she offered them to him. "I wonder if you can return these to her for me? I won't see her again for a few days and I'm sure she'll need them sooner than that. There's life in them yet!"

Zack accepted the slippers, adjusting his expression so he didn't look as confused as he felt. "Of course. What are you two working on?"

And how the hell does she have time to help you when I work her as hard as I do?

It was Christine's turn to be caught off guard. "Oh, I thought you knew? She's been helping me work out some new choreography for about a week now…on nights when she doesn't have voice lessons, of course. I get a muse and she gets some extra practice."

"I see."

"I'm sorry," she said. "I don't mean to overstep. She assured me I wasn't overextending her. We thought it might be helpful, too, with the limited time you two have to rehearse for the Tonys…"

His brows lifted, his brain comprehending what was happening. *She's cheating on me with another teacher.* Stupid notion, of course. He was proud of her for taking initiative, but his ego took a beating at the thought that Mina hadn't asked *him* for more help.

"She's picking things up quickly." He hoped his voice conveyed appreciation. "I think the extra practice is making her more confident. I-thank you."

Christine smiled. "Thank *you*. She's brilliant." She turned on her heel. "I see you're really embracing the off-season," she joked without looking back. "But a little more hair looks good on you, Zack!"

Chuckling, he raked his fingers through his longer locks, then rubbed his chin. He hadn't even noticed the extra stubble there. He could hear his mother now, "*You work too hard, mijo. I worry about you.*"

He examined the small satin slippers he held, frowning at the slightly off distribution of brown color…and then his brow smoothed. *Christ, they're dyed. She dyes her shoes…*

Apparently, there was a person on the planet who worked harder than him. And lately, all work and no play did *not* make him feel like a dull boy.

～

Sophie was keeping room service at Mina's hotel busy that night. The two picked through a smorgasbord of filet mignon, an assortment of salads, fruit and fresh rolls laid out on Mina's bed. They watched *Camille* on a DVD they'd rented from the public library. Dessert had already been dispatched.

"*Dieu*, what is it about Colin Firth that is *so* hot?" Sophie swooned.

"Will you focus? This is research. I need to get into my character's head."

"And *I* need to get into *his* character's *pants*!"

Mina snorted. "This movie is old, he doesn't look like that anymore."

"You're right, he's hotter now. Seriously, what *is* it though?" Sophie forked another bite of steak. "He's not conventionally handsome, and we see perfect bodies all the time…"

"Charisma," was Mina's simple answer. "It's his eyes. The way he walks, the way he speaks…Warm. Like his words are hugging you."

Sophie sat up straighter at that. "Wow. That was really profound."

"*Merci*."

They ate and watched the film in silence for all of two minutes before Sophie spoke again. "What is with the hugging thing anyway?"

Sighing, Mina paused the movie. "What?"

"Hugging. It's weird. People pressing their whole bodies up against each other like it's the most normal thing in the world. It is *not* normal."

Her twisted up face made Mina laugh. "It's normal here. I'm still not used to it."

"I wouldn't mind hugging Colin Firth."

Mina smacked Sophie in the shoulder playfully. "You make everything sexual."

"That may be true, but I'm right about hugging. It's very sexual. Americans are just a bunch of perverts."

"*Oh mon Dieu*, you're insane."

"Yeah well, better than smacking the shit out of him," she teased.

Mina felt the blood drain from her face.

"Too soon?" Sophie continued without mercy.

"It was a *reflex*!"

"Response."

"What? I had no idea that he was going to…to-"

"*Toucher ton chatte.*"

Mina gasped, tossing her fork away and straightening her spine.

Sophie nodded, as if her suspicions were confirmed. "He touched it and you *responded*."

"It wasn't like that! I didn't enjoy it."

Sophie shrugged a slim shoulder. "It was a shock, so I don't blame you for hitting him. But you've experienced uncomfortable scenarios before without losing your temper. Hell, we usually laugh this stuff off." She eyed Mina quizzically. "Tell me you would have responded the same way if you weren't so aware of him?"

Mina looked away.

"I thought so." Sophie softened her tone and stroked Mina's hair. "There must be another reason he has you so on edge. I've never seen you this way before, *chère*. So wound up. It can't just be sleep orgasms."

"You're never going to let me forget that, are you?" Mina groaned.

"Not until something more entertaining happens to one of us. Stop changing the subject."

Resigning herself to an uncomfortable conversation,

Mina looked toward the ceiling. *"Chai pas...* I try not to think about it because it's so distracting."

"Come on. It can't be that bad."

"Non, not bad. *Strange.* It makes me feel crazy, like this thing with Étienne."

"I told you." Sophie took Mina's hands in hers. "You are *not* crazy. What happened was horrible. We don't even know *why* it happened. And as much as I know you love me, you and Étienne shared something not even I can understand...but I know it was real."

Mina stared down at their hands. "Something about Zack reminds me of Étienne."

"Zack?" Sophie looked intrigued.

"He asked me to call him that, the night we met. Ordinarily I wouldn't have obliged—out of propriety, of course, but something happened that I didn't tell you about. Something..."

"Strange."

"Like déjà vu. But not in the sense that I'd met him before." Mina swallowed.

"Not. Crazy."

Nodding, Mina took a deep breath. "I was lost in my own head, I guess. For a second, it really did feel like Étienne was standing there with me. Speaking to me. It was so strong, when I turned around and saw Zack standing there, I was confused."

"Merde," Sophie breathed. *"Réincarnation?"*

"Non, not quite." Mina bit her lip, thinking. "I don't know what to call it. It just felt like a connection. Like the way I felt when I met Étienne, but different."

"Of *course* it's different. You weren't attracted to Étienne, not in that way. Even before you knew he was gay."

"*Non*, not in that way."

"I see why you're such a mess. You lose someone you have this insane connection with, probably thinking you'd never feel it again, *oui?*"

"*Oui.*"

"And then it happens again when you least expect it, with someone you're attracted to, and you're working very closely with him almost every single day. Touching each other, breathing all over each other. Now I understand why you keep running away."

"I don't run away. I'm still here!"

"You do," Sophie insisted. "You've had a few rough rehearsals, and you're giving up. Whenever it gets too hot, you snap. And then you run."

Mina's sigh was ragged this time, as if she was releasing two weeks' worth of tension from her lungs. "I don't know what else to do."

They both startled when three solid raps sounded at the door. "Room service."

"*Un moment, s'il vous plaît!*" Sophie called, hesitating a moment. "It's passion. Like anything else. We do what we've been instructed all our lives. We use it." Giving Mina's hand a squeeze, she went to collect their dessert.

⊰

Rehearsal…2 Weeks Before the Tonys…6:05 pm

They were just forty-five minutes into rehearsal and already Zack was contemplating throwing Mina out of the window. Fat good that would do, though. The infuriating little cat would just land on her feet. *On her fucking toes. Always the toes.* Maybe he'd suspend her upside down by her toes instead…

Closing his eyes, he massaged the tick between his brows. "Stop."

"What?" She looked up at him with wide eyes, controlling her heavy breaths. "That was better, I think."

The tick had migrated to his forehead. "Your toes. You're pointing them again."

She frowned, her hands on her hips. "I-It's not something I was consciously doing."

"Because it's ingrained. I show you something and you think, 'I know what that is, it's an arabesque, I recognize those shapes.' But it's completely different shifts of weight, completely different upper body contortions," he explained patiently.

"I know this." Her words were clipped. "This is week three. I understand the fundamentals well enough. I just… haven't mastered it yet. It still feels so…awkward."

He took in her tense body lines, her chagrined expression, and softened his tone. Bringing his hands to her stiff shoulders, he gently massaged until she started to relax. "You're doing what feels natural to you. The ballerina in you can't resist trying to make the moves look pretty. It's my job to push you into *bigger* shapes. Push you out of your comfort zone. Okay?"

She blew a long breath. "Okay."

He turned her at her waist to begin again.

Two hours into rehearsal…

"I can *hear* the five…six…seven…eight in your head, *petite*." Zack halted their movement.

"I can't help it!" Mina snapped, catching her breath. "It's how I learn the steps in the beginning."

"It's not enough," he insisted. "The quickest way to pick it up is by listening to the music-the rhythmic phrases and the melody. You're not carrying out certain steps at certain times like a robot. You're telling a story."

"*Bah.*" She positioned herself again. "I don't know how anyone learns this way."

"That's the idea." He grinned. "Shucking convention."

"Is that why you changed her name?"

"Whose name?"

"The courtesan. Her name was Marguerite."

Someone's been doing her homework. "That's what Alexandre Dumas named her in La Dame Aux Camélias. She's Violetta in the opera version. In real life, her name was Marie Duplessis. I'm calling her Camille."

"How very *américain.*"

"Artistic license, *petite*. Stop stalling."

"But-"

"Quiet. Move."

Three hours, thirty-six minutes into rehearsal…

Mina was exquisite. She could control every part of her body, it seemed, even the thick, curled lashes that fringed her pretty eyes. And it was driving Zack *insane.*

"Your torso should be slightly bent for that turn, *petite*, and it's still too stiff. Use your muscles, it's what they're there for."

Mina whipped around, clearly annoyed by his needling. Well, that was too bad.

"You say 'relax,' and then you say 'engage,'" she snapped. "It's impossible!"

"I promise you it's not. You're still overthinking it."

She sucked in a breath, and he prepared to be cut at the knees, probably with a biting response about men who don't like women who think, when her expression relaxed.

He angled his head at her. "Well?"

"Fine. You're the teacher."

"That's right, I am." It was petty, but tough shit. She was being a brat.

"You don't have to say it like that. 'That's *right*!' I just said you're the teacher."

"Do you always have to have the last word?"

"What? *Non*!"

Zack dropped his gaze to her foot, which tapped the floor wildly like Thumper the bunny. "You're about to pee your pants, you want to say something so bad."

Mina gasped. *"You can't say that!"*

"What?"

"'Pee your pants!' It's inappropriate."

"Maybe, but it's true. Look at your foot."

She looked down at her wayward appendage and froze, her head lifting in defiance. "Doesn't matter. I can't say what I want to say."

"Because I'm the teacher?"

"*Oui.*"

"Good." He turned her around by her shoulders. "Move."

Four hours, twenty-two minutes into rehearsal…

Zack held Mina in a daring hold. She was upside down, the length of her elegant back pinned to his torso, her long legs over his shoulder. She clung to him with just one hand on his calf, her muscles straining as she curved her body into a graceful bow.

He felt her body twist just slightly as she angled her head, and immediately knew what was distracting her. Again.

"Dammit, *petite,* you're upside down! Stop looking in the fucking mirror."

"*Ugh!*" she cried as he twirled her upright and set her on her feet. "Don't *do* that! I need some kind of notice before you just…*throw* me around! The blood rushes to my head and I have to catch my-"

"What is *with* you today?"

"What?"

"We've wasted at least a third of our time going over technique—technique you were nailing two *days* ago. You're distracted. Off your game. And I want to know why."

"It's nothing," she mumbled, walking to her gym bag to remove her towel and pat her face.

"I didn't catch that." His back stiffened at the way she strolled away from him with such aloofness.

Whirling around, her face was dewy and flushed, her nostrils flaring. *"It's none of your business!"*

"It damned well *is* my business if it's affecting my show!" His voice had risen to match hers, strengthened by the pressure of having to whip her diminutive ass into shape in such a limited amount of time. "I have to push you to get results!"

"*Oui*, well, there is pushing and there is throwing off a *cliff!*"

He threw his hands up. "It's impossible to adjust my teaching method to suit you when your behavior changes from day to day! Which Wilhelmina Allende am I arguing with right now? Let me know and I'll try and be more genteel."

She gasped. "You don't have to be such a—such an *ass!*"

"And you don't have to be so fucking *neurotic!*"

They squared off, their breaths loud in the sweat-dense air. Then Mina slung her bag over her shoulder and stormed out.

No, he thought, immediately regretting his words. Mina Allende did not "storm." She did not stalk. She slipped away with silent dignity. And yet, he felt like he was standing in the aftermath of a hurricane.

He noticed a pretty brunette standing in the hallway when he left the studio. Mina must have breezed right past her in her haste to get away from him. He cursed inwardly. Based on the petite woman's stunned expression, she'd witnessed the explosive *whatever*-that-was he'd just had with Mina. Thankfully, since it was nearing nine o'clock, she was the only person privy to the unfortunate spectacle. He tried to move past her, but she stepped directly into his path.

Despite being a sweaty, seething mess, he attempted a courteous smile. "Excuse me," he said gruffly, stepping aside.

"Wait," she said. "My name is Sophie Danis, from the Paris Opera Ballet. I've danced with Mina since we were little girls and I… I-" She seemed at a complete loss.

Registering her mellifluous accent in his brain, and then her actual words, harried as they were, he extended his hand politely. "Sophie. Pleasure to meet you. I'm afraid you've caught me at a bad time-"

"I know." She offered a rueful smile. "I couldn't help overhearing you, and I'm sorry to intrude, really I am, but no one knows her like I do—not since Étienne died—and I really think you should…"

"Miss Danis…"

"Monsieur Coen, *s'il vous plaît.* Today would have been his birthday."

He cursed. So *that* was the trigger for Mina's strange mood swings…and their more frequent battles of will.

Sophie must have taken his silence as an opportunity because she spoke again at a mile-a-minute, breathless and red-faced. "Several years ago, when we were still new to

Les Étoiles, Mina was filmed for a documentary. *'Une étoile dans la ville de lumière.'* It's on YouTube. I just think, if you could get to know her, you'd understand. *Enchanté.*" She didn't wait for his response, hurrying away to catch up to her troubled friend.

He didn't bother checking the time that night. Dinner was his cheat meal, the one meal he didn't plan. Tonight, it was Stromboli from Peppino's a couple blocks away. He'd reluctantly ordered a mixed salad to go with it—the only vegetable option on the menu—and tried not to think about the risk of contracting E. coli.

Sitting up in bed, a video with English subtitles playing on his laptop screen, he ate straight from the takeout box, smiling at the title above the video.

"A Star in the City of Light."

Fitting.

The documentary was a drama as engrossing as any movie. Its star stole every frame with a gentle magnetism that was equal parts confidence and vulnerability. He watched with increasing fascination as a younger, less jaded Mina embraced her new title with the tentativeness of a fawn learning to walk. He read the captions as hungrily as he ate, eager to gain insight into a woman whose motivations had eluded him since the day he'd met her.

It wasn't the camera following her around and capturing what went on behind the curtains, at rehearsals, and during performances that enlightened him. It was the quick interviews between scenes, when the narrator asked the starry-eyed ballerina the most probing of questions:

"Was it difficult, assuming that title?"

Mina was glowing with youth and ambition, her hair

pulled into a bun on top of her head. "Yes," she answered, her eyes shining with honesty. "At first it was very difficult."

"How so?"

"Well, it isn't something that happens easily, overnight. The title is…flattering…and I know I've earned it, but it doesn't suddenly make me a better dancer. I'm still the same dancer, with the same flaws, the same body. I still have to push myself."

"I imagine it's very competitive. Is it easy to make friends?"

"It can be difficult at times—there are so many of us, and it's so hierarchical." Her smooth brow creased with a tiny frown. "But we grew up together, so I suppose it's like any family. Some of us are closer than others."

"Ah, the principal dancer, Étienne Lemaire."

A blush filled Mina's fuller cheeks.

Today would have been his birthday, the brunette had said. Zack unconsciously sat up straighter, watching Mina with keen eyes.

"He's the most beautiful dancer I've ever seen," Mina said with undisguised admiration. "And my dearest friend."

"You love dance."

The narrator's statement seemed to ring true, so Zack wondered at Mina's bemused expression. After a full minute, she spoke again.

"People grow out of people and things they claim to love all the time." She shrugged. "I don't understand how something so profound can be so fickle. I'll never grow out of dance. It's just a part of me. It's…consuming. It overpowers love."

"Wow." The narrator was obviously taken aback by such a statement from someone so young. "I think you already answered this, but I have to ask, why? You say it's part of you, so I assume there are other things you are passionate about. Why dance?"

"I'm naturally very shy. In the movies, when you see some-one like me—the introvert, or the nerdy one, perhaps—she always has a makeover to change the way she looks and acts, so others will accept her." Taking a deep breath, she looked at the narrator straight-on. *"I just…I get carried away by the music, the movement. When I'm on that stage, I get to be the butterfly. Anything I want to express, I can, and everyone is listening to me. Watching me. But I'm still me. Inside. Still the introvert when I leave the stage and take off my makeup."*

Mina blushed again, and Zack got the impression she'd never shared so much of herself with the public before… and he was pretty damn sure she hadn't done it since then. He felt privy to the most precious secret, and his chest tightened at the wistfulness in her voice.

"How long will you do this?"

"Dance isn't what I do. It's what I am. It's what I'll be until I can't anymore."

"And then?"

"And then…" Mina hooked her thumbs together, flutter-ing her hands like a butterfly.

"A metamorphosis."

"Yes, into a teacher."

"We've talked about the physical demands, and thanks to your letting us follow you around, we've seen it first-hand. But what of the emotional demands?" the narrator went on. *"How does this profession affect your self-image?"*

Mina shifted in her seat. She clearly wasn't comfortable with this question, and Zack was intrigued.

"It can be quite hard. It's so competitive. And you're always working in front of a mirror, always examining what flaws to work on. You push yourself, flex your muscles—your arms,

your feet, your back—everything. I don't think it's possible for a dancer to feel absolutely confident with her body."

"But on tour, you're on stage a lot. No mirrors."

"So, I'll look for my silhouette...on the floor...and I use it to correct my movements. If I see that my foot is wrong-"

"I don't imagine Wilhelmina Allende's foot is wrong very often."

Mina grinned. "No. No, not often."

Zack set the empty takeout box aside and clicked his laptop shut, smiling in satisfaction. He'd gained a new understanding of Miss Allende. He knew exactly how to get through to her. But first, he had some groveling to do.

CHAPTER SEVEN

ZACK'S CHILDHOOD HOME should've had a revolving door. It was *always* full—of family, friends, neighbors—or kids from the recreation center where his mother still taught group salsa classes. Parties were a regular thing, especially for holidays like today, with *bomba,* soul and pop music playing, people dancing, and the tantalizing smell of food cooking and stewing and frying and baking.

The two-family red brick row house in Sunset Park, Brooklyn vibrated with Fourth of July merriment rivaling the veritable block party happening outside. He could already hear the pandemonium inside before he reached the front gate. As soon as he stepped onto the landing, Isaac, the toothless ragamuffin from two houses down, opened the door and poked his head out in greeting.

"*Tio!*" He launched himself at Zack's legs. "What did you bring me?"

"How 'bout 'hello' first, *pana*?"

"*Qué es la que, Tio?*" the little ankle-biter amended with a grin. "What did you bring me?"

"Better." Zack mirrored Isaac's infectious grin. Digging

into his pocket, wrinkling his nose for good measure, he presented a shiny red diecast car.

"A corvette! I'm gonna go show Titi!" He took off flying through the foyer and disappearing around a corner.

Zack chuckled. "Titi" could be any one of the women whose animated voices echoed from the kitchen, but he was pretty sure the pudgy human hurricane was referring to Zack's own mother, who was no doubt the ringleader of whatever mischief was happening behind the swinging double doors.

He passed through the living room, where a few more children (some relatives, some belonging to neighbors) were watching cartoons, to the dining room, where several men were playing a rowdy game of dominoes, and a sweaty Manuel Otero was kicking their asses.

"What's with the suit, *papá?*" Zack teased, kissing Manny's finely-lined cheek. "It's a holiday!"

"I'm on the city council, *hijo*! The city asks you to give a speech in the park, you wear a tie. What can I say?"

"Manny's sweating all over the place," a long-time friend of the family complained. "Stinking the whole place up."

"It's not sweat," Manny countered. "It's drool. I'm drowning here. Can't smell anything over what's coming from the kitchen. Who's gonna go in there and see what's holding them up?"

"*Bochinche!*" a few chimed at the same time, and they all laughed and rolled their eyes.

As if on cue, laughter pealed from the kitchen and Zack grinned. The ladies *were* gossiping, but the men didn't really mind. It was as much a beloved tradition among them to complain about the gossip as it was to play dominoes.

"I'll go check it out." Zack headed toward the kitchen.

Just as he was about to enter, the doors swung wide, and Isaac darted out, wide-eyed with red cheeks and wildly tousled hair.

"Don't go in there, Tio!" he said, deathly serious. "They PINCH!"

"I'll be careful," Zack promised, but the little one had already scrammed.

He took a few sobering breaths, knowing *exactly* what he was walking into and questioning his sanity for it, then stepped through the double doors.

And *whoosh*…

Sensory overload.

The hot air hit him first. Though the windows were open, the walls would start sweating any moment from all the pots going on the stove and in the oven, and the finished dishes keeping warm on the countertops. And then the smell…rice and beans and roasted pork, Puerto Rican tamales and chicken stew…the heavy scent of rum in whatever concoction the ladies had obviously had a few of. Then sound.

He dropped the grocery bag he was holding as his mother and four "aunts," some related and some not, descended on him. They fussed over him and cooed in the rapid-fire Spanglish they'd adapted since he was ten years old. He recognized them only by their voices because they came at him all at once. Tucking his head down, he squinted his eyes at the affectionate assault.

"*Aaaayyyyy, cariño!* You're back! And so handsome!" Titi Ana cooed, mussing his hair.

"*Sí, guapo,* but *flaco.* Needs to eat,*"* Titi Clarita said, pinching his ribs and arms.

"Handsome…but what's this?" Titi Isabel asked. "*Muy*

velludo," she tssked, rubbing the stubble on his chin with her fingers.

"*Sí,* but I *like* him hairy," Titi Yara approved." He looks like a *man.*"

There were kisses to his face, hands in his hair, fingers pinching his cheeks…and someone pinched his ass.

"That's because he *is* a man," Carmen Otero snapped, mercifully tugging her son away from the clucking hens. "Strong and sweet, like his father."

Zack rubbed his pinch-reddened face and grinned. "I can't believe you *still* haven't told *papá* I'm adopted."

His aunts howled with laughter, but Carmen was removing her sandal. "You think he doesn't know that, *mijo?*" She swatted him in the shoulder with it. "He was there! He signed the papers! I'm talking about things you don't inherit from DNA."

"No way, eh?" Yara quipped, getting back to whisking the eggs for her famous cheese flan. "He definitely didn't get those hips from his birth father, but those eyes! So green."

Carmen sucked her teeth. "Sit, *mijo,*" she commanded Zack, pointing to a stool. "You need to eat."

"I eat three thousand calories a day, *mamá*, I don't need-"

She cut him off, feeding him beans and rice, her hand cupped beneath the heaping spoon. It was fine. It was his cheat meal.

"You burn it off so fast," she complained, setting a full plate in front of him. "It's a wonder you don't lose weight and catch pneumonia."

Zack stifled a laugh, fearful of getting her shoe again. She had a preoccupation with feeding him whenever he came home and was in constant fear of him developing pneumonia. She really needed to stay away from Google.

"Did you bring my Adobo?" she asked, turning back to the stove to stir something.

His *abuelita* left her place at the sink, where she'd been the entire time, rinsing dishes and humming to the *merengue* in the background. She didn't say anything, just cupped his face and planted a kiss right on his lips, then put an ice-cold rum-laced drink in front of him and waited.

"*Sí*," he said to Carmen, putting the grocery bag on the counter. "With the red lid, not the blue."

Then he gave the drink a sniff. *Rum, fresh lime, pineapple juice.* It was an el Presidente. He caught Abuelita's knowing wink as she turned back to the sink. She might *look* harmless, but she made killer drinks, and he knew to sip slowly.

Carmen grabbed the bag and eyed Zack's plate. Satisfied he was making progress with the food, she turned back to her task, talking all the while. "When are you coming back to the rec center, *mijo?* Your program is doing so well. *Six* older boys signed up for dance this summer! But the kids miss you. It's been so long this time. We never see you anymore."

"I'm here every Sunday, *mamá.*"

"*Bah!* You know what I mean!"

"Soon," he promised, forking more food into his mouth. "And I want to bring someone with me."

All the women, even Abuelita, turned to look at him with interest.

"*Aayyy, chica bonita!*" Yara, the chattiest aunt, chimed in. "Dances like a dream."

"*Muy bonita*…but she's skinny too," Clarita said. "All that twirling around keeps the curves away."

"Titi," Zack said playfully. "She's fine the way she is, probably eats more than you."

"*Eh?*" Carmen's thin brow rose, a hand on her wide hip.

The aunts all took that as their cue to pretend they were busy, but their heads were all inclined in his direction.

"What?" Zack innocently forked some sweet fried *plátanos* into his mouth.

"Don't *what* me, *mijo*! Tell me, how are things going with the Parisian girl? Is she like you expected?"

He finished his mouthful and sipped his drink, already feeling full. Then he met his mother's impatient stare. "In some ways, she is. But in other ways…" He ran his fingers through his hair. "It hasn't been easy. Her training was probably tougher than *papá's* military days," he joked. "It's been difficult breaking her in. But I think…I think I have it under control now."

"*Control?*" Carmen scoffed. "That's your problem, *cariño*. You think you always have to be in control. You don't trust anyone to share it with you."

When the aunts turned from their tasks to tssk and nod their heads in agreement, Zack knew he was in for it.

"You *never* control your partner," Carmen continued. "You *lead*. Come on…" She set two mugs of *café con leche* on a tray and motioned with her hands for him to follow her. "Come talk to *mamá.*"

Zack followed behind her obediently to the sitting room—the one reserved for special occasions with its plush furniture, a piano that had been in the family for three generations, family photos, and a tapestry of The Last Supper on the wall above the sofa. He smiled inwardly. *At least she finally took the plastic off the couch.*

"Sit." She set the tray on the coffee table and sat next to him, taking his hand like she'd done when he was a child. "Tell me what's wrong."

"I knew it was going to be challenging, training a classical ballerina to do the stuff I'm doing. I *welcomed* the challenge. I thought it would be *fun.*"

"Is it not fun?"

He nodded. "Some days, it's incredible what we do. When she's present…when I can tell she's with me and she's giving me everything, I have no doubt in my mind I made the right choice. But some days I can tell she's someplace else. No matter how much I encourage her, how hard I push her, she just locks up. Loses focus. She gets unsure of herself and turns into this screaming, stubborn person. She *completely* shuts me out."

"Someplace else?" Carmen asked. "Where would she go?"

"That's just it, I don't *know.* It's clear something's bothering her—something I can't ask her about because it's personal. Of course I'm worried we won't be ready in time, but I have an understudy for just that possibility." He shook his head. "I want her to know she can talk to me. That she can trust me. I'm not sure she thinks she can. If she won't trust me, we won't be as great as I know we can be. And that's why I chose her in the first place."

Carmen's eyes widened at that. "Why *did* you choose her, *mijo?* Don't tell me you got sucked in by a pretty face."

"Well, I'm a visual person and she's very…visual."

She laughed, squeezing his hand. "Tell me."

"It's not easy to explain. There was just something about her."

"*My mijo?* The *writer?* The one who is about to open on Broadway can't find any words? *BAH!*"

Zack shrugged. "I couldn't take my eyes off her. It's that simple. Before I even saw her in Paris, I only watched one of her performances—all of thirty seconds of it on Alex's TV. I found her intriguing. She took the role into herself until it wasn't a role. That kind of passion? The kind that makes the audience forget they're watching a show? I dunno…" He rubbed his chin, then threw up his hand. "I just got this—this urge. I *had* to dance with her."

Carmen took a few sips of her *café con leche*. "If you say she's Camille, then she's Camille."

Zack started to speak, but his mother held up her hand. "Don't second guess yourself, *nene*. This ballerina…"

"Mina," Zack offered.

"Mina…She's uprooted herself, come all the way here—away from her family, away from everything she knows. She's like you, when you first came to live with me and *papi*. Everything so new and exciting, and a little bit scary, too. *But…*" She took Zack's chin in her hand. "She did those things because of *you*. Because she *does* trust you, *mi tesoro*. Or at least, your reputation. She wouldn't have come if she didn't."

She was quiet, giving him time to process her words, as she'd done since he was a child. He sipped the coffee, thinking about what he'd learned of Mina so far…She dyed her ballet shoes. She snuck in extra practice with another choreographer. She picked herself apart in the mirror every chance she got. Every move she made, every thought, every spoken word, seemed meticulously controlled.

Well, except when she's cursing at me.

She kept her insecurities to herself until they had her wound up so tight, there was no conclusion but to eventually fall apart. Looking up, he found his mother studying him. She was the seasoned teacher. And a woman. She would know what to do.

"What now?" he asked.

She sat up straighter to deliver her verdict. "Pretend the floor is like a map, *mijo*. And the steps are all the stops along the way, *bien?*"

Zack nodded.

"She is too focused on the vehicle and the weather and everything else, trying to get to certain places on the map. So now…now, you *lead. You* take the map. You drive the vehicle, so she can stop concentrating so much and just enjoy every stop."

"*No se, mamá*," he teased. "You sure *you're* not the writer?"

"*Bah!*" She straightened her clothes, clearly flustered. "I've been around you too long! Come…You need to eat some more."

Later, Zack stopped by the dance theater to post his fliers seeking skilled dancers to volunteer some time with his youth at the rec center. The dance theater had been open for camp earlier in the day but closed its studios to evening classes in observance of the holiday. He went to unlock the double doors, but they were already open. Frowning, he left the fliers on the front desk to go investigate.

He walked for just a minute before faint music met his ears. Following it, like a child after The Piper, his brow smoothed. The ambiguous sound grew clearer with each step. He recognized those yearning notes, the haunting strains of "Élégie" by Jules Massenet for *Manon.*

How long had it been since he'd heard that music? It had to have been years, longer still since he'd danced the choreography. But it was filed away with every other piece of music, every other step. His mind simply double clicked to open it up and it all came pouring out…

Manon, a woman torn between worldly wealth and

true love. It was a ballet so special, so intense and beautifully tragic, few companies included it in their repertoires… *Including this company.* Intrigued, he followed the sound until it reached its true volume, just outside studio six.

He wasn't particularly quiet stepping into the studio, but its sole occupant was moving in his direction without appearing to notice him at all. Christine must have let her in. Made sense. It wasn't a holiday for Mina.

Immersed in the music, she moved with feline grace and a flawless line, from her perfectly aligned fingertips to the tips of her pointe shoes. He admired the supple arch of her back, the gorgeous curve of her feet and her beautiful arms; but it was her exquisite face twisted in agony that rooted him to the floor for countless seconds, until she stopped abruptly, stumbled, and started up again.

Again, she danced like her body was made of water… and again she faltered, like she'd missed a step. The clumsiness was so unlike her it was jarring, and he tried to ascertain its cause. He studied her feet more intently this time, not for their shape, but for the steps. He watched the way she gained momentum, as if going into a lift, then abruptly stopped…the way she'd lean and lift her arms as if supporting them on something.

No, not something. Some one.

His mind put the pieces together. It was her expressions: They were far too honest to be an act, and she seemed completely unaware of him and her surroundings. It was her steps: She stopped short when the choreography called for a *partner*. She was dancing the pas de deux, from the first act of *Manon.* And she was dancing it with a ghost. He didn't need to be a rocket scientist to figure out who the ghost was.

Jesus.

He couldn't remember the last time he'd felt his heart break, the last time he'd experienced sorrow so acute, his body physically ached…but his heart was filling with empathy to the point of rupturing, and his breaths came heavy and uneven. Before he could stop himself, he was moving toward her—slowly, not wanting to startle her. Another file in his mind clicked open, and he was moving his steps in time with hers.

Her steps brought her toward him again. Looking into eyes that were normally dark and soulful, but now looked vacant, his breath caught. For an uneasy moment, he searched for some sign that she had come out of her stupor and didn't want him there. But she lowered her eyes and timidly bouréed toward him, silently giving him permission to dance with her.

Gingerly, he walked around her as the piece demanded… *five…six…* and spun her into his body, as if overcome with burgeoning love and desire. He was Des Grieux and she was Manon, and he swept her from her feet as she literally walked on air. His touch was attentive, adoring, and she responded, allowing him to support the weight of her body in increasingly daring lifts—lifts he knew would make her freeze up in rehearsal but were so seamless now. His eyes watered with emotion.

It could be this easy, this effortless…

He blinked it away and stayed with her, their movements becoming faster and more urgent until the final moment of repose, when they stared, enraptured, into one another's eyes. Except the moment felt strange, as if the universe had shifted somehow, blending reality and fantasy, and he couldn't discern what he was feeling, what he was reading in her eyes…or whose eyes they were.

"Zack?" she whispered, her eyes wide and equally searching.

"*Petite?*"

"Why?"

"Why?" He frowned, still trying to catch his breath.

"Why me? Why haven't you fired me? Found someone better?"

It was the second time he was asked the question that day, but it wasn't any easier to put into words, especially not now, after what they'd just shared. The exhilaration still flowed through his veins, still raised the hairs of his neck, made his nostrils flare with the effort to breathe. So, he said the first thing that came to mind. It was all he could manage.

"Because you do this thing sometimes when you dance. You flirt with the time. You're off by just a hair, milking the music for all it's worth…It's so subtle, no one knows what it is when it's happening, they just *feel* it."

"I-I didn't think anyone noticed. I just wanted to have something that was mine…"

"I noticed. I'm sure I could find someone easier, *petite,* but I couldn't find someone better."

She shifted awkwardly a moment. When she looked at him again, her eyes had taken on a sheen, and she attempted a small smile. "Truce?"

He nodded. "Truce."

୶

The sun had just begun to set, and Mina squinted as its weakening rays streamed through gaps in the clouds and filtered through the leaves. It was nearing eight hours and a half, but the air was still warm and sultry, seeping through the cracks in the sidewalk and filtering up. Her legs burned deliciously from her brisk ten-minute walk from the subway stop to Alex's beautiful, tree-lined street in Brooklyn. Brownstones towered above her in rich, earthy tones, and she couldn't help but admire their charm, even as her heart pounded in her chest.

Alex had told her more than once she could stop by anytime. Still…*I should have called,* she reprimanded herself for the thousandth time. She'd given herself a few pep talks just to get out of her hotel and onto the train. And now, as Alex's steep staircase rose from the pavement in front of her, she stopped, doubting herself again. What would be her excuse for stopping by? And so *late?*

She closed her eyes, letting the noise of the city around her absorb the panic creeping into her thoughts. Opening them again, she took the stairs slowly, until she stood at the landing in front of an ornate door. She quickly rang the bell before she gave in to the foolish urge to turn around and go right back to her hotel. There was a motion behind the thick stained-glass pane, the heavy sound of locks moving, and then the door opened. She gasped.

"Zack?"

He looked as shocked as she felt, opening the door wider as if to convince himself she was really there. "Mina."

Caught off guard, she had no time to stop her eyes from moving over him, drinking in the way he looked outside the studio, dressed down in a completely different way. He wore only a pair of gym shorts and a sleeveless shirt. The thin gray cotton stretched across the muscles of his chest and shoulders, and her eyes lingered there before trailing over his narrow waist, over his lean hips and the taut muscles of his thighs.

She remembered the way those strong arms had held her, and the way those hands had lifted her against him only a few hours ago. She hadn't been able to really see him then, the way she could now. Her eyes met his again, and she knew he was remembering the same thing.

"I'm sorry," she stammered. "Alex told me it was okay to stop by. I should have anticipated he might have company."

"No need to apologize. I'm renting the room upstairs, so bumping into me is inevitable, I'm afraid. Alex is out right now, but you're welcome to-"

"Oh, I'm sorry." She realized she'd just apologized again. "Sorry." She winced, unable to stop the word from tumbling from her lips once more. Her mind was working overtime to formulate some excuse, but the truth came quicker. Easier. "I just…I don't know anyone else here. Everyone back home is asleep, and I-I didn't want to be alone."

She chanced a look at him again, but his gaze held an unexpected warmth, not at all the annoyance she expected.

"It's okay." He stepped back and opened the door completely. "I'm someone, you know. Maybe not as wise or eccentric as Alex, but I might do in a pinch."

Mina eyed him, still hesitant. He was obviously trying to lighten the moment, it was clear in his voice. But his expression was missing the lopsided grin that usually accompanied his humor. His brows were lifted slightly, and he shifted his weight. It was as if he wasn't just being polite. As if, maybe, he really was hoping she would come in.

"Okay." Her voice was barely above a whisper.

Stepping a few feet inside, she absently admired the foyer. It was wide, with open entryways on either side. One led to a library, the other to a sitting room, both furnished with a stately elegance that was distinctly Alex. The ceiling had to be twelve feet high, and an impressive chandelier hung above a spiraling staircase down the hall and to her left. She turned around at the sound of the door clicking heavily shut and stopped breathing.

Zack was a half meter in front of her. How had he moved so quickly? So *quietly?* She felt the smallest hint of warmth from his body, caught the faintest whiff of his clean scent as she breathed, and was overcome with the urge to get closer. To experience the same comfort his nearness had given her before. Her mouth worked silently as she stared at him.

"I'm here, *petite.* I'm someone you know."

Her eyes welled suddenly and spilled over. He took a step forward and stopped, probably thinking she'd panic and flit past him out the door. She looked at the door. He wasn't far off in that assumption.

"I'm here," he said again carefully. "Just take what you need."

Letting her purse fall to the floor, she stepped closer, and for the longest moment she just stood there and watched his chest rise and fall in deep, measured breaths. Then she lifted her hands to his chest to feel the movement beneath her palms. Strong and steady. Before she knew what she was doing, her hands moved down and around his waist, and her head nestled against his chest.

She felt his deep sigh, and his arms go around her, soft and strong. His body was already familiar to her after so many hours of rehearsal, his scent and movement. He was as close to home as she could feel in that moment. Tightening her arms around him, she pressed herself into his warmth, clinging desperately to that feeling for count-less seconds, until her tears grew to soft sobs and her body went boneless.

He lifted her the second her body sagged against him, one arm beneath her knees and the other behind her back. Car-rying her to the sitting room, he sat on the soft, button-tufted sofa, cradling her to his chest. She released every-thing she had in convulsive gasps, wetting his neck and wrenching at his gut for minutes on minutes. He couldn't imagine what she was feeling, couldn't think of anything to do but rub her back and squeeze her gently every now and then to remind her subconscious that he was there.

He didn't know how much time had passed when her tears finally subsided and the shaking in her body faded to little tremors. She hadn't moved her face from where it was tucked into his neck, and her breathing had slowed, the rise and fall of her chest matching his now. He thought she might have fallen asleep, but when he relaxed his shoulder to let her head fall gently into the crook of his arm, she was staring back at him.

Though a little red, a little swollen, her eyes were com-pletely free of their invisible shield. He sucked in a breath. It was like having a mirror held up to his own soul…

"Cariño," Carmen had whispered to him when he was ten. *"I've never seen someone so young with eyes so old."*

Recognition.

That's what beckoned him closer, drawing his head down until his lips touched her forehead. It was all he would allow himself in the moment, a comforting kiss. He meant to be quick about it, but his lips lingered, pressed to her warm, dewy skin for a few seconds before he forced himself to pull back. She had other ideas, though, tensing in his hold for a split second before her arms came around his shoulders and pulled him back to her, her lips brushing his.

It wasn't a kiss. Not really. It was the softest of touches, like a feather being dragged along the sensitive skin of his lips. They tingled in her wake, parting in anticipation, his eyes drifting closed. He felt her hands glide along the sides of his neck and sink into his hair, her fingers grazing his scalp. Groaning, he tightened his hold on her.

She brushed her mouth over his again…and again, and again. Slowly, and so maddeningly soft. He nudged his nose against hers, wanting more, but he felt the warmth of her breath leave his face and knew she'd pulled back.

Slowly, his eyes opened. It was dark outside now, but the light from the foyer guided his gaze across her beautiful face. Her hair was pulled up and he could see her large, expressive eyes, the delicate arch of her cheekbones, her soft, pillowy lips.

He knew better. He *knew.*

He knew the compatibility of their bodies, that where he dipped, she curved, that even the hardest parts of her were soft against him. He knew how far she could stretch, how much she could bend, the controlled power in her smooth limbs. But when her hands dropped to his arms and gently squeezed, he still loosened his hold, still let her sit up, still let her maneuver her limber body until she straddled him, her thighs hugging his waist, her hands smoothing up his chest and along his neck to cradle his face.

Curving her lips into a smile, she brought her face close, running the tip of her tongue along the seam of his parted lips. He made another sound, low in his throat, sliding his hands up and down her waist from hip to breast. She flicked her tongue into his mouth, touching it to the tip of his and pulling away.

"We can't do this, *petite*." But she swallowed the last word, her tongue gliding past the tip of his tongue and retreating again.

"We can. " Pressing her lips to his jawbone, she practically purred as her cheek grazed his chin.

She left a trail of light kisses and playful flicks of her tongue from his jaw to his earlobe, and his fingers flexed at her waist, his breaths harsh and ragged.

"You make me crazy all the time," she murmured. "Until I don't recognize myself. I know you can make me feel good, Zack. Take away my shy."

Her accent seemed magnified, lilting the edges of her vowels, dragging out the others…and threatening his already-fragile restraint.

"You think I'm being nice to you just to get my *dick* wet?" He was being gruff, but he needed to break through the sweltering haze of arousal. "I'm not an animal, *petite*."

"*Non, tu es un animal,*" she insisted, grazing his earlobe with her teeth. *"T'es un lion."*

The sound he made was louder this time, feral, like a growl. She shuddered against him and he cursed into her mouth, enveloping her lips with his. His tongue moved against hers, and her skin bloomed in his hands. He circled her tongue with his and she sighed, knotting her hands in his shirt, pulling him harder to her. Tasting the faint remnants of wine, he sucked it from her tongue. Gasping, she gently nipped his lower lip and slipped her tongue in again. Over and over he tasted her…slow, but insatiable.

He let her control the pace with her hands in his hair,

her fingers massaging his nape. He kissed her deep and hard, then she gripped handfuls of his long strands and gently tugged, slowing their mouths to lazy kisses. Shuddering, he trailed his hands firmly down her sides to her hips, helping her grind against his erection, molding her curves more perfectly to his body.

"Fuck, I'm in trouble." Smoothing his hands over the rounded curve of her ass, he squeezed tentatively, feeling her out. "So much trouble."

He squeezed again, harder this time, enjoying her little whimper before he forced his hands to touch her somewhere else. Because he couldn't handle much more, or he'd haul ass up three flights of stairs to see what other sounds he could rend from her lovely throat. Returning his hands to her sides, he caressed up and down, increasing and decreasing the pressure, circling his thumbs over her ribs just beneath her breasts. All the while, his lips never left her skin. They brushed her cheek, pressed hotly along her neck, and slowly down. She trembled as his lips brushed the delicate line of her collarbone, and he lifted his head to look at her.

"So much fucking trouble," he gritted through his teeth.

Her mouth was open, her head tipped back as short, shallow breaths left her lips. Her breasts seemed to grow right in front of him, lifting and pushing against his chest. Helping her shrug out of her cardigan, he slid it over her shoulders and down her arms.

"Jesus, *petite*." *The skin I can see.* He trailed his fingers along the top swells of her breasts, dipping them into the valley that disappeared into her camisole, then replaced his fingers with his mouth.

"*Lion,*" she moaned, and something in him snapped.

He tugged the straps down until the soft, golden brown flesh was fully exposed, the pretty peaks stiff and ready for his touch. But he teased her, deliberately avoiding them, caressing the sides of her breasts, cupping and gently squeezing. The more he gave her, the sharper her cries grew, until she was writhing wildly in his lap, and he was dangerously close to coming on Alex's expensive couch. Cursing, he shifted his hips to adjust himself and avoid a mess, determined to get her to shatter for him instead. Licking his fingers, he swirled them along the dark skin around her nipples, dipping his head to blow over the dampened skin.

"Zack…" She strained against him, squirming as moisture seeped from her leggings to the soft fabric of his shorts.

Her scent wafted up between them and he breathed her in, practically tasting her on his tongue. Panting now, his hips flexed uncontrollably. *The skin I can see,* he reminded himself, dipping his head. She cried out, something shrill and completely unintelligible, the pain of his hair twisting around her fingers spurring him on. He took care to gently knead the breast he didn't devour, alternating between licking and swirling her nipples with his tongue and sucking them into his mouth. When he grazed her with his teeth, she went rigid in his arms, taut as a tightly coiled spring, and then suddenly, gloriously, she released.

"Lion," she gasped, shuddering against him. *"Gentle, gentle, lion."*

Zack rubbed her back until her tremors subsided, stiff with his own desire, his eyes glued to her dewy face.

"Petite?" His voice was hoarse, tentative.

It was fascinating, the way he could see the exact moment the euphoria left her face and awareness swept across it like a cold, sobering wave.

"*Oh mon Dieu…*" She snatched her camisole back up to cover herself, scrambling from his lap.

Grabbing her cardigan from the floor, she quickly turned away. She was nearly to the door with her purse over her shoulder by the time Zack could move, but he was still painfully aroused, and with his hair mussed up as it was, he was sure he looked like a crazed predator.

"Wait," he called softly from a few feet behind her.

"*S'il te plaît,*" she begged from the door, her back to him. "Don't say anything."

"Mina, that was…*incredible.* I've never seen-"

"I have to go." She wrenched the door open and fled, and Zack was in no condition to stop her.

Chapter Eight

MINA WAS EATING her way through half a loaf of fried bread smothered in a syrup of wine, orange juice and sugar, when her phone chirped from deep in her bag.

"Look who finally decided to call," she said, piling more food into her mouth.

"You texted me fifteen times," said Sophie.

"Sixteen!"

"I'm not the one who moved to Siberia! It's six hours into the future here, you know that. Just leaving rehearsal—which, by the way, has not been easy since you left. The director thinks we're all conspiring to leave. Anyway, I figured if you were dying, you'd call."

Mina choked. "I can't decide which part of that statement sounds stupider."

"Someone's in a mood today. How's the new apartment?"

"Crowded. *Maman* sent an army to decorate this morning so I'm eating a monstrosity they call 'French Toast' at a restaurant I don't even know the name of."

"It'll probably kill you," said Sophie. "And Siberia?"

"Hot." Mina took another bite and emptied her brain in a torrent of food-muffled words. "So hot. And crowded.

People everywhere, all the time…walking, standing in line, sitting on the train…"

"It must be very inconvenient to encounter actual people in a densely populated city-"

"So many people, but I still feel alone."

"Oh, Mina…"

"I *like* being by myself. I left my apartment this morning because I wanted to be by myself! But…sometimes I don't want to be." Mina's stomach cramped, and her hand flew to her mouth. "I think I'm going to be sick…"

"Take a deep breath, *chère*. Stop binging."

"I know. I'm so *stupide*. This is the first time I've eaten today." Taking a tiny sip of water, controlling her breath, she willed the lump in her throat to sink back down. "*Bon Dieu,* I feel disgusting. I have rehearsal today. I have to face him, Sophie."

"Deep breath," Sophie said again softly. "What happened?"

Mina moved her gaze from the sea of people passing by the restaurant window. They were walking too fast, and nausea crept back into her throat. Closing her eyes until it passed, she took another deep breath. "Last night, I didn't want to be alone. Monsieur Verenich said it would be alright to stop by if I wanted…I should have called…"

"Monsieur Verenich? I'm confused…"

"He wasn't home. Zack opened the door. He lives there. He has his own floor."

"*Merde!*"

"I wasn't going to stay, but he insisted. I had nowhere else to go, and I… I just wanted something familiar."

"So… you and him, alone…"

"*Oui.*"

"The suspense is giving me an ulcer. Just tell me!"

"We…hugged."

"*Tramp!*"

Mina burst into laughter, uncaring of the heads turning her way. Let them stare. The tension in her body eased a little more with every gasping breath. "And kissed."

"*Putain!*" Sophie swore. "I *told* you, hugs are sexual."

"It wasn't like that, not at first."

"*Non?*"

"He can be such a… such an—"

"*Connard.*"

"*Oui,* an ass…but last night, something happened. He was the man I met in *Paris* after the show. His voice, the way he looked at me…Everything from that night came back, and it felt like he was pulling me to him without touching me."

"*Mon Dieu.*"

Mina sighed. "It was…bliss."

They were quiet a moment. Then Sophie spoke again. "He has such a presence, Mina. It's intimidating. I almost apologized for breathing his air."

Mina laughed. "That's ridiculous!"

"It's *true*. I… don't be mad…"

"What?"

"I… *merde*…I may have asked him not to be so hard on you—"

"*Sophie!*"

"I *know*! It was *stupide* and impulsive and completely unprofessional…but you keep so much inside you. It's not healthy. I just wanted him to see you like I see you, *chère.*"

Mina groaned. "I can't *believe* you! What did he say?"

"*Nothing!* I didn't give him a chance. I was so nervous…

I told him about that documentary we did years ago, when you first got promoted. Then I ran after you."

"Now it makes sense."

"What does?"

"Why he was so nice to me. I sat there and cried in his lap like a toddler!"

"Slow down—"

"And then I kissed him. He tried to stop me, but I kissed him anyway. *Bon Dieu…*"

"Okay, just…wait," Sophie said. "Calm down. Did he kiss you back?"

Mina's body blossomed all over, the answer to Sophie's question playing in her mind. Like a scene from a favorite movie, she remembered every action, every line. She touched her fingers to her lips. "Yes," she breathed. "It was so good, Sophie. When he kissed me, I felt it everywhere."

"Everywhere?" Sophie gasped. "He went down on you?"

Mina's floor muscles contracted at the thought of Zack's slow, deep kisses on her neglected core, and a tiny moan escaped her lips.

"*Wilhelmina Fiona Allende, you better not be turned on right now, I swear to God!*"

"*Non.*" Mina's voice was distant, husky. "Above the waist. Everything above the waist."

"Oh my…neck?"

"*Oui.*"

"Shoulders?"

"*Mmhmm.*"

"Boobs?"

"*Everything*, Sophie." Mina licked her lips, trying to phrase her next words. "He made me…It was so good, I didn't control it."

"You had a boob orgasm? *Oh. Mon. Dieu!*"

Mina blushed furiously, her fingers and toes tingling, her hands flying to her cheeks. "It's never happened to me before."

"Well, *merde*, me neither. How did it feel? I must know everything. You're the only one getting any action at the moment, and sleep orgasm guy just made you—"

"*Okay,* I'll tell you! Just…stop calling him that."

"*Allez, chère.* You're shy, but you're not a prude. We learned about sex in primary, watching people paw each other to death along the Seine."

Relaxing her posture, Mina focused on the pedestrian light changing from 'Stop' to 'Go.' "It was like…when you're having sex, and you feel it building and building, but when it happens, it's…*gentil.* Not so intense. Your whole body radiates, and it lasts *forever.*"

"*Bordel,*" Sophie breathed.

"I know."

"Then what?"

Mina pushed food around on the plate with her fork.

"*Mina?*"

"I was so embarrassed. I didn't mean for it to happen."

"You ran." The silence seemed to answer Sophie's question. "You have to stop running."

"I can't face him."

"Be a grownup. Go to rehearsal."

"I'll call in sick."

"Don't be ridiculous! You haven't done that once your entire life."

"But—"

"I'm not listening anymore. Congratulations, *chère.* I'm happy for you."

"Wait! Sophie—"

"Ciao."

⚘

3:55 PM, Five Days Before the Tony Awards

Polishing off his banana and discarding the peel, Zack strolled into the studio. He arrived early each day, using the time for marking, ensuring each step was absorbed in his muscle memory. Keeping his movements light, he rose to his toes wherever there was a jump and motioned with his hands wherever there was a turn, conserving his energy until Mina arrived.

Alex and Harper were there, too, and Carla, the brilliant cellist working with Harper to compose the music for the production. Harper sat at the piano, and Carla in a folding chair beside him, her enormous cello resting against her thigh. They stopped playing whenever Zack needed to work out timing or tempo. Alex took notes from Zack about which points in the routine to watch most critically during rehearsal. It was getting down to the wire, and all the parts needed to move in perfect synchrony for Sunday's show.

Facing the door, Zack was first to notice when Mina arrived. He stopped moving and stared at her openly, a smile tugging the corners of his mouth. She was so quiet, moving with feline grace to set her gym bag on the floor in a corner. Today, the feline wore a black hoodie that swallowed her whole, the hem stopping beneath her butt, the zipper to her neck, the hood pulled over her head. She peered at him from beneath the hood, but stayed in that corner, the point in the room farthest from him, he noticed with increasing amusement.

It was clear she had no intention of removing the gargantuan sweater, so he hiked his brow and let his grin stretch from ear to ear. Lifting her chin, she glared back, folding her arms. His answering chuckle alerted the others to her presence, and Harper gave her a wide smile.

"That you under there, Little Bird?" he teased. "You're gonna love what I made for you."

"Hey, you work for *me*," Zack said, but Harper's expert fingers were already fluttering over the keys.

Carla's cello joined in like a deep, soulful voice. Zack tilted his head, eager for Mina's reaction to the mellifluous sound filling the studio. He wasn't disappointed. Her body rocked side to side through the first strains, then she sighed and closed her eyes, wrapping her arms around herself.

Yes. What she heard made her want to be held, and it made him smile.

Harper hadn't simply taken Chopin's score and added a beat to make it contemporary. He'd plumbed its depths, revealing every secret, shortening and lengthening the melodies, twisting them and adding his own, until something completely unique emerged. *Magic.*

It was "A Song for Camille," and by the time Harper and Carla finished playing, a simmering energy crackled in the studio. Zack's heart beat double time, the hairs of his arms and neck standing on end. He saw it in Mina's eyes when she opened them again. They were ready to dance.

Mina joined Zack and Alex for quick instructions while Harper and Carla reviewed their notes.

"I hope we're on the same page today." Alex looked from Mina to Zack. "I know it's an unsavory part of the business, but sometimes partners have to put their hands in rather…personal…places to guarantee safe execution of the lifts, or for more contemporary pieces, to set a mood."

He addressed them both, but Mina was keenly aware that his exposition was for her benefit. It was beginner's fare, partnering *un- zéro-un*, and the fact that Alex felt compelled to remind her made her cheeks heat painfully. Zack's eyes burned a hole in the side of her face, but she refused to look at him, shifting her weight from one foot to the other.

"Sincerest apologies for what happened, Mina, but I assure you we're all professionals here. I can say with complete confidence I've never seen Zack drop a partner. In his efforts to catch you, his hands might slip and… well, better to be groped than dropped, my dear."

"I understand." She wanted to forget the embarrassing debacle ever happened.

Louder, so everyone heard, Alex said, "Right, so it's Act Two. We're in the Lady Camille's boudoir. You're very much in love, and things are about to…happen." Turning back to Harper and Carla, he was oblivious to Mina's mortified groan.

"Take off that ridiculous sweater."

She jumped. Zack was alarmingly close to her ear. "How do you keep doing that? Sneaking up on me like… like a—"

"Like a lion?" he murmured, lifting his hands to her shoulders, gently massaging. "You're so tense. Sorry about Alex—he meant well, but I think what he said might qualify as sexual harassment. For the record, I'll never grope you unless you want me to."

"Connard!" She meant for the insult to sound much harsher, but it ended on a moan, her traitorous body melting into his hands. "Why did you cover the mirrors?"

"Because you bully yourself." His warm breath tickled her cheek. "It is *July.*"

She cast a quick glance behind them at the others. Were they looking, a massage to a ballerina's tense shoulders wouldn't seem out of the ordinary. Still. She lifted her shoulders to shrug him off and turned to face him. "I'm cold."

"Bullshit. It's seventy degrees in here. Pretty state-of-the-art, these climate-controlled studios…"

She glared at him.

"I have to see your body, *petite,* watch your muscles moving. You know that."

"I think you've seen enough," she snapped, then felt the color leave her face. "*Merde!*"

"So that *is* what this is about."

"No." She looked nervously at the others again.

"Liar. Are we seriously gonna pretend you didn't come in my lap?"

Mina gasped, her arms going limp at her sides. She stared at his smug, infuriatingly handsome face as he unzipped her hoodie, watching his eyes move slowly over her body in her leotard and wrap skirt. Then, to her abject horror, she moaned.

"Ssshhh, don't wanna go telling the whole world now, do we?" With a wink, he tossed her hoodie into the corner with her bag.

"We'll start from the second phrase," Alex's voice cut in, and Mina nearly leapt from her skin.

Moving to her mark, she lowered her voice so only Zack could hear. "That can't happen again."

"Can't?" His tone matched hers. "It wasn't hard, *petite*." Getting into position, he took her by the waist and looked square into her eyes. "And now, I'm intrigued."

"*Enfin*, don't be."

"*Aaannnd…*" Alex motioned to Harper and Carla for their cue.

"I can't help it." Zack moved his hands higher, to her true ribs, flexing his fingers there. "You intrigue me."

The piano started up. What she saw in his eyes made her lashes flutter furiously. He grinned, the *connard*.

"*…Begin!*"

Launching herself into Zack's arms, her stomach pulled into the delicious knots of life at the feel of his fingers digging into her waist, his strong torso hugged between her thighs.

"*Wonderful elevation, Mina.*"

Alex's voice reached out to them from a distance, like a foghorn through heavy haze. Her subconscious picked it up, but she was fixated on Zack. Judging by his severe expression, he was fixated on her, too.

"*Your movements are still too tight. They need to be bigger. Much bigger. Don't be afraid of really finishing off, to the ends of your fingers, so the gestures really show.*"

They positioned themselves again, and Mina jumped from the midlife of the beat, her arms engaged a second earlier, stretching the movement to her fingertips. When Zack caught her this time, her arms came around his shoulders in an exaggerated motion, and she turned her face into his neck. "I've only just begun to intrigue you?"

"*Sharp head!*"

She lifted her chin a bit.

"*Sharper head.*"

Adjusting obediently, she sucked in a breath, jumping to assist Zack as he hoisted her up to sit on his shoulders, his face pressed to her abdomen. Her cheek touched the top of his head, her face trained to show utter bliss.

"Wonderful!"

"No." Zack turned his face up with sensual drama, touching his forehead to hers. "Since Paris."

Paris?

"Watch your expression, Mina."

She braced herself on Zack's shoulders, letting her legs fall gracefully beneath her. He gave her a quick toss, catching her waist again and setting her slowly to her feet.

"Yes! Great improvisation there, Zack! Nice playful element in such a serious piece. Note that for next time so you don't look quite *so startled, dear."*

Spinning her around, Zack bent her over, her feet and fingertips flat on the floor. Her heart pounded like war drum, flooding her face with heat. He smoothed the palm of his other hand up her back, and she started to come up slowly.

"Not so straight, Mina. Use your whole body, so it's more sensual. It's got to come from that foot, dear. Push off…Good."

Mina leaned into Zack's body, letting her head fall back onto his chest, her face turned up to his. "I don't understand." She controlled her breathing. "What you said to me that night—"

She couldn't finish her thought, because he'd drawn her arm up, rubbing his stubbled chin along her sensitive skin.

"Show the inside of your arm, Mina. It's very soft, very sensual. Everything should be exaggerated."

She adjusted her arm.

"I said you were performing. The curtains closed, and you were still pretending." Zack touched his lips to her arm in the choreographed places, kissing his way up to her elbow.

She stopped breathing.

"Excellent tension there, dear."

Taking two stylistic steps back, Zack stretched out his arm. Only his hand touched her, supporting her neck in his palm.

"Jesus, stay with her, Zack."

Mina engaged every muscle to keep her body straight, and fell back, her feet sliding slowly along the floor. Zack went down with her, lowering her to the floor by her neck until she lay on her back, then kneeled beside her.

"So then, why…?" She tried not to frown, conscious that she was supposed to be acting, and made sure her chest heaved convincingly.

The music faded to softer strains. *"Go ahead for the kiss."*

Zack was over her in a flash, supporting all two meters of his muscular body on just his arms, like a pushup with his feet off the floor. "Because through it all, I still saw you."

She gasped, then his mouth was on hers. In a whisper of time, mere seconds, a million things happened: Her eyes drifted shut, and her other senses exploded. His lips were soft, insistent, the heat from his body making her back arch, her chest seeking contact with his. Her nostrils filled with the musky scent of him, and his hair tickled her brow. His tongue flicked her bottom lip and her stomach clenched, her lips parting to taste his breath. But he kept it from her, sucking it in quickly and shoving off, pulling her up from the floor by both of her trembling hands.

"Holy *shit!*"

"Yes, thank you, Harper," said Alex. "Well…you don't need to practice *that* part, do you?" Clearing his throat, his gaze flickered over them. "Splendid! Let's take it from the next phrase, then we'll start from the top."

They went through it again. And again…and again, until Zack was satisfied that Mina no longer hesitated before a jump, and her face stopped giving it away when she was about to be thrown into the air or whipped around with her head inches from the floor.

Something else was happening too, and it thrilled him more than he cared to admit. She shivered when he touched her—usually her waist, her neck, that hidden gem along her spine that made her jerk from the lightest brush of his fingers there—but she'd *finally* stopped flinching. It was…nice. Snapping from his reverie, he braced to catch her again.

"Run *to him, Mina…sharp pirouette. Look at him all the way down, you've got plenty of time…Great.*"

Maintaining the all-important eye contact the entire time, he kissed up her hand and her inner arm, laying his head against her breast for their close embrace.

"*And hold it…really try and fix that position, just for a moment.*"

Her heart beat out the time against his face, filling his nose, his mouth, with the musky scent of vanilla and sweat…

"*Steady her with your right hand, then snake that left one after the lift. That's good. That's fine…Real passion within the moment, you two…a bit of music when you draw her back in… Take your time, now. That's a* real *stroke of her breast there…*"

Fuck.

She shivered again, and his fingertips throbbed where

they met her skin. He was soaked in sweat, worse than any rehearsal he could remember. His limbs tingled with the effort not to break character, drown out Alex's commands about how to touch her, and follow his own instincts…the way he'd done last night. He squeezed his eyes shut against the stinging sweat.

"Grab her wrists…"

He did.

"Mina, let the music take you down."

She did, right in front of him, her wrists captive in his hands. Her head tilted back, far enough for her eyes to meet his, and her legs parted into a split.

"Come in, Zack, right on top of her. Don't be shy."

Laying her down again, he collapsed on top of her. "Sweet, merciful, baby Jesus," he breathed into her chest.

A breathless giggle escaped her, and her eyes were dark and shiny, half covered by her long lashes.

"Well, much better today. Not perfect, but better."

High praise from Alex Verenich.

"Ho-leeee *shit!*"

Higher praise from Harper.

Zack helped peel Mina from the floor, then bid the others farewell. Alex left with Carla.

"I am so in love with the music, Harper," Mina gushed. "I was lost in it, truly."

He preened like a peacock—almost looked like one too, in his colorful designer duds. "Just wait." He collected his sheet music and satchel. "For the real deal, we'll have *four* cellos, another piano, a synthesizer, smoke and mirrors, a pony—it's gonna be this, times a *thousand.*"

Kissing his cheek, Mina smiled. "I can't wait."

"Alright, Little Bird." He turned to Zack. "I'd polish that ending a little though, looks a little sloppy."

"Fuck you."

"Maybe next time." Harper grinned, then left with a tip of his imaginary cap.

Probably a trilby.

Shaking his head, Zack turned, expecting to find Mina scurrying to the corner to snatch up her bag and the hoodie she'd obviously lifted from a sumo wrestler on the train. Instead, he collided with her petite body, catching her with an arm around her waist to keep her from flying, her arms clutching his sweaty shirt at the same time.

"Ooof!" Her eyes looked enormous, and her hair was a frizzy mess trying to escape her bun.

"That's the most inelegant thing I've ever heard you say."

She gave his chest a shove.

Stroking her back, he quirked a brow. "I thought you were shy?"

"I thought you were intrigued?"

"I am."

Her shiver didn't go unnoticed. "I *am* shy, but I'm not a corpse."

"I don't think that," he said stiffly.

"Don't you?"

"I think I'm too old, and too your boss, to tell you *any* of the thoughts I've been having lately."

Her breath hitched, and she stared back at him with unmistakable need in her eyes. His awareness of her sky-rocketed, and all he could think about was the feel of her soft body pressed to his, and her even softer lips parted millimeters from his own. Moving her hands between them and over the planes of his chest, she tentatively shaped his

129

arms and shoulders. A class let out down the hall, the commotion snatching them from the moment, cooling their warm embrace to a sweaty hug the instant they hurriedly pulled away.

He wrinkled his nose. "You stink."

"There he is." She was noticeably breathless. "The charming little *connard*."

Letting go a full-belly laugh, he studied her. Her skin glowed from exertion, and maybe something else, his ego hoped. "You think I'm an ass? Never would have guessed."

"Oh, I've thought worse—even said it, behind your back."

He grinned. "Go home. Shower. We're not done yet."

She cocked her head.

"While 'better' from Alex is a rave review, I know what your best looks like, and I won't be satisfied until you give it to me."

"I don't…think I understand."

"Dress for a night out." He patted her rump lightly, not in a remotely sexual way, and she went to the corner to collect her things. "I'll pick you up at nine-thirty."

"Pick me up?"

"You're not meeting me anywhere alone at night, *petite*."

"Ah, *chivalrous connard*."

"Don't you forget it."

❦

"It's *three* in the morning, Mina. This better be good."

"We hugged again."

Sophie groaned. "Well, I try not to kink shame, but you're stepping dangerously close to sexual deviant territory."

130

Mina held her phone to her face with her shoulder, slipping on her heels. "His hugs are nice. He squeezes just right. I feel it in my toes."

"Are you...*swooning?* Wow, now I'm feeling torn about the hugging thing. *J'ne sais pas...*Next time, maybe try it naked."

"Sophie!"

"*Je dis ça, je dis rien.*"

Mina scoffed. "You never *just say* anything. Anyway, we're going out—" She pulled the phone away so that Sophie's squeal wouldn't rupture her eardrum.

"What, like right now?"

"In a few minutes. It's not a date."

"It's after *nine*. That's practically a booty call."

"I'm serious! It's for work."

"So, he wants to throw you around after hours, too."

"*Sophie.*"

"Not my thing, personally. Being thrown terrifies me, and you volunteered for it."

"I did not *volunteer*. I'm being paid. *En fait*, I'm hanging up now."

"I hope you're wearing pretty panties. The new ones!"

"*Salut.*"

Zack almost tripped off the curb outside Mina's apartment building when she walked outside. Her fancy black dress had one shoulder and sleeve and wrapped around her slender neck like a choker. Her long legs were bare to mid-thigh, her slim feet arched high in strappy red heels with flames licking up the tops of her feet to her ankles.

"Hi." She said it like a woman who *knew* she looked good, peering at him with her big, smoky eyes.

He couldn't stop staring at her feet. They looked as buttery soft as the rest of her, and he had the strangest urge to take her oddly-proportioned toes into his mouth for a taste. "*Jesus, petite.* I said, 'dress for a night out.'" He scanned her body again. "That outfit screams 'fuck me with my shoes on.'"

That little gasp was growing on him.

"*Pardon.*" She accepted his arm. "Must have been lost in translation. You like my shoes?"

"I'll have to brush up on my conversational French. I *love* those shoes. Never take them off."

"I'll consider it. They make my feet look pretty."

"Suddenly, I have a foot fetish."

"I think there's a compliment in there somewhere, so… *merci.*"

Before he could think better of it, he brushed her loose waves over her shoulder and pressed a kiss to the creamy brown skin there, then led them toward the subway. "You're stunning. *Too* stunning for where we're going."

"And where is that?"

"Someplace too mercifully dark to see your sexy feet."

The warehouse in Brooklyn housed three massive dance floors crammed with hundreds of sweating bodies. The bouncers took one look at them and let them skip the line. Walking through the doors, Mina was hit with thick, sultry heat. It was dark. Very dark, but for flashes of strobe lights alighting on wall-to-wall bodies. They moved like they were in a trance, the bass thumping so hard, it shook the building and seemed to beat from within their ribs. Clutching at Zack's arm, another nocturnal animal bumped into her, his eyes practically rolling to the back of his head in pure ecstasy.

She tugged Zack's arm until his ear bent to her lips. "Are these people on drugs?"

His body shook with laughter. "Better than drugs, *petite*. This atmosphere is like a high. You forget about how you look or what you're doing. The music goes right through you and you just *move*."

She wasn't sure *how* they were able to move—the floor was sticky. Watching a trio of dancers doing something that looked illegal, she tried not to think about the biological hazards stuck to the bottom of her Italian leather shoes.

She squinted against the purple and blue light. "This place should come with an epilepsy warning!"

A flash of purple lit his face, highlighting his freshly shaven jawline, the sensual curve of his lips, and she completely lost her train of thought. Her eyes trailed his body slowly, progressing a little more each time a strobe lit him up again. He looked sexy and dangerous in this light, like a demigod in all black.

"It's great, isn't it?" sexy demigod's lips asked.

Her mouth suddenly went dry. "Not the word I'd use. I think I need a drink."

"Uh-uh, no alcohol. This is homework. No cheating."

"But I'm *French!*"

"Nothing I can do about that." He shrugged his shoulder against her retaliatory slap and led them through the sea of bodies.

Stopping somewhere in the middle, where writhing bodies pressed against them on all sides, he brought his hands to her hips and pulled her to him. Instinctively, her arms went around his shoulders, holding onto him, she convinced herself, for fear of slipping into the human sea. Besides, it was the only way she could *hear*.

"Zack…"

"No mirrors, *petite*." He gave her an encouraging squeeze. "No one's looking at you but me."

Then he looked at her.

Bon Dieu, did he look at her.

He studied her body like a map of the cosmos was hidden beneath her skin.

There was nothing lustful in his eyes, only wonder—a desire to be completely attuned with her and the way she moved. It was sensual by nature, in the way it made her feel stripped down to her being—her very existence—and only he could see. It made her feel sexy and fearless…and *safe*.

Staring into the shadows of his face, she lifted her arms above her head to do as they would. The bassline came at her from every direction, throbbing through her veins, exiting from the points of her fingers and toes. The darkness made her bold, and a new energy rose inside her. The atmosphere became heady, making her more drunk on it with every breath, until she moved her entire body like a boneless addict chasing the next beat.

For a full phrase, he continued to watch her, and there was something in his expression, in the intensity of his eyes, that made her lightheaded: she was the Mina he'd been waiting for, the one he'd seen in Paris beneath the façade of the makeup, the fancy dress and the grand chandeliers of the Palais Garnier…the one who had cried on his shoulder and come apart in his arms. Comfortable in her own skin.

Winding her body, she slinked her arms like reeds in a slow breeze, meeting his eyes with every flash of light. He rubbed his cheek along hers, following her movement with his hands, feeling every muscle beneath thin fabric and sensitized skin. He stroked her stomach with his palm, and she sucked it in hard.

"Sorry, *petite...*" He kissed her cheek, then seemed to indulge himself a moment, running his hands along her hips until they settled on her waist. "That's not what this is, what we came here for."

She melted at the sincerity in his voice, in the warmth of his touch. "What did we come here for?"

His grin spread against her cheek. "Trust falls."

CHAPTER NINE

The eve of the Tony Awards

MINA STOOD STAGE left waiting for her cue. Pressure. That's what she felt watching the other dancers take flight across the stage. Acerbic, precise and athletic, they were an acute reminder of how much she'd been coddled. Three *weeks* of one-on-one rehearsal to learn technique, and these veritable gladiators executed it like they could do it in their sleep.

Closing her eyes, she waited for his voice: the dreamy, soothing tenor that always reminded her to never tell a lie. Her heart grew heavy at an alarming rate, like the Hulk inside her chest, trying to pound its way from its cage. She doubled over, trying to catch her breath.

Oh mon Dieu.

His voice wasn't coming. She hadn't heard it all week. Not *once*. She had been so caught up in the dance, learning her lines and lyrics, the excitement and nerves…and Zack. It was hard to breathe. *She couldn't hear.* Her heart was so *loud*. Her eyes stung, and her skin was clammy.

She'd erased him.

Étienne was gone.

"Mina?" someone called to her from far away. *"Mina!"*

Mina jumped at someone's hands on her shoulders. Not so far away, then. She recognized that face. An expressive face with thick black lashes and a cupid's bow to die for. The face had a name…*What was her name?… Kyoko!* The gymnastic dancer with springs for legs and a switchblade for a mouth. Mina liked her.

"Quick!" Kyoko yelled to someone backstage. "Help me get her to the dressing room. I think she's having a panic attack."

Kyoko and someone else—someone strong from the easy way she was half walked, half dragged—assisted her to the dressing room and into a chair. The room was like a cluttered walk-in closet, covered in costumes and boxes of costumes, shoes and hats and wigs. The vanity was a mess of makeup and cream, false lashes and hair products, and the lights were blinding. She shut her eyes, vaguely aware that her other savior had left the room.

"That's it, honey. Breathe," Kyoko said in her raspy tone. "You look like you could use a drink."

Mina managed a weak smile, finally getting her breathing under control. "If it's stronger than wine, I'm not allowed. Mrs. Perez says no hard liquor or caffeine."

"Good, cuz I got water, and water." Grinning, Kyoko handed Mina a bottled water. When she seemed satisfied Mina was drinking enough, she leaned her hip against the vanity. "Perez used to get on me, too. Said I needed to be less Betty Boop, more Pearl Bailey—no room in the theater for pipsqueaks."

Mina's laugh tore from her like a cough, scratching the back of her throat. "Betty Boop? *You*?" She couldn't imagine Kyoko with a high-pitched voice. She was so…*sultry*.

"Yup, I sounded like one of the Chipmunks before Perez put some bass in my voice. We're dancers *first*. Not even singers come with perfect pitch."

"I—*merci*." Mina's smile was tight, but genuine. "But I can't help feeling embarrassed. It's different for me. I was imported for this role. People expect…*perfection*."

Kyoko lifted a feathered headdress from the vanity, crowning herself with it. "My first solo role, I puked all over the place—one of the other dancers slipped in it, had to dance in that smelly costume for two hours. She won't talk to me to this *day*, the bitch."

"Why didn't she change?"

"Budget only covered one costume. They wiped her down and changed her tights, but it was a bust: They needed a *hose*. Anyway, you learned the routine in four hours. I've never seen a prima bank those moves so fast. You got nothing to worry about."

"I have *so* much to worry about—lines, lyrics, steps. I'm afraid I'll forget something. Or move wrong."

"You might," Kyoko said flatly. "But you're an actor. You fake it like a porn star and the audience won't know any better."

A male dancer popped his head in. "There she is. They're looking for her. She missed her cue."

"Thanks, Captain Obvious. She'll be out in a minute."

"No need to be rude." Coming all the way into the room, he looked Mina up and down. "They called five so Coen can yell some more."

Mina winced. "This is my fault. I should get out there."

"In a minute," Kyoko said. "Make sure you're okay."

"How are you, Kyoko?" He still ogled Mina.

"Still gay, Sebastian."

"*Bonjour.*" He reached for Mina's hand. "Sebastian, since Kyoko insists on being rude."

Kyoko scoffed. "She speaks English, numbnuts."

"So, Mina…" He ignored Kyoko. "Are you finding your way around okay? If you want, I can show you—"

"Lemme save you a headache, honey," Kyoko cut in. "Are you single?"

"Yes," Mina said.

"Are you looking?"

"For what?"

"For a nice, soft penis to warm your cu-"

A voice cleared in the doorway, sounding commanding even without forming actual words. "I'll take it from here." Zack waited for Kyoko and Sebastian to clear the room.

Kyoko squeezed Mina's shoulder on her way out, and Mina gave her what she hoped was a more convincing smile in return.

"You okay?" Zack closed the door behind him. "Word travels fast in here."

"I'm fine."

"I don't believe you." Moving to stand in front of her, he took her hands and pulled her up. "C'mere."

She hesitated. In an effort to *try* and be more professional, they hadn't touched each other in days, apart from choreographed holds and lifts, and hugs still felt so…*personal.* Intimate.

"It's not like that, *petite*." He seemed to read her mind. "I just want to see where your head is."

Closing her eyes, she let him wrap her in his arms. In seconds, the warmth and familiarity of his body, the security of his strong arms, helped to calm her ruffled nerves. The tension left her muscles, and she let him support her, allowing her arms to circle his waist for just a minute as they listened to the bustle outside the door.

"I usually work well under pressure," she murmured into his chest. "I don't know what's wrong with me."

"This is different. We've all been there, transitioning from dance to musical theater. We're happy to work with you, you know that."

"I *do* know that." Straightening, she pulled his arms from around her with some reluctance. "That's the problem. I feel like I'm being…indulged. I—they won't respect me if I don't prove myself, if you—if you go easy on me."

"When have I done that?"

"*Enfin,* I messed up my line—twice—and you were nice to me. You yell at everyone else—"

"I do not yell."

"You *yell.*"

He rubbed his temples. "It's down to the wire. We're all feeling a little pressure. You've had less time to memorize the script, and I don't want you to feel singled out."

"I know…but as the lead, I *should* be. I need to—"

"Earn their respect."

"*Oui.*"

"And you're sure you're okay?" He nudged her chin up with his finger, seeking the truth in her eyes.

She nodded.

"Then you got it, *petite.*" Pulling her to him again, he kissed her forehead, then moved to open the door.

"*Wait!*"

He cocked that left brow at her. It was so sexy, it wiped the English language from her memory.

"*Dis-moi…*" she started to say, then his sexy left brow

met his less-sexy right, and she tried again. "Tell me to never be dishonest."

"I don't understand."

"*Please.*" She imagined how she must look to him: sad, desperate - maybe a little insane. But thankfully, he took mercy instead of questioning her further.

"Never be dishonest. Now get your ass back out there."

They ran through the number again, and this time Zack watched Mina use her jitters to power her performance. When the accompanist cued her for the song, she poured herself into it, metamorphosing into Camille, the Lady in Red. The opening number for the Tonys was seven minutes long, and she was only on for two minutes in the first half, playing the innocent country girl who escaped an abusive father with nothing but the ratty clothes on her back, to start a new life in the city.

The other dancers and the chorus line were Parisians young and old, the stage the bustling streets of Paris. Armed with nothing but beauty and determination, Camille's sweet, lusty voice filled the theater. Her fellow courtesans flourished behind her, beckoning noble souls to come, for a price, to taste and see what they had to offer.

"From your diaphragm, Mina," called Mrs. Perez. "Really belt it out."

"Use the stage, Mina," yelled Zack. "You're not doing hard choreo during the chorus, so interact with the audience more, really move around."

They started again.

"You're late, Mina," said Will, the assistant choreographer, from the aisle. "Try and keep up."

Zack zeroed in on her feet.

"Mina—" Will started again, narrowing his eyes. "Bloody hell…what are you-? That's incredible. What are you doing, darling?"

He turned to Zack. "What *is* that?"

"Flirting." Zack's gaze flickered to Mina, who looked decidedly pleased with herself, then back to his notes.

"Flirting?" Will scratched his prominent brow.

"With the time," Zack said, as if Mina's quirk was standard practice. He signaled to Harper at the piano. "Let's see that again."

Neal, Zack's stand-in, played the dashing but fatefully unwealthy Armand Duval, who fell in love with Camille at first sight. The young man's eyes gleamed with obvious appreciation and approval.

Method actor, that one.

"She's an elegant little thing, isn't she?" said Faye. She sat beside him, front row. Her role was administrative, but her importance was tantamount to the entire production not falling on its ass. "There's something so…vivid about her."

"Well, she's a courtesan, not a hooker from Murray Hill."

"Not that we're knocking hookers from Murray Hill."

"Little more heat, ladies and gents," Zack barked. "This is more genteel than Murray Hill…" He looked sidelong at Faye. "…but it's still the nineteenth century red light district. Sell sex. Keep it classy. I can appreciate it's a little contradictory, but I trust your artistry."

The dancers snickered. The unity was there. They were already acting like a tight-knit family after a three-day whirlwind of read-throughs, blocking, and grueling rehearsals. Made sense, bonding after a traumatic experience.

Zack grinned. "On eight…"

They started again.

"Nice diversion there, Jason Bourne." Faye leaned in. "But all that yelling doesn't hide the Tex Avery wolf in your eyes every time you look at her."

"What are you rambling about?" He didn't care that he sounded rude. He'd worked with Faye for three and a half years. They'd long discarded their filters.

"Nothing." She kept her face forward. "I try to stay out of other people's business—"

"A fantastic character trait."

"Just reign in the wolf. The media hounds will sniff him out and we don't need that kind of publicity."

"Noted." He looked at her then, giving her an appreciative smile. "They've got nothing on your nose. You're a shark."

"Damn right." She still watched the stage, but the fine lines near her gray eyes and around her mouth indicated her smile. "Wouldn't have made it far in this business without it."

"I'm grateful." He squeezed her arm. "What's next?"

"Final costume fittings in two hours. Pre-party starts at eight—your tux is in your office. All set for dress rehearsal at Radio City tomorrow. We're up first, before the cast of the umpteenth *Grease* remake."

"They'd be a tough act to follow." Zack turned to yell at his stand-in. "That's good, Neal. I've seen enough. Take five, everyone."

Faye lifted a brow at him. "Suiting up?"

"Time to reprise my role." He stood up. "I promise not to howl and beat my head with a mallet."

"Atta boy."

❧

The pre-party at the Ritz later that night was in full swing by the time Mina arrived. There was a small stage set up outside, where Tony-nominated cast members performed snippets of songs from their favorite Broadway hits. There was a bit of fanfare upon her arrival, a firework show of flashing lights and press yelling at her from every direction. The photographers loved her, scrambling to capture her svelte body in her mini cocktail dress the color of merlot, and her face (which made no effort to hide her delight at sharing the red carpet with The Muppets…Miss Piggy was giving her a *serious* run for her money).

She answered their questions about her transition to Broadway, and how she was adjusting to American culture, though they seemed far more enthused about the veteran American headliners with whom she also shared the red carpet. That was fine with her. She held her own, wooing them with her accent and self-deprecating humor before exiting to the ballroom inside.

The theme was Old Hollywood, with a live band and incredible vintage lighting. Stars she recognized from stage and set formed dozens of high-profile clusters, filling the air with exuberant conversation. Waiters weaved through the crowd with trays of glasses exploding with champagne bubbles, and elegant amuse bouche. The scents permeating her nostrils were rich, and she thought about swiping a few more of the decadent treats from the next tray that passed when a flash of gold caught her eye.

"Hey, honey," Kyoko said breathlessly, sidling up beside her at the bar.

"Kyoko, you look gorgeous!"

"Thanks." She beamed a little at Mina's praise, then gestured toward the hors d'oeuvres table none-too-subtly with her glass. "I think she's warming up to me."

Riha, the costume designer for the show, sparkled in her salwar kameez…and she was piling a tower of mini quiches onto her plate.

Mina leaned closer to Kyoko's ear. "Can you be sure it's not the wine?"

"Don't know." Kyoko drained her glass. "Only one way to find out though." She kissed Mina's cheek. "You look yummy, babe, too yummy to stand here all alone. Go mingle."

And she was off on her quest, leaving Mina *contentedly* alone, *merci beaucoup*. Her eyes scanned the room at the exact moment Zack walked in, and she nearly choked on her champagne. He wore an impeccable black suit, with just a hint of a white dress shirt showing beneath his buttoned jacket and tie. The tailoring showed off his height, the width of his shoulders, the lean line of his hips and thighs. He wasn't alone for a *second*, constantly stopped for animated conversation with colleagues and adoring fans.

He must have felt her staring, because his eyes drifted to hers and held, and heat rose on her skin. They weren't touching, and yet, they were. The room and everyone else in it disappeared, and there was only them, eating each other alive with their eyes. Hands trembling, she handed off her glass to a blur of a passing waiter. She felt a stifling need to escape his hungry lion's gaze and the cacophony of laughter and inebriated chatter.

Drifting for a few minutes, she followed the maze of the first floor away from the ballroom, until she reached the end of a long wing of hotel rooms where it was reasonably quiet. Then she was being spun around and pressed up against the wall.

"*Zack!*"

He cut her off, crushing her mouth with his.

Maybe it was his own obvious need that drew hers out…parting her lips, making her head tilt left, then right, her body shivering in satisfaction when she finally achieved the perfect angle. She whimpered, he moaned, his hands racing over her until she was writhing and murmuring mindlessly, trapped between him and the wall.

Scrambling into him, she dragged her nails down, then up his back, sending shock waves down his spine, making him rock into her. His heart thudded faster with each movement and sigh, pounding a hectic rhythm in his brain. He breathed her name against her lips, into her mouth, the sweet, soft skin of her neck.

"*Zack…*"

It was so sweet and intoxicating—his name on her lips, her warm and welcoming, her hot and ravenous. He drank it all down until he was lightheaded, until his lungs burned for air.

"You're so gorgeous, *petite,*" he panted, still holding her beautiful, flushed face in his hands. Her chest heaved, pleasure shuddering over her expression. "*God*, if you knew… if you knew how hard it is for me…not to think about the way you feel when we dance together…not to touch you when you look like this."

She sighed, and he kissed her again, struggling to regain some control, but her body began to move, elegant as a minuet, erotic as her character's title. Melting into him, she fisted his suit jacket in her hands, driving him mad with a thigh between his legs.

Someone's key card opened a door, its mechanical sound registering in the air like a fog horn, and Mina yelped, hiding her face in Zack's neck.

"It's okay." He sent a quick glance down the hall. Whoever it was had stepped quickly into the hotel room, probably to avoid an uncomfortable encounter. "It's okay, *petite*. They're gone."

"*Bon Dieu,*" she moaned, moving away slowly, trying to smooth her clothes. "I—it could have been worse, Zack. It could have been someone important—someone we know."

"Christ, I know that." He dragged his fingers through his hair. "I know. I'm sorry."

She was skittish, like a deer in headlights. "I can't—I don't want to be that girl. I don't want the first impressions of me dictated by *les tabloïds*."

"I know," he said gruffly, silently cursing his blood-filled extremities. Any other time, he would have laughed at the thought that arousal made men stupid, but it didn't feel funny now. Not at all. "I have nothing to say for myself, *petite*. I lost control. But given our…positions…the way we were standing, I'm sure we weren't recognized."

She looked at him warily, still visibly shaken, her fingers at her lips. Truthfully, neither of them were A-list celebrities, and paparazzi weren't hiding behind trash cans for a money shot. Still, it was careless to get caught up with so many cameras around.

To lose control.

"I'll cool my heels, for both our sakes, okay?" He resisted the urge to touch her again, haul her to him for a reassuring hug. "I promise, *petite*."

Taking a deep breath, she let it out slowly. "Okay."

"You go ahead back to the party. I'll follow in a few minutes."

She nodded and started to walk away but paused just after she passed him. *"Merci...*for what you—what you said." The vulnerability in her smile seized his heart mid-thump. "I feel the same way, when I dance with you."

A distinct feeling of déjà vu overwhelmed him as he watched her retreating form. Just like the night he met her outside the Palais Garnier, he was left alone, staring after her for minutes after she'd disappeared.

∾

Hours before the Tony Awards, stars from Broadway's biggest shows gathered at Radio City Music Hall for a final dress rehearsal in front of a live audience. The two hosts were beloved veterans in the industry, finding a way to parody most of the nominated musicals, softening the blow of sound and technical glitches (of which Zack's number had its fair share). By one in the afternoon, rehearsal finally closed out with the synchronized dance moves of the *Grease* cast in their flashy red jackets. Performers filtered out, abuzz with performance day excitement.

∾

The Tony Awards

It was ShowTime.

Mina had performed her two-minute song and dance with the other courtesans in the first half of the opening act, and her body still hummed with adrenaline. She'd flown from the stage to her dressing room, where a blur of hands skillfully peeled her from her courtesan gown. Riha had cleverly infused the costumes with Eastern influences, lending a richness to the fabrics and prints that conveyed a life of excess without the restrictions of ribbing and petticoats. The same hands carefully removed Mina's artfully coiffed courtesan wig, let down her hair, and fluffed it out. Then, they slipped her into her short, minimalist red dress, and shoved her back out for her bedroom pas de deux with Zack.

Performers were all around them, bustling backstage and in the dressing rooms, and waiting in the wings, feeding on the nervous energy, until it was their turn to take to the stage. Lifting her hand to her chest, Mina felt for her heartbeat in the dipping neckline of her costume.

"You were amazing out there, nice and strong," Zack said in her ear. "We don't sing for this part, so whatever it is inside you, give it to me with your whole body. I want all of it, *petite.*"

The thirty-second warning came. Shivering, she looked out at the rest of the *Lady in Red* cast, an explosion of bodies and voices finishing up their part of the opening act on stage. She started to turn inward, absorbing herself, becoming Camille.

Fifteen seconds.

There was a rush of movement, the cast clearing the stage in a small stampede. Then, a flurry rose in her chest as Harper's gorgeous composition poured into the enormous space.

"Tell me." She sounded far away to her own ears, like she was hovering over herself, watching from outside her body. "Tell me again."

"Are you gonna tell me what this is?" Zack's breath tickled her ear, gently disturbing her straightened tresses.

She looked at him then, at his freshly trimmed hair and clean-shaven jawline, lingering on his expressive green eyes, and the smooth, hairless breadth of his naked chest. "I-I can't. Not yet."

Five seconds.

"*Petite-*"

"*S'il te plaît...*"

Three seconds.

"Never be dishonest."

Dancing on stage with Zack was a miracle.

It was a slow, provocative number, with intimate holds and daring, dizzying arcs. They were all fluid feet and legs and spines, wheeling torsos and tangled limbs. His panto-mime felt real, as convincing as a sonnet, tricking her heart into believing him desperately in love with her, fueling her own performance. They fought and cried and made love on that stage. In a room full of voyeurs, an entire lifetime played out in a single dance.

And Mina had never felt so free.

For Zack, everything after the performance happened in accelerated motion. He'd swept Mina up and kissed her cheeks, then they were engulfed in cheers and embraces by the rest of the cast. Next, they were whisked apart backstage by stylists and makeup artists eager to get them into their evening clothes.

He didn't need to look for Mina when the biggest night of the season came to an end, because he was flanked by two of the loudest women in New York City. One of them had a train a mile long, and an obnoxious voice that called out to Mina in the elaborate foyer of the music hall.

Drinking her in as she descended the curving stairs,

the pulse in his neck pounded against his restricting shirt collar. There was a flash of silver at her feet, and her shimmering emerald gown split to reveal the endless, exquisite perfection of her legs. Her satiny brown skin was on full display in the deep, plunging V at her neckline. Her eyes danced, and her mouth smiled as she made her way over. She turned to Vera and he nearly choked to see an identical V at her back.

"Vera," Mina greeted with cheek kisses. "Lovely to see you again."

"Oh, you look *splendid,* dear! On stage and off!" Vera raved. "Everyone's talking about it. You keep that energy up through the season, you'll be a shoo-in for next year's awards."

Mina flushed, and her beauty made his gut ache, a bittersweet blend of desire and ecstasy and pain. "Mina." There wasn't much he could do about the thickness in his tone. "My mother, Carmen."

Carmen turned to him briefly. *"Muy hermosa,"* she said with wonder. "Blushing, too. *Tan humilde.*"

Mina's skin deepened further. *"Merci.* It's an honor to meet you."

Carmen gasped, letting go his arm to take both of Mina's hands in hers. "You speak Spanish?"

"Sí." She looked meaningfully at Zack, a teasing smile at her lips. *"Espero que él dijo sólo cosas buenas acerca de mí."*

Carmen laughed, then seemed to remember she was in mixed company. "Forgive my rudeness, Vera." She looked back at Mina with warmth. "Yes, of course, he's said *wonderful* things about you, *only* good things. I'm just happy I got to meet you before you left to dance the night away. I'm too old for that now, so, *lo siento,* but this is *hola* and *adios.*"

"I have to run too." Vera was already moving toward the exit. "I see a lifelong friend of mine and I *must* flag her down. Enjoy the rest of your evening."

They watched her go in a burst of noise and rumpled fabric.

"Ridiculous, exhausting woman," Carmen muttered, shaking her head.

"*Mamá*," Zack warned.

Carmen sucked her teeth. Mina made a strange noise, like she was trying to stifle a laugh, drawing his attention to her face. He noticed the faint circles under her eyes for the first time, the subtle slouch in her typically immaculate posture. She was exhausted.

"I'm just escorting my mother to her car," he said. "Wait here. I'll take you home."

"*Merci.*" She exchanged cheek kisses with Carmen. "I hope to see you again soon."

"I hope so too, *linda*. Goodnight, Mina."

When Zack returned, he offered Mina his arm. "It goes without saying, you look amazing, *petite*."

"So do you," she said shyly, taking his arm. "I appreciate the gesture, but I'm not sure—"

"It's not uncommon for cast members to leave together. But since you're worried, we'll try something else."

"Won't I be keeping you from the after parties?"

"I think the adrenaline is starting to wear off, so I'm heading someplace a little less—*Broadway*."

"I didn't know there was such a place. I—Could I come along? I don't want to go anywhere too crowded, but I don't want to be alone."

Her eyes sparkled as much as her dress, and he couldn't resist hamming it up. "Oh, there *is* such a place." He flagged down a town car. "A magical place that doesn't turn into a drunken *vaudeville* hour after midnight."

"Sounds fantastical."

"You have no idea." He saw her safely into the back of the car, then instructed the driver. "Fifty West Forty-Fourth, between Fifth and Sixth. Park until I get there."

"Zack?"

"I'll see you in ten." He shut her door.

CHAPTER TEN

FORTY MINUTES AFTER Zack swooped her up in his Audi from the nearby parking garage, away from cameras and onlookers, he turned onto a familiar street. Mina hadn't anticipated their destination at all. Coming here above-ground was so different from riding the train.

"You didn't have to lure me here with fairytales," she said. "I would have come anyway."

"Is that so?"

"*Oui,* I like you well enough."

"That's encouraging." He parked close to the curb. "But I wasn't spinning tales. Come on."

He got out and came around to open her door. Giving her a hand to help her out, he didn't even *try* to hide his admiration of her legs. "Look up," he said when they were safely on the sidewalk.

"Where?"

He pointed to the rooftop of Alex's brownstone. Craning her neck, she saw green shrubbery jutting over the ledge, a profusion of plant life sprouting and spilling down the limestone façade of the building. Sprays of colorful blooms and the pale bark of small trees glowed in the moonlight.

The street, in contrast, boasted very little green apart from the trees that lined it.

She hadn't noticed it at all the last time she'd come, but then, she'd noticed little of anything through her haze of emotional turmoil. Looking back at him again, she lifted a brow. "Wonderland?"

"Better, and you won't have to fall down a rabbit hole to get there."

"Thank God. I'm wearing the wrong shoes for that."

Predictably, his gaze took the scenic route down her body, ending at her strappy silver heels. "You're wearing *exactly* the right shoes. I'm committing those to memory with the 'fuck me' ones."

"I'm so glad you like them. After all, I choose *all* of my shoes with you in mind."

A grin tugged the corners of his mouth, and he reached for her hand. "Good, because I have a deep, dark closet where I hang photos of your sexy feet on the wall and come back to stare at them later."

She tensed, pulling her hand away.

He grimaced. "You're right. Bad joke. You're safe with me, *petite.*"

"That's not what I—that's not why." She surveyed the street with obvious unease.

"Stop worrying. It's Brooklyn, not Los Angeles. Paps aren't following dancers around unless they're on a red carpet."

Looking around again, her shoulders relaxed, and she let him lead her inside.

Flipping on the light in the foyer, Zack felt for the light switch at the base of the stairs, then took her up the steps without letting go of her hand. The chandelier at the landing lit their way to the second floor.

"*Oh mon Dieu!*"

"You okay, Alice?"

"I was just…admiring the rabbit hole. Alex is a *very* stylish rabbit."

All around them were gilded mirrors, floor-to ceiling, but for the wall directly opposite, where natural light from two ten-foot windows flooded the deep mahogany floor during the day. There was a baby grand piano, and a golden barre stretching from corner to corner in front of the windows. There was even a powder room just off the hall.

Zack's heart did calisthenics at her stunned expression. "I forgot what it's like seeing this place for the first time."

"This is the most gorgeous studio I've ever seen. Is Alex secretly a billionaire?"

"Publicly a millionaire. This studio is in high demand, booked even in the off season. Hopeful parents pay a steep price to get their kids private lessons from the legendary Alex Verenich."

"It really does feel like Wonderland. It should be in a magazine."

"It is." He marveled at her face reflected in the mirrors. Her beauty was almost *too* much in the elegant space, and images of her draped over the baby grand in her gown, or en pointe in the center of the floor filled his mind. He *had* to have her photographed here. He cleared his throat. "It's his sanctuary in the middle of a teeming metropolis."

"*Bravo*. You sound like a writer."

"I fancy myself one too. Would you like a tour?"

"I don't know," she said in a coquettish tone, fanning her face with her hand. "It's so sudden and unexpected."

Laughing, he tugged her to him, enjoying her quick gasp, pecking her lips playfully. "Tonight's your lucky night. Turns out, I'm a playwright. Improv is my middle name."

"It's a very respectable name." She relaxed into his embrace.

He moaned quietly at the feel of her soft curves pressed gently to his frame. "I've already forgotten it. What were we just talking about?"

Pulling back, she gazed at his face. "Your eyes are cloudy. Like sea glass. You look just like the Cheshire Cat."

"Seems appropriate."

His voice was gruff. Again. The fullness in his throat remained, even after several attempts throughout the evening to clear it. He'd begun to sound chronic, with his mother threatening to bathe him in a vat of VapoRub by the time the ceremony had ended. The fullness became fuller as he lost himself in Mina's expression. Wonderment etched itself all over that alluring face. And welcome. He did not need her looking soft and welcoming and full of wonder. *For Christ's sake.* Giving her waist a quick squeeze, he reluctantly let her go.

She stepped back, flushed and breathing deeply, a hand at her chest. "Tell me, cat, which way should we go?"

The fullness threatened to suffocate him at the husky tone of her voice. Clearly the air up here was affecting her, too. It took him a few more breaths to recover, but when he did, he grinned. "Depends on where you want to end up."

Mina gaped, pressing a hand to her chest. The entire third floor housed a stunning library, with a small theater in the back. There was a fireplace, built in mahogany shelves, and an en-suite bathroom. "A theater in the library?"

"Complete with noise-canceling headphones," he said. "Someone reading in here wouldn't hear a thing."

"I'm in love. I want to live in this library."

Zack chuckled, tearing her attention away from the hundreds of gorgeous, leather-bound books.

"I mean it. If I lived here, I'd never leave."

"Then it's my great fortune you don't." He approached the third flight of steps. "I'd look ridiculous prancing around onstage singing to myself."

She broke into laughter, stumbling subtly.

Looking back at her with creased brow, his eyes trailed her frame. "Are you okay?"

"I'm okay." The butterflies in her stomach mated and multiplied. This was the fourth floor. Zack's floor.

"Old building," he said by way of explanation. "No elevator."

"I don't mind."

Flipping on the light switch, he let go of her hand, removing his tuxedo jacket and draping it over a chair. She didn't gasp this time—couldn't because she was breathless. It was far more intimate than simply knowing where he slept, confirming with a single glance that two could fit in his well-made bed. It was that the master suite occupied the entire floor and was the unquestionable lair of a creative mind.

She took in the room slowly...the stacks of books on the floor beneath the windows, the guitar and keyboard in one corner, the sheet music on its stand covered in scribbled red notes, the who-knows-what-draft of a script on the desk, countless notebooks, and at least a dozen poster-sized inspiration boards on easels along the walls.

One of the boards enticed her feet to move until she

stood, dumbfounded, in front of it. Her face, her body, the entire essence of who she was, was tacked to that board. She was dressed for a different role in every photo, held in position or frozen in flight, but every emotion on her face was genuine—immortalized in stunning captures at just the right moment. There were sketches of costumes, and choreography carefully drawn out step-by-step. She fingered the swatch of ruby red fabric beneath her head shot and a scrap of paper that read simply, "Camille."

The warmth from Zack's body sent prickles down her spine seconds before he spoke. "What do you think, *petite*? Did I get it right?"

She shivered, unnerved to be in his head, to see for herself the irrefutable evidence that he knew her. He *knew* her, and she hadn't told him a single thing.

"I think I need some air." She faced him, too tired to mask how shaken she felt. "Do you know where I might get some?"

His eyes were sharp, penetrating, like they could read every thought in her mind. To her relief, he softened the intensity in his features, giving her an easy smile. "I know just the place."

They climbed a narrow staircase to a narrower landing in front of a windowed mahogany door. He flipped the switch beside it, and the most enchanting sound filled the space—a classical piano being played near a lake, surrounded by trees and birds…in a light rain? Biting her lip, she tried to identify each sound she heard.

He stopped short. "If you're sick of classical music, I can turn it off. Alex's taste is impeccable, but pretty predictable."

"*Non,* I—I like it. It's beautiful."

"Used to be a ladder and a hatch door where we're

standing." He undid the lock. "Alex had the stairs and door put in a few months ago."

"It's lovely, but a portal would have been much more Wonderland."

He opened the door and the music followed them out onto the roof. "I agree. Luxury is a real buzzkill."

Mina hardly heard him. The lush life thriving in this new stratosphere sucked her in. It worked *against* nature, a tiny corner of respite from the unremittingly loud, distracting city below.

Wordlessly, he took her hand again and led her farther out. They walked in comfortable silence, free-falling the rest of the way down the rabbit hole, to a serene garden that reminded her of a Japanese tea house. A multitude of flowers flourished in planter boxes, pots and undulating borders. There were Japanese maple trees, and statues and artifacts obscured by twisting vines.

"Alex collected these during his travels to Asia." He narrated the last stop on the tour. "Some are from Thailand, some from China…Burma, Japan."

She recognized four of the statues. They were varying interpretations of what Buddha looked like, some skinny, some fat. She reached out to touch a short statue of a monk holding a long staff. "What's this one?"

"Ah, Jizo Bosatsu. Protector of travelers and children, and all the sorry souls trapped in hell. Some say he awakens us from our dreamlike world of illusion."

Something *precisely* dreamlike colored his voice, enticing her to meet his gaze. Her chest tightened at the way he looked at her, like it wasn't a look at all, but an embrace.

"Then let's keep going," she said. It seemed it was contagious, because it affected her voice, too. "I like this dream."

Deeper in the garden, what appeared at first to be small pools of clear water, were skylights allowing light to the fourth floor below. They stepped across pavers that were brushed and polished to look like Tuscan stone, following its path to the edge of the garden.

"Wow," she whispered. "This is…" She struggled to find a word, even with three language banks to choose from, staring at the softly lit oasis in front of her.

Beneath a pergola made from Indian columns and covered in vines, was a seating area with deep cushions, patterned pillows and a richly colored Persian rug.

"It's breathtaking." Feeling his regard on her again, she met it instinctively with her own, reading his thoughts as easily as if he'd said them aloud. She pursed her lips. "Really? Of all the times to hold your tongue, you choose now?"

"I think my thoughts right now are obvious." He stroked the back of her hand with his thumb.

"Be kind to me. Tell me anyway. I'm not immune to vanity."

Releasing her hand, he touched her face, trailing a cheekbone with the back of his fingers, then let his hand fall to his side. "You are an obstinate, unrelenting smartass who sometimes makes me want to quit the business and open a distillery…but unquestioningly the most breathtaking woman I've ever seen."

Dieu, her lashes fluttered like a speeding camera shutter, making everything around her appear in slow motion. Her involuntary nervous system gave out on her, so breathing took some effort…as did speaking. "I-I'm choosing to ignore the first part, because the second part was really beautiful."

"*You're* really beautiful."

Breathe. "That's better."

Smoothing his hands down her bare arms, he brushed them over her palms, tickling her fingertips with his. Then he lifted her arms and draped them over his shoulders. "It was good, wasn't it? But this is better. Way better."

"Mmm," she hummed, letting him lead her in a slow dance. The music hung in the air around them, so soft it felt confined to the rooftop, like no one could hear it but them. "Your mother was lovely."

"My mother is…a *lot*." He said it warmly, though. "She likes you, which I'm sure you noticed."

"*Oui,* she's not subtle. It's very easy to like her, too."

"Good, because she teaches dance at the recreation center where I grew up. She's been begging me to bring you with me the next time I come…and the kids would love to meet a real life, superstar dancer."

"They've met you."

"Yeah, well, they don't get out much. Besides, I'm not as pretty."

"You mispronounced, 'breathtaking.'"

"Apologies."

"Of course I'd love to stop by." She searched his face a moment, biting her lip.

"*Petite?*"

"Your mother is Latina? And your father…?"

"Puerto Rican. So is my father." He grinned. "You obviously aced biology—and Spanish, too. My mother is beside herself. You'll probably get a marriage proposal from her on my behalf."

The butterflies multiplied again. It was getting crowded in her stomach. "I…"

"Breathe, *petite.* You're turning a lovely dark shade of pink."

"It's because of your bad jokes," she sputtered, catching her breath again. She looked out beyond the roof to the buildings surrounding them, towering over them. "So, you were adopted?"

"Boring story, really. Pretty uninspired. My mother was a teen when she had me. My dad skipped out on her. I was in the system by three—foster care nomad. I was just some ruddy kid, invisible to starry-eyed parents looking to adopt chubby little cherubs."

He tightened his hold, and Mina's heart broke a little, making her rub her fingers soothingly through the hairs at his nape.

"*Petite…*" he groaned.

"Sorry." She stilled her fingers, the butterflies taking flight en masse, fluttering into her chest. "Please, go on."

He cleared his throat, and it occurred to her that he might be nervous. This tall, strong, self-assured man was tripping over his tongue and, *Dieu,* it was so *cute*. She softened her eyes.

"Fuck, you're gorgeous." He licked his lips. "Let's see, typical troubled kid story, so we'll skip to my redemption… I started at the local rec center in the summer when I was nine. Swimming, basketball—standard stuff to keep me out of trouble. Then one day, the Latin dance teacher needed a strapping young lad to even out her class. She saw something in me—hips like a hula dancer, impeccable rhythm, luxurious head of hair…"

"Is that all?"

"I'm being modest."

She smacked his nape.

"Whatever it was she saw, it helped me work through the adolescent anger every foster kid seems cursed with. We fell in love in that way adoptive parents and kids do." He shrugged. "Sort of like falling in love with a puppy in a pound. It just felt…*right.* The ink dried when I was ten. My parents helped me find scholarships for my dance education, paid for the rest…and here I am."

"I don't think it's uninspired at all," she said. "It's very stirring."

He didn't say anything else for a minute. Then he took a long, slow breath, like he was making his mind up about something.

"What?" She brought her arms down slowly to rest on his chest. They were no longer dancing.

"How did it feel, *petite?*"

The anticipation in his expression told her he wasn't just talking about the excitement of performing on an awards show. He looked *vulnerable.* Like he was invested in her response. Like his heart was wide open.

It made her want to hand over hers.

"Dancing with you felt…like learning I could fly," she said softly, enjoying the stunned pleasure on his face at her words. "Like I didn't know I could fly until that moment, and then you took my hand and said, '*Allons-y*'— 'Let's go, *petite.*' Then, it felt like the sun was at our backs, and the wind was in our hair…and everyone else was watching us from the ground."

A sound left his throat she couldn't identify. Primal. Needy. Like he was starving. "That was quite a description. Very evocative."

"It's okay, if you didn't feel the same way." Her rapid heartbeat called her a liar. "I just wanted you to know."

"I *did* feel the same way. I felt it when we were dancing, and when I saw you come down those stairs in this dress."

His hands smoothed up and down her waist. "I felt it in the car, downstairs, on the sidewalk…And I feel it right now."

His fingers dug gently into her hips, his voice so deep, she was sure she'd feel its vibrations for days. They spread through her chest and up into the roots of her hair. It was embarrassing how happy it made her to hear his words.

It was too much.

"Zack—" She flinched, lifting her face toward the sky. Another tiny droplet hit her face, and another, and another. The clouds seemed to form from thin air. "*Oh*! *Non*!"

"Don't worry." Taking one of her hands from his chest, he led them back over the pavers, ducking under the pergola.

"*Merde*!" Her bare toes hit the framework, pain shooting halfway up her shin.

"Shit. I forgot this thing is slightly elevated—in case it rains." Lifting her to the longest couch, he set her down gently.

"It's—I think it's okay."

Ignoring her, he took her legs into his lap and deftly removed her shoes. He massaged the offending leg, working the muscle with his hands until she sank into the cushions with a sigh.

"Old injury?"

"*Injuries*." She winced. "Stress fractures, mostly. I can jump on my legs, spend hours on my toes, but if I hit them the wrong way—*ah!*"

"Breathe."

Breathe. He'd been reminding her since they'd arrived. It was quite a task with him so close, but she managed it anyway, looking out into the garden. Trillions of droplets fell now, but slowly, like a shimmering curtain. The air cooled and stirred, masking the stale smells of the city heat with a cocktail of damp earth and Japanese chrysanthemums from Alex's potted Eden. It was a perfect summer rain.

Her leg felt better already, but she didn't want to tell him that. It felt too good. She looked down at his hands in case mind reading was among his many skills. "You're a choreographer, a playwright, a composer, and a masseuse? You make me feel so unaccomplished."

"I'm also old. You have plenty of time." He gripped her calf with one large hand, his other over her shin, twisting them away from each other, moving toward her ankle.

She closed her eyes. "Why do you live here, with Alex?"

"That one's easy. My job pays a pittance. No pressure, *petite,* but my whole life is riding on you bringing the house down on opening night."

Her startled moan cut off her response. It was low and deep, strangled from somewhere in her belly. His hands ceased their sorcery on her foot, but the sensation still thrummed like electricity through her body. Her gaze shot to his.

Watching her intently, he slid his hand up her leg, lingering on her tight, muscular calf. He continued moving up, and her breath caught, his hand tightening on her thigh. Every molecule in the air seemed to be humming, not just with physical awareness—it had long gone past that—but a sense of wholeness, of profound connection. And she knew she wasn't alone feeling it. She saw it in his darkening eyes.

Need.

"Mina."

She couldn't blink because his face was closing in on hers, his lips brushing lightly against her cheek, sending tremors through her nerves that made her whole body tremble.

"I want you," he murmured, his lips tracing the line of her cheekbone. "I want you so fucking much, it takes effort to think of anything else, but I'll cool it, *petite*. Just say the word."

With a soul-deep sigh, she closed her eyes, nudging her nose against his. *"Non."*

CHAPTER ELEVEN

ZACK FELT, MORE than heard her. Felt her melt against him, filling and surrounding him with her *yes*. Smoothing his hand up her abdomen, he felt it tremble and tighten. He rested his palm between her breasts, over her rapid pulse, watching the rise and fall of her chest with her quick, shallow breaths. His eyes drank in her big, expressive eyes, the arch of her cheekbones, the pout of her mouth…Then his lips were on hers.

Their moans collided as their mouths fell lazily together, soft and open. Slowly, his tongue moved over hers, touching the tip, circling it, licking the roof of her mouth, drawing from her another shuddering moan. Her mouth was pliant and sweet, her tongue velvet and searching. Blood coursed through him hot and thick, and he reached for her hand, bringing it urgently to his lap.

"*Petite.*" He was hoarse, going mind-numb as she rubbed him until he was panting from dire need of the very thing she was giving him. "*Jesus…Jesus…stop…*"

Clutching her hand as gently as he could, he took deep, steadying breaths. Except they weren't steadying at all. They fueled his roaring blood with more oxygen, leaving him with whole-body vibrations he desperately needed to stop, but also continue forever.

He wanted to take his time.

Slipping from beneath her legs, he laid her down carefully, an arm cradling her back, parting her legs with his knee. Then he was over her, crushing her, the muscles and planes of his body meeting glorious curves and softness. His lips enveloped hers in wet consuming kisses, like he was dying of thirst, even as she gave him water, one excruciating drop at a time.

"I want to taste you, *petite.*"

Clutching his shoulders, she dug in with her nails, circling her hips against his erection to soothe the ache in her center with delicious friction. He felt so good, she sobbed, not realizing he'd tugged her dress straps down, exposing her breasts to his hungry gaze…until his lips wrapped around her nipple, his cheeks hollowing slowly. She gasped, shuddering violently as he caressed her side from breast to hip and back again, molding her in his hand.

"*Fuck,* don't you dare." In one swift motion, he was on his knees on the Persian rug, shoving her dress up, tugging the wet scrap of lace down her hips, taking her legs over his shoulders. "I can't *believe* you'd cheat me out of this," he growled, kissing her navel and moving lower, his hair caressing her stomach.

Holding her open with shaking hands, he nuzzled her with his nose. Her back bowed, and hoarse, incomprehensible pleas left her lips.

"I love those sounds, *petite,*" he murmured, heating her wetness with his breath. "So sexy."

He teased her with light licks, and fluttering dips of his

tongue. Tension spread through her body, tightening everything until it felt like she'd splinter under the pressure.

"*S'il te plait.*" Clutching the edge of the cushions, she pressed herself to his mouth.

He repeated his soft suction a few more times, and she bucked, whimpering in French, heated relief coursing through her shaking body. She came down from it gripping his hair, pulling his mouth from her sensitive core. He was next to her in a flash, taking her face in his hands.

"My God, you're so hard up," he said against her lips. "It drives me crazy."

"Only with you. Takes me longer by myself."

His face drained of color.

Giggling, she wrapped her hands around his wrists. "What?"

"Gimme a sec, *petite*. I think my brain just short circuited."

"Men. Is it so hard to believe women like to give themselves pleasure as much as you do?"

"Not at all." Pulling her into his lap, he nuzzled her neck. "I'm a card-carrying feminist. I just didn't expect you to be so direct." He ran his hand up the inside of her thigh, cupping her where she was warm and wet.

She moaned. "I-I am capable of intimacy, you know. It takes me some time, but when I'm comfortable with someone, I talk about everything."

Pulling away to look at her face, he twirled a wavy lock of her hair around his finger, then slowly released it. "Coincidentally, that's *exactly* how much I want to know, but I need some things first. Promise me you'll still be here when I get back."

She kissed his nose, then stiffened. "Alex! Is he—?"

"That party animal won't be back until six in the morning."

Her body went boneless, draping itself, half undressed, across the couch. *"Oui,* I'll be here. I can't move."

Laughing, he gently disentangled himself and left her alone with her fluttering heart, the winsome music, and the calming rain.

He returned some minutes later with a comforter, condoms and wet wipes. He'd removed his bowtie and belt, and opened his shirt, the air cool on his naked chest. When he reached the pergola, Mina bit her lip, her eyes glued to his torso. She moved her hand down her body and between her legs, clamping her thighs together with a moan.

"Miss me?" he teased, spreading the blanket down over the rug.

"Oui." Her voice was husky, her eyes hooded.

He nodded to the condoms. "In case you're not on anything."

Standing, she reached behind her to undo her zipper, stepping out of the amazing dress as it pooled at her feet. "You think of everything."

"I'm a thoughtful guy." His voice sounded far away, his eyes devouring her naked body. "They're new, *petite.* It's been weeks for me."

She came to him without a hint of shyness, smoothing his shirt over his shoulders, humming as it dropped with a whisper to the floor. Her fingers traced the smooth ridges of his abs, and he sucked in his stomach. She grinned. "New? So, this is premeditated?"

"More like *anticipated.*" He shuddered as her arms

went around his waist, hugging every inch of her skin to his. "Very, very anticipated."

"How many weeks?"

"Eight, give or take." Wrapping his arms around her, he rubbed his hands up and down her back. "Should we call my mother? She thinks my slaving over this production is preventing me from settling down."

"*Non,* I'm quite satisfied with your answer, *merci.*"

"You sure? I think now is the perfect time to give you a detailed history of my considerable experience in this—*oh shit...*"

She squeezed his ass at the same time her teeth tugged his lobe, her tongue flicking over the spot, her breath wetting his ear.

"*Fuck,*" he moaned.

"*S'il vous plait.*"

He took her mouth again, loving her with his lips and tongue and teeth, urgent but not hurried. It was just the two of them in an empty garden. They had all the time in the world. Undoing his pants, he pushed them down with his briefs, brushing kisses on her face wherever he could. Walking them to the center of the blanketed rug, he lowered them with a supporting arm around her waist.

He kissed across her chest, scraping her nipples gently with his teeth, toying with them before surrounding them with wet heat and suction. Her hands were wild in his hair, tugging his head away, then pulling him back to her, her breathless sighs tickling his forehead. Delighted laughter left his chest this time when she came. It seemed swifter and less intense than before, but she was grinding her hips up, taking his heated arousal between her thighs, and he couldn't breathe.

"Stop that," he groaned, quickly opening and sliding on protection. "Wait for me, dammit."

"I can't help it," she panted, her head falling back.

Trailing his open mouth over her throat, he licked her chin, capturing her lips again. "Look at me…look at me, *petite*."

He waited for it, the reflection of his own desperate need in those open, bottomless depths, and then he took her slowly. Crying out, she opened her legs wider and let him in again. Tracing sensual patterns on her hip with his fingers, he moved inside of her in deep, easy thrusts.

"Mina…"

The feel of her, silky and soft and warm, gripping him so tightly made his eyes water, blurring her beautiful face.

"I knew it would be like this." The tremble in his voice would have been embarrassing, if not for her own needy sounds. She started to flutter around him, and he blinked, hard. "I knew it when we danced *Manon*."

Tightening her legs around him, she dug her heels into his lower back, guiding him with gentle hands on his ass. "I knew it…before…that…"

Her grip tightened suddenly, and her eyes flashed pure, mindless pleasure before snapping shut.

"No, no, no… look at me, *petite*. I want to see your eyes when you come." He reached between them, moving his fingers in time with his rhythmic thrusts.

Sighing brokenly, she showed him eyes glassy and black. He saw himself in them, the ravenous look on his face, the wild disarray of his hair.

"*Lion!*" she gasped, bucking her hips against him.

He cursed into her neck, shuddering as she squeezed and pulled him into herself, until they fused into a single mass of pure, writhing ecstasy. Eventually, his breathing slowed, and she stroked his sweat-slick back softly, whispering soothing adoration in his ears.

Full consciousness took the scenic route back to his brain, but when it returned, he whispered against her throat. "When did you know?"

Almost an entire minute passed with no reply, so he lifted his head to look at her face. As he suspected, she'd been holding her breath. "*Petite-*"

"In *Paris*," she said in a rush. "On the loggia.*"

Her answer should have stunned him, but it didn't. He remembered that night vividly, as if it'd happened minutes ago, and he realized she was right. She'd looked incredible in the moonlight and smelled even better. He remembered how soft and smooth her hand felt in his for the brief moment he'd held it…But mostly, he remembered the unfettered passion in her eyes, when the rest of her had been so composed, and how badly he'd wanted to manipulate it, to see it poured into something *he'd* created.

Reality had surpassed the dream. He'd touched and tasted it, drawn it into himself, and he wasn't ready to unpack the feelings tightening his chest in the aftermath. He had a sneaking suspicion she wasn't, either.

Tempering his expression, he gave her a lopsided grin. "Yeah, well, you're an overachiever."

If relief had a sound, it was her laugh. "And you, are an-"

"Asshole." He kissed her cheek. "Yeah, *petite*, I know."

Afterward, he lay with his head in her lap, blowing raspberries into her belly button. He lifted his head to admire her breasts. They were flawless little mounds, her dark nipples pointing slightly up.

"God, your tits are amazing. Two perfect mouthfuls." He took a nipple between his teeth for a playful tug.

"Leave me alone." She gripped his hair, tugging gently. "I need to recover."

He gave the side of her breast a lingering lick, then returned his head to her lap and gazed up at her. Stroking her hair, his fingers snagged in one of her sex-mussed tresses. The rain had finally stopped, and the moon seemed to glow brighter, illuminating her face.

"What?" she asked with a tiny frown.

Her arm was draped across his chest, her fingers lightly tracing his ribs, and he curled a hand around her wrist. "How does an American get into one of the toughest ballet schools in Paris? *Parisians* can barely get in there."

"Good thing I was already a French citizen, then."

"So, your mother?"

"*Oui.* She met my father in Tokyo, of all places. She was there on business. He was on a break from training in Okinawa. It was one of those crazy things. They fell in love in a week."

"Wow. Love at first sight?"

"Something like that…Four months later, they were married. I was six when they divorced. He died two years later, during an extended tour."

Stilling her fingers, she looked away. He followed her gaze to a single, fat droplet of rain on the edge of a nearby leaf that would fall *any* second now. "Who would you stay with when your father was away on duty?"

"*Papa's* family is from Virginia. I stayed with them. When he died, they fought for custody, but I begged to live with *maman*. So, I moved to *Paris* and started at the ballet school right away."

"I'm sorry." He raised her hand to his lips for a kiss. "We don't have to talk about this if it's too traumatic, *petite*."

"*Non,* it's okay. I needed the distraction—and discipline if you ask *maman*. It was difficult at first, but eventually, I got better. It became…everything to me, even though I was always aware that I looked different."

Automatically, he looked at her hair. It was *gorgeous*, every thick, dark strand, every wayward curl…but, admittedly, a stark contrast to the textures that crowned the heads of his previous partners. "I get that. Was it hard for you, being different?"

"Not all the time. I think puberty was the most difficult time. It happened early for me—I was nine when my cycle started, when my body began to change." She shifted awkwardly, but she kept talking. "I was *scared*. The body requirements are so strict, especially for girls, even at eight years old. I felt like everyone was watching me, staring at my body all the time to see if my breasts would grow too big, or my hips too wide. That's when I became fully aware of how different I was, because people expected me to lose my lean shape—as if black women only come in *one* body type."

Rubbing her arm, silently reassuring, he let her talk. He sensed she needed it, and he enjoyed listening to her, being privy to her closely guarded secrets.

"I suppose it's madness," she said, "that I thanked God for not giving me 'too much' of the attributes most people find beautiful on a woman."

"Not madness. It was your reality. We've come a long way since Balanchine decided skin and bones was somehow ideal, but we still have a long way to go."

Moving her arm, he sat up, taking her face into his

hands. "You're incredible and determined and soft and strong—and *beautiful*. No fucked up, Jurassic ballet standards should ever make you doubt it."

He *loved* the color her skin turned when she blushed.

"I-*merci*. I know that now."

"Doesn't hurt to be reminded."

"*Non*, it doesn't." She pecked his lips.

"It was a pretty inspirational speech, wasn't it?"

"Very." Her eyes turned into molten, dark pools. "Zack?"

"*Petite?*" he whispered, opening his arms to help her settle in his lap.

Moving against him, her thighs hugged his waist, her voice a husky sigh. "Again."

Chapter Twelve

THE HOURS JUST past played over and over in Mina's dreams. Touches, whispers, laughs, moans. Her name was whispered in her ear, a kiss pressed to her neck, and she couldn't determine whether it was real, or a dream. Then she heard her name again, uttered, barely spoken, felt another lingering kiss. She shivered. The bedroom was draftier than her own, the sweet, rain-washed darkness all around her settling over them peacefully. Strange, the stillness. She was used to the noise of the city, the finest place to be alone among crowds.

But she wasn't alone now, nor was she dreaming. Strong arms tightened around her, and wonderful pressure warmed the length of her body.

A hug.

He pressed himself to her, so close she felt him pulse along her thigh.

A naked hug.

Sophie would be proud.

He must have sensed when she'd completely awakened, because he released her, applying light pressure to her shoulder until she lay on her back. Half in shadow, the muscles of his torso were back-lit by the faint glow of the street outside the windows.

Beautiful.

His hair was a thick, silky mess from sleep–and from her fingers, his tawny skin so tempting to touch. Every move of that glorious flesh against hers had given away his strength, and a gentleness she'd never experienced with anyone else. His eyes were shadows, too, but she didn't need to see them. She'd seen enough in the last several hours to take to her grave. They'd be a fascinating contradiction now, her favorite facet of his expressive eyes. Steely with intensity, soft with…something else.

"We were hugging," she murmured.

"We were doing a little more than hugging, *petite.*"

She giggled—or something like a giggle. It was hard to tell what mangled sound she made with her bottom lip caught between his teeth. "I-I'm not used to it. I like it."

Pulling back a moment, he grinned. "Are you so deprived?"

She shrugged, and his eyes caught the movement, then trailed slowly down. Her answer was lodged in her throat.

"You talk in your sleep," he said gruffly.

"What did I say?"

"Nothing intelligible." Stroking his knuckles down her cheek, he toyed with a lock of her hair.

Wincing, she smoothed her hair. She could only imagine the sight she made. Sleek and wavy hours before, it was undoubtedly a sweated-out mass of thick, tangled curls. His ego must be soaring. He settled between her thighs, gently pressing her into the mattress.

A strangled cry left her throat, and he chuckled softly.

"Yes, I remember you like being smothered. It's slightly morbid, as kinks go, but I can roll with it."

Her groan was part pleasure, mostly mortification. She felt his grin spread over her jaw in a brush of a kiss.

"Don't worry, *petite,* you're still a mystery to me."

Drawing their hands above her head, he intertwined their fingers. They were almost nose-to-nose, and his eyes were clearer—warm jade and inquisitive.

What is it? they asked. *That gasp wasn't like the ones I pulled from you last night.*

How could he know the difference? How could he know her so well when she hardly knew him at all? She thought of the inspiration board right across the room, shrouded in darkness, covered in her face, her body, her heart…and shut her eyes tight. He'd been decoding her cipher since the night she met him…

Even now, you're performing.

You don't trust yourself.

You're distracted. Off your game. And I want to know why.

You do this thing sometimes, when you dance-You flirt with the time.

You bully yourself.

Through it all, I still saw you.

He used what he learned to push her buttons, open her up, take what he wanted and stow the rest away for later. Soon, she'd have no secrets left. Soon, she wouldn't be intriguing anymore…He kissed her back from her thoughts. Back to the now. Holding her hands to the pillow easily, he slanted his mouth over hers in slow, wet slides. The past stopped haunting her when Zack kissed her, when he breathed into her mouth, fed her his tongue, sucked hers into his. It registered in the pit of her stomach, tightening her insides and curling her toes. His eyes were on hers when he pressed in gently, filling her a little, and then a little more. She clamped down on him and he surged deeper, shuddering, breathing hard.

"Sorry, *petite.*" He touched his forehead to hers, sinking her further into the mattress with each heave of his chest against hers. "I'm pretty much a horn ball in the mornings, and it doesn't help that I've been dreaming about you for weeks."

"About this?"

"This. Not this." His expression was intense again. "Nothing. Everything. What you eat. What you sleep in. What you think about when you get that far away look in your eyes. How you stuff all of *this…*" He kissed her hair. "…into those little buns you wear all the time." His nostrils flared like he'd just finished the Boston Marathon. "Just… *you.*"

Her heart separated into a million pieces, fluttering around in her chest, then flocking back together so she could breathe again. "Inside? Or out?"

"What?" He breathed the word, rolling his hips.

She tightened around him involuntarily, and a prominent vein throbbed in his forehead. She needed her answer before he lost the ability to form coherent sentences. "You said I'm still a mystery. Did you mean inside, or out?"

Sighing, he let go her hands to trail his down her sides. He fitted them to the dips at her waist, squeezing gently, grinning at her whole-body jerk. "Both."

He dropped another kiss on her lips. "Gonna take some time to figure you out."

Sinking his hands beneath her, he lifted her hips from the bed, groaning into a smooth, easy rhythm.

"H-how much t-time?" she babbled, wrapping her legs around him, bracing for the ride.

"I've had *hours, petite.*" He spoke with effort, his breathing ragged. "I'm inside you again, but I'm pretty good at foresight. I can tell you…I'm gonna need more. Much, much more."

He finished the proclamation in her mouth, slipping his tongue in for a silky twirl around hers. Lifting one of her legs over his shoulder, he increased the angle, deepening his thrusts.

"*More,*" she repeated—begged, actually—over and over…and over.

Their mouths landed slick, lazy kisses wherever they could reach, savoring each other like their skin was coated in honey. It was slow and slumberous, like a dream. He moved with such controlled power, holding her leg steady, his breathing heavy and slow. Her composure long gone, she squeaked her pleas in a slur of French and English, until the pressure had her sobbing…until a few more lazy rolls of his hips made any sound at all impossible. She caught his expression before her eyes rolled shut as she came, arching sharply, shuddering into his chest.

Delirious.

Because of her.

Pure radiation emanated through her body, slow-burning through every nerve. Her hands slipped on his sweat-slick shoulders, and she dug her nails in, needing something to hold onto. A sound wrenched from him—guttural, like he was in pain, and he finally lost his composure, his head dropping to her shoulder, his large body shaking in her arms. It didn't seem to matter to him that her muscles had turned to mush, or that her limbs were spread out most ungracefully beneath him. Clinging to her, he hooked his arms under her armpits, beseeching The Divine between kisses on her neck.

Mina scrunched up her nose, thinking about her makeup. "This is the sweatiest hug. I probably look like a raccoon."

He fell on top of her with a husky laugh. "A stunning raccoon."

"I'm serious! We are stepping dangerously close to dirty romance novel territory."

Still laughing, he rolled off her and strolled into the bathroom. "Explain yourself, woman."

Following his gorgeous retreating back with her eyes, it took her a moment to remember what she was talking about. "*Em*...You know, a sex marathon. *Cock* this, *pussy* that—I can't help it. I always imagine a rooster chasing a cat. It's disturbing, like that skunk, Pepé Le Pew..."

His laughter was full-body this time, shaking the bed when he climbed in and stretched on his side.

Admiring the way his abs rippled and folded as he laughed, she went on. "Multiple screaming orgasms. *Chatte* so sore it needs ice."

"First of all, screaming?" He propped his head on his hand. "I distinctly remember something that sounded like a strangled cat, but no screaming, tragically. We'll have to work on that."

She swatted his shoulder. "I can't scream with you inside me. I can't breathe."

Looking her over with the smug satisfaction of a cat that had just thoroughly licked his bowl clean of crème, he grinned. "Fair enough. *Chatte*?"

"A woman's...nethers."

"*Nethers?*" He collapsed onto his back, dying from laughter.

She hid her grin, feigning long-suffering patience. "When did you…? I didn't hear anything." Her question was directed toward his penis.

"I put one on while you were admiring my chiseled face and my dreamy eyes."

She groaned.

"I have ice, *petite*."

"That's very kind of you, but I don't need it."

His face fell. "My ego just took it hard…in the nethers."

"Just as well. It's already big enough."

He turned onto his side and tugged her hand, pulling her onto her stomach so they were face-to-face. "Your words are laughing, but your eyes aren't."

She closed her eyes.

"Hey." He held her chin in his hand, and her eyes drifted back open. "Talk to me. You don't regret it, do you?"

She stared at him, at the raw vulnerability in his expression. Taking his hand from her chin, she kissed it. No matter how strong her reservations were, she couldn't lie to that face. "*Non.* How could I? That was—I've never…"

Frowning, she sifted through her dating memory for a point of reference. Not finding one, the silence stretched, but it wasn't uncomfortable. It seemed to say more in the absence of words than anything she was capable of now.

"It's okay," he said finally. "I feel the same way. I'm not sure how we rewind after tonight."

"The alternative is impossible."

"Complicated. *Batshit,* maybe. But not impossible."

"How?"

Pulling her closer, he kissed the anxiety from her lips.

"At four in the morning, I'm stupid, as a rule, but I've also been thoroughly fucked, and the most beautiful woman I've ever seen is naked in my bed." He emphasized his statement with a slap to her ass, grinning as she made the strangled cat noise again. "We see each other every day, *petite*. We'll figure it out. Okay?"

He said it with such confidence, her lungs emptied again with relief. She rubbed her cheek against his. "Okay."

Zack stared at her with obvious appreciation when she emerged from the shower. "Thank you, for not wearing a towel."

"I dried off with it. Why would I want to wrap myself in it?" Scanning the floor with her eyes, she bent to search under the bed for her underwear. "You've seen everything."

"Well, now I have."

"I can't find my—" Standing straight again, she froze. "*Zack...*"

Her lacy panties dangled from one of his fingers. "These look expensive."

"They *are*." She held out her hand.

Making no move to return them, he lifted them higher, craning his neck for a better look. "Then I'm sorry for almost ripping them. These are *racy*."

She couldn't help her amusement at this new side of him. Or perhaps his humor had always been there, channeled into driving her insane rather than getting her to smile, which she did now. "You didn't notice them when I was half naked on the roof?"

"You were half naked. I wasn't looking at your clothes."

"What were you looking at?"

He dragged his eyes up from her toes. "Your eyes."

185

Snorting, she lifted her dress from the back of the arm chair and stepped into it.

"I love your eyes," he said. "I've never seen anything like them. When I first met you, I swear your eyes were telling me to come here and fuck off at the same time."

She sifted her arms through, then turned for him to zip her. He obliged, kissing her back before zipping her up. Pulling her to him for a cuddle, he turned his face into her neck. "You washed me off only to smell like me again."

"I'll bring my own lotion next time."

"I *forbid* you to bring your own lotion. And I forbid you to ban me from showering with you again."

Turning in his embrace, she lifted her arms to his shoulders, heat filling her face.

He frowned. "Don't tell me you're still shy?"

"*Non*...but I didn't plan this. I didn't have anything for the shower...for my hair." Her face heated again. "I stole a plastic bag from under the sink."

"Plastic bag?"

"*Oui*, you don't have a shower cap."

He looked at her like she was reciting astrophysics in ancient Greek.

"I couldn't get my hair wet," she explained. "I would have been forced to leave here looking like you'd given me electric shock treatments instead of multiple screaming orgasms."

His eyes flashed at her. "You can't breathe with me inside you, let alone scream. I heard it from the horse's own mouth."

Merde, there was that shivering reflex again. "I imagine there's a first time for everything."

"*Petite*...."

"What are my eyes saying now?"

Studying her a moment, he held her hips, digging in gently with his fingers. "They're saying, *Kiss me.*"

"*Oui.*"

He didn't do it right away. Instead, he spoke with his eyes, stating his intent, making promises. They dropped to her mouth and stayed there for seven seconds—she counted. Seven seconds felt *much* longer when her body was vibrating, when sounds that were more animal than human left her throat. Finally, he bent his head and plied her lips softly with his, teaching her for untold minutes that there were infinite nerves on the surface of her lips, that he could isolate each one with his tongue, make them tingle with pleasure. Never had she experienced this without tongue in her mouth, or elsewhere, accompanied by copious amounts of heavy petting. Never had she felt so utterly filled, so *thoroughly* kissed.

Pulling away, he chuckled, massaging her waist. "You're purring."

"I think we've established that you think I'm a cat." She was more than a little breathless. "Are you going to give me back my underwear?"

"*I'm* wearing underwear." He lifted her panties from the bed. "*These* are… "

He brought them to his nose.

"Zack…"

He sent her a wicked look.

"Don't…"

He took a long, slow drag.

"*Nom de Dieu.*"

"How attached are you to these?"

"They're dirty."

"Still waiting for your point."

"You're disgusting."

"Sentimental." He handed her the delicate scrap of lace with obvious reluctance.

"*Merci.*" She stuffed them in her evening bag.

Air left his body like he'd been kicked in the stomach. His face said as much, too. "You're about to ride commando in my car?"

"What?"

His Adam's apple moved in his throat. "Nothing. I hope you left me some hot water."

Zack took the longest route to Mina's apartment, but even cruising the slow lanes on two of the world's otherwise most homicide-inducing highways brought them to her neighborhood much too quickly. The console read five-thirty, but the sun wouldn't be up for a couple of hours. He stole glances at Mina whenever street lights turned her skin gold. She looked like a movie star.

"Where did you get that hoodie, by the way?" he asked. "It's not exactly your usual style."

"How would you know?"

He threw her a disbelieving look. "Wild guess. Old boyfriend?"

The far-away look returned to her eyes, right before he turned back to the road. "Something like that."

She said it so softly, he almost missed the catch in her voice. Almost. "Étienne?"

"*Oui.* But he wasn't my…we weren't lovers."

"But you loved him."

She gasped, and he glanced at her again. "Sorry. Love him. You love him."

Looking out of her window, she wrung her hands together.

"It's okay, *petite*. We don't have to talk about it."

She was quiet for a long time, until he thought they'd continue the rest of the drive in silence.

"We were soulmates." Her voice was quiet, distant.

"I think that means something a little different here."

"I believe there are many kinds of soulmates because there are many kinds of connections."

It was quiet again as he pulled to the curb a few yards from her apartment building and put the car in park.

"Maybe that's crazy. I sound crazy," she whispered.

She was starting to pull away, second-guessing herself for opening up to him, and he needed to win the competition with her thoughts. Undoing her seatbelt, he pulled her across his lap. "Intriguing," he said, kissing her again.

CHAPTER THIRTEEN

VERA TETLEY RULED her empire from her sumptuous castle on the Upper East Side. The mega mansion was made up of two apartment buildings, gutted and renovated with a courtyard at its center. Stepping down into the sunken stone terrace in the middle of the courtyard's lush garden, Zack felt like he was entering a great room in a witch's palace.

By some sorcery, the sounds of the city beyond the limestone walls were nearly shut out, and all he heard was the sound of tinkering china, and the steady stream of water pouring from the marble lion's head mounted on the garden wall behind them.

It was a sweltering eighty-five degrees when he'd left Alex's brownstone for the theater an hour ago, but it felt like a balmy seventy-five in Vera's garden.

Yup, sorcery.

He'd been summoned by the witch—plucked from the street by an old man in a monkey suit who seemed to know only a handful of words, "Vera Tetley would like a word." That was it. Then Mr. Monkey Suit kindly held open the backseat door and waited for him to slide in like a good little lad. Disappointingly though, unlike the monkeys in

The Wizard of Oz, this one couldn't fly, so it took an eternity to arrive at Vera's fortress at mid-fucking-day. He'd sent an apologetic text to Faye alerting her that he'd be significantly delayed, which earned him a very eloquent

????!!!!

He replied,

I've been kidnapped again.

She replied,

Vera.

…

Affirmative.

…

Fuck.

…

Indeed.

His phone remained silent for a few minutes, and then vibrated again, with Faye's assurance that the assistant director and choreographer could wrangle the zoo animals for as long as he needed.

Faye, lovely Faye. Moon of my life, my sun and stars…

…

**Game of Thrones? Nice. Say hello to
Norma Desmond for me.**

He set his phone down, trying to silence his scolding brain.

You missed lunch. Turkey on wheat. Extra veg and olive oil. Grapes. Yogurt.

His leg bounced in irritation.

It's fine. You're in control. Swap lunch for dinner. Make lunch your cheat meal.

Besides, the more pressing matter was that he was forty minutes late for the first out-of-studio rehearsal for *Lady in Red*. The cast had been split into groups the last three weeks, and he was excited to get everyone together in the same place, see all the moving parts working together.

By the time the illustrious lady swept in on her broomstick a cool *twenty* minutes after he'd arrived, he was over an hour late, and not in the mood for her antics. He cursed under his breath.

"Zack-a-ryyy, *darling*! I'm so glad you could join me!" she gushed, breezing onto the terrace like a heavily-scented hurricane.

"Vera." He managed to show appropriate levels of deference with a kiss to her outstretched fingers, then pulled out her chair. "I wasn't exactly in the neighborhood, and it didn't sound much like an invitation—"

Her face fell, and so did the thick liner around her eyes, giving them a slightly sinister shape. "*Oh poo!* Don't get your tutu in a twist, Coen!"

Before he could respond to *that* little gem, the south wall of the kitchen, made entirely of glass and bronze, retracted, a handful of servants filing out like penguins with trays of pastries stuffed with chocolate, creamy cheese, fruit preserves…

Eye of newt, toe of frog.

The pulse at his temple gained pressure with each tray set on the table.

For crying out loud.

Adjusting the silk turban on her head, she straightened to allow one of the penguins to lay a cloth napkin in her lap. It was a fucking Mad Hatter party. At that thought, his heart lurched. He'd been making a lot of internal references to *Alice in Wonderland* over the last two days which, coincidentally (or not), was exactly how long it'd been since he'd left Mina on her doorstep. She'd looked so beautiful, and happy, and tired, and confused—and *scared*. She was very likely freaking out after the turn of events that weekend.

He hadn't called her, sensing from their last kiss that she needed her space. The kiss had felt so *final*, a lingering press that seemed more like "Goodbye" than "See you later," or "I'm scared-as-shit but we'll figure this out." The need to see her felt almost physically painful.

Curious.

Massaging his temple, he squeezed his eyes shut briefly against his train of thought. "I'm keeping about a hundred and fifteen people waiting—"

"Let them wait! They're on my payroll, honey. Thanks to the Actor's Equity—which I *fully* support, of course— they'll be compensated for their time whether they're working or picking fleas from each other's backs."

Zack swallowed an exasperated sigh.

Vera didn't swallow hers. "Money talk is so *vulgar.*" Remarkably, she sounded genuinely aggrieved. "I thought a little noon tea would be nice."

He glanced at his watch. 1:07 p.m. Then he looked back at Vera. Dressed in art deco from head-to-toe, emphasizing her already-emphatic words with swirling hand motions and exaggerated lifts of her shoulder, she really did embody Norma Desmond's eccentric persona—even with the grating chain-smoker's quality to her voice.

He winced.

No need to be a dick.

It's not like she was intentionally rude; she was just blissfully out of touch. It would never occur to her that anyone's time was as important as her own. She spooned the yellow center of a soft-boiled egg into her mouth at a snail's pace between a recap of her conversation with her neighbor (former Mayor Bloomberg) that morning, and he was sorely tempted to funnel the rest of her food into her mouth, so he could move things along.

"What's on your mind, Vera?" he asked more politely, tapping a tiny silver spoon on the edge of the table. —He'd reflect on the irony of that later. "Are you backing out? Am I gonna have to dance in the street at the mercy of kind strangers with spare pennies to chuck into my hat?"

She frowned, increasing the number of cracks in her thick mask of foundation. "Oh, for God's sake, Zachary, don't be so dramatic!" She wiped her chin, then waved one of her penguins over without turning her attention away from him.

Within seconds, a timid young penguin materialized before them with a short stack of newspapers and, at Vera's nod, set them in front of Zack. He smiled sympathetically at her before she disappeared as quietly as she'd come.

Vera considered him thoughtfully. "I thought you'd like to see the early buzz for your show. You've even managed to pull The Morning Metropolitan out of hiding. They only ever trouble themselves with the arts if an actor breaks her neck or sleeps with a director."

Zachary coughed, choked, then redoubled his coughing effort until his eyes watered.

Jesus.

"Good Lord, are you alright?" Vera motioned another penguin. "Water! What is it? Allergies? They just cut the grass this morning and I don't think the air's settled just yet—"

"I'm fine." He dutifully sipped the water. "Forgive me. I enjoy going toe-to-toe with you any other time—"

"It's alright, Coen, I know you're eager to be rid of me, but some news should be delivered the old-fashioned way. Face-to-face."

She said it with a mischievous smile that wrinkled her cheeks but didn't quite spark in her eyes. Zack frowned. Vera's eyes *always* sparked, whatever her mood. It was unlike them to burn out. That's when his senses sharpened, homing in on the penguins shuffling about in his periphery, manning their stations in a house much too large for one person. He recognized something in her faded eyes he hadn't experienced in many years, but could never, ever forget.

Loneliness.

Vera had the dance and theater circuits, her social circles, infinite influence, and enough money to circle the globe a million times, but she was lonely. The ten-year-old inside of him wanted to reach out and hold her hand. Grown-up Zack sensed Vera would find pity undignified. Instead, he cleared his throat, and lifted a newspaper from the stack. Giving it a snap to straighten it out, he smiled warmly at her before reading each bolded headline she'd circled in red.

Lady in Red is filled to the gills with fresh star power. -USA Today

*Bare-bones in the best way, stripped down
to the marrow. – The New York Times*

*Coen and Allende are flint and tinder, striking sparks
throughout the entire performance. – The New York Post*

*Evocative, provocative, rousing, arousing. If Coen's opener
is any indication of what's to come this Broadway season,
audiences will need Xanax and cigarettes. – Newsday*

"I see the Tribune is in rare form," Vera croaked. "The new critic makes Ben Stein sound like Robin Williams."

Zack tossed the last paper on top of the stack, giving her his first genuine smile since their meeting began. "Thanks for that, I haven't had time to read anything, mostly because I hate reading critiques—"

"Zachary—"

"But the unanimous use of the most time-honored clichés must be a good sign. *Sizzling, scorching, electric, hot…*"

"I don't give a rat's ass about reviews either, tell you the truth. Look how wrong they were about *Wicked*. It's what the audience wants that matters, which is why I invited you here, Coen. I have faith in you, you know that. We've known each other a long time."

His left brow lifted at the gravity in her tone. "Vera?"

"I refuse to be at the mercy of some burned-out critic who could wake up on the wrong side of the bed and decide it's not only risky to turn a ballet-turned-opera-turned-play *back* into a ballet, but stupid."

Just like that, the throbbing returned to his temple. "To be fair, it's a *musical…*"

"It's been on Broadway before—"

"As a play, not a musical."

"I also refuse to be at the mercy of theater owners who decide what to book and what to evict," she continued without so much as a blink. "It's about *real estate,* darling."

"I'm afraid you've lost me."

"*Lady in Red* won't be playing in any pint-sized theater on West Forty-Fifth. It'll play in front of thirteen hundred people, in one of the few houses that are actually *on Broadway.*"

"*On* Broadway?" He leaned forward. "Correct me if I'm wrong, but aren't those big, shiny houses completely booked? Not to mention, exclusively owned by about four organizations? How'd you swing this?"

Vera looked so smug, so incredibly proud of her secret, Zack could *hear* Norma Desmond's voice saying, "*Alright, Mr. Demille, I'm ready for my close-up!*" in the long, dramatic pause that followed.

His heart pounded so fiercely, he thought it might dislodge and get stuck in his throat. "You're killing me."

"I bought a theater."

Zack choked again, peering at the madwoman in stunned disbelief. "Incredible, the way you said that, as if you just told me you bought a new pair of shoes."

"Well, technically I bought a landmark hotel and flipped it." She cracked *her* first genuine smile. It turned the corners of her eyes—and her thick black liner—back up, framing her mouth in rows of parentheses. "Renovations are ahead of schedule. Tetley Theatre will be ready in time for previews."

Right. Sure. Absolutely.

Also, holy fucking shit.

Of course, it was entirely plausible that Broadway was teeming with relics just waiting for billionaires to snap up and turn into their pet projects…and plausible, still, that the small army of workers it would take wouldn't squeak to the press.

Plausible, but not probable.

"Why?"

She scowled. "I realize you young people speak in abbreviations and acronyms, but I need you to elaborate, sweetheart."

He wondered how many more endearments were left in the English language she hadn't employed in the last twenty minutes. There couldn't be many. He made a mental note to be more mindful not to sound like a condescending ass in the future.

Except maybe "petite."

He grinned. It was his favorite. He'd be loath to give it up.

"Zachary!"

He came to, clearing his throat. "I'd have to be living under a rock not to know how much you love the arts, and that your contributions to them over the years have probably kept a lot of institutions from closing…This isn't just about profit or control for you, I get that. But this feels like a little more than charity."

"Handsome *and* astute, I see." Her hawk eyes looked him over, searching, narrowing—then softening with what looked like recognition. Whatever she saw must have earned her faith, and she let go a sigh. "I've loved the performing arts since I was a little girl. While my father troubled himself with business and selfishly trying to make a boy heir with the woman who nearly died giving birth to me, I busied myself with ballet and theater. I didn't have the natural talent, but I've always had a passion for it. This gives me something to do in my old age. When your play is established, I'll find myself another. My *father's* legacy is Tetley Media Group. *This* will be mine."

The clouds didn't break, and a chorus of angels didn't rush in singing *hallelujah.* Vera didn't suddenly seem less absurd, or out-of-touch, or obnoxious, or proud…but she *did* feel more accessible. More…human.

His lips twitched. "Since I'm tacky and classless and have absolutely no shame for it, how much is this pet project?"

"About a hundred million dollars."

The wind left his body in a sound like, "*Huh.*"

When his wits returned, he spoke again. "And the manager of the theater we've already contracted with?"

The light of mischief returned to Vera's eyes. "The idea that happiness cannot be bought is a lovely sentiment, but deeply flawed."

Well. That was that.

Mina did *not* have sexy feet. It was something she'd grown to accept, and even be proud of. She didn't need sexy feet, because she had warrior feet. Warrior *princess* feet. The feet of an incredible athlete. The feet of a prima ballerina.

So why was she sitting on a bench in Central Park, staring at her feet? Her subconscious sat down beside her on the weathered bench, leaned in close and whispered, *You know why.*

She shivered, though it already felt like a sauna at half past ten, despite the cloudy sky and the shade of lush trees where she sat along the edge of the Harlem Meer's tranquil water. The air gifted her with the sweet scent of hydrangea and summer rain, Mother Nature's apology for being so humid.

Slipping her feet from her two hundred-dollar shoes—ballet flats designed by an orthopedic surgeon that had substantial arch support, plenty of room for her toes to wiggle, and cushioning that felt like layers of fluffy clouds—she stretched her legs out in front of her. She examined her abused appendages, seeking some characteristic that might be considered conventionally attractive to any sane human being, let alone sexy. She'd learned to hide her imperfections with artfully-executed straps and well-placed appliqués. Perhaps it'd been enough to deceive eyes the color of the ocean on a stormy day, green with tinges of blue, gray and silver...

Her subconscious rolled her eyes. *Oh, so we are poets now?*

Merde.

Her subconscious was *annoying.*

Frowning, she flexed her toes. Her feet were slender, strong, beautifully curved, and at size seven and a half (though they shrank to size seven during the season), they were long for her petite frame—perfectly proportioned for ballet. All her toes were about the same length, nearly square in shape. "Peasant's feet," Madame had called them in Third Section. Mina used to *hate* them. They reminded her of Shrek's feet—until she'd risen en pointe for the first time at twelve years old and realized what good fortune the genetics gods had gifted her with...

The pressure distributed more evenly when she danced on her toes than it did for other dancers. It certainly didn't make it easy. She was still prone to the delightful spectrum of injuries and annoyances that befell ballerinas—stress fractures, purpling flesh, blisters that brought tears to her eyes at the slightest touch. But at least she'd been able to avoid painful cracked toenails and bunions.

Small mercies.

Her Shrek feet had made her triumphant at sixteen years old, when she'd taken to the bare stage of the Palais Garnier, before eleven unsmiling faces staring at her from the empty orchestra section, to dance for her life. Or at least, that's what it had felt like—her heart pounding so violently, she could feel its relentless pulse from her fingertips, to her battered, silk-bound toes.

Twelve years later, she still heard the director's voice sharply commanding, *"Begin!"*

It had been like the voice of God—resonant, authoritative, with an omniscient tone that was both a promise and a threat. She'd heard it loud and clear: she had *one* chance to advance to the rank of *premier danseur*, and this was it. Taking a deep breath, she'd closed her eyes and meditated on three simple words:

Never be dishonest.

They'd proven a soothing balm to her anxiety, rendering one of the greatest performances of her life from a moment of pure fear and desire. At the end of the piece, Mina had stood onstage on legs she hardly felt, listening to the deafening sound of her quick breaths echoing in the hall. Terrified and uncertain, she'd scanned the faces of the veritable jury for any expression whatsoever.

An *eternity* had to have passed, because her breathing had slowed as much as her nerves would allow, the sweat on her body had cooled and dried, and the silence had become excruciating.

"That's all," the beak-nosed director had said stiffly, and her heart had sunk to her toes.

Just as she was about to weep, he cracked an almost imperceptible smile. "I've never seen a dancer so young execute Odile's thirty-two fouetté turns so flawlessly. Well done, Mademoiselle Allende."

A whisper went through her, and her heart slammed into her rib cage, snatching her from her reverie. Goosebumps rose on her arms and neck. She went on high alert, quickly scanning her surroundings. Seconds later, she relaxed her posture, smiling politely at a young woman having a jog along the path with her dog.

It was stupid, really, feeling like she was being watched. She'd been on edge since Sunday night. Of *course* she was being watched. Never mind that New York was one of the most populated cities in the world—She'd just performed on one of its biggest stages, and she would only become more recognizable after opening night. A ripple, then a splash, went out over the water, drawing her expectant gaze to its surface.

There you are, my elegant friend.

Looking affectionately at the magnificent bird as it glided into view, she admired its long, graceful neck and stark white feathers. It turned and looked right at her, a slippery aquatic plant dangling from its beak, and she giggled.

"Oh, you are a 'him,' aren't you?" she whispered, recognizing the large black knob at its forehead. "At least, I *think* you're a him. You were down there a long time."

As if on cue, it craned its neck and lifted its wings slightly, spreading its feathers in a display of its impressive wingspan. Mina's brows lifted at the stunning creature's proximity warning.

Absolument a 'him.'

She was well-acquainted with the mute swan, feeling an odd sort of kinship with the lovely bird. In *Paris*, whenever she missed her *papa*, she'd watch for them along the Seine in the Nineteenth Arrondissement, admiring them as they cleaned and shook themselves along the water's edge. They were the quietest of their kind, a fact her *papa* shared with her when she was a painfully shy little girl.

"You see?" he'd told her. "One of God's strongest, most beautiful creatures is soft-spoken, too. They don't have to be loud to leave an impression. *Never* change who you are to please someone else, do you hear me?"

Sniffling, she touched the back of her index finger to her nose to halt the trickle of moisture there. It was *exhausting,* being haunted by two ghosts. Or perhaps she was conjuring them herself, desperate to hold onto two of the most important people in her life.

That's not the only reason you're upset, her meddling subconscious goaded.

Mina laughed without humor, and the swan craned its neck at her again, holding her in his stately stare for a few heartbeats. He must have concluded she wasn't a threat to him or his territory because he didn't bother preening again before ducking his head into the water.

Zack doesn't want to change you.

She tapped her foot, exasperated.

Fine! So what if he likes my feet?? What of it, then?

She wanted to scream at how pathetic she was, obsessing over such an insignificant detail. But her heart told her it was more than what it seemed on the surface, beating faster each time she replayed his compliment in her head.

In the short time she'd known him, Zack had never

spared her feelings. He was honest to a fault, painfully, *infuriatingly* so. But as brutal as he could be, he was equally as generous with his praise, leaving her breathless at his brazen admiration. He hadn't been mocking her or playing to her ego when he'd given her compliments.

Oui, her subconscious said. *You're catching on…*

Her heart did a sad little pirouette. It was much, much more than him merely liking her feet. It's that he'd seen them for what they were, in all their perfect imperfection, and still found them beautiful.

He sees you *in your perfect imperfection, and he thinks you're beautiful.*

Letting her tears fall this time, they streamed hot down her face. What was the point of stopping them? Few people interrupted her tumultuous thoughts, walking their dogs or taking a morning stroll, so she could succumb to her pity party in peace. She'd held back all night, and through the morning, through her workout and pointe class. Better to let go and cry it out now, so there was nothing left when she told him she couldn't do this.

Admittedly, she'd taken this role in a desperate effort to escape her haunted life, but the ghost had followed her here, and performing at Radio City Music Hall—exposing her soul to millions of people tuning in on Sunday—had yanked her from limbo and plunged her back into the world of the living. No longer transient in her own existence, she had a taste of what could be, and it awakened a hunger in her she'd been missing for so long it felt like someone else's memory. She couldn't get distracted. Not now.

Mina's eyes jerked up, her heart leaping into her throat. *Where'd he come from?!*

The hooded figure hadn't made a sound. He just stood there, shifting his weight for a beat…

She opened her mouth to ask what he wanted, then hesitated. It was obvious from the way he hid his face that it was nothing good. Perhaps she could dissuade him with—he was so fast, lunging at her before she could gather her wits.

"*Non!*"

Pain stabbed the point where her arm met her shoulder as he practically ripped her arm from its socket trying to snatch her beloved Chanel bag. She cried out again. It was fight-or-flight. Acting against everything she knew to be smart, against self-preservation, she kicked at him and clutched the bag with both hands to keep him from making off with her…everything.

Everything is in this bag!

It was the only thought in her head in the heightened moment, her every breath and motion powered by a shock of adrenaline. Instinctively, her eyes traveled over his tall form in search of the tell-tale bulk of a weapon. Saliva tinged with bile flooded her mouth at that thought, and she choked, but she held on through the fleeting fear that he might hurt her, through the ache in her shoulder…

"Lady, *please*!" her assailant gritted. "Just let *go*!"

She froze at the first sound of her attacker's voice—deep, but pitchy, cracking at the word "go." Her eyes flew to his face—partially hidden in shadow, but unmistakably missing the angular features of a fully-developed man.

Oh mon Dieu…

Her lips parted in shock.

He was just a kid. And he looked *scared*.

Taking advantage of her distraction, the youth shoved

her away, giving her bag another yank. Another piercing pain shot through her arm, and she wailed, letting go of the bag in defeat. Seconds later, he was gone, disappearing beyond a bend in the path.

She struggled upright, new tears quickly pooling in her eyes, blurring her vision. Shaking, sobbing, her arm throbbing, she felt along the bench for anything that might have fallen from her bag during the struggle. Her mind was going too fast for any single thought to stick. Coming up empty handed, her sobs intensified. Her eyes darted left and right and behind her, seeking out a good Samaritan, widening at the thought that her attacker might return, then clouding again when she found there was no one. Her throat was too dry to scream for help, backed up by a lump she hadn't the strength to swallow down. She looked despondently over the water again.

Nothing.

Even her silent companion had abandoned her.

CHAPTER FOURTEEN

WHEN ZACK WAS eight, he'd run away.

It was Thanksgiving Day, and he'd broken a dish (while running through the house again) that belonged to Foster Mom Number Four's mother-in-law—an ugly, misshapen glass bowl with painted flowers on it he'd later learned was called a gravy boat.

A fancy dish for gravy?

Stupid.

The sentiment was something he'd felt compelled to say aloud and earned him "ten licks" from Foster Dad Number Four. He couldn't remember ever feeling so *angry*—which was saying something for a kid who was always angry. He'd taken the second-story window to the fire escape, down the ladder, and quickly along the sidewalk to the subway while everyone else was preoccupied with champagne and trying to outdo each other's thankfulness.

Assholes.

He still remembered his excitement when the subway doors opened at Times Square, and the circus that greeted him as he took the stairs two at a time and stood gawking at his first glimpse of Broadway and Forty-Second Street. Balloons the size of Godzilla, floats carrying his favorite heroes, and laughing, deliriously happy people had filled the streets for blocks and blocks. The sky opened up and rained down streamers and confetti. Police rode horses in this magical place, and everywhere he turned, another vendor sold a new, mouth-watering treat. His eyelids had stuck open like window shutters.

It was *exactly* as he'd imagined.

The fact he was escorted back to Foster Home Number Four in the back of a police cruiser instead of on horseback, and the wonder of Broadway had been slightly over-sold by the Macy's Thanksgiving Day Parade, was inconsequential. He'd been bitten by the theater bug, and it was a malady of the incurable kind.

He would never be able to recreate the exhilaration he'd felt that first time, but damned if stepping into the theater to rehearse his first musical on Broadway wasn't a near-perfect second.

The theater was an absolute *circus* by the time Zack arrived well after two o'clock. Members of the chorus line were doing vocal warm-ups in the wings, filling the air with a blur of idiotic sound. Some principals were bouncing stage banter off one another in the aisles, quick on the draw with one-liners and exaggerated expressions, their obnoxious voices mixing with the vocal warm-ups to form a sound like a swarm of mosquitos in the amplified space.

He grinned, feeling the familiar rush in his veins. It was *glorious.*

"*On eight!*" called Will, the assistant choreographer.

Like little marionettes, dancers who'd been slouching against each other and gossiping in low tones snapped to attention. They moved into position, risking life and limb on a floor glossy with sweat, waiting for the count. It came, and with the music, they sprang to life. This was his tribe, a sentimental pack of theater fanatics trapped in eternal childhood. It was a quality he looked for in every cast and crew member, from stagehand to star.

Speaking of… He studied the slight figure lifted precariously over his understudy's head. *Where* is *my star?*

The young lady was about the same build as Mina, her hair pulled into the same neat bun, and her skin glowing like the moon on a clear night. Pretty, but his leading *Lady in Red* looked more amber beneath the stage lights.

Dammit.

He'd anticipated some distance from her once they'd left their bubble of euphoria and re-entered the real world. He was prepared to be hit with her metaphorical emotional wall.

Or her literal hand.

But not showing up at all?

Unacceptable.

It's not that he couldn't empathize with a healthy melodramatic freak-out. He'd been caught up in his own version of it for two days. Like now, for example:

The two actors in the aisles with their animated expressions and body language looked like live-action Tweedle Dee and Tweedle Dum. Working with Pete to tweak the script last night (again), and polishing the choreography (again), and consulting with the costume and stage designers over the last two days, had been more of the same.

It was his trustee childhood defense mechanism springing to action, his brain transforming his retinas into fantasy lenses. He could escape into the fantasy for hours and still be aware of the real world around him. It was like…sleep walking. But the fantasy wasn't enough to suppress the little thud his heart did when he thought of her. Yet, *he* was here. It was a trick of the trade to be able to multitask, and he expected it—*demanded* it—of his people, too. No excuses.

Two days. He missed her. And now he had the added pleasure of being annoyed.

Professional annoyance. Not the deeply personal kind.

Right.

He cursed.

"You'll have to snarl a little louder," Faye said from his left side, handing him a cellophane-wrapped turkey sandwich and a bottled water. "My ears are still ringing from the vocal warm-ups."

Relief flooded his veins.

Turkey sandwich on wheat.

Making a grateful noise from the back of his throat, he ripped open the sandwich and tucked into one of its diagonally-cut halves. "I know why *my* understudy is up there," he said between chews, "but barring a natural disaster—which I can categorically dismiss—or broken legs, Mina should be the one with her ass in mid-air right now."

Faye angled her head and stared at him blankly. "I take it tea time with Norma was unpleasant?"

He scowled, taking another bite and scanning the theater again. *In case she's hiding in the orchestra pit? For fuck's sake…*

"On the contrary," he grumbled through another mouthful. "Vera bought a theater."

"Huh." Incredibly, Faye didn't bat an eyelash.

"My exact response."

"Did it come with a unicorn or a two-headed dragon?"

"Not that I recall, but I'm sure there's still time to put in a request."

"Slow news day, then." Dramatic pause, and then, "Interesting read-through earlier. Can't say I've ever done it without the two leads in attendance before."

Zack tried to smile.

"Yikes." Faye grimaced. "I don't think I've ever seen a human's lips curl back like that—like a dog baring his teeth."

Grunting, he polished off the rest of the sandwich.

She lifted her hands, palms-out. "Okay, fine. Let's play Where's Wilhelmina, shall we?" Sticking two fingers into her mouth, she whistled loudly. Several heads snapped up. "You." She waved over one of the dancers who'd been breathing through a take five. Then to Zack, "I've seen Mina with this one a few times, maybe she knows something."

The quick-witted principal dancer with a gymnast's body sprinted over, then put her hands on her hips to open her chest a little more. A few seconds later, her breaths came easier, deeper.

"Kyoko," said Faye. "Have you heard from Mina today?"

Kyoko seemed suspiciously uncomfortable.

"At ease, cadet." Zack joked. She obviously knew something but coming in too hot would get him nowhere. "No one's in trouble. But if something's up, I need to know."

Kyoko swallowed, her uncertain gaze flitting between him and Faye. "That's the thing, I haven't heard from her all day. We were supposed to meet up for brunch and come here together."

"Where and when?" Zack asked.

"On Eighth, like eleven o'clock."

"Cross street?"

"Between Forty-Eighth and Forty-Ninth."

"Maybe something came up?" asked Faye.

"Nah, you don't understand." Kyoko shook her head

emphatically. "Mina might be the most anal chick I've ever met. She's never late for anything, not even eggs. She would have called."

Zack nodded. *Anal* was an understatement. Death could call her up with a date and time and Mina would show up five minutes early. He tried to ignore the distinct drop his heart made to his stomach. "Why didn't you say anything earlier?" Faye nudged him, and he tried again. "Did you try to contact her?"

"Four times, but it went straight to voicemail." Doubling over, she moved her hands to her knees.

Zack's brow ticked. "When's the last time you ate?"

"Yesterday."

He bit back a scolding remark. "Get out of here. Eat something."

"But—"

"See you tomorrow, Kyoko," Faye said firmly, but gave her a reassuring smile. "We'll get to the bottom of it."

"Yeah, no problem."

Zack pulled out his phone and quick-dialed, ignoring Faye's penetrating look. It didn't ring even once before Mina's softly accented voice asked him to leave a message. Cursing, he hung up and tried another number.

"Who's up next?" Faye pulled out her own cell.

"Physical therapy."

She nodded. "I'll try Perez. Mina's usually up last for vocal training, but it's worth a shot."

Fifteen minutes later, calls to Mina's apartment building, gym, the studio where she took classes, and the costume department proved fruitless. Zack's hackles were *way* up by the time he called Alex and the man hadn't seen her, either.

"Fuck me." He turned on his heel and left the auditorium.

Faye followed behind him to the lobby, not saying a word as he tapped out the last number anyone wanted to dial. Her eyes matched his thoughts exactly:

I've got a bad *feeling about this.*

The line clicked, and a deep, authoritative voice sounded on the other end. "N.Y.P.D."

Ten minutes further, and the end of Zack's rope had unraveled, caught fire, and disintegrated to a steaming pile of ash. "*What the hell do you mean you can't do anything for twenty-four hours? Have you checked emergency dispatch again? I've been on hold for five* minutes!"

Pacing in front of the glass doors, he absently watched the sprinkle of rain pick up to a steady stream. Faye had already wrapped rehearsal, and the only remaining personnel besides the two of them were cleaning the theater. He turned away from the doors to throw a homicidal look at the janitor who chose that *exact* moment to switch on the vacuum.

Faye scurried to shut the theater doors, and Zack snapped into his phone. "I *told* you, she did *not* run away. She has no family in the area. She isn't seeing anyone, abusive or otherwise. She keeps to a schedule like a *clock,* generally within a five-mile radius. She's ten pounds soaking wet, but she's kinda hard to miss. There are thirty *thousand* of you. I'm pretty sure you can spare *two* to patrol the goddamn radius!"

"Zack," Faye said tentatively.

"*Do* not *put me on hold again!*"

"*Zack!*"

"*What?*"

Faye nodded toward the entrance. "Ten pounds, soaking wet."

Three things happened when Mina walked through the doors of the theater.

First, Zack's expression went from livid, to shocked, to wild-eyed concern. It was like watching a silent film. Well, almost. For some reason, sound reached her ears like it was traveling through Jell-O.

Second, his eyes ran through an impressive color spectrum. Forest pine, maybe? Then emerald, then that cloudy sea glass that reminded her of holidays lounging on the beach in Nice, and swimming in the warmth of the Mediterranean Sea. The memory made her smile, just before the third thing, when her heart sped up like she'd been running a triathlon, and everything went hot and fuzzy.

"Jesus," he said.

Then the world went black.

"Pulse is coming in strong, but she's dehydrated," a sharp, feminine voice said. *"Get me a—wait, there she is. Pupils look good. I need an oral rehydration solution. Help me sit her up."*

"Nnnaagragh." Mina tried to speak, but her brain was slow to catch up and her tongue felt thick.

The calm, reassuring face of a medic came into clarity—and so did Zack's deep, measured voice from somewhere outside the ambulance.

"Is it standard practice to put people on hold, or is that unique to your precinct?"

"I apologize for the inconvenience-"

"Incompetence."

"Mr. Coen, if I could just ask a few questions…"

Then Faye's soft, *"She's awake now."*

214

Mina shivered. She was soaked in rain and sweat, which formed an uncomfortable film over her skin. It had been so *hot* outside, but it was a refrigerator in the back of the ambulance, and the lights made her headache feel like her brain's hemispheres were trying to split from each other.

Merde.

Squeezing her eyes shut, her sense of smell sharpened. She *desperately* needed a shower.

"Mina, right?" said the blond medic, draping a small blanket around Mina's shoulders. She didn't look much older than her. "I'm Tara. You were out for a few minutes. Your vitals are good, but you're dehydrated, so we've administered an IV."

Mina looked down at the tiny tube that narrowed into a not-so-tiny needle and disappeared into the back of her hand. Heat rushed to her cheeks, and moisture filled her mouth. *"I-"*

"Bucket."

A small blue basin was held under her chin, and she retched and retched, until her abs constricted painfully, and her heaves came up dry.

"Jesus."

"Sir…"

"Is she okay?"

"I'm still checking her, but it looks like she's gonna be fine…"

There was some commotion, and then Tara blew a resigned sigh, shifting to her left to continue her examination. The ambulance shook a bit, then shrank to the size of a shoe box as Zack's athletic frame filled the limited space. He came to a squat in front of her, his eyes glued to her face. "Are you okay?"

"I'm-" Mina tried, then winced. She sounded like she'd

been out of it three years instead of minutes, her voice small and hoarse.

"Drink this." Tara handed her a pouch with a straw. "Deep breath…"

Mina winced again as the medic's expert hands reached her shoulder, then obediently sipped, aware of Zack's sharp eyes moving over her face and body, then back up to her shaking hands. Acute humiliation at him seeing her so haggard brought a new kind of heat to her face. *Enfin…* he wasn't exactly Fred Astaire, either. There were shadows under his eyes, and his hair stuck out in places it usually lay smooth, like he'd run his fingers through it more than once. His jaw was so tense, it could have been made of steel and bolts.

But more than any of that, was the way his body filled the space. He wasn't threatening—not to her. He was like the swan, she realized. Raising his wings, spreading his feathers. Protecting her. She felt a lump in her throat. After feeling so small and scared and powerless, she welcomed the flood of relief in her body at the sight of him. Despite her earlier resolve to end things before they began, she found herself fighting the urge to throw her arms around his neck and squeeze.

"I'm…" She almost said, *I'm fine,* but that wasn't true. She'd never been a good liar, and she was *so* tired. "I… don't know."

"What happened, *petite?* Where were you?"

"In a minute," Tara's voice was kind, but firm. "Almost done, Mina. When was the last time you ate or drank?"

Mina shifted her eyes to the left, away from Zack's penetrating stare, to the back of the ambulance where Faye and two officers were observing quietly. Faye looked particularly rapt, her gaze going back and forth between Mina and Zack like a ping pong ball.

Merde.

"*Eh,* this morning." She forced her attention back to Tara. "It was early. I… think I had a banana before the gym…and a green juice a-after pointe class."

"Do you remember what time it was?"

Mina still felt a little shaky and sipped the salty-sweet concoction in the pouch again. "Nine hours."

"Nine o'clock?"

"*Oui.* Sorry. Yes, nine o'clock."

Tara glanced at her watch and marked something on a clipboard. "Good. That's very good, Mina."

"What time is it now, *s'il vous plaît?*"

"About two-thirty. We're treating you for heat exhaustion, exercise-related collapse, and dehydration."

Another medic—male, about the same age, handed something to Tara, and the crackle of plastic filled the ambulance.

"Your shoulder's a little tender," she said, gently. "Is it an old injury, or relatively new?"

Ice cold met her shoulder and Mina jerked, then relaxed, hazarding a glance at Zack. She was pretty sure he hadn't blinked since he'd entered the ambulance. "New," she said quietly, and the clamp on her finger began to beep in time with her quickening pulse. "I was—it happened so fast. He took my bag. He pulled so hard—"

"*What?*" Zack boomed.

Mina flinched. He filled her vision completely, his hands on her knees. "You're saying you were *mugged? Jesus,* are you ok?" His frantic eyes moved over her face, her hairline (which probably looked like the matted fur of a black sheep) and trailed her body again. "*For Christ's sake, why didn't you lead with that?*"

Lynn Turner

"Just grasping at straws here," said Faye, "but this might be why."

He ignored her. "Did you see the guy? Where were you? Did he hurt you?"

"We'll get to that," Tara snapped, waving him out of the way. "I think we should get you to the hospital for an x-ray—"

"*Non!*" Mina was exhausted. She couldn't stand much more poking and prodding. Besides, she didn't need x-ray confirmation. She was certain her shoulder *was* sprained. It was nothing. She'd had much worse.

Tara's expression softened. "You aren't the first stubborn dancer I've treated. Let's make a deal," she said to both Mina and Zack. "You need to *rest*. Forty-eight hours, minimum."

Mina gasped.

"*Forty-eight hours,* no hospital. I'll send you home with some ice packs, which you can use as-needed. Make sure you get plenty of fluids, and…" she directed her scowl at Zack "…try and keep the stress to a minimum."

Unfazed, Zack looked Mina over again, then nodded, as if assuring himself she was whole. "I'll be right outside, okay? I'm *right* here."

Giving her knee a squeeze, he ducked from the ambulance.

"Mina?"

Mina watched until he stepped out of view with the officers again. Faye gave her a sympathetic smile and followed suit. Seconds later, muffled voices filtered into the air, blending with the surrounding noise of the city.

"Mina," Tara said again. "Are you hurt anywhere else? Other than your shoulder?"

Mina trembled at the horror of the underlying ques-

218

tion. "*N-non.* Just my shoulder. He took my bag and then he ran."

Tara clasped Mina's shaky hands. "It's okay. You're okay. You were lucky, you know. This is one of the hottest summers on record. We treated a couple of two-hundred-pound marathon runners last week who weren't so lucky." She patted her hands and signed another form. "I'm clearing you to go home. You okay to give the police your statement?"

"*Oui,* I can do that."

"Good." She smiled, handing off her clipboard to the other medic.

Sitting with her legs dangling over the edge of the ambulance, taking unenthused nips at a peanut butter protein bar, Mina answered the officer's questions. There was no ignoring Zack's imposing presence, and honestly, his ticks were fascinating. She recorded each one in her mind, stowing them to obsess over later.

"What is your full name?"

"Wilhelmina Fiona Allende."

Curious left brow.

"How old are you?"

"Twenty-eight."

Jaw muscle tick.

"Where were you?"

"Central Park."

"Were you alone?"

"*Oui.*"

Jaw muscle. Vein in left temple.

"Walk me through. What brought you to the park? What were you doing when you were attacked?"

"I had to get out of my apartment. I… I needed to get away from…myself. I didn't want to be alone."

Adam's apple. Jaw muscle. Left brow.

The officer scratched his jaw. "So, you were meeting someone at the park?"

"Non. I went to see the swans. I… needed to think."

Knowing, all-pervading stare.

Merde.

"I see. You went to the lake, near the Conservatory Gardens."

"Oui."

"About what time was that?"

"Half past ten."

"Did you notice anything strange before the attack?"

"I—I had a strange feeling…like I was being watched. It's—*stupide.*"

"It might not be. Most of these cases are crimes of opportunity, but people who stick to a predictable routine make easy targets."

Tightened jaw. Thin lips. Green eyes cooling to black.

She looked away. "The park isn't part of my usual routine."

The officer scribbled some notes. Zack stared a hole into the side of her face.

"How long have you had this feeling?"

"A couple of days, I think. I don't know…" She bit her bottom lip. "I'm a private person, so it may be my anxiety about being recognized."

"Let's not rule it out. Can you remember what your attacker looked like?… About how old was he?… What race?… Any identifying marks or tattoos?"

She couldn't help herself. She looked at Zack again.

Brows, lips, jaw, Adam's apple…clenched fists.

She sighed. The rest of her statement took twenty minutes.

"And you walked here, without stopping anywhere else, from the Conservatory Gardens to Times Square?"

"*Oui.* I had no keys, no phone, no money." She didn't look at Zack this time. The hopelessness in the aftermath of the moment caved in on her, and she swallowed down a sob.

"How long did that take?"

"Almost two hours. I-I got lost a-a few times."

Muffled curses.

"Is there anything else you can tell me?" The officer was no longer looking down at his notebook.

Mina hesitated.

"It's alright, take your time."

"His eyes were—he looked scared to me. I know it sounds ridiculous, but it's almost like…he didn't *want* to do it. He said *please.* What kind of thief says please?"

"You said he was young. It might have been his first time."

She nodded, eager to accept the first logical explanation, even as her stomach lurched in apprehension. Her entire body sagged, and she buried her face in her hands.

"Is that enough?" Zack asked, but it sounded more like, *That's enough.*

"I think we have what we need for now." The officer nodded once at his partner to confirm. "I suggest you cancel your credit cards and get new locks. Try not to go anywhere secluded alone."

Chapter Fifteen

MINA PROTESTED WEAKLY against Zack taking her home, and when he unceremoniously told her to shut up, she didn't argue any further. She didn't even call him an ass, which was concerning. It was fine with him that she didn't speak much on the way to her apartment. He seemed to have lost his flair for quick, witty conversation anyway. At five in the evening, there was no parking available, because of course everyone in New York City owned a car for the express purpose of hoarding a parking space for all eternity. Muttering a string of curses, he prepared to circle around again.

"What are you doing?" Mina sat up straighter, wincing.

He dropped his eyes to her shoulder, then back to her face. "Looking for someplace to park."

She stopped fidgeting with her seatbelt. "*Non,* you can't come up."

"I'm coming up."

"Zack-"

"You were *mugged.* I just want to make sure you're safe, *petite.* Then I'll go."

Worrying her bottom lip with her teeth, she seemed

at war with herself for a few seconds, then relaxed. "Fine. There's a garage underneath the building. The entrance is on the street opposite."

"Where am I going?" he asked when they were underground.

"I'm unit eight—over there."

He pulled into the narrow space and switched off the engine. Gently, he brushed his fingers through the mess of curls at her hairline, grinning when they snagged on a tangle. "I don't think you need to worry about anyone recognizing you."

"Connard!" she snapped, turning her face away.

There it is.

His heart twisted.

He hadn't seen hide nor hair of her in two days, and when he finally did, both were in a sorry state of affairs. For the first time since meeting her, she appeared as small as she was. It was like she'd shrunk, turning inward and folding in on herself. Her eyes looked exhausted and wary…but there was a healthy flush to her face. The fire was still there, however faint.

Thank God.

"Atta girl."

She was more than a little wobbly when she stood from the car, so he bent and scooped her into his arms, shutting the door with his foot. "Come on, Bambi."

"Espèce d'idiot! Je m'apelle Mina!"

He chuckled, as much from amusement as from relief.

Yup. Still there.

Walking them through her front door, he promptly kicked it shut and leaned back against it, supporting her easily in his arms. "Good management here at least. I wasn't expecting them to change the locks in a timely manner."

"You weren't expecting it?" She sounded incredulous. "You said *incompetent, lazy,* and *criminal negligence* in the same sentence when you yelled at him on the phone—you said if I was abducted or murdered, he'd be an accessory—"

"Jesus. You heard all that?"

Her body shook softly. *"Everyone* heard it."

They fell quiet. His thoughts spun like pennies, racing through the events of a day that felt like three, wobbling faster and faster until coming to an abrupt stop. So much had happened, but there hadn't been time to do anything but react until now.

"Mina?"

Great, I sound completely unhinged.

"Zack?"

"Are you okay?"

"I'm okay." Her body stiffened, but she didn't try to stand up, or demand that he put her down.

His heart did a slippery swirl in his chest, because the war within her filled the silence as surely as if she was fighting it aloud. It felt like the moment in the car when she was deciding if she'd let him in.

God, what a perfect metaphor.

Painfully perfect. Genius, really. Too bad he wasn't in any condition to appreciate it. He flinched instinctively as her warm hands framed his face.

"Are you?" she asked.

He sucked in a breath in wonder at the woman he held. After the ordeal she'd suffered, and the tedious hours following—she was asking him if *he* was okay? That was it. His brave front, his tenacity, his strength—were all decimated by two whispered words. Tightening his grip on her, he bent his knees, sliding with her to the floor, touching his forehead to hers.

"You scared the shit out of me, Mina."

"I know."

"I feel like a tool for even saying it, knowing how scared you must have been." He rubbed her back gently. "Knowing how—*annoyed* I was, at you—before it was obvious something was wrong. I thought you were avoiding me."

She averted her eyes.

Not far off the mark, then.

"So many scenarios ran through my mind before you walked through those doors," he said. "Each one worse than the last. And then you just *dropped,* and my heart fucking stopped. I was annoyed, and you were out there—*Fuck.* I'm so sorry, *petite-*"

"Sshhh." Stroking his cheeks with her thumbs, her warm peanut buttery breath tickling his face, she pressed her lips to his.

He fell head-long into the kiss, drowning in the musk and heat of her, breathing her breath, feeling the warmth and fullness of her lips against his, the pitter patter of her heart against the violent pounding of his own. It was blessed relief. Life tasting life and being unendingly grateful for it. She flinched a little, reminding him of her sprained shoulder, and that he was squeezing her in his need to have her closer. Proof positive she was whole and here and fine.

"I'm fine," she said, as if reading his thoughts.

"You're fine." He tested the words, letting them hang in the silence, then caught a whiff of her natural aroma tinged with the odor of sweat and city sludge.

She must have felt self-conscious, because she crinkled her nose and looked down at her soiled tank top.

"Tell me what you need," he said.

"A hot bath, preferably with a pillow."

He was on his feet in one smooth motion, with her still latched to him like a tree frog. "Clearly, you're not well, and I'm gonna have to supervise you so you don't drown in your tub."

When he'd seen to it that Mina was neck-deep in warm, sudsy water (he'd misinterpreted the French label, so she was going to come out smelling like her shampoo from head to toe—which he didn't see as a bad thing), he navigated to her kitchen to see what he could throw together for her to eat. She'd fight him on it, but he'd win.

Opening the refrigerator door, he recoiled. "Christ, it's a *botany* experiment in here."

Sifting through the wilted, the moldy, and the possibly fermenting, he failed to salvage enough ingredients to make anything substantial, so he tried another tack. Twenty minutes later, food was on its way, he'd rid her fridge of anything suspiciously green and fuzzy, and discovered the cleaning supplies in her hall closet…tucked in a corner, away from her *impressive* collection of shoes. The flaming red ones screamed for him to touch them, so he did, even if it made him a foot-lusting perv. The points on the heels were sharp enough to qualify as weapons. He'd spent decades dancing on his toes but walking on those things without sustaining major injury was pretty damned impressive.

And hot.

Very hot.

He grinned.

The apartment was beautiful in an interior decorating

226

magazine sort of way: classic, feminine, chic. But it was obvious she didn't spend much time here. It wasn't untidy but being Carmen's son meant being able to eat from the table and floor and seeing the whites of his teeth on any shiny surface. So, he got to work. When his complimentary housekeeping services brought him to Mina's living room, he straightened and smiled.

She had an actual chaise. A *fancy* one—cream, with buttons and intricate carving on the legs. This was where she lived when she was here, where a cozy blanket was thrown across the back, and a book lay open and upside down on the seat. Much like the sexy flaming shoes, the book was too enticing not to touch. It promised to reveal a secret about its reader: the kind of words she liked to fill her mind with.

"She Came to Stay," by Simone de Beauvoir. He arched his brow at the cover's description.

Kinky.

And smart.

And so, so complicated.

Fitting.

Hearing the shower come on, he stopped a moment, inclining his head toward her bedroom door. There was something else they had in common: showering after a bath. The coffee table was home to at least three more books of varying degrees of satire and scandal, a remote control, a couple of dirty tea cups, a stack of French magazines, and a miniature swan made of fancy aquamarine glass.

Cute. She must have a thing for swans.

Trying to ignore the way his jaw locked up at the way her sightseeing excursion had ended that day, he wiped down the table and picked up the books, preparing to shelve them. The setting sun pierced through the windows and caught on something on the bookshelf, sending rays of light in every direction. Squinting, he walked over to the shelf.

So, it *wasn't* the world's biggest diamond. He picked up the little swan figurine, crystal-clear and multifaceted—and *heavy*. This thing could double as a weapon, and from the looks of it, an *expensive* one. These weren't his mother's knick-knacks, that was for sure. By the time he finished the room, he'd counted at least a dozen tiny swans. Murano glass, crystal, porcelain, silver, gold—and likely materials he was too unsophisticated to identify. He lifted a figurine from the television stand, next to a photo of Mina and the man she wouldn't talk about—not with him.

He swallowed, a physical reaction to the idea of being in some kind of twisted competition with a dead man. It was hard to dismiss, especially when they looked so cozy, cheek-to-cheek, wearing smiles that spoke of years of inside jokes and long, intimate conversations. Clearing his throat, he examined the weighty ornament of obsidian glass. Two swans faced each other, their long necks curved, their heads touching to form a heart.

"That's one of my favorites."

Zack startled a little and turned around, then tried not to look like a teenage boy seeing a pretty girl half naked for the first time—especially one in dire need of food and sleep. Outwardly, he may have succeeded, but inside, there was a wolf in a suit and tie, whose eyes had bugged out of his head and fallen to the floor.

Coming close, she gently took the figurine from his hand. "Étienne bought this one for me," she said softly, turning it in her hand. "From the airport in Sydney. It reminded him of that movie, The Black Swan."

She offered a sad little smile, and Zack couldn't keep his eyes from wandering over her lips and the loose, springy curls of her hair.

"He hated that movie." She followed up her sad little smile with a sad little laugh. "He thought Natalie Portman was beautiful but made a terrible ballerina."

Zack fought to keep his eyes on her face. But again, it was hard. She wore the most absurd, ineffectual pajamas he'd ever seen—mere scraps of silk that covered nothing but the essentials, and even those made shadows beneath the delicate fabric of her shorts and cami. He frowned at the purpling on her left shoulder. When his eyes returned to her face, she was watching him, and it took the will of a thousand men not to react to the longing in her eyes.

Down, boy. She's tired.

Hungry and tired.

Hungry and tired and just fucking got mugged.

Loud knocking sounded at the door, ending his internal pep talk.

Thank. Fuck.

"I ordered food." His voice sounded like sandpaper.

"I'm not hungry."

He tried to ignore the fact that hers did, too.

"Tough shit." His lips tugged at the corners, and he went to answer the door.

As it turned out, she wasn't a botanist, or a vegetarian. The lady just needed someone to feed her.

"It's a good thing you're the fourth highest paid ballerina in the world, or you'd starve…or die from inhaling spores," he said, taking a bite of his own food.

Mina glared at him for an impressive stretch of time, until she'd finished chewing and swallowing a bite of scrambled egg-stuffed crepe. "I would not starve. I'd go out, or order in. I don't have time to plan and make all my meals."

"Fair enough."

Finishing before her, he settled into the comfortable silence on the chaise beside her. He'd crossed his legs and was thumbing through one of the magazines when the crystal swan glinted again. "Where'd that one come from?" He nodded toward the bookshelf. "The sparkler that looks like a baseball diamond."

She laughed, taking a sip of green juice and licking her lips. "*Papa* gave me that one, after my very first ballet."

"I thought he died when you were eight?"

"*Oui,* he never saw me dance," she said sadly. "But he took me to see *Swan Lake* for Christmas a year before he died. I know it's cliché to call it magical, but I was just a child, and the lights, the costumes, the tiaras—All the dancers looked like princesses, and they moved so beautifully, like they were floating."

Zack succumbed to the sparkle in her eyes, his heart doing the swimming thing again, and he suspected she'd had the same effect on her father when she was a little girl.

"He made an affair of it." She looked past him, out of the window, obviously lost in her memories. "He got my hair done, bought me a new dress, and right before we left for the theater, he gave me that swan wrapped in white tissue paper."

"There must be a dozen of them here. All of them, gifts?"

"Some of them. Some of them, I bought for myself." She picked up the pretty blue swan from the coffee table. "My newest one, from Milan, after my tour as Giselle."

It took her twenty minutes to finish eating and detail the origins of each miniature swan. He witnessed her mind transport to every locale she mentioned in her tales, riveted to her expressions, her voice, and the way she moved her hands when she was excited. She was like a swan herself—an origami swan, coming apart fold-by-fold to reveal the steps that made her.

"What about you?" She searched his face. "What was your first show?"

"*Phantom of the Opera*, when I was twelve."

"Carmen?"

"*Mmhmm*, and Manny. I was teased by some kids at the rec center for my dance tights. I was so upset about it, I swore off ballet. *Mamá* and *papá* wanted me to see what was possible. They wanted to show me how strong and powerful and skilled those dancers were—how much they were admired."

"Did it work?"

"What do *you* think?"

Her lashes fluttered, and he gave himself a mental high-five.

She sniffed. "You certainly don't lack any confidence."

Lowering his crossed leg, he shifted his body and moved in closer, inhaling her all-over shampoo scent. "Should I?"

Her breaths came audibly now. He couldn't say he didn't like it.

"*N-non.*"

Wrapping his hands around her calves and lifting her legs across his lap, he heard her breath catch. It was nice to know she wasn't immune to him, even if she had concocted some grandiose plan to cut him off. (He wasn't sure about this, but he was sure of her apprehension about any sort of relationship.)

She covered his hands with hers, resting them on the

smooth skin of her thighs. "I like your confidence. I want to know where it comes from, who it comes from." She lifted her eyes to his. "I want to know you."

His heart did the slippery slide into a back-dive, then a three-quarter twist, and landed on a handstand. "What do you want to know?"

"How did you meet Vera?"

Biting his cheek, he thought back years and years. "I don't think I remember, exactly. She's as much a part of the performing arts as the venues where they're put on—and probably just as old."

Mina swatted his chest, and he caught her hand, bringing her fingers to his teeth for a nibble.

"It's true," he insisted. "Try and remember. I dare you."

She perked up, probably at the chance to one-up him, but seconds later, she sported a tiny frown.

"*Exactly*," he said. "People don't meet her, so much as she finds them. She singles you out if she sees something extraordinary." He gave her a meaningful look. "It was her and Alex who convinced me to cast you."

She gasped. "You wanted someone else? Did you settle for me?"

"I—had some reservations, *none* of which had anything to do with your talent."

Her face unequivocally demanded explanation, and he sighed. "It had to do with some rather…" *Fuck.* There was no way he was going to say anything that didn't paint him a complete douche. "I was an idiot, *petite*. I'd seen a bunch of news stories in the last year with your face splattered all over them below salacious headlines surrounding the death of your friend—in *very* tacky font."

She stiffened. "I… it's not what you think."

"A great cliché in movies, but I'll admit, it falls a little flat in real life." He couldn't help the bite in his tone.

Mina winced.

"Shit." He ruined his hair with his fingers. "I'm sorry, *petite*. That's not fair. I know it's not."

It grew quiet again, one of those moments where he wasn't sure she'd talk again, or maybe slap the taste from his mouth.

"If I keep it to myself," she said softly, "it can't be perverted the way you saw in *les tabloïds*. Even the truth is twisted to sound sleazy. We partied, *oui,* but no more than anyone else. I suppose my truth is too boring to them, so they paint me as a socialite who only made *Les Étoiles* because of affirmative action. My truth is…I miss him. Every day, I miss him. I don't want to share his memory with strangers."

Am I a stranger?

Mercifully, the thought didn't reach his lips. That's not what she meant, and he knew it, but there was still a nagging stab in his chest that there was some truth to it. This was one of her origami folds he hoped she'd be comfortable enough to show him someday. For now, it was enough that he was here. It was enough that there was trust. She must have read his resignation, the apology in the stroke of his fingers over hers, because when she spoke again, all trace of timidity was gone.

"When Vera showed up at my mother's apartment in *Paris*, I almost agreed without knowing what I was getting myself into. She mentioned you, and all I kept thinking was, *This is it. This is my chance to get out of the box and try something new and exciting.*"

"And now? How do you feel?"

"*Enfin*, I was scared. I'm *still* scared. But anything worth doing is a little scary."

"You have incredible instincts, Mina. You just have to trust them."

She stiffened.

"What?"

"You hardly ever call me Mina. *Petite*, things I can't repeat…arbitrary characters from ancient cinema-*eeek*!"

He attacked her ribs with quick, merciless fingers. "Eight years is hardly ancient." He tickled her until she was cry-laughing and desperate for breath.

"*D'accord*! *Arrêtes*! *Please*! *Okay, okay, okay*!"

Remembering her shoulder, he cursed. "I'm sorry. Is it-"

"I'm okay." When she could breathe again, her abs still contracting in aftershocks, she met his eyes with curiosity. "How did you come to be a playwright? No matter what, I will always be a dancer first. It's like it's in my blood. If I could choose only one thing, I would choose dance. But you…" She turned his hand over in her lap, tracing the pattern of the broken M on his calloused palm with her fingertips. "You write as well as you dance. You sing as well as you write. I suspect the choice isn't as easy for you."

Wow.

"What?" she asked this time. "What did I say?"

"The most *intriguing* thing. It didn't occur to me until just now, but I think you're right. They're all equally a part of me, and I've loved them all since I was a kid."

There was that curious spark again.

He kissed her fingers. "I can't remember who said this, but I think it's mostly true, that the artist is born in an unhappy child. Some kids have teddy bears, or security blankets—I had my imagination. If shit got bad, I'd make something up and disappear. I could control where, and when, and who, and what. Having that control when everything else made me feel powerless was everything. It stayed with me, I guess. And now I do it for fun."

It wasn't pity he saw in her endless brown eyes, but recognition. Their childhoods were vastly different, but the fact they'd experienced similar loss and loneliness at points in their lives felt—comforting.

"Those notebooks in your room," she murmured. "There must be a hundred of them."

He nodded. "Comics, poems, plays—some of it is just ideas or characters scribbled down. I'll have to live a thousand years to get to them all."

"Tell me, what was the first musical you ever saw? – *Non*, I have a better question…"

Chuckling, he hiked a brow at her in curiosity.

"What is *the* musical? The one that started it all?"

Letting go a deep, contemplative breath, the lyrics came back to him clear and vibrant as day. "I was eight when I saw *Les Mis* on TV when I lived with Foster Mom Number Two. There had to be six of us in that house—it was a *zoo*. I was sucked into the story—*outraged* for the guy who went to jail for so long, just for stealing bread. But he got out. And when he did? Nobody wanted to cut him a break, so he had to make it on his own."

She yawned, obviously running out of steam. Her eyes were glassy, and her words came slower. "You related to him. The hopelessness, and the feeling that no one would help you?"

"You could say that. But I also related to the hopefulness. It gave me hope that he changed his fate. That, and I got to tear around the house screaming the words to 'Master of the House' at the top of my lungs."

Another yawn. "Very inappropriate. I wasn't allowed to sing it because of the words *whore*, *bastard* and *inebriate*."

"Oh? What did you sing?"

Shifting awkwardly, she seemed to be losing her battle with fatigue, a full-body stretch-yawn combination laying her out like a cat. "I didn't. Not really. I had voice lessons until I made *les Étoiles,* but I had to give them up after that. Ballet was too demanding. Besides, musicals were still very much an *américain* tradition when I was younger. The lyrics didn't translate so well."

He tssked, easing from underneath her. "That's very sad. How lucky you are that a playwright swooped in to save you from a mediocre existence."

Covering her with the blanket, he lingered a moment, tangling his fingers in her curls, brushing a kiss on her cheek. Whatever she responded faded into mindless babble, and then soft, steady snores.

Chapter Sixteen

"*MINETTE,* I KNOW you are upset," Mirielle said, "but I can go right now to avenue Montaigne and buy another bag—like *that*—easy! Tell me, *where* will I find another Wilhelmina? Huh? *Bon sang!* You *must* be more careful."

Mina winced. Her mother rarely used strong language, reserving it for tax collectors and people who walked slowly on busy sidewalks. The white floral textured tiles of her mother's kitchen ceiling filled her tablet screen, like a stage curtain drawn to hide the commotion behind it—a pour of liquid, glass settling on granite, the continual clink of a spoon against the inside of a tea cup…*stir, stir, stir…*

"I know, *maman.* I'm sorry."

The tiles disappeared in a blur, and then Mirielle's deeply concerned face was close enough to count the freckles on her golden-brown skin. They were concentrated on the bridge of her nose—slightly narrower than Mina's own, a trait Mirielle inherited from her Swiss mother. It was so unlike Mina's, which was closer to her father's smooth sienna complexion, like the tempting brown tops of the little cakes from her *mémé's* bakery, dusted with almonds, pistachios, or curls of dark chocolate.

That she could see her mother's freckles made Mina frown. "No makeup, *maman?* It's four-hours-ten—"

"*Alors.*" Mirielle sighed. "That's because I've been home all day, trying to see if we can sue *ces idiots* at *Zut Magazine* and *Rumor Has It.*"

Mina cursed.

"I don't want you to worry, *okay?*" Mirielle scowled. "They're trash. I only mentioned it because I didn't want you to stumble on it yourself. I wanted you to hear it from me, so you know that I'm handling it."

"What is it this time? Am I unpatriotic? Dating a drug dealer? Or perhaps they want to dust off my alleged steroid use, because of course, I cannot possibly be so good without them."

"*Minette-*"

"It helps me to know."

"*Oui,* I know that. Even as a little girl, you always looked at the needle when *le docteur* would stick you—you never closed your eyes or looked away." She licked her lips. "I know I am not the most...nurturing...of mothers—"

"*Maman...*"

"It's true, I can admit that much. Still, it's my job to protect you."

It wasn't often the subject of their relationship dynamic came up, mostly because Mina sensed, even as a child, that her mother was a perfectionist, that the addition of a tiny, messy, needy human into her ordered life had been difficult for her. It was her *papa* who read her to sleep at night, pressed kisses where simple band-aids sufficed, and had tea with Mina and her dollies.

When she was six years old, he'd told her his heart was weaker than her mother's and would break if he lost his little girl. It was a precious gift, he'd said, that her mother agreed to let him keep her for the school year and bring her to *Paris* for summers and holidays.

"I know, *maman*," Mina said. "But knowing *does* protect me. If I don't know, I'll be blindsided. I'll lose focus from worrying."

"Okay." Mirielle nodded. "It's a blessing and a curse, I suppose. You are so much like Derek that way. Sometimes, he made me feel I was the only person in his world—but then, sometimes, he would get in such a state, he tuned the whole world out. It could go up in flames all around him and he wouldn't notice."

Something squeezed Mina's heart at the pain in her mother's voice, and though she tried to quiet her thoughts, they shouted at her anyway.

Is that what you think of me? That I am the reason you and papa did not stay together?

She toyed with a tassel on her bed pillow. It was another rare thing, her mother speaking so intimately about her father.

"*Maman?*"

Some of the clouds cleared from Mirielle's eyes, sharpening her chestnut gaze a little. She lifted her perfectly arched brows in question.

Mina's heart knocked against her ribcage.

Merde, just ask!

"When I was six… that first summer I came with *papa*, and we all went to see *memé* and *pépé* in *Aix-en-Provence*…I—I was making a crown of lavender flowers with *memé* in the garden, and I saw you and *papa* by the fountain. You were crying, and then I saw you kissing and—I thought you would get back together, but you never did."

"Oh, *minette*." Mirielle's voice was as soft as it went. "That summer was very difficult. I don't know what you think, but it wasn't an easy decision for me to leave you. My parents have been married a very long time. *Papa* moved to France for a better life. It was difficult being a black man in Tunisia.

Maman is white, but she was not French—still a foreigner to people here back then. They faced a lot of discrimination. They told me they couldn't understand why, if they overcame difficult times, your father and I couldn't do the same. They invited us to stay with them because they thought we were having typical marital problems—whatever that means. They knew your father and I still loved each other. But sometimes—sometimes it's not enough to love someone. For life? That takes sacrifice. He loved it in Virginia. I missed *Paris*. He wanted more children, and I did not. I could not lose myself. I'm sorry, *minette*.

I just couldn't do it."

Mina nodded.

"I don't regret having you," Mirielle said softly. "You know it's the truth."

Oui, she knew. Which is why she wouldn't cry. The truth was too precious, and crying might compel her mother not to share with her again. Besides, she'd never intentionally caused her pain. After all, she was here answering questions about her father to avoid revealing the latest tabloid rubbish.

"Okay," Mina said. "I'm ready."

"Okay." Mirielle rubbed her eye with her middle and ring fingers, a tell Mina recognized as supreme annoyance (one step away from strong language). "Just a few weeks ago, those *connards* printed that you and Étienne were involved. Now, it seems, after digging up what is likely the only photo of you two together in existence—at an opening night party, no less—they think you are a better match for Monsieur Angelo Bernard."

Merde.

Mina squinted at the sunlight pouring into her room at the late morning hour, casting a shadow of hundreds of fluttering leaves across her bed covers. She felt a sudden compulsion to count them all, one at a time.

Mirielle lifted a brow. "That is not the response I anticipated."

"*Maman...*"

"Appropriate responses to this *absurd* claim might be, *par exemple,* shock, profuse denial, or perhaps even justifiable anger at the suggestion you were inappropriately involved with one of the wealthiest, most influential men in the world—"

"*Maman, s'il te plaît...*"

"I usually don't meddle in your love life, but you'll understand if I make an exception for a stunning lapse of common sense—"

"He was a regular donor to the ballet. He—"

"*Putain de bordel de merde!* He was found *dead* alongside one of your closest friends! *I* know *who he was, minette!* I worked for Christie's nearly twenty years. I've auctioned that man's *furniture.* It doesn't matter that he supported the arts, Wilhelmina. All anyone will say is that *my* daughter, who worked hard all her life to become a ballerina, *screwed* her way to fame with the man whose name is on *two hundred-franc bottles of wine*! Had you aimed a bit lower, this would be an overnight scandal—forgotten in no time. But *this?* Even by French standards it is... *sensationnel.* That he was murdered in cold blood means a lot more trouble for us than the suggestion of an affair—*Nom de Dieu*! Stop crying, *minette*. It's no use to anyone now."

Mina tried to stop, but she couldn't. The guilt was too powerful. She didn't mind the tears so much—they blurred her mother's disapproving stare. It was the sobs that were unbearable. Her body was wracked with them, her throat full of them, and she choked.

"*Minette…*" Mirielle's voice was softer, coaxing. "*Minette*, calm down. Just…*tout me dire*, Wilhelmina, so I can try to fix it."

Tell you everything? How can I? I've kept this secret so long, giving it up feels like… betrayal.

She pulled a few tissues from the box on her nightstand and wiped her nose. "I can't. It could hurt people."

"It's too late for that. Besides, it's you who will be hurt the most if you don't let me help. I can call Noémie to assist with public relations—"

"*Non, maman.* You don't understand." Mina shook her head hopelessly.

"Help me understand."

Mina took a deep, ragged breath…then another, and another. She managed to control her breathing, though the tears still flowed. "It wasn't me. I-I wasn't the one involved with Monsieur Bernard."

"*Mon Dieu!* Why didn't you say so in the first place—"

"It was Étienne."

Mirielle gasped, and then there was silence. The leafy shadows on Mina's bed fluttered. Their branches swelled up and down, swayed left and right. She hadn't heard the wind outside until now.

"*Minette*, I—I'm so sorry, *chère*. I did not know."

Mina shrugged. "No one did. I couldn't tell you, *maman.* I couldn't tell anyone."

"Not even *la police*?"

"*Non.* Especially not them. Étienne came out to me in complete confidence. He wasn't ashamed of it at all, but he was very private. I couldn't betray him that way, not so he would become a suspect in death—Those *bâtards* in *les tabloïds* would have *salivated* to spin it that he murdered Monsieur Bernard in a crime of passion. It would over-shadow everything he's ever done."

"So you martyred yourself? It's a noble thing to do, but a useless one for someone who is no longer in need of protecting."

"Is it useless, *maman*? Tell me how he'd be remembered? If it got out that Étienne was in the closet with a man who owned thousands of hectares worth of vineyards and *three* castles? No one would care how beautifully he danced. You *know* it's true."

More silence. More watching the leaves dance to the wind's eerie song.

Mirielle took a deep breath. "*D'accord.*"

"*Okay?*"

"Tragically, you are right, so I don't begrudge your rea-sons. But I'll have to relay this information to *la police*—"

"*Non…*"

"We have no choice, *minette.* You needed to protect Étienne. I need to protect you. I understand you're still grieving, but you must consider the possibility this infor-mation may help to find the people who did this."

Mina sniffed. "I told *la police* Monsieur Bernard spon-sored a few dancers, including Étienne. I-I told them that's why Étienne was at his estate. To sign a contract. It was p-partly true."

"*Allez,*" Mirielle said gently. "That's enough for now. I need to talk to our lawyer, and call Noémie."

"Okay."

"It may not be a bad idea to start talking to someone again."

Mina laughed humorlessly. "So they can say I'm crazy again? Impossible to work with?"

Mirielle ignored her hysterics, keeping her voice calm and even. "Think about it, *minette.* No need to decide right now. In the meantime, I'll take care of this. Say nothing to anyone. The performance from the Tonys still makes news here, and those swine cannot stand that you left *Paris* to be *une américaine* star. On the bright side, at least they aren't still comparing you to Sylvie Guillem." She smiled an ironic smile. "You know you've made it when you have *les tabloïds* all to yourself."

"Something tells me you haven't been obeying doctor's orders."

Mina walked through the door of the rec center, from blindingly sunny day to colorless, dark gym.

"Cat got your tongue, *petite?*"

She squinted. "*Non,* I'm waiting for my eyes to adjust to this cave so I can glare at you."

Zack chuckled, taking her elbow to steer her away from the squeak of sneakers, the slap of hands, and the clash of body against body on the court. "Today is an *excellent* day for sunglasses."

"*Oui,* it's perfect," she said drily. "I'm sure my mugger will look *fantastique* in them."

"Son of a bitch," he muttered.

She tilted her head, her brow quirked in agreement, but said nothing else. They crossed the gym the short way, behind the basketball hoop. She flinched as the ball ricocheted off the backboard and someone yelled "*Brick*!"

"We're up after the game," he explained, leading from the gym and into a brightly lit hallway.

They walked away from the sound of aerobic machines coming from a workout room at the other end of the hall, past some offices and restrooms, to an inconspicuous door at the end of the hallway. He let go her elbow to fumble for keys in his pocket...in his back pocket, which was lucky enough to exist over the generous, perfect curve of his *beau cul.* A little zing rippled through her body, like her veins were made of copper wire, and her blood was a live current.

She stumbled. "A-after the game?"

He twisted around to face her, and her eyes tracked the movement hungrily, moving up from his butt over his tight waist, to the muscled length of his torso and chest. His T-shirt was light gray and looked impossibly soft, like it'd been laundered a hundred times, thinned to a worn perfection that left little to the imagination.

Bon Dieu.

"The gymnasium doubles as a studio," he explained, opening the door to a storage room. "When they're done playing ball, they mop up court and set up the mirrors. We keep the mirrors in here."

Mirrors?

How could she think about mirrors when every groove and swell of muscle on his torso was practically embossed on his shirt? It was a work of art—like the kind she had made as a child, scribbling over a sheet of paper to reveal the beautiful pattern of a leaf's veins underneath it. She was close enough to reach out and trace over the pattern with her palm, to feel some of that hardness give a little at the press of her fingers…

"You keep the mirrors in a closet?" Her voice sounded strange.

At that, he did a slow scan of her face, of her dark mass of spiraling curls, then looked down her body. Her breath caught and held as she tracked his gaze to her lips and throat, then to the shoulder and collar bone left bare by the draping neckline of her silk top. His eyes lingered there, until she could feel the gentle stroke of his fingers.

Her skin prickled.

She was more covered up now than she'd been in the studio in past weeks. Still, she felt so much more…exposed. Her pale pink top was more fitted below the neckline, grazing the peaks of her breasts, cinching her waist, hugging her hips and upper thighs. Skin-tight black denim stretched down to cropped ankles, and her feet breathed in three-inch heeled sandals. She'd chosen her outfit carefully. She was French, after all—there was a standard. Part of her was thrilled for him to see her in something other than sweaty leotards or glamorous evening clothes.

To see all her colors and textures.

The hardness and softness.

Darkness and light.

To see…*her.*

By the time he finished, her whole body felt licked, from neck to toe. The heat of it made her shiver in a way that was entirely unquestionable.

Merde. Her skin flamed, and she focused on the pulse in his neck.

"How are you, Mina?"

How dare he ask her how she was in that low, velvet voice? A voice that said, *I know exactly how you are, you little liar. Thinking you can stay away. Thinking you can resist this thing between us.*

Predictably, her subconscious was delighted to chime in, *Look at you, panting like une chienne in heat!*

At least if she *were* a bitch in heat, he'd be kind enough to mount her from behind and hump enthusiastically until they both quivered in satisfaction.

Merde. Merde. Merde.

Her eyes ascended slowly from his neck. His stared back, dilated to almost completely black, only slightly rimmed with green. She gasped. Had it been only three days since she'd seen this beautiful beast? Since she'd smoothed her hands over so much soft skin and taut muscle? Dug her fingers into him, absorbing all that power and dexterity until he'd spent himself inside of her? Her fingers tingled and curled into her palms.

"You thirsty, *petite*?" The corners of his mouth lifted in an arrogant smile.

How can you tease me when you just ate me with your eyes? she screamed inwardly. Outwardly, her features were soft. She was quickly learning how his game was played.

Giving him an alluring smile, she whispered, "*Lion.*"

He cursed, and before she could blink, he'd dragged her through the door, across the small storage room, and through another door into the light of day. It was a secluded little corner of the world, suitable for a smoke or a bit of fresh air. A quick glance around was all she had time for, taking in the few square feet of fenced-in sidewalk and little else, before Zack's presence overtook it, wrapped her up in its shadow, and pressed her back against the rec center's sun-warmed brick wall.

He locked her in with a hand to the wall beside her, above her head, and the other on her bare forearm. "Ten-to-one you haven't been home licking your wounds."

The challenge was spoken so gently, her breath caught, and she stood there staring at him mutely, picturing his tongue flicking over her wounds. He must have taken her silence as defiance because he tilted his head a bit, studying her more intently.

"You don't want to tell me." He ran his hand slowly up her arm to the swooping neckline at her shoulder. "Well, I can guess."

His fingers slipped beneath the silk, his knuckles brushing the length of her collar bone—which sent a shock of sensation through her so violent, she shivered all over. Curving his lips in a sultry smile, he tugged the neckline to the side, exposing her right shoulder. Frowning, he traced his fingers softly over the fading blot of a bruise, then pinched the joint. She winced slightly but didn't flinch.

"Good, you've been staying off that arm," he murmured, tickling her shoulder with his breath.

He dropped a kiss to the sore spot, then spun her around, pressing the length of her body back against his. She gasped, her hands shooting to the brick wall for support—though it didn't help much, with her butt cradled in his thighs and his arm tightened around her waist. Bending his head, he stroked her soft, voluminous curls with his cheek, from her temple to her neck, the new growth at his jawline scraping gently at her sensitive skin.

"I love your hair like this, *petite*," he breathed, and her whole body dissolved in desire. "It smells amazing." He tugged the supple neckline again, exposing the nape of her neck and a hint of her back, both of which he kissed. "You felt the need to wash it again since last night?"

He drew his fingers down the length of her spine, and her back arched involuntarily. "*Oui,*" she whispered.

Pathetic response, of course. She should have balked at his condescending tone, defended her right to practice *excellent* hygiene as often as she liked. Unfortunately, her brain cells seemed to be suppressed by the nerve endings in the rest of her body.

"Hmm." Nudging her legs wider, he released her to pat her body down, starting at her waist with a squeeze, then her thighs, and the still-sore muscles of her calves—which made her jump. "Uh-*huh.*"

Standing, he turned her back around in one svelte move, resting his hands at her waist. "Tender calves, heels that don't qualify as stilts…You went running—*far,* from the looks of it. You were told to stay put for two days, but you couldn't last *one.*" He shook his head. "You are *hurting,* aren't you, *petite?*"

She groaned—partly because he'd found her out, and partly because his voice got deeper, and his fingers dug into her waist at *hurting,* like he *knew* what he was doing to her and had the nerve to find it *amusing*.

Connard.

There was nothing funny about the way she was hurting, the way she was hot and damp and weak with arousal, the way her nipples tightened and brushed against unforgiving silk, the way he lowered his gaze to stare at her obvious reaction—as if her breasts had sent smoke signals to his eyes…the way his eyes held no trace of green anywhere when he pried them from her nipples and locked them on her lips…

"*So what?*" she snapped, resisting the urge to fold her arms over her chest.

"So, you're *frustrated*," he said gruffly, dropping all hint of humor. He pulled her body forward, his chest expanding on a deep breath. "So am I. I'm hurting, *petite*. I'm dying of thirst, too."

And while her body was still shuddering desperately from that confession, he opened his mouth over hers.

Grasping the back of her neck, he buried his hand in her hair, positioning her the way he wanted, then moaning in satisfaction. At the first flick of his tongue, she sighed, her body swaying fully into his. He tasted so warm and vivid—so *alive,* and *Dieu,* she *needed* that feeling, wanted to bury herself in it until it seeped into her bones, sample it until it was imprinted on her tongue.

They kissed on and on, with stroke of tongues and gently scraping teeth, lips pressing and rubbing together. Her hands wandered mindlessly over the muscles of his back and abs and chest, her fingers flexing, digging into him. He felt so *good,* so hard yet graceful, his muscles contracting beneath her touch, his hard breaths snatching air from her lungs. Holding her tightly against him, between him and the wall, he hauled her to her toes, pressing her hips to his lower abdomen. She nipped his bottom lip with a frustrated growl.

It wasn't enough.

He was too tall for the pressure she needed. Further irritating her—they had on too many clothes. Sucking in a ragged breath, he pulled back to look at her. What must he see? Did her eyes look like his now? Dark and needy? Was her face as desperately naked? Whatever he saw made him grab her hips and press her back to the brick wall, wrapping her legs around him. She gasped, and he sought her lips again, his mouth so greedy.

"Mina." Her name was gruff along her skin, just like his hands, which rubbed the soft silk of her top over her skin, massaging it into her muscles and ribs and breasts.

The sky dimmed a little, like the sun had dipped behind some clouds to give them more privacy. Behind that fence, shrouded in Zack and the minutes before dusk, and wearing clothing that felt like neither armor nor costume, Mina felt—free. The feeling spiked her blood until she felt drunk on it, until her lips and hands moved uninhibited wherever they could reach.

Pulling her kneading hand from his chest, he kissed each finger, then her palm, then her wrist. "I've missed you," he murmured, breathing into her palm, scraping it tenderly with his teeth.

She shivered.

Really, it was such a winsome thing to say. Such an enticing idea, that he'd grown fond enough of her to ache when she wasn't around. That maybe, just maybe, when he was alone in bed at night—or on the couch, slashing scripts with his red pen—he wished for a warm, welcome body to curl around his…and for that body to be hers. She made a soft sound, and he took her mouth again.

She trembled as his hands slipped under the hem of her top, running hot along the fine bones of her ribcage. "I've missed you too."

He stroked her abdomen, then slid his hands up, his

palms cupping her breasts. They kneaded, then kneaded harder as her back arched. "I knew you would understand."

"*Oui.*" Arching again helplessly, she pressed herself against his thigh, his hands growing hungrier on her breasts. "You like me."

"God, yes."

"*Beaucoup?*"

"Very, very much."

Bon Dieu, but she ached. Seeming to understand, he gripped her hips and dragged her firmly up and down his thigh. Need burned through her—hot, searing, relentless. The smoke signal came from low in her belly this time, drawing his dark eyes to her face. He ground her against his arousal with bulls-eye precision, circling his hips, rocking her. The friction made her eyes water, and she clutched the front of his T-shirt in her fists.

"Yes," he said hoarsely. "I missed you like this. Just like this."

Unzipping her pants, he slipped his hand into her panties, finding her easily, then pressing, stroking…

A heavy click sounded on the other side of the door, followed by a heavier slide. Zack cursed, jerking his head up. Mina froze in fear, but it was too late: she'd already begun to fall.

"*Merde!*"

"Shhh, it's okay, *petite.*" He pressed the heel of his palm against her, rubbing firmly. "Ride it out, I've got you."

When she stopped shaking, she scrambled down from him, taking quick, steadying breaths. He chuckled, and she shot him a look of annoyance.

"*Arrêtes!*" she spat. "This isn't funny."

"Relax, *petite.* No one comes out here. They're probably looking for something in the closet."

They straightened themselves out as best they could, dispelling the haze of arousal. Well, as much as a few seconds could allow.

"Eyes up, pervert." He nudged her chin up with his thumb.

A completely unsexy sound—like a horribly muffled sneeze—ripped from her throat.

"Okay?" He searched her face, his other hand on the doorknob.

She managed a nod and nothing else, stepping back for him to open the door.

Carmen was halfway down the hall, pushing a very large wooden apparatus on wheels toward the gymnasium.

"Whoa, *mamá,* lemme get that for you." Zack finished locking the storage closet, then slow-jogged to catch up to Carmen.

She looked at him with surprise, then at Mina, then at the storage closet door. "So nice to see you again, Mina. Looks like you and *mijo* have something in common. Neither of you knows how to take a day off."

There was mischief behind her smile, which stopped Mina in her tracks.

Oh. That's *where he gets it from.* Mina's answering smile was automatic. "I-I want to be here. I'm so flattered that you invited me."

"Don't be flattered, *linda.*" Carmen stopped fussing with the apparatus, rooting Mina to the spot with the full force of her direct gaze. "Everywhere you go, you belong. Every praise you get, you've earned."

Wow. Raw, unfiltered conviction wrapped around the

words like gift ribbon around a plaque. *Here you go, doubt-ful heart,* it said. *Keep me somewhere safe, so you can take me out and read me whenever you start to question yourself.* That wasn't even the part that brought heat to Mina's face—the first sign of her *irritating* tendency to cry whenever she felt the tiniest drop of emotion.

Non, what moved her was that Carmen had said it like it was the most ordinary thing. Like there were people who walked around in the world with absolute confidence that they belonged, that they were good enough exactly the way they were.

Mina considered herself confident enough, but she'd never looked in a mirror and not seen something to improve upon—unlike Zack, who, despite the darkness he'd endured as a child, carried himself as though every *centimètre* of space on the planet existed solely for him to occupy.

Now she understood why.

He cleared his throat, because obviously she was a drama queen, overreacting to someone being nice to her, and she needed a moment. "I thought I'd show her around before introducing her to the kids."

Carmen's brow lifted in the exact way that Zack's often did. *Vraiment,* it was *fascinating.*

"I see." She planted her hands on her hips. "You were showing her the breathtaking view of that rickety old fence and the brick wall next door?"

"*Mamá…*"

"Oh please! Don't try to pull the wool, *mijo.* Manny and I go back there all the time."

Zack groaned.

Mina's cheeks flamed.

"Anyway," Carmen said. "It's none of my business—"

Zack scoffed, but seemed to have the good sense not to say the *Since when?* written all over his face.

Carmen turned away from them and back toward the apparatus, positioning herself to push it down the hall again, speaking over her shoulder. "I can handle this thing. There are a few more T-shirts from the summer intensive program in the office in case you two don't want to look like you were in a back-alley brawl."

Mina grimaced at the horribly misshapen front of Zack's shirt. She could identify *exactly* where her fists had been because the fabric across his chest boasted two little whirlpools made of wrinkles.

Pride kept her from even glancing at her own shirt. Instead, she glared at Zack.

"What?" He didn't look embarrassed at all. "You were making sex eyes at me."

Grunting, she lifted her chin.

He shrugged. "If you don't want people to know about us, keep your sex eyes to yourself."

CHAPTER SEVENTEEN

Mirrors.

THE WHEELED APPARATUS turned out to be mirrors.

Mina gaped. There were six of them, each two meters tall and a half-meter wide, in wooden frames connected by hinges. When Carmen had taken them from the storage closet, they had been folded together like an accordion to save space. Stretched out now, with a barre in front of them, the shiny basketball court was transformed into a makeshift little dance studio.

"Manny and *mijo* built it a few years ago, when Zachary first started the new summer program," Carmen explained.

Late comers took their places along the wall and on the bleachers, likely hearing about her visit through word-of-mouth. Mina turned her attention from them to Zack—who was herding about thirty kids ranging in age from six to twelve—into a semi-circle on the gymnasium floor. It wasn't a publicized event, but camera phones were out nonetheless.

"Zack started it? Not you?"

"*Sí,* it was his idea." Carmen beamed at her son, who was telling jokes and laughing with the kids. "We do it every summer for free, because some of the kids can't afford to pay. Most can't afford dance clothes, so we rely on donations and support from the community."

"The summer? And…after that?"

Carmen spoke candidly. "I get one, maybe two every year who have enough natural ability that I can mentor them, catch them up in time to apply for scholarships. The rest? If I see them next year, I'll be surprised."

Mina gasped, pressing her hand to her stomach. "But…" She blurted the word, because her insides felt like a lava lamp—like her organs were floating around in molten liquid. "How can you introduce them to something so beautiful, only to tell them they cannot continue?"

The warmth in Carmen's wide brown eyes intensified to a spark, her voice a whisper. "*En boca cerrada no entran moscas.*"

Mina stared at her mutely.

"You have no *idea* what that means, do you, *linda*?"

"I understand the words, just not what they mean. 'Flies don't enter a closed mouth?'"

"*Sí.* It means, 'Sometimes, it's best to keep your mouth shut.'" She gave her a meaningful look, then went to join Zack in front of the kids.

Even with her own foot shoved down her throat, Mina observed the way Carmen radiated around Zack, how incredibly proud of him she was—how fiercely protective.

Oh.

Merde.

Zack, who stood there so charismatic and relaxed, had been one of these kids. Hungry and full of potential. Potential, but not money.

Without Carmen to keep him from slipping through

the cracks, where might he be right now? How different—
and *small*—would the world of ballet look without him to
stretch and redefine its boundaries? Without someone who
refused to accept that the genre was confined to the styles
of only a handful of choreographers? Someone who saw a
classic like *La Dame Aux Camélias* and re-imagined it for a
contemporary audience—and for the lead to look like *her*.

Mina's heart sank to her stomach, and she suddenly
felt half her usual height. Strangely, the smile on Carmen's
face looked genuine when she introduced her to the kids,
and Mina knew instinctively that it was. *Everything* about
Carmen was real—her warmth, her frankness, her laughter,
and obviously her love. To someone like her, an apology
was nothing more than empty words.

Mina had not been sure of what she would say to these
children before she'd arrived. She supposed Zack might lead
the discussion, open it up to some questions, and she'd take
a few pictures. Now, she was determined to share a little
of herself, to show Carmen that her privileged upbringing
hadn't made her so out-of-touch, she couldn't connect with
these children.

Or that you can't connect with Zack, her annoying subconscious said. *Not that it would bother you for her to think
that, simply because she knows you like his hand in your pants.*

Impeccable timing, as always. She tried not to groan.
Unlike her subconscious, people could hear *her*. And see
her. *Naturellement,* he was looking at her now. *Non,* not
at her, or through her. It felt—had always felt, from the
first time they'd met—like he looked *inside* of her, past
skin and muscle and bone. That's why she'd raised a leaden
shield around her heart, so his gratingly precise x-ray vision
couldn't see what she wasn't willing to share. Taking a deep

breath, she lowered the shield—just a little—smiled and took her cue.

"Your accent is funny."

Zack met Mina's quick eye contact.

Is he serious? she telepathed.

Don't look at me, he telepathed in return. *Serve it right back.*

She cut her eyes back to her heckler. "Funny, that's *exactly* what the French children told me when I arrived with an *américain* accent."

"You were an *American*?" The kid stared at her like she'd said she was from Narnia.

Several people laughed.

"I *am américaine.*" She lifted a fine brow. "It is a lifetime honor, so I'm afraid you are stuck with me."

"Ever heard of Beyoncé?" another one challenged, obviously unconvinced she hadn't been hatched, or cultivated in a petri dish.

Mina narrowed her eyes playfully. "I'm from *France*, not Mars."

With that, the little band of misfits was hooked. Zack exchanged an amused glance with his mother—who seemed to be fighting a smile and losing—then folded his arms over his chest and watched Mina work.

"I come from one of the oldest ballet schools in the world…"

Jesus.

Maybe it was her impeccable posture, or the way her voice had risen to reach the people in the back, but the hard, echoing surfaces of the gym seemed to magnify her accent. The subtle huskiness of her tone became less subtle, her words blending into one another, lending a steady, lyrical sound to her voice that seduced her listeners with its rhythm. It was like hearing her speak for the first time again, sending his pulse racing in his chest.

"I was the only ballerina of African descent in any of my classes, the first to join my company. I had friends, of course, but it was…a unique kind of loneliness—the kind you can feel even when you are not truly alone."

Zack's heart stuttered—from pure shock—at those words, at the pain in her voice and in her expression when she said them. Of all the methods he'd considered for extracting information from her (including possible use of tethers), wide-eyed, ruddy kids weren't one of them.

"It hurt me," she said, "to feel underestimated sometimes. Like greatness was neither expected, nor required of me. And then, sometimes, when I exceeded expectations, to feel like I was being evaluated with a more critical eye than my peers. It was not until I was preparing to compete for an apprenticeship, that I realized the advantage my experiences had given me. You see, in ballet, your body and every movement it makes, is placed under a magnifying glass— no matter *who* you are, no matter what you look like…no matter where you come from. When everyone else around me grew sick from the pressure of competition, I remained strong. The kind of scrutiny they were preparing to endure? I had already endured for years."

Zack felt a whisper tickle up his forearms, the back of his neck, even the skin of his legs. Goosebumps. Her passion was tangible—like he could reach up and pluck it from the air. It was almost too much, being exposed to the full intensity of her soul when he'd grown used to getting just a glimmer at a time.

"If you choose this path, it will be hard," she said. "It will hurt, and sometimes you will want to give up. I just want to say, *don't*. Don't ever give up, no matter what you decide to do. Would you like to know why?"

At their nods and softly uttered yeses, her face lit up with her smile. Holy *shit*, did it light up. It wasn't until that exact moment that he missed her smile, when he realized it was her first smile since she'd started talking. That's how bright it was.

"In French, we say, '*Petit a petit, l'oiseau fait son nid,*'" she said. "It means, 'Little by little, the bird makes its nest.' With patience and persistence, you can accomplish anything."

It wasn't a speech, but it felt like one. The room erupted in applause and whistles, and a little girl sporting two fluffy puffs of hair on either side of her head rushed forward, nearly knocking Mina over in her eagerness. Zack recognized the smallest ballerina in the program that summer. She belonged to one of the gym's regulars.

"That's Charley," he said. "Six years old, youngest of five, only girl, and obviously raised by wolves…"

Charley giggled, and Mina moved into a squat, bringing them eye-to-eye.

"You're the same brown as me," Charley said, which made everyone laugh.

Holding up her hand, Mina examined the back of it with feigned concentration. "I think you're right."

"And, we have the same hair…I think." Charley frowned. She looked like she wanted to say something else, but hesitated.

Mina went to her knees. "Did you want to ask me something, *chère?*"

Charley moved her head closer, whispering something in Mina's ear. When she pulled back, Zack saw Mina's face again—a strange mix of shock and curiosity. They stared at each other long enough that it was almost awkward, and he started toward them to rescue Mina from whatever put that look on her face when she held up her hand to stop him. He paused, gaping along with everyone else as Mina smiled into Charley's eyes, gave her a subtle nod, and bowed her head.

Charley lifted one of her little hands and tentatively stroked Mina's hair, sifting several of the spiraled strands through her chubby fingers. Mina's eyes welled up, but she stayed stock still, waiting for Charley to finish her gentle examination.

"Well?" Mina asked when Charley dropped her hand again.

"You're just like me," Charley said. "I *knew* it!"

That drew some much-needed laughter, and after Mina graciously answered a round of questions, Zack decided to complete the rescue mission he'd started several minutes ago.

"Okay, we have time for one more. You—Snaggletooth," he said affectionately to a girl missing all four of her front teeth. "Bonus points if you don't ask to *pet* the special guest."

The girl giggled, then shyly asked her question. "Hi, what's your dream role? Thank you."

Mina tensed up, as if the girl had asked what bra size she wore. It was subtle, the way her posture got a little straighter, her chin a little higher. He quirked his brow at her, opening their telepathic communication line again. *What's that about, petite?*

Averting her eyes, she turned back to her audience, her smile a little too perfect. "Forgive me, I don't think anyone has asked me that question. I think, because I've been fortunate to have danced as many roles as I have... I-it's a great question."

Expert Stalling Tactics, an abridged version, with annotations by special guest, Wilhelmina Allende...

Her words stalled, but her face didn't. It seemed painted in two shades: sadness and happiness. Red and gold waged war on her skin.

"When I was six years old, my *papa* took me to see *Swan Lake*. I was in awe of everything about it, especially that a single dancer got to play two roles—the black swan, and the white swan—such a range of emotion and technique...Since then, I have always dreamed of being the Swan Queen."

With that, Zack's heart tripped hard and fell, hitting every rib on its way to his toes. This time, his telepathic communication said:

What.

The.

Fuck?

Then the door to her heart slammed shut, the sound of it echoing off the rafters, and question time was over. Mina was a champ, though. For half an hour, she endured questions about her Frenchness that were, at the least, curious, and at most, semi-insulting (not from *his* kids, thank God). After posing for selfies with anyone who asked, she was understandably ready to go. She tried to hurry ahead of him, but Zack kept up with her easily.

"How is it you've never been the Swan Queen?" he asked. "Weeks ago, when we danced for Alex's class, it felt like you'd done it a million times. The way you moved—it's like it wasn't a memory at all. Like it was mapped in your DNA."

"I do not want to talk about this, Zachary."

"*Zachary?* Are you shitting me, *petite?*"

Her speed-walk into the parking lot out back was comical, since she was riding with him to his mother's house for dinner.

"That is your name, *oui*? Just like Mina is *my* name, and how I would appreciate being addressed in *public*."

He looked around the near-empty parking lot. It was six o'clock, but daylight streamed through the trees and a persistently overcast sky. Security was locking up. Other than the two of them, there was just a guy tossing his gym bag into his trunk and getting into his car. A few stragglers were smoking something that smelled illegal across the street, but they weren't paying them any attention. She tugged on the passenger's side door handle, to no avail. Cursing, she spun around, looking *thrilled* to see him standing right behind her.

"I am not *shitting*." Leaning against the door, she crossed her arms over her chest. "I just don't want to talk about it, *okay?*"

"No," he said. "*Not* okay."

"*Putain!*"

"Sticks and stones, *petite.*"

See, this was supposed to be the part where she crinkled up her cute little nose and called him an ass in her sexy pissed off voice. For the record, she didn't.

Instead, her eyes locked with his.

Her hands balled into fists.

She shook like a leaf.

And though she'd been walking fast, unless she'd also done fifty jumping jacks in the last sixty seconds, she shouldn't have been breathing so damn hard.

"Shit," he muttered.

Unlocking the car with his keyless entry, he opened her door and shuffled her in, then jogged around to the driver's side, sliding in and closing the door. Keening noises roiled in her throat, building, but staying obediently put as she looked to him for… What? Permission? *Oh.* Starting the engine, he hiked the volume as the radio came on, then checked their three, six, and nine o'clocks for any potential onlookers.

"We're good, *petite.* Go ahead and let her rip."

So, she did.

She ripped.

And ripped.

Then ripped some more.

No words, just noise. She screamed until the tears he'd seen in her eyes a few times during her non-speech to the kids finally streamed down her cheeks, until her tightened fists relaxed, until she fell back in her seat, boneless and damn-near hoarse. He kept his face forward the entire time, checking his periphery, giving her a moment. She needed that, he sensed. To have someone with her so she wouldn't be alone, but space to exorcise whatever demons plagued her. Wordlessly, he handed her some tissue from the center console, sneaking a glance to ensure she was okay. A minute later, she flipped open the sun visor mirror and started touching up her face.

"Oh no." He flipped it back up. "Uh-uh. We're not about to just ride off into the sunset after a screaming banshee just crawled out of your throat into my car. Talk to me, *petite.* For God's sake."

The minute hand on the console changed again. And again. God, this was torture.

"Mina," he said softly. "Please?"

That brought her head around quick, her eyes mapping his face then falling to his hands gripping the steering wheel. He hadn't even noticed he was doing it.

"You're…asking me?" She looked incredulous.

Okay, that was fair. He did make a habit of demanding things from her—in the studio, on stage, and the few times he was lucky enough to have her in his arms. Leading. Maybe it was time to let her do that.

"I'm asking, *petite*." He let go the steering wheel, letting his left hand fall to his lap, his right resting between them, palm-up. "I'm asking you to trust me with this—with whatever is hurting you."

She stared at his hand.

"How about some collateral?" His voice was low, earnest. He was beginning to understand her more, that sometimes she needed a full minute to process things. "How about I tell you this doesn't freak me out? That I wasn't holding onto the steering wheel because I thought you were crazy."

She lifted her eyes to his. *Go on,* they telepathed. *I'm listening.*

"How about I tell you it's because I used to scream just like that when I was a kid, into my pillow, until Carmen and Manny took me home? That I used to wet my bed for a year after?" Her soft palm slid over his, and his fingers curled automatically around her hand. "I was eleven before I woke up to dry sheets, because, for all the heroes I'd made up in my head, there was at least one monster. I'd have the most…*vivid* dreams. Lots of kids have monsters under their

266

beds." He swallowed his hammering heartbeat down. "One of my monsters tried to come *into* mine."

Mina gasped and shuddered, her eyes mirrors of his pain. "Zack, I—I'm sorry. I'm so, so sorry." She winced. "I feel…*stupide.* I shouldn't- "

"No." He squeezed her hand. "That's the point, *petite.* You *should.* Okay? You can't keep carrying everything on your own, letting it bottle up like that. You wanna know the ugliest monster in my head? Foster Mom Number Three. She was wearing the skin of a good guy, like the villains in Scooby Doo." Angling his head, he studied her face. "What does your monster look like, Mina? No monster is too small. Tell me. Let me help you rip the mask off the son of a bitch."

Her laugh had cracks all through it. Pain dripping through the humor, washing away some of the madness. Taking a deep breath, she let it all go. "My monster is… the most beautiful thing I've ever seen. She wears a feather crown, and a tutu so shiny with diamonds, so full of feathers that, when she dances, she looks like an angel floating in the clouds."

"Odette," he said. "From *Swan Lake.*"

"*Oui,* I've wanted to play her since I was six, since my very first ballet, when *papa* gave me that crystal swan." Her smile had the same hint of sadness she'd worn at her apartment when she'd shown him the figurine. "Every time I look at it, as much as I feel love for my father, and comfort at his memory… it tortures me, too. Taunts me."

"Because you think you can never have it."

She nodded.

He ached for her, his free hand curling into a fist. "You can't really believe that, can you? You were incredible as

Giselle. You have the speed, the stamina, the precision… Not for nothing, *petite*, but you're *intoxicating* to watch. It's what made me come to Paris for you."

"So then, why? Why is it, no matter how many roles I dance, how much I succeed, how much I improve, when I go out for the Swan Queen, it's always, '*Désolé*.'" She'd deepened her voice, screwing her face up like a stuffy old man. "'I'm sorry, *chère*, you're just not the right fit.'"

Zack sighed. "I—can't answer that, not with any kind of certainty. I can't explain why some choreographers are obsessed with this antiquated notion of uniformity, when other art forms seem to be evolving much faster."

She sniffed. "It is so unfair, to see dancers I've bested, get the role I'm rejected for."

Jesus. That explained why she was always looking in the mirror. Second-guessing. Obsessing. But the normal tendency of a dancer to find something to improve upon had fuck-all to do with this. No, one of the most gifted ballerinas in the world was having a mental breakdown because she couldn't measure up to a standard no amount of rehearsing could meet. And it made his blood boil.

"It *is* unfair," he said. "It's *bullshit*, but if you let it, it'll drive you nuts. Besides, what's the alternative? You stop?"

"*Non!* M-my heart beats for this. If I could not dance, I think something inside of me would die."

Releasing her hand, he lifted her chin, seeking her out. Checking for that constant, driving hunger that made her eyes so powerfully compelling. She didn't let him down.

"For so many dancers, the Swan Queen is the end-game," he said. "You are nowhere *near* that yet. It can happen anytime. It *will* happen. No one persists like you do and fails. I believed what you said to those kids in there.

268

They believed it, and I know you believe it too, or you'd have run right back to Paris after our first rehearsal."

"I do," she whispered. "I do believe it."

"That's it, then, *petite*," he murmured, kissing her eyelids. "Little by little. Okay?"

She nodded stiffly, because he still held her chin hostage.

"Good." Nuzzling her nose, he let her go. "Let's start with dinner."

Chapter Eighteen

ZACK GAVE HER a safe word.

Pineapple.

Then, he told her that Carmen and his aunts were like the Sanderson Sisters from *Hocus Pocus* on a good day, and the four horses of the apocalypse on a bad day…right before he walked her through the front door.

En fait, it was wide open when they arrived, and Mina found herself plunged in the middle of an intense conversation as soon as she stepped through it.

"Why'd you put cheese in this, Carmen? You know I'm vegan since I had that stomach flu!" someone complained—from the kitchen, Mina assumed.

"For the *last* time, Yara, you are not vegan, you're *lactose intolerant.*" Carmen sounded exasperated. "The *cheese* is vegan."

"Yeah, well, you didn't have to make it on my account. *Cagar más arriba del culo*, okay? Tastes like crap on a cracker, you ask me."

"Good thing I didn't ask," Carmen said flatly. "And I told you to speak English, none of that New Yorican *espa-*

ñol. You're gonna make the poor girl's head spin when she gets here."

Yara huffed. "She's gonna have worse problems, she eats this. Cheese doesn't even stretch—watch…" (Silence.) "Looks like glue."

"Someone should put glue in your lipstick," Carmen snapped, and cackling filled the house.

Mina's hand flew to her mouth. Whatever it was couldn't be so bad. It smelled delicious. The entire house smelled delicious, like she could lick the walls in any room and have a five-course meal.

Zack pulled her back against him with his big hand on her abdomen. "In case you didn't catch all that—they talk pretty fast—Titi Yara thinks *mamá* is out of her depth," he murmured in her ear, sounding amused. "She was cooking all day, trying to impress you."

Impress her? After her blunder at the recreation center, Mina felt guilty that Carmen had gone to so much trouble. Hopefully she'd be able to get Carmen alone and apologize…Zack pressed a lingering kiss to her neck that made her body clench, and she spun away from him.

"*Zachary*!"

"What? You're already out of the bag, kitten."

She flayed him with her eyes, whispering through her teeth. "I will slap you."

"I believe you."

A blur whizzed past them, stopped, then doubled back. "*Tio!*" a cute little boy yelled.

Zack's entire face brightened. "This is Isaac. Say hello, Isaac."

"Hello, Isaac," the little one parroted, grinning wide.

Mina couldn't help her smile. "Hello. How are you, Isaac?"

"Good," he said politely, but he was obviously eager to talk to Zack. "I got a C on my quiz at summer school today. *Mami* said I have to tell you, so you can talk senses to me."

"You mean 'talk *sense* into you.'" Zack looked very stern.

Mina hid her amusement behind her hand again.

"What did I tell you about Cs?" Zack asked.

Isaac's eyes lit up. "Cs are common, but Bs are *bad ass*, and As are aaaaaa-*mazing*!"

"*Mijo*? You better not be teaching that boy to curse again!" Carmen's voice rang out.

Isaac darted behind them and out the door, faster than anything Mina had ever seen.

Then Carmen yelled again. "Stop stalling! Bring Mina."

Zack shut the door, removing his shoes. Following suit, Mina tried not to stare at all the family photos on the walls, and on every flat surface of furniture as he led her through the house. In the sitting room, something tall and shiny stood out among the trophies and baubles behind the glass of an antique display cabinet.

Mina gasped. "Is that…?"

Zack's grin practically split his face in half, and he moved to open one of the cabinet doors. Lifting the golden-hued statue carefully, he extended it toward her.

"*Oh!*" She couldn't possibly…could she? Oh, but she *had* to. When might she get another chance? With both hands, she accepted the polished statuette with reverence, turning it over and over in her hands, stroking the wings on the lady's back. "It's *beautiful*," she murmured. "So heavy."

His eyes danced over her face. "It *is*. You're groping six and a half pounds of sexy Emmy award right there."

Mina exhaled heavily. "I wish I could whistle. I'd do it right now."

"I'm filing that away as a rare and interesting fact."

She rolled her eyes. "What's she holding?"

"It's an atom. The lady is the designer's wife, his muse. He intended it to symbolize television as art *and* science."

"It's so strange. Seeing it up close." She traced the inscription with her fingers. "I knew you'd won, but now it feels...*real. Ah*!" She thrust it at him. "Take it back...I feel like I shouldn't hold it too long."

"It's nice." He accepted the statuette and replaced it in the cabinet. "But *we're* real. The work—that's real. Pretty statue or not, I never want to lose sight of that."

She met his gaze, unable to hide her admiration.

"Thank you, *petite*."

"For what?"

"For what your eyes just told me."

Claiming her hand, he led her through a formal dining room that looked like no one ever used it, it was so pristine. Photos were in abundance there, too, and Zack was in at least half of them. One of them caught her eye as they were about to leave the room.

"Is that Camila Morera?" she gasped.

The dark-haired beauty was older than Mina in real life, but much younger in the photo, wearing a strapless gown that showed off her *incredible* shoulders. Next to her was an equally young, leaner, tuxedo-clad Zack...with considerably more hair. Wincing, he turned the photo face-down and gently prodded her with a hand to the small of her back. But Mina planted her feet.

"*Oh mon Dieu*, it *is* her! You used to *date* Camila Morera?"

"No. Our mothers are friends. We did the old program at the rec center when we were kids, and I took her to prom."

"What's the difference?"

"You jealous, *petite*?"

"Of you, *oui*." She enjoyed the flash of surprise on his face. "She's one of my heroes. When I was in Third Section, I saw her in an interview for the New York City Ballet. She said, '*Breasts* is not a bad word. I won't apologize for having them, and I'll never powder my skin again to look lighter.'"

He smiled.

"What?" She asked.

"I was just thinking, you're what Camila Morera was to you, to so many young girls, and you have no *idea*."

He said it with an intriguing blend of awe and amusement, like everyone in the world knew exactly who she was, and she was still trying to figure it out. It might have seemed patronizing, if it was up to her brain to sort it out, but her heart was in it, too, absorbing the warmth in the spaces between the words until it grew plump and content.

Heartwarming. That's what it was. She wasn't sure what to do with all the warmth emanating from him and washing over her. *Dieu,* his eyes were so gorgeous from this close, a sea of warmth. Her entire being vibrated with the urge to leap from her body and swim in it.

"*Mijo!*"

Her heart jumped into her throat.

Zack bent his head, whispering in her ear. "Pineapple. Don't forget."

The second they stepped into the kitchen, they were swarmed, and it was all Mina could do to keep up.

"No *wonder* we never see you anymore, *cariño!*" said

a woman who looked like a younger Carmen with blond highlights in her hair.

"Titi Yara," Zack said affectionately.

"*Sí—que linda.* It's her eyes, so serious," another aunt swooned.

"Titi Ana."

Oh. He was identifying them for her.

Ana was tiny—shorter than Mina but hugged like a bear. "Not serious," she mused. "You're an old soul, aren't you? If you told me you were a hundred years old, I'd *believe* you."

Mina yelped.

"Nice tush, too," said the one who'd just pinched her butt. Her skin was deeper than the others, her hair short and nearly as curly as Mina's.

"*Titi Isabel.*" Zack's lips twitched.

Isabel angled her head, presumably to get a better look at Mina's...*tush.* "What is it, *linda*? Pilates?"

Mina already felt dizzy (it was more likely the strong scent of rum wafting into her nostrils than the eccentric aunts). "*Eh,* I-I train approximately six to ten hours a day..."

"Probably genetic," Isabel concluded dismissively.

"What's the matter with you?" Carmen snapped. "She's not a prize horse, *okay*? Come, *linda*." She pulled Mina from the fray. "You need to eat."

"*No!*" Yara dove for the counter, grabbing one of the casserole dishes dotting the counter top and plopping it into the sink.

A small, elderly woman standing at the sink, whom Mina hadn't noticed before, turned to scowl at Yara.

"*Lo siento,*" Yara said. "But it's a matter of life and death!"

Mina's laughter surprised even herself, and everyone turned to look at her. "I'm sorry." She shifted her weight nervously. "I'm sure it's delicious. Everything smells delicious, really."

"It *smells* like a mixology lab in here." Zack gave the elderly woman a pointed look. "Abuelita, *normal* families drink *coquitos* for *Christmas*, or at least have a reason to—"

"I do not need *any old reason* to celebrate, *nene*." An enormous smile spread over her kind, time-worn face. "It's enough you're here. Anyway, the doctor says I have to watch my blood pressure, so I use coconut cream liqueur— no dairy. It's *flaco,* skinny *coquitos,* okay? You'll like it, it's healthy."

Zack chuckled and embraced her. "Just a guess, but I don't think that's what the doctor had in mind."

"*Bah!*" she huffed. Then, to Mina's amazement, she came and reached for her, kissing each of her cheeks. "Celebration for you too, *mami*, I saw you dancing on the TV." She gave Mina a quick appraisal. "You need to eat."

Releasing her without another word, she took one of the dishes from the counter, heading for the table in the open dining room. The aunts seemed to take it as a silent command, and followed suit, filing after her one-by-one with casserole dishes in hand.

"Carmen…" Mina touched Carmen's arm.

Carmen looked at Mina sympathetically. "They like you, *linda*. The *less* you hear your own name, the more you are loved. *Mijo's* grandmother was married to my father for fifty-two years. She's always bragging about how they were so in love, they *never* addressed each other by name."

Mina's rapid heartbeat had nothing to do with nerves, and everything to do with the way Zack looked at her before he lifted a casserole dish in each hand and strolled from the kitchen.

"I—*non*, I don't mind," she stammered.

Petite, petite, petite, her subconscious sing-songed. Mentally shooing her away, she turned to find Carmen watching her.

Merde.

Thanking the universe for skin that (mostly) camouflaged the heat spreading over it now, she tried again. "I wanted to apologize, for earlier. I didn't mean—"

"It's forgotten, *cariño*." Carmen cupped one of Mina's cheeks in her slightly calloused hand. "I meant what I said to you in the hallway. You're humble, and you should never lose that—but you *must* stop apologizing for living. *Okay?*"

Mina smiled tearfully. "Okay."

There was enough food on the table to feed a corps de ballet. Abuelita sat to Mina's right, making it her mission to pile a little of everything onto Mina's plate.

"You're not allergic to anything, are you, *mami*?" Abuelita asked, hovering a wooden spoon over a seafood dish.

"*Non*," Mina said. "That looks incredible. What is it?"

"It's my *sweet* mofongo with shrimp and mango *sofrito*," Abuelita said proudly. "I make it with green *and* ripe *plátanos*. Sometimes I do sweet potato, but not for summer—here you go."

Isabel—sitting across from Mina—would not be outdone. "Here, try my rice and peas. It goes with everything."

By the time the ladies were through, Mina's plate was full to heaping, and she needed a moment to decide what to try first.

"Friendly reminder I've brought a *human* to dinner and not King Kong," Zack said dryly.

"Oh, it's okay," Mina said. "Whenever I visit my *grands-parents* in *Aix-en-Provence*, I always feel like a goose being prepped for foie gras."

Abuelita chuckled. "Where is that, *mami*?"

"*Le Midi*, the South of France. *Pépé* is a *professeur de mathématiques* at the university there. He's *Tunisien*, and a great cook—though *maman* complains his food is too spicy. *Mémé* has a *patisserie*. I can never stay too long, because they feed me too much. I wouldn't be able to fit my tights."

Yara laughed. "That's the most I've heard you talk so far, *linda*."

"*Sí*," Ana said. "That accent! Let's keep her talking. I can listen to her all day."

Zack's left brow reached for the ceiling.

"What?" Mina was aware of the four pairs of eyes on them now.

"I swear I walked on broken glass, then jumped through a flaming hoop before I learned something about you other than the fact you can do a double tour with your eyes closed, when most men can't do that."

"You didn't ask." Shrugging, she dug her fork into the rice and peas.

"*Oooohhhh, I like* her," said Isabel.

"Me too." Zack whispered it so only Mina heard him, then louder, "Where's Titi Clarita? And *papá*?"

"Manny is on his way," Carmen said. "He had a community organizing meeting today. Clarita has a date."

"This is the *fifth* date," Yara informed the table. "I told Clarita to take condoms, just in case."

Mina choked.

"You okay, *mami*?" Abuelita asked, as if she hadn't heard a thing…or she had and wasn't scandalized by it at all.

"*Oui,* I'm fine." Mina was an adult, after all. She could handle someone talking about safe sex…at the dinner table.

She met Zack's amused gaze. It distinctly asked, *Pineapple?*

Lifting her chin, she gave him a look that said, *Non.* Then out loud, "I'll just…slow down."

"He's younger than her," Ana said. "I only date older men. They're happy just to get some—they don't expect me to do gymnastics like you young girls, *linda.*"

Mina choked again.

"*Ana!*" Carmen spat. "You're gonna kill her, you keep on."

Abuelita put a rum-scented drink in front of Mina, which Mina gratefully brought to her lips. She heard Zack's soft laughter but refused to look at him again. She did not *need* his pineapples, *merci beaucoup.*

By the time Manny showed up, everyone else had finished the main course, Isabel had informed Mina of a switchblade that masqueraded as lipstick (so the next time someone tried to mug her, she could cut the bitch), and Zack had asked Mina about pineapples no less than seven times. Yara, the self-proclaimed Queen of Desserts, was serving her luscious *piragua de crema de mango con vainilla*—mango vanilla cream shaved ice. Carmen had his plate full before he'd loosened his tie and sat down.

"How was it, *papi*?" Carmen asked.

"I think it went well." Manny tucked a paper towel into the collar of his shirt. "We had great turnout this time, more young people in attendance than I've seen in years— lotta people fired up after that voter purge we had last year.

I'm starting to think anger is a better motivator than peer pressure and promises."

"It's true." Yara nodded. "Happy people don't vote. Pissed people picket."

"Okay, Doctor Seuss," said Ana. "Maybe you should write a children's book, teach kids about voting."

"That's not a bad idea, actually," said Zack.

"*Sí*," Isabel said. "And a safe sex book. 'No glove, no love.'"

"*Come on*, that one was for our generation," Yara said. "You gotta use something *fresh*, like, 'Cover your bony before she rides the pony.'"

"Wrap it up or you'll fill her cup," Ana joined in.

Yara didn't seem impressed. "I like, 'Cloak the joker before you poke her.'"

"That's *terrible*," said Carmen.

"Yeah, seriously." Isabel looked exasperated. "Those are too hetero. We need to be more inclusive. Like, 'Protect your bits before you hit.'"

"Mind your middle before you diddle," said Yara.

Even Abuelita took a turn. "Make sure they like cake before you bake."

Mina burst into laughter.

Ana went again. "Check the weather down south, or you'll scorch your mouth."

Manny looked toward the ceiling. "Oh, for God's sake—*Ow!*"

Mina jumped.

Abuelita had somehow reached behind her *and* Zack and whacked Manny with a wooden spoon. "You know better, *nene.*" She scowled. "Don't take the Lord's name in vain."

"*Lo siento, mamá.*" Manny rubbed his shoulder.

Mina was doubled over. They had been utterly ridiculous all evening long, so Abuelita's hard limit being *Jesus* made her break.

"Maybe *you* need some cake, *mami*." Abuelita grinned.

Oh…mon Dieu. She couldn't breathe.

Zack bent over to gloat in her ear. "Craving any fruit, *petite*? I recommend pineapples. They're in season."

Straightening and collecting herself, Mina pressed a hand to her stomach. "*Non, merci,* I'm full."

"So, Mina." Manny seemed eager for sane conversation. "How is it working with *mijo* so far? He giving you any trouble?"

"*Oui*." Mina threw a side-long glance at Zack. "He's pushy."

"*Hey…*" Zack started to protest.

"And *mean*," Mina continued. "But…after learning his technique, I'm sure I can do anything. I'm stronger than I have ever been, and I have him to thank for that."

Zack looked like he might fall from his chair. "Will wonders never cease?"

"Stop teasing her, *mijo*," Carmen scolded. "You didn't always admit you needed help, either."

"Yeah," said Isabel. "Remember the time he couldn't figure out how to use a dance belt?"

Zack groaned. "Any time you're ready, *petite*."

"*Non*. I want to hear. Dance belt?" she asked innocently, leaning forward.

"You know damn well what a dance belt is," he murmured.

"Hush." Mina waved him away.

Seeming resigned, he leaned back, folding his arms across his chest.

"What was he, twelve? Thirteen?" Isabel asked.

"Thirteen," Carmen said. "He'd just started partnering classes, and these things—they're not like jockstraps at all. They offer *no* protection if a girl's foot slips or a turn goes wrong. They're like thongs men wear under their tights to lift their buns and make their junk look good."

"Thanks a lot, *mamá*." Zack massaged his temples.

"*Hush, mijo.* Anyway, he spent a whole *week* miserable and in pain, until he finally admitted he needed help stuffing everything in there the right way."

Mina caught Zack's pained expression and couldn't resist. "So…everything was just…flopping around?"

"*Sí*, hanging low and looking messy—But I asked one of the older boys to show him how it's done, so he wouldn't be *too* embarrassed."

"We wouldn't want that, would we?" Zack muttered.

Mina bit back more laughter.

"It's not an issue anymore, for the record." Zack straightened his shoulders, which pushed his chest out, and Mina looked down his body automatically.

"Of course not." She lifted her gaze back up to his.

"Although, I may consider full-body armor after a few weeks of dancing with you."

"*I'm* the one who needs armor. In case I fall from one of your crazy lifts."

He looked hurt. "I have *never* dropped you."

"*Non*, but it doesn't mean I won't fall."

His expression darkened, his eyes pinning her to her seat. "I'd catch you."

Her pulse sped up at the double entendre, her mouth clamping shut. *Merde*. Perhaps she was reading into things. Perhaps it wasn't a double entendre. She couldn't think with him looking at her like that, like he was trying to forge a path through her nervous system and into the far recesses of her mind. Like it was *absolument* a double entendre.

Manny cleared his throat, and Mina turned to see everyone staring at them—most of them with amusement. Everyone but Manny.

"How's the grant proposal writing going, *mijo*?" Manny asked Zack, bursting their bubble completely. "I thought you'd come by the community organizing meeting and throw your hat in the ring."

The room fell quiet. So quiet, the sound of Manny's fork hitting his nearly empty plate was like two cymbals crashing together. Mina noticed the other women's eyes were focused on that fork, too. But not Zack's. His were dark and unreadable, and though his body language seemed relaxed, his jaw looked tense.

"Not now, *papi*," Carmen said softly.

"It's going great," Zack answered in a casual, upbeat tone—the kind people used when they did not feel at all casual or upbeat. "Almost finished, in fact. Just ironing out a few more details before the submission deadline."

Mina knew it wasn't her place, and interfering was rude, but her need to *know* overcame any trepidation. "You're writing a *grant*? But…where in the world do you find the time?"

Zack's expression softened for her, his lips curving into a reluctant smile. "Somewhere between midnight and six in the morning."

Mina couldn't hide her astonishment. "What is it for?"

"*Mijo* wants funding for a dance school for the kids." Carmen was obviously proud, and probably wanted to lighten the air a little. "We'd have our own studios, a library, tutoring and computer labs…"

"It's ambitious," Manny cut in. "It's more realistic to pitch for more funding for the program at the rec center. Get an afterschool program going year-round."

"It's not enough, *papá*." Zack's voice had an edge to it.

Abuelita and the aunts busied themselves with clearing the table, clearly having witnessed this conversation before. Mina's hand instinctively reached for Zack's underneath the table, giving it a reassuring squeeze.

He didn't look at her, but he squeezed back. "This community shares two million dollars between all its nonprofit programs for low-income youth. That's *great*, I'm not downplaying that accomplishment, but for kids who are serious about pursuing dance careers, it's not enough."

"It was enough for *you*, *mijo*," Manny said. "You went through the same program, worked hard, and got everything you dreamed of. You saying these kids can't, too?"

Wiping his hand over his face, Zack sighed. "I'm *grateful*, *papá*, but I'm an exception and you know it. This grant would cover university-trained dance teachers, partnering with local dance theaters to work with their choreographers. Gifted students would get scholarships to dance academies, increasing their chances of pursuing real dance careers from about impossible to abso-fucking-lutely."

"*Mijo*," Carmen tried to interject…

"No, *mamá*. I appreciate the doors you guys opened for me. I'm just trying to open more, a little faster."

"And you refuse to let anyone help you," Manny said stiffly.

"How's that?" Zack asked, just as stiffly.

"Zachary…" Mina tried, but he'd released her hand, his hackles up—a lion primed for a fight.

Merde.

Abuelita and the aunts were frozen at the kitchen counter, apologies on their faces. Giving them a brittle smile, Mina could only sit there helplessly.

"You don't let people open doors anymore," Manny accused. "Even when you know someone with a key—you'd rather *kick* them down yourself."

"What's wrong with that?" Zack fired back. "What's wrong with taking control instead of waiting for someone to give it to you?"

"That's your problem right there. You have to be in control of *everything*. All, or nothing—even the food you eat—"

"*Papi*!" Carmen protested.

"Same thing, same time, every day. Right, *mijo*?" Manny asked flatly.

"*Pineapple*," Zack bit through his teeth, then looked at Mina. "Let's go."

Chapter Nineteen

ZACK SAT ON the grass in Sunset Park with Mina, watching two Doberman Pinschers walk their little girl.

"*Oh mon Dieu!*" her face lit up with delight. "How adorable."

"Yeah, until those two take off after a squirrel and she turns into a kite."

Everything in him seemed to smile with her laughter, as bright and vivid as the sun's final rays of the day. It was a mild evening for July, so families and couples were spread out everywhere, on blankets across the park's grassy hills, to watch darkness fall.

From their vantage point, they could see clear across the bay, where Lady Liberty stood with her torch aloft, and Jersey City behind her. Zack pointed them out for Mina, identifying the tips of Ellis Island and Governors Island… and the skyscrapers of Lower Manhattan stretching into the sky. Beneath them and closer in, were several church spires, and water towers atop pale brick row houses, blending with the colorful awnings of the diverse restaurants in the heart of Brooklyn.

Impulsively, he threw an arm around her shoulders,

hugging her against his side. Her contented little sigh kindled something in his heart. Maybe it was being around his family, and the kids at the rec center, and romping around his childhood haunts with her that made him want…more.

He longed for nocturnal strolls and late-night picnics with her in summer; for winter nights exploring new restaurants and theaters, huddling in close to each other in puffer coats, their arms circling each other's waists. They'd laugh, their breaths coming out in cold puffs of visible air, shivering their asses off until they ducked into their shared apartment, where the rent was too fucking high, but the location was perfect. They'd strip off their clothes and fall into bed, wrapping themselves in the silk and warmth of each other's skin, simultaneously dreading and looking forward to the next day, when they'd wake up and work themselves *silly* doing exactly what they loved…

The sun slowly descended toward the horizon, turning the sky a bright, intense yellow that was hard to look at for too long. Squinting, she looked away from the sunset and caught him staring at her. Her beautiful, upturned face was awash in gold, highlighting her gorgeous brown skin and illuminating her eyes, until she looked like a bronzed statuette—his very own muse. The city seemed to come to a standstill, if only for a few seconds, along with the beat of his heart.

Holy shit.

He was falling in love with her.

Days and nights with her played out in front of him as if from an old movie reel, its film so long, it stretched out over the water and disappeared into the skyline.

"The light is back in your eyes," she murmured. "I didn't like seeing it burn out earlier."

"You have no idea," he whispered.

Her brows pinched together. "Are you going to tell me?"

"Yes."

Truthfully, he'd rather be stripped ass-naked and strapped to the airship mast at the top of the Empire State Building than explain his tenuous relationship with food to her. He could think of a million things he'd rather be doing, and every one of them was identical.

Her breath caught. "Are you going to kiss me?"

"Yes."

"Zack—"

"Shut up, *petite*."

"*Connard*."

He smiled a slow, deep smile, his free hand coming up to take a handful of her curls. Indulging himself a moment, he sifted their spiraling softness through his fingers, then tugged her gently forward. Even narrowed on him, her eyes were so beautiful, reaching deep inside of him and warming his soul.

"I wish you wouldn't." She cast a wary look to the side without moving her head, then her gaze fell to his lips, and her breaths came shorter. "*Dieu*, but I wish you would."

Shielding her profile with her voluminous hair, he dipped his head. "How's this?"

She sighed.

"Is that a yes?"

Her eyes drifted shut, and she closed the distance between their lips. "*Oui*."

Pleasure moved through his body in soft, undulating folds, the kind that spoke of profound contentment, rather than desire. Everything he wanted—everything he needed—was right here in his arms, yielding to him with every soft, elated breath.

Yes…yes, yes.

Sliding his fingers deeper into her hair, he cupped her head in his hand, fitting her to his mouth, stroking her tongue with his. He enjoyed how soft and pliant her lips felt under his, the playful way she nipped his bottom lip every so often, tugging gently with her teeth.

Subconsciously, he'd wanted this since the first time he'd met her. To get close to so much beauty and passion. To harness and mold it, channel it into something he'd created, and unleash it to the world. He hadn't anticipated she'd be the one to get under his skin, spiking his bloodstream, flooding his veins.

She was fast becoming vital to him, like his next heartbeat, his next breath. Kissing her felt just as vital, so he melded his lips to hers until night fell completely. Until stars dotted the sky, the delighted screams of children quieted, and the older crowd dwindled to lovers seeking a romantic place to cuddle. Her hand slipped under his T-shirt and over his chest, kneading softly over his heartbeat. Then, pulling away slowly, she looked up at him with wonder.

"Wow," she whispered.

"Swooning is satisfactory." His voice was raspy. "More kisses are also acceptable."

She gave a soft laugh (God, he loved the sound of it), then tucked herself into his side, leaning back to look at the sky. "So many stars."

"Said like someone seeing stars for the first time."

"*En fait*, it feels like I am."

"The sunset in Paris must be *such* a disappointment compared to this."

Laughing again, she pinched his waist. "I *love* the sunset in *Paris*. The closest thing to this in *Paris* is in *Champ de Mars*, on the grass, where you can *feel* the *tour d'Eiffel* beside you. Drinking red wine, of course."

"Of course." He was enchanted by her voice, her accent made stronger by nostalgia for her home.

"But my favorite place to watch is on the Seine. You can see the *tour d'Eiffel*, and the Île de la Cité…and the towers of Notre Dame. The water turns orange, and then red, and when it gets dark, you see how the city gets its name."

"The City of Light."

"*Oui*. The lights come on all over the city. It's beautiful, but it's so bright, you can't see the stars."

"So, what you're saying is, despite being—*arguably*—the most romantic city in the world, the sunset doesn't compare to the one you just watched with me?"

"I—"

"That's very sweet, *petite*." He nuzzled her neck, chuckling at her exasperated little growl. "*Mmmm*…When you don't smell like sweat, you smell like flowers." Unable to resist, he licked the pulse in her throat.

"Your flattery needs work."

He would have had a ready response, if he hadn't buried his face in the sweet spot between her neck and shoulder, now breathing her intoxicating scent into his lungs. It drove him crazy, a mix of piney shrubs and spicy herbs and sweet flowers.

"God, what *is* that?" he murmured. "It smells like you, but stronger. Every time you let me close enough, I want to bite you, then lay my head here and fall asleep." To demonstrate, he gave her clavicle a little nip that made her body jolt.

"My scent makes you behave like a sleepy *lion*? *Allez,* your compliments are getting worse and worse."

Damn, but he *loved* when she called him a lion. "*Petite…*"

She shook with more of that sweet, soft laughter, tucking her legs in so she sat cross-legged. "I smell like *Le Midi*. The same way my *maman* and *mémé* smell. Perfumers like to bottle it up and call it 'lavender,' but my *grand-mère* calls it '*garrigue*.' It's just…the smell of the South of France. It's all of it together—the flowers, the wine, the earth, the air. *Mémé* found the only perfume that even comes close to it. She gave it to me when I joined *Les Étoiles*."

"And the name of this magical potion?" He pulled back to look at her.

She acted demure. "Sometimes a woman likes an air of mystery."

"Fair enough." Laying on his back, he rested his head in her lap. "Tell me something that isn't a mystery— Don't bother with scars or identifying marks. I know all about those."

Swatting him, her dark eyes smoldered. "You know *of* them, not *about* them."

"Touché." He moaned contentedly as her fingers played in his hair.

"*Oh*, you great big cat." Biting her lip, she thought for a moment. "When I was nine—only a year after I started at the ballet school—I had terrible pain in my left ankle whenever I pointed my toe. The doctors said an extra piece of cartilage between my Achilles tendon and my heel had hardened to bone."

"So…surgery?"

"*Oui*, to remove it. But not until I was ten. I danced on

it for a year, and by the time they removed it, it had fractured. *Merde,* it was excruciating—so swollen and irritated. But, with physical therapy, I recovered in a few months, and I was able to catch up."

"That's not too bad." He'd been absently caressing one of her ankles as she spoke. His hand curled around it now, his thumb stroking the smooth, indented skin of her tiny scar.

"*Non*, but a year later, the same thing happened to my right foot."

"*Jesus*."

"I was devastated. During my recovery from the second surgery, I had to watch my peers move up to the next section, while I stayed behind. '*Just take notes,*' Madame told me. But I screamed at her, '*Non!* I can dance in my boot!'"

"Good to know you were always so difficult. I'd hate to think you've been giving me special treatment."

"*Allez*." She laughed, but her cheeks flushed, like she wasn't particularly proud of anyone thinking her difficult. "Anyway, I caught up—I made the top four that year. I've had injuries since then, but no more surgeries. What about you?"

"Mostly maintenance work…couple surgeries on my knees and ankles over the years. I was lucky not to have the Achilles curse, or problems with my back giving out— ballerinas might *look* like waifs but lifting solid muscle over your head every day makes a male dancer's shelf life pretty short."

That made her incline her head a little, looking at him intently. "So, musical theater was your retirement plan?"

"Oh no, nothing like that. So much of career success in theater is about luck—getting the right opportunity at the right time. I've always wanted to do it, but I had *no* delusions I'd get more than the supporting roles I've done over the years. I dreamed about putting on my own productions, but the reality of it still hasn't completely sunk in yet. Honestly, I hope it never does. I don't want to lose this feeling."

"What feeling?"

"It's a little like being out of your mind. Or high. It's so exhilarating, sometimes I can't sleep. It's…overwhelming. Like I don't have a choice. For better or worse—whatever the quirks and challenges—this is what I want."

Mina let go a dreamy sigh. "Sounds like falling in love."

A thunderstorm roiled in his chest, his hand tightening around her ankle. She didn't seem to notice, lost somewhere in her own head. Then he remembered what she said in the documentary he watched weeks ago, when the interviewer suggested that love was what compelled Mina to dance:

People grow out of people and things they claim to love all the time. I don't understand how something so profound can be so fickle. I'll never grow out of dance. It's just a part of me. It's…consuming. It overpowers love.

Consuming.

That's exactly what he felt pursuing his dreams, the euphoria of chasing something that gave him great pleasure, that made him *feel*, and feel important. And it's *exactly* what he felt right now, falling in love. Gazing up at her now, at the wistfulness coloring her features in the soft light of the park's lamps, the storm in his chest continued.

What would it take to have her look at him that way? To feel for him that way? To get her to see that what she described in that interview years ago was precisely what it meant to be in love? Or, maybe she already knew. Maybe, in the years since she'd given that interview, life had taught her differently…

"Have you ever been in love, Mina?"

At first, he thought she hadn't heard the question. Then, he felt the tension in her body, and she looked at him like she'd been caught putting Play-Doh in gum wrappers.

"It's just a question, *petite.*" So why did he sound like a guy who'd spent his last dime on a lottery ticket, holding his breath and waiting for the winning number to be read? "I want to know you."

That made her smile, her body relaxing again—as much as a ballerina with near-militant training could relax. "I came close, once. I was twenty-one. We met at a *café*—a cliché I adored almost as much as I adored him. It was romantic, and *awkward*. He dropped his coffee when he saw me, and it made me feel so beautiful. I loved how he made me feel."

"Can't say I blame the poor bastard. So, what happened?"

Taking a deep breath, she turned away from him, toward the night skyline. She was quiet so long, he almost let her off the hook. But he needed her to share some of her secrets. To let him see some of the cramped, dark spaces she didn't show many people. To let him see that, maybe, she was becoming invested, too.

"*So* many things…" She kept her eyes from him, which was fine with him, so long as she talked. "He wasn't a dancer, so he was jealous a lot…of my partners. There's a lot of caressing, and pained expressions, and tight, pro-longed holds. In a company, you're surrounded by beauti-ful people all the time. It made him insecure. Then, he'd see me injured a lot, and he'd ask me, '*Enfin,* why don't you just stop?'—Can you imagine?"

There was fire in her eyes.

"Or, I'd want to talk about things, just to vent. Like how, sometimes, even my hair made it harder for me than other girls—trying to stuff it into a bun without snapping all my hair ties—and he'd use that to try to convince me to quit. Eventually, he stopped asking. When we broke up, he accused me of choosing dance over him, and I wanted to scream, '*You gave me an ultimatum! You backed me into a corner!*' But I just said, '*Oui,* I am. Because if you loved me, you wouldn't make me choose.'"

"Wow." Taking her hand from his hair, he held it to his chest. "It's hard, trying to explain to someone who doesn't dance, why you love something that hurts you. I get that."

"You do?"

"Mmhmm. I've fallen in love a few times. Falling is easy. It takes hardly any effort. Maintaining it is hard. Maintaining it with someone who doesn't understand you is just…impossible."

"So…" She traced circles on his chest with her fingers, pinning him to the grass with her stare. "When was the last time you were in love?"

Bonus points for remembering to breathe. "A few years ago. We worked together."

"Was she your partner?"

"No, but we were in the same company. It was convenient, and fun, and we never fought about not having enough time together. Strangely, it was during that time that I stopped having my sexuality constantly called into question. I never understood how ballet could be perceived as gay when every single classical piece features hetero leads. Male dancers who are anything but cis and straight are the greatest actors in the business."

"Oh, I know. A dancer who isn't heteronormative playing a classical lead role has to be a *fantastique* actor. I used to joke about it all the time with—" Her hand flew to her mouth, and her body locked up again.

"Étienne," he guessed. "It's okay, *petite*. You've told me already you two never dated—not that I'd have a problem if you had—*Fuck*…Not that it would matter if I had a problem with it." He blew a harsh breath, massaging his closed eyes with the heels of his palms. "*Jesus Christ.*"

Her soft laughter pulled him from his pathetic, clusterfuck of a verbal hamster wheel. "It's okay."

Wondering something, he opened his eyes. "Have you ever dated a partner?"

"*Non.*" She looked grateful for the redirect. "Have you?"

"Not until you. Have you ever dated someone in your company?"

"Of course. It's convenient, like you said. After getting out of a performance late at night, I'm *exhausted*. The *last* thing I want to do, is go to a bar and try to look cute to pick up a date."

More bonus points for not saying she didn't need to try. (It was true, though.)

"*Alors,*" she said. "It's difficult to find someone outside of the dance world who understands how…*weird* and wonderful the lifestyle is. But if things don't work out with someone in the company, it can be…complicated." She frowned. "Wait…why didn't it work out?"

He laughed—not because it was funny, but because she sounded like she'd find his ex and kick her ass. Stupid as it was, his heart wagged its tail. "It's complicated, *petite*. *People* are complicated. We gave each other what we needed at the time—companionship, loyalty, sex, laughter. It was enough, until it wasn't, and we mutually decided it was over."

"What do you mean, 'until it wasn't?'"

"She had an opportunity somewhere else, and I knew I could live without her."

She gasped. "That's a *terrible* thing to say!"

"Maybe, but it's true."

"You're so much like Carmen. So direct. Almost abrasive."

"Does that bother you?"

"Sometimes." She gnawed her lower lip for a few seconds, tracing his eyebrows with her index finger. "But it's comforting, too."

"Oh?" His brow arched beneath her touch.

"*Enfin,* it's part of who you are. It tells me you're not a flatterer. So…when you pay a compliment, I know you mean it." She drew her index finger down the bridge of his nose, stopping at the bow of his lips. "When we left your parents' house earlier, as…angry as you were, you still kissed your father's cheek."

"Wow, that was some segue, *petite*."

"*Merci,* I learned it from you."

Groaning, he sat up and faced her. "So, we're really doing this, huh?"

She took his hand and held it in her lap. "Only if you want to. I don't want you to feel obligated…"

"I don't." He looked around. Only a few people remained in the park, and he didn't want to tempt fate by making themselves easy targets. "But let's take this conversation to the car, okay?"

"Okay."

They walked briskly to Zack's Audi, and the console

read ten thirty-seven by the time they got on the highway. He held her hand as he drove, a U2 song playing faintly on the radio. It felt so natural with her. Talking to her, listening to her, making her laugh…kissing her, touching her, making her come…pushing her buttons, and getting pushed right back. She challenged him, but she also made him feel important.

Vital.

"Back there, with my father," he said. "I'm sure it sounded intense, but I don't want you to think I have anything less than the utmost respect for him."

"I know. I can tell."

"We just…don't see eye-to-eye sometimes. Manny—he's old-school. Working class, son of immigrants. He worked his *ass* off to give me a good life—and not just me. Everyone in the neighborhood knows if they ever need anything, Manny is the guy. Even if he's struggling himself, he finds a way to help others. Shirt from his own back, etcetera."

"Like he helped you."

"Precisely. But he's a Bootstrap Believer—You know, you can do anything if you just, pull yourself up by your bootstraps. That's part of it, but a huge part of success for kids like me is *opportunity*. I mean, I was a *white* kid growing up in Brooklyn. If someone tried to tell me I had some advantage over anyone else when I was a kid, I would have fought them, literally started a fist fight. Because what part of getting my ass kicked by some punks, being abused by foster parents, or being stuck in the foster system at all after my own parents tossed me away like lawn clippings, is privilege?"

She sniffed, and he turned to see her wiping away

tears. "I understand. It's so complicated. Like when I try to explain my challenges as a black ballerina, but my parents were well off—I went to boarding school."

"Exactly. People like Manny just don't see that kind of nuance. Everything is cut and dry, black or white. They can't see gray, and if you told them there was an entire gray *spectrum*? I think their heads would explode."

"*Oh mon Dieu*, that sounds exactly like *maman.* She did her best raising me, and I love her so much, but I still find it difficult to relate to her."

"Oh, trust me, I know. I had to negotiate your contract with her. Remind me never to get on her bad side." He grinned. "I see some of her in you, you know. When you're handing me my balls, for example."

She laughed a little, then sobered. "I think it's incredible what you're trying to do. For me, dance was so much more than learning a pretty art. It taught me discipline, and self-confidence, how to work with all kinds of people…I get to travel the world, and I can't imagine a better way to connect with who I am, the world around me, and in a strange way…the universe."

He couldn't resist glancing at her again, to see the passion play out on her face. "I know what you mean. For these kids, a dance school could be a springboard out of poverty. As a white guy, my story makes me *interesting,* like street cred is sexy. But for these kids, it's a stumbling block—the world counts it *against* them. Manny wants them to pull themselves up by their bootstraps. I'm just trying to supply the boots—slippers, if you will."

"So *do* it," she said with conviction. "Maybe in time, Manny will come to understand your vision. He'll see that you both want the same thing, and it's okay if you take a different path to get it."

Turning into the parking garage at Mina's apartment, he pulled into the number eight spot and switched off the engine. "What he said about food—"

She squeezed his hand. "Zack, you don't have to—"

"No, I do. I want to. I wish it hadn't come up this way, but if you're going to understand me, maybe it's best for you to know."

Saying nothing, she simply nodded.

"Food was one of the ways I was punished by Foster Mom Number Three." The pulse points in his body pounded like opposing war drums. "She'd send me to bed without dinner, because I fought her when she tried to— take advantage of me. I never tried to tell anyone, because she'd threaten to send me back. It might sound crazy, being afraid to *leave* an abusive home, but enduring her seemed easier than being thrown back into the system. She'd even tell me, if I was bad, they'd send me out of state."

"Oh mon Dieu…Zack…"

She looked distraught, and it made his chest ache. He could still hear Foster Mom Number Three's voice:

You're ungrateful. This is your third *foster family. You really think you're gonna get any more chances? You think you're fucking Huckleberry Finn, or Oliver Twist? Get out of your fairytales, boy. It won't get better than this.*

Squeezing his eyes shut, he continued. "At first, controlling what I ate felt normal. All the guys I knew were doing it—meal planning, designing special workouts to stay fit, but not bulk up too much. One week, when I was touring in Italy, I ate the same thing every day—mostly because it was convenient and cheap. I was trying to get used to an unfamiliar place, and my Italian was *horrible*. Completely by accident, I discovered it had this…calming effect on my mind. The routine. Knowing I would eat the same thing, at the same time, every day…it gave me back some control. I don't do it all the time, just…high-stress situations."

"Like writing, choreographing, starring in, and directing a musical?" She cupped one of his cheeks in her hand. "It's nothing to be ashamed of, Zack. When I first became an *Étoile*, I'd hold my father's figurine before every show. It gave me peace of mind, too. Soothed my nerves. If anything, coping mechanisms show our strength, not our weakness. They show we are self-aware, that we want to be better."

His body heated quickly, and he felt the sting of tears in his eyes for the first time in longer than he could remember. "I meant it when I told you I missed you, *petite*," he said, stretching one of her soft curls.

"I believed you," she said. "In French, we say '*tu me manques.*'"

Letting go, he watched the curl spring back into place. It was deeply satisfying to watch. *God,* he loved her hair. "I'm a little rusty, but that sounds more like, 'you miss me.'"

"That's what it *sounds* like, but the way the verb works, it translates to, 'you are missing from me.'"

"That's very romantic."

She looked away. "Perhaps that's *too* romantic."

"You know that's not true." Bringing her hands to his lips, he kissed her knuckles. "I enjoy being with you. You feel it in the way I kiss you. The way I look at you. I hope you remember that when things start to get crazy, and I'm yelling at you in rehearsals, and the only time we have together is clandestine moments in whatever nook or cranny I pull you into."

Her eyelashes did the fluttering thing, a tell he was quickly growing to love.

"I like *this* directness," she said.

"Good. Keep that in mind when I have to shut down one of your tantrums."

"My *tantrums?*"

"And anger management problems."

"*Bah!*"

He grinned. "You slapped the shit out of me."

"It was a-a mistake!"

"Plus, you're stubborn," he went on. "At first, I couldn't tell if you had a superiority, or an inferiority complex—"

"This isn't romantic at *all*." She flushed, snatching her hands away, crossing her arms over her chest. "I hope you don't write poetry."

"But…I came to realize, it's neither. It's passion, *petite*. It makes me want to kiss you, to see what that passion tastes like in different places—in the studio, onstage, in the car… your place, mine…in the grass with you on your back and your eyes giving me back the sky."

She gasped, her bottom lip quivering in shock.

"I'd much rather be slapped by you, than kissed by anyone else."

"Zack," she moaned.

"For the record, I'd prefer you kiss me, but both leave me reeling."

Gripping his shirt in both fists, she pulled him to her with almost superhuman force. "Zachary."

"Yes, *petite?*"

"*Shut. Up.*" And she kissed him.

Chapter Twenty

THEY KISSED IN the car, and from the car to the elevator, and from the elevator to the hallway, where he backed her up against the wall next to her door, sinking his fingers into her hair on either side of her face.

"Zack," she whispered, feeling his response shudder through his body.

"I love how you say my name."

Her gaze moved slowly down the length of him, his arousal pressed against her lower belly. Sliding his hands down to the curve of her hips, he pulled her to him snugly, pressing his fingers into the sore muscles of her butt, a reminder of just how far she'd run that morning. Stroking his abdomen, she enjoyed his sigh, and the way his muscles contracted under her touch. He took her mouth again, until it was soft and open and malleable, the muscles of her lips so weak from kissing, they could barely press back. Until their kisses were silky slides of lips and tongue, hot and wet and messy.

"Come to bed with me," she whispered.

"You know I want to, *petite*." As if to emphasize his

claim, he squeezed her inner thigh. "But I don't think it's a good idea."

"Why not?"

"I know what's coming in the weeks ahead. I think…a cooling off period, just for a little while, so we—so *I*—can focus…might be a good idea. If I come in there with you, I'm not leaving until morning."

"Are you trying to talk me out of it?" She swirled hot kisses on his neck, cupping and rubbing him firmly with her palm. "Or into it?"

Groaning, he pressed himself into her hand, as if he couldn't help himself, letting her rub and rub him, until he cursed and gripped her wrist, gently pulling it to his lips. "I don't have anything on me, *petite*."

"We don't need it." She kissed his chin, his cheek… "I'm on the pill, and I've been tested recently—*Pas de problème*."

"Me too."

"Oh, you're on the pill?"

"No, smartass." His fingers dug into her thigh. "No problems for me, either."

Her lips touched the corners of his mouth as he said it, and he shuddered, flexing his body into hers.

"Fuck it," he growled, pulling her up off the floor and kissing her again in earnest.

Shifting, he pressed her up against her apartment door—and stumbled, *hard*, through it, the door swinging wide. Their curses tore from them at the same time, and she clutched at him desperately to keep from falling to the floor.

"What the fuck…" He lowered her to her feet, immediately tugging her behind him.

It took her a few seconds to process that it was an

instinctive move to protect her, because her body was still shaking free of arousal.

And because her apartment had been completely upended.

Drawers and cabinets were open and emptied, their contents scattered—some broken—on the floor, and all over the countertops. Books and photographs and trinkets from the shelves had been thrown to the floor like garbage, the coffee table and chaise flipped upside down. Papers were strewn all over like giant confetti, and the television was turned on its face on the floor. She recognized the Bordeaux-red of her passport atop a messy stack of papers, the national emblem of France emblazoned on the front.

Roaring flames licked through her body.

Her blood ran hot.

Her heart beat painfully in her chest.

Screaming a string of French curses, she dove to the floor.

"*Mina*! *No!*" Zack was next to her in a flash, plucking her from her hands and knees like she was a rag doll.

"*Non!*" she cried, flailing. "*Let me go*! I have to find it!"

"We're getting the fuck out of here." His long strides already carried them into the hallway. "Whoever did this could still be in there."

"*L'aisse-moi*! *S'il te plaît,* Zachary!" she screamed, struggling to no avail. "*Please, let me go!*"

"Everything okay?" someone asked, peering through the crack of her chain-linked door.

"Call nine-one-one," Zack barked, ducking Mina's hysterical assault. "Goddammit, *petite*! Stoppit!" Grabbing her arms and pulling them down, he restrained her tighter.

"*Stop*," he said gentler this time. "It's a crime scene, Mina. You can't touch anything."

He was right, and fighting him was futile anyway, so Mina went limp, trying not cry—Only because the neighbor across the hall had her hawk eyes narrowed on Zack, and Mina realized the woman probably thought he was kidnapping her.

Putain de bordel de merde.

"You okay, miss?" the woman asked.

Zack cursed, carefully letting Mina go and scowling at the woman. "Lady, I'm not a serial killer, okay? I'm a friend. She's been *robbed*. Will you *please* call the fucking police?"

"I think she can speak for herself." The woman looked at Mina. "You *okay*?"

"*Oui*—I—yes. *Merci*, but it's true." Mina was grateful for the woman's thoughtfulness. If the situation had been different, she might have saved her life. "We came here together and found my apartment vandalized."

Zack hiked an angry brow, and the woman nodded, disappearing into her apartment.

The police arrived in seven minutes.

"Good thing we weren't being stabbed to death," Zack said tersely. "Or we'd already be hacked to pieces and stuffed into the walls."

Wisely, they did not respond. Maddeningly, because it wasn't a crime-in-progress, no one was missing or murdered (and left at the scene), and the intruder wasn't kind enough to sustain bodily injury during the break-in and leave a trail of blood for DNA analysis, there wasn't much the officers could do.

As soon as the officers finished their walk-through of her apartment, Mina trudged through the mess to take note of what was stolen. Puzzlingly, the thief had made off with her laptop and tablet, but nothing else. To her immense relief, every swan was accounted for, and perfectly pristine. Though they were scattered all over the place, her expensive jewelry and shoes were also accounted for, along with several pieces of designer clothing, and decorative pieces her mother had probably spent far too much money on. Mina clutched the swans from her father and Étienne, as the officers took her statement.

"Jimmy-proof lock," the female officer (Warner) said when she'd finished taking Mina's statement. Angling her head, she frowned. "Looks new."

Zack scoffed, and Mina quickly spoke up. "*Oui*, the manager replaced the lock after I was mugged yesterday."

"We need to talk to him," the male officer (Rodriguez) said to his partner. "Rule out anyone with a key."

Warner shook her head. "Looks like the perp picked the lock—substantial scratching around the keyhole and the thing's brand-new. Probably used some kind o' twist flex tension tool, and a standard hook pick to get in."

Mina shivered. The whole thing made her feel so… *violated. Bordel!* They'd plundered her *underwear* drawer, touched all over the utensils she put in her mouth, tore apart the bed where she slept. She didn't spend a lot of time here, but it was her sanctuary. Nothing had given her more relief after her mugging, than to seek asylum in her apartment, and now she didn't feel safe at all.

She gasped. "Do…you think the two incidents are connected?"

"Could be," Rodriguez said. "Could be a coincidence."

"I don't like this kind of coincidence," Zack said.

"Neither do I." Warner nodded toward the living room

window. "This is a high-risk neighborhood. Lotta traffic, fancy apartments. No security, but you've gotta be buzzed in. Whoever did this probably blends in. Doesn't seem threatening. They put their neck on the line to get in here, just to leave so many valuables behind."

Mina thought of something. "Why would they want my computer? My tablet? My *shoes* cost more than those."

"Could it be a stalker?" Zack asked. "Some asshole's been following her around—now he has her phone, her computer, and her tablet. He has access to photos, contacts...personal information—"

"We don't want to speculate, sir," said Rodriguez. "And we don't want you to *panic*, ma'am. It's important you keep a level head. We still don't have enough to go on to determine whether it's the same person."

It was all incredibly overwhelming, and though she was grateful to be unharmed and retain most of her personal items, it was still a horrible note to end the day on. Less than an hour ago, she was going to share her bed with Zack, and now she wanted to get as far away from it as possible.

He caught her gaze, giving her a sympathetic look, then turned to Warner. "Can you at least dust for fingerprints?"

Warner finished her notes, then looked up. "We'll throw some dust around, but I don't expect to get a decent print from this mess. Whoever did this was skilled and very organized. My guess is the perp was in and out in fifteen minutes or less."

"We'll canvas the neighborhood," said Rodriguez. "Show the sketch of your mugger to the neighbors, local bodegas, see if anyone recognizes him. Someone could've let the perp in without realizing it. If a person looks friendly enough, people will hold the door open without thinking twice about it."

"Jesus Christ." Zack swiped his fingers through his hair. "It's like being humped twice."

"Look," said Warner. "I've been doing this twenty years. Unless it's a crime in-progress, the best you can do is file a police report, including property damage, and anything that was stolen, so you can try and get some compensation." She looked at Mina. "You got renter's insurance?"

Mina nodded solemnly.

"Good. I'll see if the serials for your laptop and tablet turn up anywhere, but it's a long-shot. We'll get on the manager's ass about getting better locks—something that can't be picked in thirty seconds. If you can stay with someone for a couple days, do that. De-stress, talk to someone. Maybe get someone to help you clean up, so it starts to feel like home again."

"And stay *alert*." Rodriguez handed Mina his card. "You think of anything else, or anything suspicious comes up, gimme a call."

"*Merci*." Her shoulders sagged. "I-I will."

In the thirty minutes it took for them to take Mina's prints (for comparison), dust for viable fingerprints, and leave, Mina had two suitcases packed, she'd changed all her passwords and put a freeze on her credit cards, and Zack had helped put all her cherished photos, figurines and other effects into a box. She locked the door behind them with disdain. It certainly hadn't done its job, so what the hell was the point? She supposed a locked door might deter any opportunists looking to score some runny tights, or a decorative vase by some obscure French designer…or some *very* good artisanal cheese.

They didn't talk on the ride to Alex's house, and Mina was grateful. She felt she could communicate to Zack without words, as though he knew, instinctively, she'd rather weight the entire experience with rocks and toss it into a river in the back of her mind.

When at last they arrived at Alex's beautiful brownstone, it was well after midnight, and they quietly lugged Mina's things to the fourth floor. His room had a calming effect on her nerves. It was familiar and warm, with pieces of her imprinted on his bed, tacked to boards, and scribbled in the margins of the *Lady in Red* script on his desk. Most of all, *he* was there. He made her feel safe, and it's what she needed to feel more than anything right now.

To feel protected, to reconnect with the person who was the closest thing she felt to being home.

Without a word, he stripped them down to their underwear, then pulled the covers back so they could slide into the warmth of his cavernous bed. Opening a drawer, he shook out a few of his downy-soft T-shirts, comparing their sizes and settling on the smallest one.

"You can wear this one." He rolled up the hem to slip her head through the neckline.

She stopped him with a hand on his arm, smoothing over his bicep to the curve of his shoulder. "Not yet."

"*Petite?*" He studied her face with those beautiful, darkly lashed green eyes. "Are you okay?"

"I will be." Stepping closer, she rested her palm on his chest, over his heart. "Thanks to you."

She wrapped her arms around him as tightly as her fatigued muscles would allow, his body heat warming her chest and stomach, and the legs she lifted and wrapped around him. Sitting at the edge of the bed, he held her, stroking her back.

"*Dieu.*" She pulled away a little to see his face. "I could get used to hugging you."

"Stars, hugs…is there any other normal thing you tragically haven't been able to experience?"

She shrugged. "There is no word for 'hug' in French. People back home don't hug much, unless it's a child…" She caressed up and down his torso hungrily. "…or a lover, but never in public."

His gaze held her almost as strongly as his arms did. She stared back, caught by the sexy curve of his snarky mouth, the passion in his eyes, the strong bones of his face…and dark brows drawn together in deep concentration. Tracing over those well-formed brows again, as she'd done in the park, she savored his expression with the tips of her fingers.

"In that great imagination of yours," she murmured, "did you see me here?"

"You know I did." He smoothed a few curls back that had fallen over her brow. "Every night since I met you in that sexy white dress."

She gasped.

"Does it really surprise you, *petite*? As beautiful, as passionate as you are, that you'd star in someone's dreams?"

It took her breath away, the way his expression turned oddly solemn. The way he said the words—as if he wasn't talking about sex at all, but something that touched more than skin, delved deeper than shallow layers of tissue and bone—ignited more feeling than any nerve could detect. Something that was powerful enough, if she let it, to take the jagged edges of her soul, and fit them to another that was just as broken. There might be a scar where those edges met, but it was okay, so long as it was healed…right?

Was she ready to be that vulnerable? That *naked*? To give someone access to something much more fragile than her body?

Merde, she knew by the way it was hard to breathe, and the sting of tears around the rims of her eyes, that it was too late. Ready or not, she was falling, and she tried very, very hard not to look as scared as she felt.

"Mina."

"*Non*," she whispered. "Only that I'd star in yours."

Then he kissed her, a continuous, sleepy meeting of lips and tongues. The troubles of the moment felt somewhere far, far away, getting farther each time he nudged her with his nose, changing the angle and kissing her again. By the time she pulled back, dizzy with desire and the need to breathe, there was only his mouth, only his arms around her, in this great big room.

"How did you see me?" She rode him slowly, enjoying the tortured sounds he made as he adjusted her over his erection.

"Like this—Oh…*God*…" Gripping her butt, he dragged her harder up and down his length. "And other ways. *So* many ways."

She trailed her tongue over his lush bottom lip, pulling away before he could take her mouth again. He looked like he wanted to devour her, and it made her breathless. "Show me."

"*Petite*," he said hoarsely. "It's been a long day. A lot's happened—"

"*Please*, I need this," she begged against his lips. "I need you to hold me…take my mind off things. I need you to show me."

Groaning, he gently lifted her from his lap, turning her and settling her onto the bed on her knees, then tucking her back against his chest. The sheets were slightly cool at the first touch on her skin, but the heat from his body warmed her everywhere, driving away the chill.

"*Oh, Dieu,*" she sighed, excited to play out one of his fantasies. She shivered at the feel of him pressing against her butt. "*Oui.*"

Curving his hand around her neck, he gave her his thumb, and she sucked it softly, getting wetter at his answering moan. He removed his thumb and smoothed his hands down, down, over her breasts, rubbing them, squeezing them, circling her nipples with his thumbs. Arching her back, she danced her bottom over his erection. He cupped his hand over her pretty new panties, where she was unbearably hot and wet.

"*O-oh…mon Dieu…*"

His fingers dipped into her panties, sliding up and down between her folds, and she bloomed like an orchid for him, offering him the little nub hidden inside.

"You're so sexy, Mina." Pressing harder against her butt, he slipped his long fingers inside of her. Her muscles trembled and clenched, and he cursed. "I can't wait to be inside you, feel you squeezing me just like this."

The lusty rumble in his tone was driving her crazy, his strokes sure and purposeful—but missing the nub completely.

"*Zack…please…*"

"Sshhh, *petite*—little busy here."

Her laugh broke on a whimper, and she could only writhe in pleasure. The muscled curves of his chest were embossed on her back, her nipples rubbing against the strong, sturdy arm that held her to him so tightly.

"*S-s'il te plaît,*" she begged in French this time, riding

313

and riding his fingers, fascinated by the intense need in her own voice.

"You're not ready yet," he murmured against her temple. "I can feel you, you're almost there."

Rubbing firmly with his palm, his fingers glided deeper, her soft inner walls clinging to him desperately.

"*Oh merde…oh merde, merde, merde.*"

Finally, *finally*, he rubbed his thumb over her clit, and her body convulsed, tumbling forward onto the bed. He stayed with her, planting one hand on the mattress beside her head. In this prone position, completely at his mercy, her entire body tingled with vulnerability. It sent the most incredible heat simmering everywhere, and when his thumb circled firmly again, she felt the deluge, heard the slickness of it on his fingers.

"*Yes,*" he whispered. "Now you're ready."

Kissing her again deeply, he trailed kisses down her back, pressing his lips to the dip at her waist, and to the curve of her butt cheek as he pulled her panties down and off. She cried out at the pinch of his teeth there, shuddering at the delicious bite. A moment passed, filled with the sound of their breathing, the dip of the mattress as he removed his briefs. Then, arching over her and pulling her tightly to his chest, he slid into her body. She tensed and tightened instinctively, and he groaned, breathing heavily against her cheek.

"God, *petite.* You don't know what you do to me, do you?" he said hoarsely, pulling back and sliding into her again.

"*Oui.*" She shuddered, swirling her hips to meet him. "The same thing you do to me."

He groaned and filled her again—so full, she gripped

the sheets, close to coming already from the ecstasy of his hard precision, the way he controlled her body so easily, and the way he so clearly enjoyed her. Squeezing her breasts, he thrust his body a little rougher, a little deeper into hers. She clenched down on him once, hard, then shuddered violently, sobbing softly into the sheets. Turning her onto her back, he spread her legs, caressing her until she finished.

"*Oh mon Dieu,* I'm going to die."

Chuckling, he kissed her, all over her face, brushing her hair out of her eyes. "You're not dying. You're just exhausted."

"So." She wet her lips, arching to press against him seductively. "Why don't you put me to sleep?"

"That, I can do."

He stroked in her, slow and deep, her body moving instinctively into his rhythm, absorbing every jerk of his body, every groan, every sigh. Curving his arms underneath her this time, he wrapped her up closely—*hugging* her.

And she absolutely *melted.*

With a soft moan, she gripped him with her arms, her thighs, and very deliberately with the muscles hidden deep inside her body.

"*Petite…*" Even at a whisper, his voice was strained, his hips moving much less gracefully.

"I love when you hug me like this," she whispered close to his ear. "I love how your skin feels on mine."

The breath rushed from him, and he came, his shudders running all through her as he whispered her name. She was so tired, it was like a dream when he finally released her, when he wiped her with a warm cloth, pressing kisses like reverent *Thank yous* on her belly. Covering them with the duvet, he curled up snugly behind her with his face nestled in the fluffy pillow of her hair, and they drifted off to sleep.

CHAPTER TWENTY-ONE

CURIOUS, THE WAY fear and excitement triggered the same heart-dropping sensation.

Zack felt both. It was like being on a roller coaster and sensing the acceleration on the first drop. Like his stomach had been wrenched from his body and left on top of the mountain, his heart falling into its place.

It was finally hitting him.

Lady in Red was happening.

Presently (nine o'clock in the morning), the lady was flying through the air in Alex's luxurious second-story studio, photographed by Luc Davies, the renowned dance photographer they'd flown in from London. They'd agreed on a minimalist approach, with Mina appearing by herself in a stunning, ruby-red chiffon gown that would be eye-catching among the many billboards in Times Square. Her pointe shoes were hand-dyed by the tireless young Amy, who was hired to dress and undress Mina for the show. For as long as Mina was on *his* payroll, her slippers would be dyed by someone else.

For fuck's sake.

After working through the lighting challenges of the

dance studio, Luc set up a white, seamless background and did some test shots, adjusting the flash units to create a white blow-away background that would enable the photos to be easily composited for the official poster, playbill, and other promotional materials. Next, he used strobes to freeze action while capturing Mina's strength and grace in motion. Zack worked with her to make sure her expression was relaxed through her various leaps and poses. The first few shots were a bit shaky, but after that, she *nailed* them.

It was the moments when she looked weightless, flying and floating—like she was dancing on absolutely nothing—that sent exhilaration zipping through his veins. By stroke of luck, or divine intervention, or magic, her eyes met his just as the long, sheer skirt of her gown caught the air perfectly, billowing red all around her as she struck an incredible pose.

His brain immortalized her before the flash did.

She was the living, breathing title of his work, elegantly posed in mid-air. Her back was arched, one arm extending to the tips of her fingers, the other stretching behind her, her silk-wrapped toes pointing toward the floor. A perfect assemblé. The beauty of it snatched his breath—almost like she was suspended in water, rather than air.

"Bloody hell," Luc swore during a few more lightning-fast clicks of his camera. "That's a wrap, sweetheart. That's the one."

Yeah. Zack's heart still pounded like a gorilla's fists in his chest. *No shit.*

Within the hour after Mina's session, the studio was packed with assistants, dressers, makeup and hair artists, press, and all the principals of *Lady in Red*. Faye was there to keep them all in check, and help maneuver them around equipment, props, luxe furniture (on which they'd drape themselves stylishly), and the ladies' voluminous courtesan gowns. Riha had designed the gowns with a modern twist, the skirts cut with a much higher hem in front, to show off the dancers' flawless legs. The men wore her Eastern-infused take on nineteenth-century Parisian fashion, their top hats, vests and shoes vibrant with prints and textures.

Zack tried to be present in the moment, but he couldn't help the flashes of time when he'd look outside himself, watching with pride and a sense of great accomplishment as the cast bonded even closer during the experience. Half of them had gone with him to Mina's apartment the day after it was burglarized, helping her to clear away the mess and get things looking right-side-up again. They'd ribbed each other and exchanged stories, and Kyoko invited Mina to stay with her for a few days. Watching them all now, a week later, he realized it had been a team-building exercise in disguise, forging a new family from a terrible experience.

Mina posed for a mournful long shot, and Kyoko got a makeup check. Sebastian flashed a huge smile during his interview as other principals checked their appearance in the mirrors. He got all the Mina-draped-over-the-baby-grand shots his heart desired—and then some. She even danced on top of it in her pointe shoes. All the while, he'd catch her watching him, too. Sometimes it was a quick glance and an embarrassed smile for being caught. Sometimes, he'd *feel* her looking, then catch her eyes tracking down his body, or staring at his mouth as he gave an interview.

It drove him *insane.*

"No judgment," Faye said from his left, yanking him back into the moment. "But if you two want to keep this thing under wraps, maybe stop the long, yearning stares."

"This *thing*?" He let her herd him toward the setup for the final part of the shoot.

"Look, I'm a feminist, okay?" She presented a stack of papers to him. It was her chicken-scrawled to-do list—an obvious prop to ward off suspicion the conversation was about anything other than work. It was Oscar-worthy, really. "The prime minister of New Zealand had a kid out of wedlock. I want to burn my bra and buy an urn for its ashes."

"I'm afraid we've veered past the point and into The Upside Down."

"It's Broadway, not Hollywood—not that you aren't interesting—but no one's gonna pay a mil for a snap of the two of you sharing a spaghetti noodle…"

"The *point*, Faye."

"It's not a big deal, until it is," she said bluntly. "You're already established. She is too, to be fair. But theater's a different animal. She's getting her feet wet here. It would be a shame for the other animals at the watering hole to talk about anything but how *fabulous* she is, *capisci*?"

Oh God, he'd dragged the Italian out of her. He'd better behave. "Understood."

"Good, get back out there, tiger."

Flashing her his perfected devilish grin, he said loudly, "Actually, I fancy myself more of a lion."

Mina had a sudden fit of coughs, and a drink of water from Amy, before joining him and the rest of the principals in a steamy series of promotional photos.

Hours later, in an enormous room wrapped in mirrors, Zack watched the woman he least wanted to see hurt, dropped to the hard, sweat-shined floor repeatedly—from every direction.

"Stay sharp, Hughes!" he yelled at Sebastian. "I'm throwing her *to* you, not *at* you. So the objective is, of course, to *catch* her."

"Shit, I know." Sebastian winced, rubbing the back of his neck. "My bad, Mina."

"I'm fine," she insisted, glaring at Zack.

Her eyes said, *Put the paws away, I can handle myself.*

He was very tempted to growl his response. Instead, he said, "Let's go again."

It was the last day of a weeks' worth of grueling studio rehearsals with the entire cast: dancers and dance captains, swings and standbys and understudies, accompanied by Harper on the piano, and Carla with her cello in the corner. Those not rehearsing a number sat or stood along the walls, watching with rapt attention. Something was always being tweaked or re-worked, and they needed to take down all of Zack's notes.

Mina was starting to look like a punching bag under her clothes. So far, they'd had energy and opportunity enough to make love twice that week, and both times, he'd seen the impressive collection of old and new bruises dotting her torso.

He'd threatened to wrap her in bubble wrap before rehearsal.

She'd threatened to share the dance belt story.

The measly leotard and footless tights had won out.

The pas de trois was risky, he'd admit, but it was such a provocative visual that, if they got it right—before Mina ended up dead (or Zack killed Sebastian for killing her)—it could be one of the defining moments in the show. It symbolized the tug-of-war between Zack's middle-class character, Armand Duval, and Sebastian's extremely wealthy character, Baron de Varville, for the most beautiful courtesan in all of Paris.

"You're anticipating too much," Zack told Sebastian. "She's not a bag of rocks, so stop worrying about getting hurt." He slapped the younger man's shoulder. "That's what all those strapping muscles are for."

That drew teasing laughter from the rest of the cast. They went through the pas de trois again. Over and over, until Mina looked like she could hardly stand, and Sebastian was able to catch her like she weighed no more than an infant. Rowdy cheers, whistles and applause went up all around the room, and Harper played "Pomp and Circumstance" for shits and giggles.

Zack didn't go easy on them after lunch. They paired up and waltzed in a circle for one of Camille's lavish parties, the men wheeling the women into the air. Zack raced around the floor with Mina, demonstrating Armand's passion by lifting her into a leap every few steps. It was a damned demanding body of work, and the dancers hit the floor so often, they joked good naturedly about it during breaks.

"Oh, I'm madly in love!" *Drop*.

"I'm dying!" *Flop*.

"I simply cannot contain the fire in my loins!" *Plop*.

But it was drama, after, all, so they didn't just fall. They dove, swooned, or fought their way down rapturously, pretending to tear off their outer garments. Zack subjected Mina to his athletic pas de deux for Act One three times, whirling her around his body and hoisting her high, her wrap skirt in his face as he stared amorously up at her. It was a pose that was *supposed* to make them appear besotted with each other, but her acting needed a little work.

321

"*Bordel!*" She was clearly feeling much abused. "Is my character not *dying* of tuberculosis?"

Several people snickered. Zack practically swallowed his tongue to keep his grin in check. Her temper wasn't supposed to be cute. Or hot.

"Technically, yes," he said. "But it's more romantic to call it 'consumption.'"

"*Nom de Dieu!* You're a *man*, of *course* you think it's romantic to throw a sick woman around."

More laughter from the cast…

He hiked a brow at her, unfazed. "If you'd like to depict Camille's fragile health more accurately, you're welcome to cough a few times."

There were snickers, accompanied by some impressive snorts. Then, to Mina's obvious delight, they did it again.

It was after dark when rehearsal wrapped, and Mina was meeting Zack at Vera's new theater at ten o'clock. Well, he *hoped* she was. Given her temper toward the end, there was a chance she wouldn't show.

Who was he kidding? Of course she'd show. The curiosity would kill her otherwise. It was just as well, because he wasn't at all remorseful for pushing her so hard. She was capable of so much more than she thought, and if he had to piss her off to prove it to her, so be it. Still, he wanted to sweeten the ache with a little surprise. There were a few minutes before she was supposed to arrive, so he was checking the rigging for the stage again.

"Everything looks good," said Jamal, the fly captain for the show, and Zack's friend since their days as theater interns. "Highs and lows on the drops are set, and the counterweights are balanced."

"Thanks a lot, man." Zack took Jamal's hand. "I appreciate it."

"Don't mention it. Nice to see you stepped your game up since we were kids." Jamal's smile was bright white. "You don't have to sneak girls backstage anymore. Boss man gets his own theater."

"Not mine, technically."

"Uh-huh. I'll just be here at the ropes. Holler at me when you're ready."

"Will do. And Jamal…"

"I'll let myself out." Jamal grinned knowingly, and Zack headed toward the stage door.

At ten o'clock on the dot, his cell vibrated in his pocket. He didn't bother checking the caller ID. "Hey, pretty girl. You ditch the security detail?"

"*Oui*, at the Metro—*Au fait*, don't call her that," Mina said. "I like Kyoko, and *la police* told me not to go anywhere alone in case some crazy person corners me in an alley and—*Merde!*" She jumped back as he opened the stage entrance door, then went on the attack. "You *scared* me!"

"Who were you expecting?" He laughed, absorbing her fists easily with his chest. "I'm teasing, *petite*. I like Kyoko, too. I like *all* you ingrates, but only one of you's getting a Christmas card."

She looked beautiful, if irritated, in a shirt dress with tiny flowers all over it. "Don't get any ideas. I'm too tired for sex, and my legs feel like rubber, *grâce* à *toi*."

"Happy to see you, too. Even when you threaten me with corporal punishment."

She groaned but let him take her hand and lead her into the theater. It took some maneuvering to get around all the big crates and boxes, coils of rope and cable every-where, ladders, lifts and tool chests.

"What a mess," Mina muttered. "Are you sure it will be ready by opening night?"

He helped her over a large metal pole in their path. "Have a little faith. Say hi to Jamal."

"*Bonsoir*," she said, looking slightly uncomfortable.

Jamal smiled ear-to-ear. "Not to worry, m'lady. Me and Zack go way back."

Zack scoffed. "'M'lady? *Really*?"

Jamal shrugged, and Mina gave him a little smile. "*Enchanté.*"

Tipping his baseball cap, Jamal turned back to the ropes, and Zack steered her along again. They cleared the backstage area unharmed, walking to the center of the large stage and looking out into the auditorium.

She gasped, her eyes enormous. "*Oh mon Dieu...*"

"Indeed."

Blowing an appreciative breath, he folded his arms over his chest and stared at the phase of Vera's legacy most people would never get to see. The floor plan was oval, rather than the horseshoe or square layout of most theaters—which was easy to see since none of the seats had been installed yet. It was a vast, empty space, surrounded by lavish décor in royal blue, pale blue, and gold. The levels were staggered, with three rows of balconies trimmed in gold leaf, French-style boxes, and a colonnade stretching up to a magnificent blue vaulted ceiling encircled by crystal chandeliers.

"It looks like a palace," she whispered.

"Yeah, it looks like *money*."

Walking to stage left, she stroked her hand down one of the heavy, pale blue velvet curtains trimmed with golden tassels. "It's so beautiful—and so different. Not red, like most theaters."

"Something tells me that's exactly why Vera chose it." He took her hand again and walked them to the edge of the stage. "That's not even the best part. What do the walls look like to you?"

Frowning, she turned her head in a slow survey of the space. "Marble?"

"*Faux* marble. It's almost entirely made of painted wood—which *means…*" Taking a deep breath, he burst into song, doing "Master of the House" from *Les Mis*.

"*Ahhh*!" Cringing dramatically, she covered her ears. "You're insane!"

"Maybe, but I can't think of a better way to test the *excellent* acoustics in this place. You won't have to worry about projecting in here, *petite*. If you mumble under your breath, some guy all the way up there in the back is gonna answer you."

"Or back here," Jamal yelled from backstage.

Mina's hand flew to her mouth, and Zack snatched her up while she was still laughing, twirling her around the stage and serenading her with the rest of the song, deeply amused at how much he was embarrassing her.

"*Allez*!" she squealed, pounding his chest. "*Arrêtes,* you fool!"

They were center stage, exactly where he wanted her. Resting his arms low on her back, he smiled into her glowing face, then turned his head to yell, "Now!"

A few seconds later, there was a mechanical sound, and Mina tilted her head back, looking straight up into the hundred-story fly tower as a massive piece of scenery slowly descended to the stage. "Zack?"

"Wait for it." He squeezed her hips.

There was another mechanical whir, the stage vibrated, and more scenery began to move onto the stage along tracks in the floor. Fifteen seconds more, and they were nearly surrounded by stunning mirror mosaics stretching twenty feet high. Only the side facing the auditorium was left open.

Zack grinned into Mina's stunned face. "Lights."

With a final whir, lights came on overhead, and a magnificent crystal chandelier came down slowly. The intricate geometric designs in the mosaics refracted light from every angle, making it look like millions of diamonds were shimmering all around them.

"Clear?" Jamal called out.

"All clear!" Zack didn't take his eyes off Mina's face. Patterns of light danced all over her skin.

"See you tomorrow," said Jamal.

"Goodnight!" Zack returned.

Jamal's footsteps faded, then there was the sound of the stage door being opened and closed, and they were alone.

"It's…dazzling," Mina murmured, "but what *is* it?"

"The mosaics are a mixture of colored glass and mirror." Zack traced the pattern on one of her arms. "The idea came to me in a dream, that night after our fight in rehearsal."

She snorted. "Which one?"

"Point taken—The one where you kept checking yourself in the mirrors."

"*Oui*, and you yelled at me."

"After which, your friend Sophie kindly handed me my ass, and I guess the guilt stuck with me in sleep."

"So, you dreamed of…mirrors?"

"Well, like always, I dreamed of *you*. Dancing in a room covered from floor-to-ceiling in shattered mirrors. I screwed up that day in rehearsal, *petite*. I was annoyed that you were so distracted by your flaws, you couldn't see how incredible you were—Are you gonna cry?"

"*N-non*." She sniffed. "Go on."

He kissed her then, because she was such a sap and he fucking *loved* it. It made him want to surprise her all the time. "I realized, by not letting you be who you are, I was stifling you, and I'm sorry for that. So, I added a scene—*this* scene. No dialogue. No lyrics. Just you, en pointe, showing the audience why you're one of the best ballerinas in the world."

She gasped. "All this…it's for *me*?"

"It is."

Turning around once, slowly, she seemed to take it all in with new eyes—eyes that were already filling with tears. He tracked her movement as she walked up close to the mosaics, reaching out to finger the broken glass. "They're *huge*. It must have taken forever to make them."

"Careful, *petite*." Coming up beside her, he watched their distorted reflections. "There's one more thing."

She looked at him expectantly.

"It won't be choreographed."

Her gasp was one of horror this time. "Zack! I *can't*…"

"You *can*." She opened her mouth to protest, and he took her small hands in his. "The singular reason any ballerina makes it as far as you have, is what she adds to the dance—not the other way around."

"But…what will I do?"

He shrugged. "I don't care if you get up here and dance the same steps every time, because I know you'll bring something new to those steps night after night. For Camille, it's a moment of introspection before she makes a big decision. For *Mina?* Consider it…an outlet. For three and a half minutes, you get to do what no one else in this show is gonna get to do."

"Whatever I want?"

One of her tears followed the pattern on her cheek, and he bent to lick it away. "Whatever you want."

A hurricane formed behind her eyes, and then she was shoving at him—very aggressively, he might add—toward the wings. Laughing, he stumbled at first, then walked backward, since that was clearly what she wanted him to do. His back hit something firm, but not hard enough to be a wall. In fact, it gave a little and he registered that they were tucked between the folds of the heavy blue stage curtain. Then, he registered the sultry look on her face, and his body temperature kicked up by about twenty degrees.

"*Petite?*" His voice was gravelly. "What are you doing?"

Giving him a sexy smile, she took his face in her hands. "Thanking you."

"I admire your enthusiasm, but—"

She cut him off, and damn.

Damn, damn, damn.

She was *hungry.* He could taste it on her lips, in the urgency of the deep, thorough sweeps of her tongue. He heard it in her shuddering sigh, felt it in the way she pressed into him, moving her body in a suggestive dance against his. Gripping her hips, he pressed her harder into his pelvis, and she moaned low in her throat before she pulled away, breathing deeply.

"*Merci.*" Her eyes were half closed and black with desire. "*Merci,*" she whispered again, kissing his neck… "*Merci…*"

She nipped his pecs over his T-shirt, a tiny pinch of pain

that made him moan, his heart thudding faster, pounding a rhythm in his brain that muffled her husky voice—but dear God he felt it. He felt it when she pushed his shirt up, rubbing it over his chest, breathing *mercis* hotly into his skin… and when she caught his eyes with a starving look, then licked slow circles across his abdomen.

"Jesus…*petite*…"

Instinctively, he knew the path her lips made down his body, the intent of her nimble fingers at his belt, the promise in her eager little moans. And he wanted it. He *wanted* to want it… more than he'd wanted anything else in his entire life.

He wanted to be sated by her.

But when her breath heated the skin of his lower belly, and her fingers teased the edge of his briefs, he felt the desire get seized by something else. It got all twisted and distorted. Turned into something ugly. Shameful. It was slipping away from him—the control he so desperately needed. His blood seemed to run cold in his veins, reversing direction and tripping everything up. He moved like a compulsion, shoving her away.

She cried out, and the sound of her distress locked his body in shock. For a moment, he couldn't think, couldn't move. He could only stare at her as she rose gracefully from the floor.

"Mina—I…" His insides twisted at the confusion, and then the hurt, on her face. "Dammit, I'm sorry."

"I—I'm sorry," she stammered, straightening herself out, shifting awkwardly. She met his eyes directly, then froze. He saw it the moment she figured it out—when little tidbits of his life from their countless conversations, and the details of all their intimate moments, stitched themselves together like patchwork pieces of a filthy, moth-eaten quilt in her brain. "Zachary…"

The cold in his veins turned icy. "Don't, *petite*."

But it was too late. Fat tears already fell from her eyes. "What happened to you?

He took a hard, shuddering breath.

"No monster is too big," she said softly.

God, everything seethed—his head, his chest, his heart and arteries and veins —creating relentless, unbearable pressure. He wanted to cut himself open for her, let them bleed. But he'd never let himself be that vulnerable with anyone but Carmen and his childhood therapists for years. Manny knew, but only because Carmen kept no secrets from him.

Besides, he'd been right to cordon off that part of his past, to avoid the pity he saw in Mina's eyes that very second. He didn't *need* pity. He didn't need saving. He'd saved himself years ago, turned the universe inside out, rewritten his story, changed his fate. No longer a victim, he was a hero.

And heroes didn't bleed.

"*Gods* don't bleed," Mina whispered, "but heroes do."

Fuck. He hadn't realized he'd said it aloud.

It was that invitation in her eyes, ever compelling.

Whenever they'd said, *Come hither,* he had.

Whenever they'd said, *Believe me*, he had.

Now, they said, *Tell me,* and he couldn't help himself.

Dragging his fingers through his hair, he sighed. He could write a comic for her, make her a truth-inducing superhero. She'd wear special tinted glasses to shield her from being inundated with the secrets of every stranger who looked directly into her eyes.

"You could tell me," she said, as if reading his thoughts. "If you wanted, if you tried, you wouldn't have to push me away. Hurt me. You could just…let me share yours."

The armor around his heart caved in, crushing him at the crack in her voice. His *heart* trusted her, beating ferociously, sending Morse code pulses to every extremity that said, *Tell her. Tell her. Tell her.* But telling her would mean he wasn't a hero anymore. It would strip away his cape. Make him ordinary. He couldn't be ordinary. He couldn't just be someone to her. He needed to be *somebody*.

He needed to be *everything*.

Wiping his hand over his features, he ignored the lump in his throat, ready to do what he always did when someone got too close. "How can you expect me to tell you something so personal when you're keeping something just as big to yourself? I've been trying to get you to open up to me for *weeks*. You *still* shut down when I ask you about Étienne."

"That's *different*! He has nothing to do with us!"

"Doesn't he? You keep him close to you like a secret. People who trust each other? They tell each other their secrets."

"*Dieu!* I'm not the one hiding, Zachary." She swiped her tears away. "*You* are. Behind your wit, and your…*charisme*." Her chest heaved a few times, and then she seemed to gain control again, her expression softening. "You've been hurt…so badly. But you still find it in you to treat everyone with so much more compassion than you show yourself."

His body jerked, his chest tightening at the precision of her arrow. "I guess you have me all figured out then, huh, *petite*?"

"*Non*," she said with a calmness he couldn't read. "That's the point. I *don't*."

"I'm sorry I hurt your ego, okay?"

Shaking her head, she looked at him sadly. "It's not my ego you're hurting."

Then it was quiet.

Demons from his past, ghosts from hers—monsters, all of them—filled the space between them in the silence. Feeding off it. Off everything they weren't saying. Growing and growing until he couldn't stand it any longer…or the compassion persisting in her eyes despite his attempt to hurt her. She'd seen right through it, and coward that he was, he fixed his belt and turned away from her with pain in his gut. Because he'd rather deal with an ulcer, than let her see him bleed out.

"Zack…"

"Come on, *petite*. I'll make sure you get home safely."

Chapter Twenty-Two

MERDE.

Four days felt like an eternity when she was being stabbed constantly. Every time Zack looked at her, it was with daggers. Or, he would play target practice with her pupils, like they were little hearts and he wanted to pierce them with arrows—which just made it worse that he *still* wouldn't talk to her. Unless he was in character or directing (yelling).

"Christ, that was *excruciating*," he yelled from the pitch-black void of the house.

Enfin, that was how it looked to Mina, anyway. With the lights on, onstage, she couldn't see a thing. *He* obviously could, because she felt his cold green daggers between her ribs.

Stab, stab, stab.

She made sure to glare in his general direction.

"We've been off-book for two days, people," he griped. "That harmony should be nice and clean—no straggling voices. *Again.*"

"Music," the stage manager, Chuck, called out, and they went through the chorus again.

The other courtesans and gentlemen artfully dispersed,

businessing about upstage like aloof city folk, leaving Mina and Kyoko downstage, closest to the audience.

"Your heart is bigger than your pocket book, Camille," Kyoko said, in character as Camille's best friend, Prudence. Her arm was hooked through Mina's as they strolled down the imaginary streets of nineteenth century Paris. "And I *love* you for it, darling. But you're in debt, to the tune of *thousands*."

Camille plucked at the vivid red petals of her invisible bouquet of camellias. "You worry too much."

"*Someone* should! The cost of making you look rich is making you poor."

"Well, as long as I don't *look* poor…"

Prudence stopped, appraising Camille brazenly. "You look *beautiful,* which is fleeting." On cue, Camille went into a coughing fit, and Prudence looked *very* concerned. "Nothing fades beauty faster than sickness, and that cough's gotten worse."

"I'm fine." Camille was all brightness and vitality. "Really, I just need fresh air. Paris is turning into a *chimney.*"

"And *you* are turning twenty-one, practically an old maid."

"Cheat, Kyoko," Zack directed from the abyss. "The audience should see your face when you say that line. Really ham it up here—and Mina, counter. I can't see you."

Oui, Mina was aware he couldn't see her because she had been using Kyoko as a human shield. For a full, glorious minute, she hadn't felt his piercing stare. Sighing, she adjusted her position.

Stab, stab, stab.

She tempered her expression to seem wistful. "I wish I could get married—for *love,* can you imagine?"

Prudence threw her head back in a sing-song laugh. "Marriage isn't in the cards, *chérie*. Not for us."

"What about love?"

"Certainly, so long as you fall in love with a rich man." Prudence took what was left of Camille's naked camellia, plucking the last of its petals. "I know *just* the one—Baron de Varville. He's desperate to meet you, and I told him I'd introduce you…"

"*Prudence*!" Camille looked appropriately aghast.

"Tonight, at the theatre." Prudence pinched Camille's cheeks, inviting a flush of color to her presumably dimmed complexion. "That's better. Wear gold. It suits you."

"Lights," Chuck called, and the stage went dark.

Everything was madness for a minute, as Mina dashed backstage with the other actors and Chuck supervised the crew setting up the next scene. She narrowly missed colliding with a stagehand, still learning where her track was, the invisible path she'd follow backstage during every show. Everyone had their own tracks, and the choreography backstage was just as intricate as any onstage, making sure cast and crew navigated the limited space without crashing into each other.

Amy materialized at her side. "How are you?"

"*Eh*, I'm not sure." Mina watched Sebastian bump into one of the hair dressers. "It all seems so chaotic, like it's going to be a complete disaster."

Amy laughed. "That's what putting on a show feels like. It *always* feels like it's going to be shit, like those last details will never come together. Because there are a million moving parts. Like props—I had to keep track of a *broom* for Fiddler on the Roof last season and it was the bane of my existence. But somehow it all falls into place."

Mina gave her a small smile. She liked her, which was great since Amy would be seeing all her bits and pieces.

"We'll do your quick-change for the next scene here," Amy said. "We only have about two minutes, so there's no time to get to a dressing room—Don't *worry*." She seemed to read Mina's mind. "Next week's tech week. It'll feel like second nature by then."

"I hope so."

"Beginners!" Chuck cued the actors for the next scene. "I need Allende, Coen, Mori and Hughes."

Mina's heart dislodged in her chest. It was time to be stabbed at close range.

It was the shittiest déjà vu, feeling Mina's little flinch whenever he touched her—which was only the quick brush of their fingers since their characters were meeting for the first time in this scene. There must be a million nerves in the fingertips, and every single one of his was buzzing. His skin was starved for her, prickling at the smallest contact. He had no fucking idea how he'd lived before meeting her, how he'd managed not to feel lonely, or gotten enough sleep at night. Let his body tell it, he *hadn't* been living, only existing.

Worse, was her wincing every time he met her eyes. It was subtle, like a little nerve tick in her face. At some point in the last couple days, he'd sensed her pity for him turn to anger, and for some twisted reason, he preferred it. He'd rather deal with her temper than sympathy, than being reduced to a victim in her eyes. Someone vulnerable. Weak.

"Keep to your marks," Chuck said, snatching Zack from his reverie. "Tetley Theatre's rigged for stage animation, so you'll be up in your fake box seats about ten feet off the stage."

Adjusting his position, Zack took a sweeping bow,

posing as the Baron du Varville—a fact the audience would know, but not Camille.

"*Enchanté*," she said demurely, offering him her hand.

Again, he clasped her fingers, and again, she reached inside him and melted his insides out. "You're the most beautiful woman I've ever seen."

Her breath caught—quite convincingly—and she snatched her hand away.

"That's not quite the reaction I'm used to getting," he quipped, off-script, and laughter filtered out from the wings.

Wincing (again), he had to feed her her next line, which seemed to fluster her further…and getting through the scene was torture.

"Let's take five," he finally said, when it was clear they weren't convincing anyone it was love at first sight.

Mina bolted from the stage.

He didn't seek her out. That wouldn't have been fair, and frankly, he had no idea what to say. Nothing he said would take the place of the conversation she wanted from him, and he wasn't ready to give. So, five minutes later, they did it again. This time, she may as well have been wearing a half mask for a masquerade because Mina was nowhere in sight. Camille took over the stage.

"You're the most beautiful woman I've ever seen," he said.

"That's kind."

"It's true, and the cleverest, too."

Fanning herself coquettishly, she set her body to seem surprised. "Are not the ladies in your circles clever?"

"Indeed, as clever as their limited education allows. It's the greatest irony, don't you think, that one such as you, snubbed by society for your profession, possesses more education than many of the finest ladies?"

Camille seemed to forget her façade, revealing her honest nature. "I don't find it ironic at all, but sad."

Armand looked stunned. "You pity the women who resent you for your beauty?"

"It's not my beauty they resent, but my freedom."

Zack fixed his expression and body language to seem quite enthralled. "Your freedom, mademoiselle?"

"Yes. I come and go as I please. I'm as educated as any man."

"But, as any woman, you depend on a man to keep you."

"I get to *choose*. I am not chosen."

There was a dramatic pause, an invisible spark kindled, but before Armand could reply, Kyoko burst onto the scene with Sebastian at her side.

"Oh, there you are, Camille! See? There she is! Isn't she lovely? Camille, this is the Baron du Varville, who is very pleased to make your acquaintance."

Camille looked aghast, collecting herself quickly, and allowing the true baron to kiss her hand. She shared a longing look with Armand, who slipped quietly from the theatre box.

They took another five, so the crew could dress the next scene, then rehearsed. Six months passed in *Lady in Red*'s timeline, and Armand and Camille met again at a party. She was the baron's mistress now, and Armand was desperately in love with her. They snuck to the garden, which would be cleverly revealed by a revolving set onstage. On one side, the lavish party would go on. On the other, Zack and Mina would play star-crossed lovers under custom lighting to mimic a starry night.

"How could you deceive me?" she cried. "You made me like you, and then you turned away."

Jesus. Either she was method acting, or those were real tears. There was silence in the wings, and a pin drop could be heard onstage.

"Because I loved you before I met you," he professed. "I followed you for weeks, certain you would not have me."

"I would have had you." She coughed, sounding progressively worse. "And now, it's too late."

"It's not too late, my darling." He touched her cheek, and she closed her eyes. "You're unwell. Come to the country with me. Let me take care of you."

"Cue music," Chuck called out.

Zack pulled Mina into a dreamy waltz, shivering with relief to hold her again, as he did every day since stage rehearsals began. If she noticed, it didn't show in her face. She was thoroughly Camille, and he sang to her his rousing petition:

Let me take care of you.

Tell me what you need.

Tell me I'm essential,

That all you need is me.

Maybe, maybe then,

There's a chance we can get by,

A chance I'll make you happy,

A chance that we can try.

Please take care of me,

Of the heart I give to you.

Don't leave it with the other gifts

From suitors come to woo;

To sit there on your vanity

like vanity itself,

And make me covet you,

when all you want is wealth.

Let me take care of you.

Tell me what you need.

Tell me I'm essential,

That all you need is me.

"Curtain," Chuck called out again, noticeably quieter.

Mina stepped from his embrace—less reluctantly than he'd written in the script—but he heard her little sniff before she walked off the stage. She wasn't the only one, apparently. Either someone was chewing hot chili peppers in the wings, or they'd nailed it.

By Friday night, Zack was confident they'd be ready for tech week. They'd had a good rehearsal. If he was honest, it had been a *great* rehearsal. Even the perfectionist in him could admit that. Still, it wasn't *incredible*. Not yet. Most of the cast had their lines down, choreography was second-nature, voices were fine-tuning, and the stage animation and scene painting were nearly complete. The biggest nightmare, according to Riha, was finishing the beading on Mina's party gown for the second act in time for previews. For that, she'd insisted, she needed two more assistants, each with tiny hands.

Grabbing dinner from a food truck, he ducked under a corner store awning to dial his mother.

"Let me guess," Carmen answered. "You won't make it to dinner on Sunday?"

"*Lo siento*, but I have to wrap up a few details before tech week next week."

"You're gonna work yourself to death for that crazy woman."

"Vera's been generous, *mamá*. It's a big risk for her, throwing money at a first-time director. It's nice to have support for my vision without feeling micromanaged."

"That better not be a dig at your father. You two need to patch things up already."

"I know, and I will, when I have time."

"*Make* time. You know he's been stressed lately, trying to make sure our little working-class neighborhood doesn't get smothered by coffee shops and chain stores. We support you, *always*, but try to see his perspective."

"I see it, *mamá*, but I'm not trying to build a dance school to 'clean up the neighborhood' or drive up the rents. It's for *us*. It'll be *part* of the neighborhood. The heart of it. A little trust would be nice."

He heard her sharp intake of breath, and was about to apologize, when she spoke again. "What's wrong, *mijo*?"

Massaging between his brows, he expelled a breath too, one he felt like he'd been holding in for days. "She knows."

Carmen was quiet, long enough for an Uptown bus to stop with a '*tss*,' unload its passengers and load up again, then pull off into late night traffic. "Are you okay?"

"I don't have a simple answer for that."

"I didn't ask for one," she said gently. "I only ever want you to tell me the truth. No matter what, okay? So, tell me the *not* simple answer."

Some asshole ducked under the awning and stood right

next to him, puffing a cigarette. Shooting him a scowl, Zack left his temporary sanctuary. He was one of a million people on their cells, dancing the sidewalk tango to avoid crashing into each other. Anywhere else, he wouldn't have this conversation out in public. Here, he could light himself on fire and they'd all just cross to the other side of the street. "Not simply? No. I don't think I'm okay. I don't think she is, either."

"What happened?"

"You really want to talk about my sex life?"

"*Oh.*"

"Yeah."

"I know you don't want to hear this," she said carefully. "*Papi* was wrong to put you on the spot like that at dinner, but what he said about you needing to be in control…"

"*Mamá*…"

"I'm *so* proud of you. As a dancer and choreographer, you've mastered your own body, taught others to master theirs…but at some point, you have to confront the reason you find a few *un*choreographed moments of intimacy so frightening."

Nearly colliding with a business woman who looked like she'd bludgeon him with one of her heels, he ducked into a phone booth—It smelled like a urinal. "I think it's pretty well documented that I *have* confronted it. Hours and hours of sitting in someone's office confronting it. I'm *tired* of confronting it. I'm ready to move past it and get on with my life."

"I'm not talking about that. I'm talking about your need to choreograph everything. Your need to be in control."

"For fuck's sake…" There was that word again.

It might have been the first time in his life she didn't

scold him for his language. "I think I can guess, at this point…but tell me, *mijo,* what is she to you?"

"Everything." It came out in a rush of breath. Because it was that easy. And hard as all hell. Mina was like a hurricane that had blown into his life and stirred everything up. "It's never been like this before. I've *always* been able to focus. With Mina…I find myself stopping everything because there's a poem, or a song, or just one line in my head that I *have* to write for her."

"*Ah, ya veo,*" Carmen breathed. "She's your muse."

It was true. She *was* his muse. She was the muse, the expression, the art…*everything.*

"Has she seen any of it?" Carmen asked.

"God, no."

"Maybe you should show her."

His pulse went nuts at the thought. He'd written most of it just to get it out of his head, for his own sanity. Showing it to Mina would put him in the most vulnerable position he'd ever been. It was frightening as fuck.

"Maybe." He bit his cheek. "But I have to fix this first."

"You know you can't fix things with her until you stop fighting yourself."

"In theory, yes. I do know that. Much as I'd love to live in theory, reality isn't so easy."

"And that's okay. If you're too afraid to be vulnerable and tell her what's in your heart, then let her read it."

Let her read it.

His mother really was a genius.

❧

"What's wrong?" Sophie asked through Mina's speakerphone. "Is my replacement mistreating you? If she is, I'll come out there and kick her ass."

Turning onto her back, Mina stared at the ceiling fan. It was dark in her room, but she'd been awake for an hour now and her eyes had long adjusted. If she focused them, she could track a single blade, as if it spun in slow motion. "Kyoko isn't your replacement. She's Kyoko."

"Good, because you already have a sassy friend with incredible hair—who, by the way, was in the middle of some *serious* REM sleep."

"I'm sorry."

She lost focus, and the fan's blade disappeared in a blur, just like Étienne had in her dream. One moment he was scolding her about the expiration date on her mascara, telling her that her lashes would fall out if she continued to use it, and the next he was gone. She sniffed.

"Say it out loud," Sophie nudged. "I can't read your mind, *chère*."

"I know, it's just…" Mina's voice sounded small, even to her own ears. For someone so physically strong, and with a will that had withstood everything life had hurled at it, her tear trigger was pretty weak. *Merde*. She was so *tired* of crying. "I'm heartbroken, Sophie."

"Oh, Mina… I'm so sorry. Tell me what happened."

She did, explaining everything as best she could without giving specific details about the horrors Zack had suffered as a child. She told her about Carmen and Manny, and how they'd rescued a special ten-year-old boy who had grown up to be a very, very complicated man. She shared how much she'd opened up to him, more than anyone else she'd dated—more than *anyone*, really—and how he was keeping her at arm's length now.

"And you're sure he's got you out in the rain?" Sophie asked. "Maybe he just needs some space to sort himself out, and then he will talk to you."

"*Non*, you should have seen his face, Sophie. It was so determined. He's the one out there all alone in the rain, and I'm just…not enough to convince him to come back inside." She felt a sob churning up in her throat, and quickly gulped it down. "If he'd asked me for space, I would feel so much better, but I don't think he intends to talk to me at all. I feel so *stupide*."

"Stop it, *chère*. You said yourself, he's complicated. And anyway, things between you have been intense since the beginning. It makes sense you'd fight intensely, too."

"I *wish* he'd fight. I'm *used* to fighting with him. It's the silence that scares me."

"Why should it scare you? You've hardly known him two months…"

"But I *do* know him, Sophie. I've spent almost all my hours with him in those two months. I—" Her call waiting beeped. "*Un moment*…The number is French, but I don't recognize it."

"I'll be here…with my eyelids taped open."

Laughing a little despite things, Mina clicked over. "*Allô?*"

"Mina? It's Noémie." She spoke in rapid French. "Your mother's been shot. She's in surgery now. I'm calling from the hospital. I'd have called sooner, but your mother didn't want you to worry. I booked you the earliest flight out of New York…"

Mina heard nothing else, because she'd dropped her phone.

CHAPTER TWENTY-THREE

NEVER HAD THE seven-hour flight across the Atlantic felt so long. Mina didn't sleep a wink. By the time she'd boarded her plane at John F. Kennedy airport, her mother was already out of surgery, so she'd spent the entire flight going over and over the details Noémie had given her.

Her *maman* had forgotten something the morning before. When she'd returned to her apartment to get it, she'd interrupted a burglary in-progress. Noémie was waiting in the car outside when she heard the gunshot, saw a man fleeing, then ran up to the apartment to find her mother bleeding on the floor of her bedroom. Surgery had been required to find the source of the internal bleeding. It turned out to be her spleen, with the bullet still inside. They'd operated to remove them both.

Mina shivered at the eerie déjà vu. The same thing might have happened to her in New York if she hadn't been with Zack the night her own apartment was burglarized.

Zachary…

Impending doom had a peculiar way of trivializing all other matters. When it seemed her mother's life was hanging in the balance, every other worry, every other gargantuan fear, had faded to specks. She hadn't even hesitated to call him last night.

"*I'm coming with you,*" he said.

"*Non, you can't. You can't just leave in the middle of—*"

"*I can. I will, if you want me to.*" He said it with absolute confidence, as if he had a plane waiting right outside Alex's brownstone to carry him halfway around the world at a moment's notice.

"*But how?*"

"*Let me worry about that, petite. Have a safe flight. I'll see you soon.*"

His flight was arriving little more than an hour after hers, and Mina still had no *clue* how he'd managed it. She landed in Paris at six on Saturday evening, and a car took her straight to Hôpital Pitié-Salpêtrière. Noémie met her in the lobby shortly after receiving her text. She'd been her mother's assistant for a decade and had become like an aunt. Looking as tall and put-together as ever, there wasn't a strand of dark hair out of place, and only faint circles were visible beneath spare makeup and a perpetual red lip, her black heels clicking on the tiled floor.

"Oh good, you remembered to change." Noémie spoke in French, looking Mina over with approval.

"*Oui.*" It was silly, worrying about her clothes and hair at a time like this, but it was comforting, too, to know her mother would probably fuss over her appearance even from her grave. *Enfin*, it was comforting until that last thought.

"It's good to see you, *chère*," Noémie said. "I'm sorry for the circumstances, but the operation was successful. If all goes well, your mother can go home in a week or so."

"So long?" Mina walked at double Noémie's pace to keep up with her brisk steps, skillfully weaving through people coming and going—visitors with flowers, nurses and doctors rushing back and forth, and departing patients being wheeled to their waiting taxis.

"*Oui*. No other organs were damaged, but bullets are dirty, so they're pumping her with antibiotics to prevent infection. She lost a lot of blood, too, so I don't want you to be shocked by the tubes."

Mina took a deep breath, steeling herself. "Is she awake?"

Noémie nodded. "And she knows you're here." She took Mina's elbow gently when they reached the elevators. "There's something you should know, before you see her."

"Tell me."

"Your mother will skin me alive—She hates when you worry. She didn't want you to see her like this, but I wanted to give you some…reassurance…before we go up there."

"Go on, *s'il te plaît*."

"After surgery last night, they gave the bullet to ballistics. This afternoon, they confirmed the bullet is *exactly* like the ones they found in Monsieur Bernard, and from… from…"

"*Étienne*." Her heart stopped—She actually *felt* it stop beating—right before it made a slow, sickening drop to the pit of her stomach. "H-how could they know…and so quickly?"

"It's a big case. Bigger than we were initially told. Apparently, they've been collecting evidence since the…for almost a year now. The bullet they took from your mother was the last piece they needed. They've already made several arrests."

Mina felt dizzy, which hardly ever happened, given the fact she twirled around in circles for a living. "Several?" She pressed a hand to her stomach. "But who? Who are they?"

"Four so far, but I have strict instructions not to stress you with details right now. Judging by the color your skin just turned, I've already said enough." She pushed the button for the elevator. "For your protection, I've made arrangements for you to stay outside the city tonight."

"For *my* protection? I don't understand."

"It's just a precaution. It's been a little while, but *la police* are aware that you were mugged…that your apartment was also burglarized. There's little evidence to suggest they're connected, but the odds seem slim that they aren't."

Mina started to protest, but Noémie was firm. "It's what your mother wants, *chère*."

Mirielle brooked no argument. Ever. It would be a waste of time. So, without another word, Mina followed Noémie into the elevator. There was a uniformed officer outside her mother's recovery room. Inside, there were fresh-cut flowers on a table near the window. A nurse administered pain medication and checked Mirielle's staples. After giving her a new dressing, the nurse nodded at Mina and quietly made her exit.

"*Minette*." Mirielle's voice sounded tired and small, and *exactly* like she'd just had major surgery. "Come here, let me see you." There were IVs in both her arms, and even the slightest movement had her face twisting in obvious discomfort. "You look well. Strong."

"Ça va, *maman*?" Mina kissed her freckled cheeks, then sat in the chair next to her bed.

Mirielle sniffed irritably. "Truthfully, I'm in agony, and these drugs make me feel like I've been hit by a train. I'd rather be miserable at home, but I'm stuck here watching soap operas until your *mémé* comes."

"I'm so sorry, *maman*." Mina tried to keep her voice

steady, but it was dreadful seeing her formidable mother so pale and run through with tubes. "I'm glad *mémé* is coming. Someone should be here to take care of you."

"Oh, *minette*. You see? This is why I didn't want you to come. You always worry. You can worry from New York. It does no one any good here."

"You're right." Mina touched her mother's arm, trying to work up the courage to ask the million questions in her head. "*Maman—*"

"Not now, Wilhelmina." She used a remote to turn off the television, wincing at even that small motion. "When Monsieur Coen arrives, you'll get your answers."

Mina nearly fell out of her chair. "*P-pardon?*"

"*Enfin*, he's here, is he not?"

"Not yet." Her face felt hot. "How did you know he was coming?"

"I checked Noémie's phone while she was asleep in that chair. She spent the night here, which was completely unnecessary." Mirielle didn't look the least bit ashamed. "She was giving Monsieur Coen the hospital address. I don't imagine many directors take impromptu international flights to check on their actors' ailing family members, so there's obviously something going on with you two."

Mina stood and started pacing. "It's complicated, *maman*."

"It must *be*. In any case, I'm glad. Stop pacing—you know it drives me mad."

"You're not going to lecture me about propriety?"

"*Non.*"

Mina folded her arms over her chest. "Why not?"

"Because I've just been shot. Because I'm *tired, minette*. And because that man might be pushier than *me*."

"You *spoke* to him?"

"*Oui*, I called him from Noémie's phone last night. I hate texting, and it would have been rude not to reply. He sounded *very* worried…about you, I imagine. He seemed confident *I'd* make a full recovery—he sent a card with the flowers."

Mina walked to the window to see the vibrant bouquet up close. Tucked beneath the vase, was a small white card:

As organs go, spleens aren't so important. After negotiating with you, I'm convinced you'll live to be 100 without one.

-Zachary Coen

Laughing tearfully, she replaced the card, then hugged herself.

"Yesterday morning, Noémie and I were meeting a former client." Mirielle's voice was shaky.

Turning around, Mina met her mother's eyes. Were those *tears*? She rushed to her side. "*Maman*?"

"I'm fine, *minette*. Just…let me finish."

Mina sat in the chair and waited.

"The client was Madame Lansac, the one who owned that Roman-era statue we sold for twenty million euros? Anyway, on my way out, the thing I forgot was…the proofs you sent me, from the photoshoot for your show. I…wanted to show them off to Madame Lansac—She's always bragging about her grandson, and I wanted to brag about you."

"*Dieu*, this is all my fault." Mina's heart was already in her stomach. Now it turned and turned.

"Don't be ridiculous. Did *you* make me forget them?

Did you send that *bâtard* to shoot me? I'm not telling you this to make you feel guilty. I'm telling you because…I don't tell you enough, *minette,* how incredibly proud of you I am."

The meaning of the words hung heavily in the air. Not the words themselves, exactly, but the fact she'd said them aloud. Her mother seemed to show the same excitement for Mina's accomplishments as she showed for a good espresso, or a perfectly baked pastry. It wasn't something Mirielle typically celebrated. It was *expected*. Hearing her say this now, after so many years starving for just such acknowledgment, somehow didn't hurt. Somehow, it was exactly what she needed to hear.

"You *hate* boasting, *maman*."

"I do. It's tacky." Mirielle carefully reached for Mina's hand, and Mina took it readily. "But I couldn't stand to hear her going on and on about her mediocre grandson who's been funneled into Oxford from his father's prep school—not when I manage the third-highest-paid ballerina in the entire world, who got there with *hard work*."

"*Fourth*-highest, remember?"

"I had my spleen removed, not my brain. Since the Tonys, we've had offers for two beauty campaigns, an athletic ad, and several perfume contracts. Obviously, you'll need to decide which you'll want to accept, but just one bumps that Tanya Rutskaya from number three, to number four." Yawning, she writhed subtly, like she was trying to get comfortable.

"*Maman*, you should rest. We can talk about this later."

"*Oui.* I need to sleep, but I wanted you to hear it from me. You really are exceptional, Wilhelmina. I love you, very much."

"I love you too, *maman*."

"When Monsieur Coen arrives, Noémie will drop you to the train. You'll stay in Burgundy tonight."

"Wine country? But—"

"Wilhelmina, I'm tired. Please don't argue."

Sighing, Mina kissed her mother's forehead, and quietly left the room.

Zack got there *two* hours later, filling the lobby with charisma made of finger-raked hair, baby-soft T-shirt and jeans that stretched over his thighs like they were made of leather. She didn't protest when he let the bag drop from his shoulder, pulling her into a fierce hug.

Her whole body flooded with relief. "You came."

"I told you I would."

"But h- "

"Ssshhh, I'll tell you later, *petite*."

She stayed like that for a minute, tucked into him with no space for Jesus, letting his warmth settle over her and her frazzled nerves. People were looking when she pulled away, and when he pressed a kiss to the top of her head. For once, she didn't care. Well, only about Noémie and the quirk of her curious brow.

"Monsieur Coen," she greeted him with a nod—and a noticeable flush.

Noticeable, because the woman worked for Mirielle, and Mina was certain one of the skills on her resume read, *Rarely flustered*.

"*Enchanté*," she said. "The flowers were thoughtful."

"Least I could do. How is she?"

"Dictatorial, which is a good sign. She sends her apologies for not seeing you, but she's already gone to sleep."

"Of course. Sorry I'm late." He squeezed Mina's waist gently. "Took a while to get squared away in New York."

"No need to apologize." Noémie's eyes briefly fell to his arm still looped around Mina, his fist full of her blouse. "You must be tired, so forgive me for rushing you, but if you have need of a restroom or the café, best to do it now. Otherwise—"

He shook his head. "I'm fine. I hope we haven't missed the train."

"*Non*, we can still make this one. I'll have the car come around now. *Pardon*." She walked away with her phone held to her face.

"It was Vera, wasn't it?" Mina asked, drinking in his face.

He sighed, and she realized how tired he looked, but, *Dieu*, he looked good. "Yes. But don't worry about it right now, okay?"

She twisted away at that. "*Why* does everyone keep saying that to me? As if I'm nothing more than a twig and worry will snap me in half? This is a *perfectly* appropriate time to be worried. In case you haven't heard, my mother was shot, probably by the same psycho who killed Étienne. We're leaving now on the chance that someone wants to shoot *me*, too. So, *bordel,* as you can see, I have every right to worry."

"*Petite*—"

"The car is ready." Noémie eyed them warily.

People were openly staring. Mina blinked rapidly, silently counting backward from ten. "*Bon*," she said calmly. "*Allons-y*."

The high-speed rail to Dijon lasted only an hour and a half, but after the eighteen hours Zack just had, it felt longer. Mina was sleeping, thank God. After their initial reunion, she'd turned icy towards him, speaking in clipped tones and only when absolutely necessary. He couldn't blame her. He deserved it, even if deep down he knew most of her ire was pure stress and lack of sleep.

Gently adjusting her head so it nestled in the curve of his shoulder, he eased the awkward angle of her neck. His heart did a little flip at her sound of contentment. At least she could be content in sleep. It had been a surprise to get her call last night, and he'd answered it for that reason— he *knew* something had to be wrong for her to break their silence first. She'd sounded hysterical on the phone, terrified her mother would die with an ocean between them and no chance to say goodbye. She'd already lost one parent. The thought of her losing the other had been just...

Eighteen hours worrying about her wrecked him worse than the eleven days he'd spent being flayed alive by her eyes. He tried not to think it. He really did. Because it was dick-ish, and completely insensitive...but he was human, goddamn it, and it had felt so *good* to hold her, to let her take comfort in him for a minute before she went back to resenting him again. He'd hoped the composition note-book burning a hole in his travel bag might help with that, but after seeing the strain she was under...it just wasn't the right time. Letting his head fall back on the seatback, he watched the scenery rush past in a blur like impressionist paint strokes on the window.

Another car waited for them in Dijon. The driver took the back roads, and it was a mostly silent trip from the historic town full of tourists and deep into the heart of Burgundy. "Bourgogne," the driver called it, the "Côte de Nuits." The landscape was beautifully untamed, full of rolling hillsides with high vines and brambles, charming little villages and country roads. It was achingly romantic, and more than once, Zack wished this had been a planned getaway—or a surprise, where he'd whisked her away for a long weekend of wine tasting and making love until neither of them could walk, or speak, or think, or move.

Instead, Mina was perched stiffly on the other end of the seat, staring out of the window. They rode for half an hour, then through the gates of a sprawling vineyard. From his vantage point, Zack could see they were at the bottom of an incredible hillside overlooking the rows and rows of twisting green vines…with a fucking *castle* at the top. There were towers on all its corners, and a pin-cushion roof of spires and chimneys. Mina jerked, as if someone had touched a nerve in her back.

"*S'il vous plaît*, is this a hotel?" she asked the driver in a strange tone.

"*Non, mademoiselle*," he answered. "It's a private residence."

She seemed anxious looking out the window now, as if trying to place where they were.

"Have you been here before, *petite*?" Zack asked gently.

"I-I don't think so," she said, not looking at him. "But it seems familiar."

It could have been a park, there was so much land—all of it manicured into geometric patches of green, its borders overflowing with colorful flowers. By the time they reached the top of the hillside, the last of the sun's rays caught the courtyard, casting a shadow across its white-washed walls, briefly illuminating a small oval-shaped plaque that sat atop a pair of burgundy colored gates that said, *Domaine de Bernard*.

Mina gasped. "I-is there a mistake?" she asked the driver.

"*Non, mademoiselle*," he said. "This is the address I was given." He let down his window to push a tiny button beside the steel gates.

Zack leaned closer to Mina. "What's wrong, *petite*?"

She looked even stiffer, if that was possible. Her chest rose and fell heavily, and her honey-brown skin took on a sickly color. "I...I know the man who owns this vineyard—*knew*. I knew him. His family makes some of the finest wine in the world. I just don't understand why we're—"

"The guests for the evening have arrived," the driver said into the intercom.

"Yes, please deliver them around front," a deep, heavily accented voice replied.

The gates buzzed open, and they entered the courtyard, pulling up behind another car parked in the semi-circular driveway. The driver "delivered" them and their bags to the front door.

Holy shit.

Zack couldn't even *see* to the top of the chateau anymore. They were too close. A doorman greeted them in French, taking their bags. He exchanged a few words with Mina, and she turned to Zack to translate.

"He says to follow him, please. We're to meet our host."

Zack lifted both brows, looking around. The outside looked ancient, but the inside was modern. It had white walls and vaulted ceilings, a double-spiral staircase and checkered marble floors, and the most lavish furniture he'd ever seen. It was *exactly* the kind of place that would require a tour guide. "Just let me know when I'm supposed to bow."

At her cutting look, he simply nodded and followed quietly behind her and the nice man in the monkey suit. They walked for maybe two minutes before being led into a room flanked by two men in all-black. There was a fire-place, a mix of modern and stately furniture, and a lean, very well-dressed man standing at its center who was either an identical twin, or a fucking ghost.

Mina cried out and stiffened like a marble statue.

"*Bonsoir, ma bichette,*" the man said with a shit-eating grin.

"*Jesus Christ.*" Zack moved quickly to catch Mina's limp body.

He lifted her and laid her gently on the loveseat. Sharp, crystal-clear blue eyes under long black lashes looked him over with keen interest.

"Étienne, I presume?"

One thick brow arched, and the shit-eating grin grew to a full-blown smile. "*Enchanté.*"

Charming little bastard. Too bad Mina was probably going to kill him…for real.

CHAPTER TWENTY-FOUR

ONE WORD.

Three syllables.

Sounded like...*fuck*...what rhymed with *ballistic*?

Best Zack could come up with was *magic stick*, and that wasn't going to help with shit. It was a little hard to concentrate on his silent game of charades when Mina was screaming a string of rapid-fire sounds he couldn't *begin* to understand.

If he thought her slap that time in rehearsal was painful, he didn't want to know what Étienne was feeling right now—She was *pummeling* the poor guy, fists balled up, throwing her whole body behind it. She might be petite, but she was pretty much solid muscle, reinforced by pure *rage*.

Étienne made zero attempts to block her, protect himself, grip those flailing arms of hers to keep her at bay. He just stood there, feet planted apart, palms up, saying, "*Je connais, bichette. S'il te plaît, chère...Mina...Je suis tellement désolé...Bichette...S'il te plaît...*"

Well, maybe it wasn't *pure* rage.

Tears streamed down her face, and she started to look exhausted, her arms landing softer...slower...until she collapsed into sobs that looked powerful enough to rip her in half. The urge to go right over there and pluck her away from him was overwhelming, but instinct held him back—instinct, and his own confusing clusterfuck of emotions.

For as long as Zack had known Mina, Étienne had been an enigma. A ghost. An unattainable ideal. Most of all, he was someone Mina obviously loved deeply enough that losing him had broken her heart. Zack knew that kind of pain acutely. A broken heart was impossible to see, but easy enough to detect. Because it hurt to breathe.

That was hard as hell to compete with—and it had felt like that sometimes with Mina. She'd kept Étienne to herself, which she'd had every right to do, but being left in the dark had made Zack susceptible to jealousy, confusion, even resentment. Now Étienne was here in the flesh. Strong, poised, and almost…painfully beautiful.

Tears were pouring from his eyes, too, and she lifted her hands to his face. He had all the angles of a well-structured masculine face, but there was a boyishness there too, in the sparkle behind his big blue eyes and the generous curve of his lips…and she mapped them all with her fingers, like she was refamiliarizing herself, testing the stuff he was made of, making sure he was solid. Making sure he was real. Then she replaced her fingers with her lips.

But they were nothing like the kisses she'd given Zack these last two months, not even in their most chaste moments. They were…adorable. After, she'd speak, he'd interrupt her, and she'd stop…he'd start, she'd interrupt, and he'd stop.

Jesus. They were finishing each other's sentences.

In a stunning moment of clarity, Zack watched two shattered souls pull themselves back together like magnets.

When the pieces finished coming together, it was clear to him what they were, what they had always been. The craziest part, is Mina had already told him weeks ago. He just hadn't understood it then…

"I believe there are many kinds of soulmates."

That's exactly what they were. They were like twins. Soulmates.

Just as he was beginning to feel left out, Mina stood with a loud sigh, throwing her hands in the air and pacing. "It just occurred to me, my daytime soap opera and my dirty romance novel are in the same room, and I have no idea how to feel about it."

With a gasp, Étienne tracked his eyes slowly up, then down, Zack's body.

Zack choked on his own damn tongue. It was a *look*, a look he was still recovering from, and all that the look meant, when Étienne turned his scandalized gaze back to Mina.

"*Oh. Mon. Dieu.* I *knew* it, you naughty girl—You're totally tapping that!"

"Have a care, would you?" asked Zack. "I'm standing right he—"

"Don't even start." Mina doubled back, jabbing her finger into Étienne's chest. "You *lied* to me, remember? I've been *miserable* all this time, and y—"

"Well, not *all* this time." Zack felt slightly affronted.

He was ignored.

"This is *exactly* why no one ever tells you anything, *bichette*. You get all worked up and start steaming from your ears."

"I—I do *not*—"

"Right there." He motioned at her head. "Steam."

"*Arrêtes*—"

"*Non.*" Étienne put his hands on his narrow hips. "I'm not done. Did you ever stop to think what a year without dancing must have been like for me?"

Mina visibly cringed.

"*Bordel, bichette*! You see? Just *hearing* the words hurts you. Imagine *living* it? —*Non,* not living. Dying. Part of me *did* die, and when I think of the work I will have to do to feel like myself again, I'm lost."

Sniffing, she walked to him slowly and slipped her hands around his waist. "I know. I-I'm sorry."

Étienne let go a sigh. "*Allez.* Enough of this now, okay?" He held her a second longer, then released her, looking at Zack. "Zachary?"

"Zack is fine—by the way, daytime soap opera?"

"*Oui,*" said Étienne. "You know, fake deaths, ransoms, secret love children."

"Right," Zack said. "Of course."

"*Bon.*" Étienne clapped. "Let's go to dinner. We'll have wine, and I'll tell you everything." Without waiting for a reply, he hooked his arm through Mina's, bending his head to her ear. "And you can tell me *exactly* how many screaming orgasms we're talking about."

"Still here." Zack followed behind them like a golden retriever.

Étienne took them to an idyllic little town with sandstone streets and Romanesque architecture towering overheard. They had dinner at a café outside in the main square, beneath the warmth of Burgundy's summer night sky. It was quaint, even with the men in black pretending to ignore them at the next table. Kids were playing in the fountains, and people were walking their dogs. During dinner,

Étienne insisted they tell him everything about *Lady in Red* he couldn't glean from the internet, and when he playfully asked for all the sordid details of their "blistering affair," suddenly the summer air turned much colder.

"*Alors.*" Étienne gave good pout. "I guess that's my cue, *oui?*"

"You don't have to," Mina said.

"I do, *bichette*. But…I need you to stay quiet until I finish, okay? That's part of the reason I brought you here." He grinned. "I thought, perhaps, in a public place, you wouldn't freak out."

She glared at him. "That's not—"

"Promise me."

Now she was pouting, too. "Fine. Go on."

Curiosity had wrapped Zack's neck in a chokehold from the moment Mina fainted. He met her eyes, silently asking if she was okay. Thankfully, she didn't ignore him, offering him a subtle nod and turning her attention back to Étienne. Zack crossed his arms over his chest, and Étienne began his story in his deep, dulcet tone.

"I loved Angelo, I should say that first. To everyone else—maybe even you, *bichette*—he was a name on a bottle. A brand. To me, he was…a champion. He made me feel important. Like the world wouldn't be the same if I was not in it."

Mina stretched her arm across the table, and Étienne squeezed her hand.

"The day he was murdered…" His Adam's apple worked in his throat. "He invited me over to discuss whether I should renew my contract in *Paris* or move to Italy…with him. He told me to take my time with my decision, and in the meantime, he had some business to take care of.

Bichette, do you remember that man—the one they called 'Monsieur Grand Cru' at parties?"

"*Oui,*" she said. "He was very popular, I remember. Everyone loved him—or rather, his parties. We went to a few of them ourselves. I—*Oh mon Dieu*!" Her eyes widened in horror. "*Oh, Étienne. Oh non…non, non, non…*"

Étienne's jaw tightened so much, a muscle ticked in his cheek. "I'm afraid so."

She gasped. "But…*why?*"

"His real name is Gabriel Ademar. He made his fortune trading in rare wine, and he had a particular fondness for Burgundy—which is how he got his nickname, you see, for the most superior grade. The problem is, he was bottling them himself, auctioning them as vintage. The year he killed Angelo—and tried to kill me—he made almost twenty-four million euros as a wine forger."

Mina had both hands over her mouth, visibly trying to keep her composure.

Zack leaned forward. "I'm guessing Angelo caught on?"

Étienne nodded solemnly. "Monsieur Ademar auctioned a rare bottle of Burgundy from nineteen seventy-one for over thirty-thousand euros, claiming it had been produced by Angelo's family, but the Bernards did not produce their first harvest until nineteen seventy-five. Angelo demanded Monsieur Ademar return the money, with whatever excuse he chose, or he would report him to *la police.*"

Taking another deep sip of his wine, Étienne looked up with tears in his eyes.

"You don't have to, *chère,*" Mina whispered, tears in her eyes, too.

"You promised me, *bichette.*"

Jesus.

Zack's hackles were up. He knew what was coming, but hearing it was still chilling.

"Monsieur Ademar showed up unannounced," Étienne continued. "He apologized, saying returning the money was impossible, because it would ruin his reputation, but he would donate to the charity of Angelo's choice. Angelo said he would only accept under the condition Monsieur Ademar would cease all forgery in the future. Monsieur Ademar pretended to consider it, then pulled his revolver and emptied the chamber."

Mina was crying softly now.

"Obviously, I survived, and Angelo did not." Étienne wiped his tears and took another sip. "For almost a year, I've been in witness protection with *maman* and *papa*, so *la police* could build their case. But Monsieur Ademar had a *lot* of money, and he was well-connected. A few months into the case, *la police* discovered he had hired a private investigator. *La police*—they work with PI's all the time. They have access to police databases…and that is how he discovered I was alive, in hiding somewhere. The private investigator got hold of my taped testimony."

"*Mon Dieu*," Mina gasped. "That's why I was mugged! Why I was robbed, and—"

"Why your mother was shot," Étienne said. "I'm sorry, *bichette*. He must have hired those thugs to find out what you knew."

"I *knew* it," she said. "I had such a bad feeling."

Zack couldn't help it this time. He took her hand underneath the table and squeezed. "Why's it taking damn near a *year* to nail this guy's ass to the wall?" he asked tightly.

"*Bordel*," Étienne spat. "It's not just him they want. It's also his known associates—the private investigator he hired, and others like him, and the dirty cops who look the other way or even take bribes from *bâtards* like Monsieur Ademar. Harvest here is next month. Monsieur Ademar is already in *Paris* preparing to tape a reality show for a food and wine channel. They're picking him up first thing in the morning, which is why I thought it better you stay here, *bichette*. It's going to be a circus tomorrow."

"I'm so sorry, Étienne," Mina whispered.

"Me too. But I'm also *relieved*. I'm *tired* of hiding. I'm ready to get on with my life. So…" He handed her a white napkin. "No more tears, okay? I'm reborn today, and you are depressing me."

Her choking laugh-sob combination made Zack's heart flip. Whatever he was feeling must have shown on his face, because Étienne studied him openly a moment, the laughter leaving his eyes, replaced with a look of fierce determination.

"I won't be accompanying you back to Domaine Bernard," he said, standing.

Mina stiffened. "*Non, Étienne—*"

"*Bichette,* I'm still in protective custody until Monsieur Ademar is indicted."

Nodding, Mina stood, too. "Will you come by in the morning? We leave for New York in the evening."

"*Oui.* For a little while. Then I have to go back."

Zack smiled. It probably wasn't enough time to catch up, but it was a start.

꧁

Mina was exhausted by the time they returned to the castle at Domaine Bernard. Another uniformed man showed them to their rooms on the second floor. *Enfin,* two floors in this place looked more like three or four. A suite of two bedrooms was prepared for them, separated by a sitting room, each with massive fireplaces and antique French beds. There was a terrace off the sitting room with a view that made her chest hurt. It overlooked a rose garden, with a maze just beyond, and a river beyond that.

Drawing the sweet countryside air into her lungs, she admired the stars. They were more and brighter than any night in Paris, and even the stars in Sunset Park she'd seen with Zack…the night they'd talked on and on then made cuddling love in his room. The night she first realized she was falling in love with him. She sighed. It was all so *perfect.* It was difficult to stomach, under the circumstances.

"Hey."

She turned to see him standing there. Watching her. "Hi."

He seemed a little unsure of himself but came up beside her on the balcony, gripping the iron balustrade with both hands. Something in his eyes softened the pout from her lips, her eyes clinging to his like they had so many times that day, seeking the truth behind his words and movements, his every expression. That he was there at all should have been sign enough of his feelings, but after what happened in Tetley Theatre, how could she trust him not to push her away again the next time things got difficult?

"Mina…"

"I'm so tired. I don't want to fight with you."

"I know, *petite.*" He ran his hand through his hair. "I know you're tired, and it's been…intense. I know it's a lot to ask but can you just…spare a few more minutes for me. Please?"

Not trusting her voice, she nodded.

Relief shuddered over his expression. "I'm sorry, Mina.

I'm sorry for hurting you instead of letting you in. For not letting you see all of me...even the shadows. You trusted me in Vera's theater, and I betrayed you by not trusting you, too. I shouldn't have accused you of hiding just because you don't wear your heart on your sleeve. You were protecting yourself, and I am so, *so* sorry you had to protect yourself from me."

Merde. He was saying all the right words. The way his deep voice shook with emotion threatened to wear down what was left of her battered heart shields. She couldn't let him do it so easily. Those shields were all she had left to protect her tattered heart.

"It's fine," she said coolly. "I'm sorry you've been beating yourself up about it. I overreacted, which I apparently do a lot. It was just...bad timing on my part, and completely out of character. I should have been more understanding."

His gaze seemed to intensify on hers, but she didn't look away. For a full minute, it felt like he was trying to read what was written on her heart walls through her eyeballs. "I almost believed you, *petite.* Next time you lie to me, close your eyes."

"I—I'm not..."

"No, it's okay. I figured you'd be skeptical." He moved as if to touch her but shoved his hands in his pockets instead. "You should know, I *did* try to tell you—maybe not all the gory details, but you still figured it out. It still scared the living shit out of me, because that's never happened before. I've never opened up with anyone else enough for them to put the pieces together."

"Zack..."

"Hang on a sec, okay?"

He seemed so earnest, she couldn't tell him no, so she

nodded. Ten seconds later, he'd jogged to his room and returned with a composition notebook.

She accepted it from his hand. "What's this?"

"The truth." He shrugged. "Every word in there is true. I started it the night we met. I never intended to show anyone, but I think…maybe you should read it."

Her fingers moved over the title hand-written on the front. "*Music Box Dancer*?"

There was that half-cocked grin. It had been so long since she'd seen it. Her stupid, traitorous heart had the nerve to *skip*.

"Seemed fitting." Leaning against the balustrade, he crossed his arms over his chest, watching her.

She wet her lips and opened to the first page…and with the first entry, the shield began to fall away from her heart:

June 16

Incredible. Inside and out of that enormous velvet box.

June 23

Smaller without the stilts. Petite, even.

June 25

She's been compressed into a diamond. Brilliant. Multifaceted. Sharp.

June 26

I think her hand might be imprinted on my face.

June 30

The lady has a temper.
Sometimes she's a quiet fire.
Simmering gently.
Her eyes are molten. Her tongue licks like a flame.
Sometimes she's a wildfire.
Scorching hot.
Engulfing.

And I can't breathe.

July 3
I wish there were a mirror that could show her what I see.

July 4
I've never hugged someone and pulled away branded.

July 11
Today, she's a quiet fire.

July 15
On the rooftop. In the garden. Underneath the rain.
Tentatively. Gently. Thoroughly.
Hungrily. Passionately. Deeply.
Slower. Faster. Again.

July 18
I can't. Not today.

July 20
When you dream you're falling, but you're wide awake.

July 23
She tries to hide her feelings sometimes, but when she sleeps, she sighs. I think it's her heart whispering to mine.

July 27
It's her pieces that slice me in pieces. Death by a thousand cuts.

July 31
Wildfire.

August 4
Every time she cries, I see how strong she is.

…

There was still one entry left to read, but Mina couldn't see it through her tears. They spilled from her like they sprung from a well deep inside her, wetting the page.

Zack gently took the notebook from her. "Dated today: 'We were never meant to be perfect. Our pieces wouldn't fit together that way.'"

Turning away, she gripped the balustrade.

"There's no corner of my heart you haven't seen now, Mina. There's no thought in my mind you don't know."

Dieu, she wanted to believe him, to believe the three words that practically peeled themselves from the pages and levitated in front of her eyes. She could believe him here, of all places, couldn't she? Here, in the quiet dark of night, in an empty castle where no one knew or cared who they were, where water droplets began to drift down, unhurried, like they had nothing better to do than kiss the leaves and vines…where the rain had all night to polish the cobbled pathway and reflect the glow of the lamps from all the empty spaces.

If not here, then where?

Finally, she let go a deep, shuddering sigh, and gave him her eyes. "*Je pense toujours à toi. Tes yeux, j'en rêve jour et nuit,*" she said in a tearful near-whisper. "*Je t'aime de tout mon cœur.*"

He did touch her then, tracing the tracks of her tears with his thumbs, until he'd followed them beneath the line of her jaw and he held her face in his hands. "What does that mean?"

Fear gripped her momentarily, but she squeezed her eyes shut and willed it away. Damn the fear. She was *sick* of it. Her mother could have died yesterday, but she hadn't. She thought she'd lost Étienne, but he was alive, and determined to take his life back. *Enfin*, she was going to take hers back, too.

"Kiss me first," she whispered.

Not hesitating a second, he scooped her in his arms, lifting her to her toes and aligning her heart with his heart, her mouth with his.

The first brushes of his lips were tentative—all whispers and sighs and shivers of relief. His lips were warm and soft, and then firmer, more grounded and sure. Sighing and melting into him, she angled her head, opened her mouth, and slipped him her tongue. He kissed her and kissed her, until the late hour didn't matter, until time and place seemed to blur, until the rest of the world and everything in it crumbled away, leaving two warm bodies, two thundering heartbeats…one hungry soul bounding toward another.

When she finally pulled away, she hugged him as tightly as he hugged her, giving him a shy smile. "Come in with me."

"So, what you're saying is, *'voulez-vous coucher avec moi*?'"

Making an exasperated sound, she frowned. "*Espèce d'idiot.*"

"I might be an idiot, but I know when a woman's telling me she's in love with me."

She gasped and slapped him simultaneously.

He burst into laughter, his hand going to his cheek.

"*Merde!*" She jumped back, her heart thumping wildly. "I-I'm sorry. It was reactionary…" Slipping her hand underneath his, she rubbed his cheek.

"It's fine, I'll just remember to buy a boxing helmet for any future momentous occasions."

That made her smile. "Y-you understood what I said?"

"Not all of it, but I think I got the gist." Grinning, he took her hand and kissed it.

"I said, 'I always think about you. I dream about your eyes day and night.'"

"That's sweet." There was no trace of humor in his tone, as if he knew how difficult it was for her to open up.

"And…"

"*And?*"

"And, 'I love you, with all my heart.'"

Pulling her close, he tucked her into his warmth as the rain dripped from the flying buttresses overhead. "I love you too, *petite*," he said into her hair. "Tell me how to love you more, and I will."

"Come *in* with me." This time, there was no mistaking her meaning.

Over pale sheets, in the dim glow of the moon and the rain-scented air coming in from the open window, their fingers laced together above her head, he kissed her unhurriedly. He kissed all over her face and neck, the peaks of her breasts and curves of her shoulders, returning to take her mouth again and again.

She'd never felt so utterly naked—inside and out—and reveled in it. Like she could drop every stitch of armor and never be pierced by another expectation or opinion, because her pride and self-worth were impenetrable. It made her entire body shiver with exquisite vulnerability.

Dieu, he was everywhere, rubbing warmth all over her, opening and exposing her, stroking and licking her.

"*Mamour*," she cried. "*Please, please, please...*"

Pre-orgasmic tremors washed over her, heat spiraling from her clit to her fingertips and toes. He slipped his fingers inside her, and her low, husky moans magnified to sharp, needy pants, goosebumps breaking out over her skin. Burying his tongue inside her again, she convulsed, crying out as everything in her seemed to dissolve and break apart.

Yet, he held her together so effortlessly.

Her eyes stung with new tears, at the scent and warmth and taste of him, after missing him for so long. Covering her body with his own, he wrapped his arms around her tightly and kissed away her tears.

"Don't cry, Mina." He said gently, clutching her to his chest.

"I can't help it," she gulped. "Any time I feel anything, I cry."

"Then cry all you want. Cry forever. Just let me be there when you do."

He pressed into her slowly, then moved again, stretching and filling her, absorbing her sounds in his mouth. Smoothing her hands over his back, she admired the feel of his muscles, the silk of his skin, the magnificent arch of his spine.

"I love your body, *petite*," Adjusting her hips the way he wanted, he kissed her again. "So much. So, so much."

She moaned appreciatively, gripping his tight butt, digging her heels into his back. They were entwined like twisted strands of rope, strong and tight. Her body started to tighten around him again at the urgency in his thrusts, the way his skin reddened everywhere, the fierce concentration in his features—like he was holding back so he wouldn't lose it too quickly. It melted her insides to feel how much he enjoyed her, to hear how good she made him feel. The tremors were already building again, low in her belly, intensifying every time he cursed or moaned.

"*Jouir pour moi, mamour,*" she whispered, rotating her hips. "Come for me, my love. Then we'll do it again."

He made an agonized sound, his hips bucking, his teeth sinking into the side of her neck as he shook from head to toe.

"*Don't stop! S'il te plaît, d-don't stop…*"

Lifting her hips a little, he drove into her again and again, chuckling at her mindlessly babbled "*Merci.*" Her breasts brushed his chest, and—like a match being struck—she came with sharp cry, her back arched, clenching down on him hard. He stroked her until the aftershocks subsided, whispering in her ear how beautiful she was.

"*Wow.*" She gripped his arms, still trembling with subtle shocks. "'I love you' sex is *way* better than 'I like you sex.'"

His laughter warmed her soul. Until he cocked his brow, and his lips twitched.

"Don't ruin it," she begged.

"I was just thinking it's a good theory, that 'I love you sex' is better than 'I like you' sex."

"*Pardon?*"

Rolling her over with him, he grinned rakishly at her squeal. "Theories are meant to be tested."

In the shower, he tested the stream of water, adjusting until it was gentle and warm, running over them like a caress. Steam thickened the air, settling in tiny droplets over their heated skin. His soapy hands traced the rivulets down her body, rubbing the warm, sweet scent all over her.

"Touch me more," she sighed, twisting his insides with longing, clouding his mind. "I love your hands on me."

Tucking her back against his chest, letting her head rest against his shoulder, he willingly obeyed; massaging her breasts, circling her belly button with his thumb, tracing over her folds with his fingers. Her throaty pleas reawakened his desire, and he pressed her hard against his erection, one arm wrapped around her, holding her tightly to his body. She tilted her face to him, offering her lips.

Lazily, he kissed her, matching the stroke of his tongue to the slide of his fingers, getting drunk on her sighs, the way her eyes slid shut, the way her breasts pressed softly into his arm, and her body melted into his, as if she'd slide into a boneless puddle if not for him holding her up. He sensed her orgasm building slowly this time, and when her inner walls clung to his fingers, he groaned, turning her easily and lifting her astride him. He pressed her back gently to the ivory tiles, giving her ass an affectionate squeeze with both hands, sliding into her soft body.

"Beautiful, *petite*. You're so beautiful."

He kissed her again, chasing, then retreating, enticing sounds rising from her lips into the steam and blending into a continuous melody as he took her in slow, easy thrusts.

"I missed you," he groaned into her throat, gripping one of her thighs for purchase. "I want to fuck you forever, *petite*. You. Just you."

A shocked little gasp escaped her, a sound he was prepared to spend the rest of his life trying to rend from her in new and awesome ways. She seemed to like his blatant declaration, because her face twisted, and she cried out, her back arching, pressing every luscious line and curve of her body against his. Shaking, her arms clutching desperately around him, the water spilling over her, she unraveled. It seemed to last forever, wave after wave of long, gentle vibrations wracking her body. He felt them all, and it was exquisite torture, her body writhing around him, her heart pounding against his, sending ripples of pleasure up and down his spine.

Setting her down gently, he drew her to him again, soaping his hands and running them all over her. She clung to his arm, still trembling, letting him wash her in the most intimate way.

Trust. She trusted him, and the knowledge had him soaring.

Also an ego-boost: her hair was in wild disarray, making her look more like a lion than he could ever hope to achieve. He grinned, despite the fact he was still painfully aroused. To that point, she was already pushing him back against the tiles and going to her knees.

"What are you doing?" His voice was thin, his heart tripping in his chest.

She smiled sweetly up at him, water dripping over her beautiful face, her hands running up the back of his thighs. "Trust falls."

"M-Mina…" His heart hammered violently now, deafening in his ears, and he gripped her hair in both hands. "I want you to, but my mind tends to…go someplace else, whenever I let someone—I want to stay here with you."

"If you don't like it, I'll stop. Trust me, *mamour*," she said softly, her hands wrapping gently around his wrists. "Let me show you how it's supposed to feel."

What shone in her eyes made him gasp. Raw, naked vulnerability, like he hadn't seen since their first kiss, like his trust meant more to her than anything else in the world. Long as he lived, he'd never get used to seeing his soul reflected in her eyes. Willing his mind to accept what his body wanted, swallowing down the remaining dregs of doubt, he relaxed his grip on her hair, shaking with anticipation. She took her time with him, smoothing her hands over his abs, then down again, trailing hot kisses along his thighs and hip bones, over his lower abdomen and the lines that arrowed to a V. Taking him into her hands, stroking firmly, she very clearly telepathed with her eyes, *I think you are beautiful too.* Then she drew him into her soft, warm mouth.

His toes curled against the wet porcelain, his mouth making unintelligible sounds as she worked him over. She didn't seem to mind that he pulled her hair so tightly, or that his hips flexed instinctively, pushing him to the back of her throat. Not even close. She moaned, like he was a delectable treat and she couldn't get enough. For the first time in recent memory, he felt no consuming need to dissociate. It was pleasurable because it was her, because it didn't feel like something was being taken from him, but given, and in giving, it brought her immeasurable joy.

And it was his complete undoing.

"Oh God, Oh God, Oh God…"

His voice echoed off the tiles, his mind and body giving themselves up, void of all control, his hands buried in her hair. It wrecked him. Turned him completely inside out, proving his love for her didn't exist only in his heart and soul. There wasn't a single atom of his body that wasn't melded with it, melded with *her*. It was ecstasy and solace. It was home.

She came to him quickly, while he was still shaking, his eyes stinging with tears, and wrapped him tightly in her arms, holding him up in more ways than one, just as he'd held her.

"*Je t'aime,*" she murmured, over and over and over. "*Je t'aime, je t'aime, je t'aime.*"

He wrapped her in a towel downy as a robe and carried her to the bed. Lying beside her, he peeled away the towel slowly, like giftwrapping he didn't want to tear. Her skin was warm and supple from the shower, and she shivered so subtly he would have missed it if he weren't already touching her.

"Having an encore?" he teased lightly, his hands floating over her body.

In answer, she grasped his wrist and pulled his hand down, sliding it between her legs.

"More," she whispered, shuddering again as he rubbed her with his thumb.

Bending his head, he licked and sucked her nipples, scraping gently with his teeth. She hadn't stopped shaking since the shower, like her orgasm hadn't finished but simmered on low, and had come back to collect. It happened quickly. Her lean, shapely body stiffened, and her eyes closed, her hips undulating against his hand. He kissed her when it was over. Over and over, because he couldn't help himself. In a castle, on top of a hill, in this antique French bed, tangled in ruined sheets, Mina Allende imprinted herself on his tongue, his skin, his heart and soul…and he would cherish her, always.

"*Merci*," she whispered, turning onto her stomach and collapsing into the pillows.

"Happy to help."

Her answer was a sleepy growl, and he chuckled softly. They were sex drunk, love drunk, boneless—entirely useless human beings. Draping himself over her back, he kissed the expanse of smooth brown skin.

"Mina." He said her name in wonder, enjoying her reflexive jerk when his lips met the small of her back. "Whatever happens after tonight, I'm yours, and you are mine."

She sighed a contented little sigh and drifted to sleep.

Point taken.

Some things didn't require words. Further, for some things, there *were* no words. And that was fine with him.

CHAPTER TWENTY-FIVE

THE SKY WAS so blue in the morning, the sun so high in the sky, the rain seemed like a dream. Mina sat across Zack's lap in the garden courtyard, intoxicated by the scent of roses and the warmth of summer, and his quick, playful kisses between bites of his breakfast.

"I think my appetite's changed, *petite*." He nibbled her lower lip, hands tightening on her waist. "Suddenly, I'm in the mood for something a little more…*satisfying*."

Someone cleared his throat deliberately, and Mina looked up to see Étienne approaching the table.

"*Bonjour*." His grin was wide. "I see this humble little *château* has worked its magic."

Mina scrambled less-than-gracefully from Zack's lap, grinning stupidly and tingling all over from her full-body blush. She kissed Étienne's cheeks. "*Bonjour, ma moitié.*"

"Sit." Zack seemed not the least bit embarrassed they were caught making out like teenagers. "Eat. There's enough food here for two more people."

"*Ah*." Étienne acknowledged him with a nod. (Étienne never exchanged kisses with anyone he hadn't met three times. It was his *thing*.) "*Oui*, Martin is an incredible chef, but his idea of portion size has a decidedly *américain* bent—*merci*." He accepted Mina's untouched plate and a glass of water.

"Thank you," said Zack. "You must've gone to a lot of trouble."

"Not at all." Étienne waved the notion away. "Angelo's family was happy to accommodate us. They're overcome to know his killer will see justice. It was a small thing, truly." He tossed the morning paper in front of Mina. "I come bearing gifts."

Picking it up, she read the headline aloud. "'Popular sommelier charged with forgery and murder.'"

She held it so Zack could see, studying the photo with a frown. Gabriel Ademar was being led from his luxury hotel in handcuffs—surrounded by a crowd of onlookers and *droves* of press.

"Smug bastard," Zack bit out. "He looks like he's posing for the fucking paparazzi."

"*Putain!*" Étienne cursed. "I'm sure he thinks his lawyers can wiggle him out of this, but his taste in guns is as rare as his taste in wine, the *connard*. Objectively, it's a pretty piece of deadly machinery. Subjectively, he's compensating for something."

"That is a *clean* shot of him," Zack observed. "Someone must've alerted the press."

Étienne nodded. "The publicity is good for *la police*. Gabriel is the biggest fish they've caught in years."

"*Ugh*, I can't stand to look at him." Mina slammed the front-page face-down on the table. "I don't think you should, either."

"Are you kidding?" Étienne took a bite of a buttery croissant. "I have several copies: one to frame above my bed, one to burn, one to leave at Angelo's grave, and one to pick up the shit of my future puppy when this is all over."

Mina crinkled her nose. "*Enfin,* I think a puppy would be wonderful. What will you name it?"

"I quite like the idea of a pug named Gary."

"*Oui,* you love it when pets have human names."

"And when humans have pet names…"

They fell quiet, lost in a shared memory.

"You two are obviously having a moment." Zack didn't sound like he minded at all. "Clue me in?"

"It's…something she said the first time I called her '*bichette*,'" Étienne explained. "It means 'little doe.'"

Mina smiled. "And when I asked why *that* name, you said—"

"Because your eyes are so big and bright. I'm surprised you remember. How long has it been?"

"Fourteen years. I remember everything."

It grew quiet again, and Zack stood from the table. "Listen, I need to make some calls." He gave Mina's shoulder a light squeeze. "Excuse me for a few?"

"Of course." Mina covered his hand briefly with hers.

Étienne nodded politely, riveted to Zack's retreating form until he moved out of hearing shot, then he leaned over the table. "*Allez,* I have been patient, '*petite,*' but that is a *lot* of charisma and sinew for one man. I'm dying to know *precisely* how dirty that romance novel is."

She felt her face turn at least three shades deeper. Zack's pet name sounded a lot dirtier when Étienne said it. "How did you—?"

"Oh please, you didn't notice I was here until I wanted you to. Long enough to see Monsieur Coen's technique isn't restricted to his fascinating choreography." He tugged her up by her hand. "Come, walk with me. I need to know when, where and how you let such a *fantastique* beast under your tutu."

She gasped. "He's not an *animal*, Étienne!"

He looked meaningfully back at the chateau. "If he isn't, then what the hell are you doing with him?"

Étienne guided her to the entrance of the circular, yew-walled maze at the edge of the rose garden. "I've never met a New Yorker up-close," he said. "I'm simultaneously disappointed and relieved Monsieur Sexy back there doesn't sound like he stepped out of a Scorsese movie."

She laughed. "I think there's a beauty to a New Yorker's accent, but most people I meet there don't have it—at least, not as prominently as Hollywood wants us to believe. And anyway, it's *my* accent anyone's ever interested in."

"How is it, *bichette*? Do you like it there?"

"*Oui*, it's—different. It's loud and colorful and awake all the time. It's…*alive*. It makes *me* feel alive."

"*Ah*. And Monsieur Sexy? Does he make you feel alive?"

Swatting his arm, she tugged him closer to her side, synchronizing her steps with his along the crunch of gravel beneath their feet. She mulled over the question until they'd turned a corner, and then another, following the labyrinth of trimmed green hedges towering above them.

"I think I've always felt alive," she finally answered. "But he makes me notice things I wouldn't see on my own. Things that make life…*more*."

Étienne's groomed brow seemed to have grown a tick. "You love him."

"*Oui,* but I've only recently said it out loud, so go easy on me."

"I only have this little bit of time, *bichette*. I can't extract information from you with my usual highly controversial and illegal methods. Which brings me to the sex."

"How on *earth* does that bring you to—nevermind…"

"Tell me. I have to know."

"Fine." She sighed wistfully. "When we're together—no matter if we're hooking up, or cuddling, or making love—it always speaks to me. It's like…when we dance together. It feels like flying, and I never want to come down."

"*Damn.*"

"I know."

"And last night? How many times did you fly?"

She let go his arm and grinned. "Four times. And once this morning, on the balcony."

Then, she took off running, her blood pumping faster every time she took a wrong turn and still evaded him. He found her, breathless, at the end of the maze, gaping at the magnificent view of the hills below them, the little country roads, and the river beyond.

Sitting on the grass beside her, he pinched her waist. "Brat. How could you make me run?"

"Because you hate it." She grinned. "Sophie sends her love. She couldn't get away—not even to see me in *Paris*."

"*Ah.*" He nodded, seeming to understand. "The season will be starting soon. Madame will be positively *militant*."

"*Mmm,*" she hummed. "Will you dance again, *chère*?"

"Of course. I've kept in shape, but I need to re-train my body. It will take some time. But I don't know if I want to return to *Paris*. It feels strange just popping up alive after everyone thought I was worm food."

"Come to New York!" Her heart did somersaults even before the thought left her lips. "I'm thinking about auditioning for a company there…after the last run of *Lady in Red*—whenever that will be. We could be close to each other."

"I don't know, *bichette*. I've been forced to stay put all this time, all I really want to do is *move*. See *more* of the world, not less of it…"

"But the American Ballet Theatre is a *touring* company!" She was getting more excited by the second. "They have short seasons in New York in the spring and fall, but they tour around the world most of the year—Oh, Étienne, you have to think about it. *S'il te plaît*. I've just got you back, I don't want to say goodbye again. I—"

"Okay, o-*kay*…" He laughed. "I'll think about it if you stop crying. *Allez*…" He lifted the hem of his shirt to wipe her face, and the breath whooshed from her lungs.

"Oh… *ma moitié*…" Lifting a shaky hand to his torso, she moved her fingers over the impressions. Two scars, several centimeters apart, marred his skin like little craters on the surface of the moon. "I'm so sorry."

"Don't cry, *bichette*. They don't hurt." There was a sheen over his blue eyes as he let his shirt down and kissed her hand. "*Mon Dieu,* I may agree to move to New York just to make sure you stay hydrated!"

Laughing, she tugged her hand away. "What about you? Have you met anyone?"

"*I* haven't," he said mysteriously. "But *Damien Moreau* has had a little fun."

She gasped.

"Don't get too excited," he said. "I'm not invested in anyone—It's hard to be, when I'm not myself, when I can't share anything true about me."

"Are you allowed to tell me your fake name?"

"Technically, *non*, but since I can't tell you anything else right now, you can at least have that."

"*Merci*. I'm happy to have it." For a minute, she was quiet, and then, "All this time, I think I was in denial. Like part of my brain just wouldn't accept you were gone. It felt like you were haunting me."

"*Alors*, it makes me feel better to know you didn't let me go without a fight."

"I *didn't*. I even impressed 'Monsieur Sexy' with the double tour you taught me."

"*Ah,* well done." His smile faded a little. "Tell me something…"

"Anything."

"Don't take this the wrong way—You know I think you can do anything…but a *musical*? Why did you do it?"

"Because I wasn't happy anymore. Because it scared me, and you always say, if it scares you, you have to do it….and because…*you* would have done it."

"You weren't happy anymore? How can that be?"

"I missed you, and it just…wasn't the same anymore."

"As flattering as that is, I don't believe you."

She frowned. "Why not?"

"Because of fate. Even if I'd never fake-died, you'd have gone to New York."

"You…don't know that."

"Oh, but I *do*. Do you remember what you said to me, the night I came out to you, and you already knew?"

"*Oui*, I'll never forget."

He smiled triumphantly. "My answer is the same. *You live in my heart*. So, I know you were restless long before my…untimely demise. You fulfilled a dream. You became *une Étoile*, confined to one corner of the sky. *Alors, Paris* is beautiful, but a gilded cage is still a cage." He touched his forehead to hers, so she felt it when he grinned. "And you needed to *fly*."

Too soon, the men in black appeared at the end of the maze, and it was time to say goodbye. The mood was solemn on the slow walk back, and Zack was waiting for them in the rose garden.

"This isn't *au revoir*." Étienne kissed her cheeks. "It's à *bientôt*, okay?"

She tried not to sniff, but—*nom de Dieu*—she wasn't a miracle worker. "I know. I just…I…" Grabbing him into a bear hug, she held him tightly and buried her head in his chest.

His body was stiff, his voice amused. "*Bichette*? What are you doing?"

"Be quiet. I'm hugging you."

She heard Zack's soft laughter but stayed exactly as she was for a few seconds longer. When she pulled away, she peered into Étienne's sparkling eyes. "Will you come to see me on Broadway?"

He gave her a flash of his perfect white teeth. "That depends: Are you still mad at me for not dying?"

෴

Étienne sent them off with a bottle of Burgundy worth half a month's rent, promising to be in touch the minute he left protective custody. Before heading to the airport, Zack accompanied Mina to the hospital to meet her grandmother and say goodbye to her mother. The eldest Mrs. Allende was a surprise: she smiled, for one, and she was chatty, with a self-effacing sense of humor. Gifting them with Swiss chocolate for the plane, she assured them she'd come see the show, along with Mina's grandfather. Mina was predictably tearful, and Mirielle was predictably... *Mirielle*. She wasn't chatty, she didn't smile, nor was she in good-humor (understandably), but she did air-kiss Zack goodbye, thanking him sincerely for coming.

He bought a turkey sandwich from the café, and then they were off. Vera, true to her word, got them seats on a charter, bumping a couple of businessmen to an earlier flight so Zack and Mina could travel together. Mina dozed most of the flight, but he had too much on his mind to sleep. While she'd spent the morning catching up with Étienne, he'd been on the phone with Faye, and then Alex, and then Harper. They were ready for tech week, but the musical—was not.

They hit the ground running as soon as they touched down—as well as two zombies could run. He kissed her goodbye in the subway station at two in the afternoon, and by six, he was with Alex in his library, along with Harper, watching last Friday's rehearsal play on the projector screen.

Zack rubbed his eyes. *Fuck.* Had it only been two days? He felt *hammered,* like he was drunk off his ass and some-one kept punching him in the head.

"You okay, man?" Harper waved a hand in front of his face, as if checking to make sure Zack was all there.

"I'm good, just...getting old—too old for all-nighters."

Alex cut his eyes at Zack but didn't comment. Likely because he knew exactly where that all-nighter had been. Zack had needed a ride to the airport, and apparently fol-lowing Mina halfway around the world had confirmed Alex's suspicions their chemistry was more than just bril-liant casting.

"This is the part I was telling you about." Alex used the remote to increase the volume.

Onscreen, Zack and the actor playing his character's father were singing their hearts out. Zack's tenor portrayed Armand hopelessly in love, his father trying to talk sense into him. Marrying a courtesan was out of the question, would ruin his reputation, and force the older Mr. Duval to disown him. But it was no use. Armand was smitten, ready to risk it all.

"It's great," said Harper. "I'm feeling the chemistry. Old dude practically stole the show—he's like Jerry Orbach in dance slippers."

Zack agreed, scratching his head. "Am I missing something? I don't see the problem here…"

"Keep watching," said Alex.

Next up, Armand Duval's father confronted Camille, begging the love-struck courtesan to see reason where Armand would not, to strike down any fantasy of marriage because it would ruin his son. Then he exited stage right, leaving Camille alone with her thoughts. Before she danced a single step, Zack sensed her emotion. It was there in her posture, her expression, the way she seemed to falter before the first movement. This was a woman tortured with an impossible decision, and when she finally moved, she danced as if caught between a dream and a nightmare. Every step, every gesture, every artful expression clicked perfectly into time and space, and he *believed* her. He believed she was confused, hopeful, impossibly in love.

When it was over, he felt completely exhausted, like he'd been deep-sea diving without oxygen, willing his body not to draw breath before his desperate kicks brought him to the surface. It was so visceral, Zack slid into a slump in his seat.

"*This* is what you needed to see." Alex paused the video. "Everything you're feeling right now, the audience will feel, too. It can't be helped. The cast is far too compelling, and Mina is…"

"A revelation," Harper finished, staring at her frozen on the screen.

"Indeed." Alex nodded. "But at this point, the audience have morphed into one, and collectively fallen into a deep depression."

"*Fuck*." Zack covered his face with his hands. "You're right. It needs…"

"A pick-me-up," said Harper. "We gotta make people wanna dance."

"Precisely." Alex leaned back in his seat. "You need to break up the melancholy with something light. Something…funny."

"Yeah, I get it." Zack wiped a hand over his face, then cocked a brow at Harper. "You up for an all-nighter? Like old times?"

"Are you kidding me?" Harper grinned broadly. "I *live* for this shit."

Chapter Twenty-Six

BY TWO IN the morning, Zack had written a bawdy, preening show of machismo in lyrics set to Harper's genius mashup of Chopin and hip hop. By four, in Alex's studio, Zack had roughly choreographed a piece for the men in the cast, a high-energy fusion of jazz, tap, and contemporary ballet. But it was missing something, something he wasn't the best at, and he'd need a few hours of sleep before going subway hopping to find it…

Later that morning, he spotted Wilson busking at the Fourteenth Street station in Union Square. Surrounded by morning commuters, Wilson's gritty rendition of Ray Charles's "What'd I Say" filled the underground with soul and the rhythmic slapping of his hands.

"Pattin' juba," Zack said appreciatively. "*Two* buckets this time? You're spoiling people."

"Ay, man." Wilson grinned, accepting a few more tips from passersby. "It's downtown. Gotta bring my A-game."

"Well, you've cleaned up and it's only…" Zack checked his watch. "Seven fifty-two."

Stuffing the money into his guitar case, Wilson packed

up his guitar and stacked the buckets together. "I ain't even close to my goal for today, so I hate to be rude but—"

"That's what I came to talk to you about," said Zack. "I want you to join my cast."

Wilson's laughter was as hard and gritty as his voice. "I'm a solo act, kid."

"Oh, like you were in San Francisco?"

Wilson froze, angling his head to peer up at Zack. "Whatchu know 'bout San Francisco?"

"I know you're Medgar Wilson, and you played the blues circuit for fifteen years before your band ran into financial trouble and split. I know the rents were high, even back then, and New York is friendlier to street performers. I know videos of you online get thousands of hits. And…" Zack leaned against a beam in the walkway, out of the way of people with someplace to be. "I know you're too damn *talented* not to be paid for what you do."

Wilson sat back on his haunches, studying Zack a moment. "Goddamn."

"Little thing called the internet—Look…" Zack crouched in front of Wilson, needing to look him in the eye. "I respect you, so you know where I'm coming from when I say you deserve better than just getting by. If things go well, you're guaranteed a steady paycheck for as long as the show runs. After that, who knows? The exposure could get you more work."

Wilson rubbed his stubbled chin. "It's a nice offer, but I need to think about it…"

"The kicker is, I need your answer now. We're in tech week, and previews start next week."

"*Next week*? Did I hear that right?"

Pulling a sheet of folded paper from his pocket, Zack

offered it to Wilson. "It's batshit, but that's showbiz. I *know* you miss it, and I need you, man. What do you say?"

Wilson opened it up and glanced at it, then back at Zack. "I ain't shucking 'n jiving in no frilly blouse and tights. What you see here is what I can do."

Well, it wasn't a *no*, and he'd kept the address to Tetley Theatre…

"That's what I want, Wilson. This *right* here. Your hands and feet. Your voice. Your *soul*. It's just one number. I'd pay you to teach my guys to pat juba like you, and you'd make a cameo onstage. Play the intro for the song—even record for the studio album."

"Well, I can't make 'em pat juba like *me*—not in such a short time. Not ever, maybe."

"Fair enough."

There was a rumble under their feet as another train approached, coming to rest with a squeak and a hiss of air brakes, the tunnel erupting with the clamor of new foot traffic.

"Fine, I'll do it." Wilson lifted his chin. "Under one condition."

"What's that?"

"I play *my* guitar."

Zack took Wilson's calloused hand. "I think we can swing that."

⁊

Mina stood stupefied in front of Tetley Theatre, gaping at herself on the enormous show poster. On the marquee, surrounded by a cache of lightbulbs not yet lit, was her name spelled in bold, black letters beneath, "Zachary Coen presents Lady in Red." The sentimental (and *very* sudden) notion she might tell her children someday that she fell in love with their father while making this show made tears fill her eyes.

"Starting to hit you, huh?" Kyoko smiled. "Come on, let's get a selfie."

After *six* selfies, Kyoko tugged Mina's arm. "I'm dying to see the inside."

They spent thirty minutes getting lost in all its blue velvet and gold-trimmed glory, joining the other awe-struck people gawking about the incredible space. They traced their fingers over the ornate carvings in the walls and columns and tested the comfort of the new seats filling the house; posed for photos and teased a couple of actors they'd caught kissing in the dressing room. Larger than their previous ones, the dressing rooms were already bursting with boxes of costumes and props. In the luxurious Beaux-Art style bathrooms, they discovered the acoustics were *excellent* for vocal warmups.

"Missed you over the weekend," Kyoko said when they'd finished making noise. "But I get it, strep throat's a bitch."

Right. Faye had told everyone she and Zack were out sick. Hazards of having to kiss your costar for a living. Apparently, everyone had enjoyed a laugh at their expense, thankful for not catching it themselves, and their stand-ins had a chance to shine.

"*Merci.*" Mina met Kyoko's gaze in the mirror, hoping she looked casual. "I feel much better now."

"Good to know." Kyoko started fussing with her perfect shiny hair. "Especially since I went by your apartment Monday to check on you and no one answered the door. Neighbor said she hadn't seen you in days."

Merde.

"And Mister 'For the record' is a slave driver," she continued, washing her hands. "I'm pretty sure he'd have just slapped on a surgical mask and been business as usual, but no one saw him around, either. Not *once* all weekend—the weekend before tech week, no less."

"Kyoko…"

"No one else suspects a thing, by the way—You two bump heads all the time, and you're never seen alone. You make sure not to show up or leave together." Turning and leaning against the vanity, Kyoko studied Mina's face. "But you also touch a lot, when you're not rehearsing. When he gives *me* notes, he doesn't have his hand on my back, damn-near-on-my-ass. Generally, when I want to get someone's attention, I just call out a name. I don't need to touch their arm, or their shoulder…or—"

"*Arrêtes.*" Mina's sweat glands were seeping. "You've made your point."

Kyoko nudged Mina's chin up with her index finger. "Hey, I'm not judging, okay? I lock lips with Riha every chance I get. And this company is like a family, *always* in your business. I wouldn't want to advertise anything, either. He seems *great* when he isn't yelling. I just…want to make sure you know what you're doing. That he isn't taking advantage of you."

"*Non*, it's not like that." Mina shook her head adamantly. "Nothing happened that I did not want. That I don't want. We're in love, but we're being discreet until after the show opens—after people see for themselves I didn't get this role for any reason other than…than—"

"Your legs?" Kyoko grinned.

Mina smacked her hand. "*Oui*, my legs. I'm famous for my extension, you know."

Laughing, Kyoko started for the door. "Yeah, I know. *Move* those sexy legs, or no amount of love in the world is gonna keep Coen from yelling at the both of us."

"It's tech week." Mina shrugged. "He's going to yell anyway."

"Fair point."

Tech week turned out to be just three days. Three twelve-hour days spent fine-tuning, shaping the look and feel of the show, growing the piece throughout. Musicians filled the orchestra pit, playing Harper's beautiful haunting score for the transitions, and his brilliantly remastered internal pieces for the scenes. There were at least double the crew backstage than actors onstage, swarming all over like worker ants carrying twice their weight in set equipment.

Costumes were altered.

Sound and lighting cues were layered in.

Quick changes and props were worked out.

Mina left the theater at dusk on day two with a dozen new scene changes to remember, feeling like she'd been stuffed into a time capsule and shot from a canon. At least her quick change before the party scene was a lot smoother. She was still handled like a rag doll, held up by two people as Amy stuffed her into her beaded ballgown and slipped on her shoes, but they'd got it down to two minutes. In bed that night, she felt more exhausted than she could ever remember being, yet there was a cauldron of energy, anxiety and excitement brewing inside her that made it difficult to sleep.

"*Vzzzzzzt…vzzzzzzzt…vzzzzzzzt…*"

Mina reached blindly for her cell on the nightstand. "*Allô?*"

"Are visiting hours over? If so, I can scale the wall outside and climb through the window."

She threw her covers off with a squeal and climbed from the bed. After a cursory look through the peephole, she opened her apartment door to Zack's slowly widening grin.

"Hey Frenchie." His voice was honey on gravel, and he looked like he'd collapse into a heap in the hallway. "Figured you might have trouble sleeping without someone to twist your limbs around like choking vines."

"*Oh Dieu.*" She slipped her hand into his free one. "Come in, sleepy *lion.*"

"I like when you call me that."

"*Allez.*" She pulled him inside, locking the door behind them. "You look like a corpse."

"You look *hot.*" His eyes trailed her body before shutting tightly closed. "I hope you never discover flannel."

Ignoring that, she cupped his cheek. "When is the last time you slept?"

He swallowed hard. "We talking more than three hours, consecutively?"

"*Zachary…*"

"I seem to remember a castle. And a ghost. Lots and lots of sex."

"*Enfin,* there will be none of that tonight." The microwave clock read half past eleven. "You need to rest."

"I'll be fine so long as we stay in the same time zone longer than two days."

Wordlessly, she helped him undress and slip into bed.

Curled over his chest beneath the covers, she was glad to have stayed in rather than gone out with some of the cast.

"Mmm," he moaned as her fingers played in his hair. "This is the only kind of all-nighter I need from now on."

"I missed you, too—the not-yelling you. I think I will hear you and Chuck yelling in my dreams. How do you feel?"

"Disoriented, honestly. All this time, *Lady in Red* has been growing in this hermetically sealed environment, and now I'm about to blow the lid off so strangers can judge it. It's exciting, but it's also nerve wracking as hell."

"*Oui*, but I know you, *mamour*…" Moving her hand from his hair to his forehead, she smoothed his worry wrinkles. "You feel personally responsible for all of us, and you're afraid of what might happen if the show doesn't succeed."

Heavily, his chest rose and fell against hers, his breath tickling her face.

"You have to let go," she murmured. "Trust the process. Trust that, no matter what happens, no one else can interpret this story the same as you, and that alone makes it special." Cupping his face in both hands, she kissed him. "Slow down. Stay a little while in the moment. *Joie de vivre.* I'm proud of you, you've worked so hard. Now it's time to *enjoy* it."

The philharmonic of late night New York City filtered through the walls. Never sleeping. Awake and dreaming. *Alive.*

"You give good pep talk, Yoda." He rubbed her back, then tightened his arms around her. "I don't know how to thank you."

Kissing his neck, she rested her cheek on his chest again. "You just did, *mamour*. Now go to sleep."

When she woke up in the morning, he was already

gone. There was a note stuck to her bedside lamp, written on a pink Post-It:

> *No act will ever be better than the one we got together.*
>
> *Love,*
>
> *Z*

Kissing the note, she slipped it into the drawer. She had an hour and a half until her ten o'clock call time, so after a good, long stretch, she went to take a shower. It still smelled like him.

⌇

Onstage, Mina slapped the shit out of Sebastian.

"*Jesus Christ.*" Zack massaged between his eyebrows. Every cast and crew member within earshot stopped to gawk toward the stage. "Stay on script, Mina."

"*Enfin…*" If elegance had an attitude, it looked like her stance. "Tell that to *l'idiote*!"

"I-I don't know what happened." Sebastian sputtered, hand to his face. "What did I say?"

"Faye," Mina said saccharinely, tapping her foot. "*S'il vous plait*, would you Google the difference between '*baiser*' and '*un baiser*'?"

"*For fuck's sake*," Zack muttered under his breath but didn't protest otherwise. Mina looked like she'd skin him with her teeth. Plus, he was curious to know himself.

"*Uh*-kay," said Faye, swiping and tapping at her phone screen a moment. "Oh…*crap.*"

"*Precisely.*" Mina glared at Sebastian, then stormed off stage left.

Sebastian jogged after her, presumably to apologize. Everyone with a smartphone had obviously looked it up, too, because gasps and muffled laughter filled the air.

"Everyone take ten," Zack said irritably. To Faye, he asked. "Do I even wanna know?"

Faye's brow answered before she did. "Let's just say it might be time to re-up that sexual harassment email."

"Fan*tastic.*"

"Hey, Sebastian can handle himself, okay? He was in *Macbeth* last year. Kid knows how to take a slap."

"I wasn't concerned, but for the sake of neutrality, maybe it won't hurt to re-up the 'How to Keep Your Cool at Work' email, too."

"We don't have a—oh, right, pull Mina aside and ask her to use her words? Will-do."

"No one betas my brain like you," he crooned. "We got enough comp tickets for friends and family?"

Faye looked insulted. "I ticked that box a week ago, I'll have you know. Even bumped into the deputy general manager this morning. We're sold out tonight, and tomorrow, and every tomorrow clear through next week."

"No shit?"

"This is a shit-free zone, my friend."

"God, you're an *angel.*" This time his tone wasn't mocking at all, and he swept a hand through his hair. "I've been a lunatic, haven't I?"

"It's just jitters. Don't *worry*. Everyone's looking sharp, and all that excitement is infectious. It's gonna spread through the audience tomorrow night like an apocalyptic plague, you'll see."

"I hope so."

It did.

The show wasn't perfect, but it *was* remarkable.

For two weeks, the cast gave their all, maintaining a dazzling, fast-paced energy, building tension, imparting the more emotional scenes with raw honesty and compassion, and recovering beautifully the few times moments went askew. It was easier than Zack thought it would be to relinquish control, to let the performance spread its wings and take flight. Because he was *in* it with his flock. Onstage, he wasn't the leader, the point bird. Onstage, they were fluid, taking turns at the front, soaring on the energy of an audience fully-engaged and invested in the story they were telling.

With each performance, moments shifted, and intentions changed. They'd rehearse any adjustments in the afternoon and perform them at night, until audience reactions to the variations implemented felt palpable, and excitement for the show mounted.

The bawdy number with Wilson garnered more laughter than Zack could have hoped for, Wilson's hard, gritty vocals blending with the crisp voices of Zack and the cast's principal males in a hilarious, blatantly arrogant song:

They say that Pah-ree is a den of debauchery,

seething with all manner of erotic immorality!

When really,

Really,

Really,

Those puritans take offense

At any kind of decadence.

Fun-hating henchmen!

jealous of us Frenchmen!

Yes, a den of debauchery,

Seething with immorality.

But really,

Really,

Really,

We're not godless, we swear it. Quite the contrary.

We like charity and verity and even missionary.

And truly,

Truly,

Truly,

They should be praising our largess,

For in Pah-ree, we find glee in both wife and mistress!

...

The choreography was short and explosive; they used their hands and bodies as instruments to communicate. Stomping, slapping and patting their arms, legs, chest, and cheeks in an exuberant pattin' juba, they had the audience in an uproar before intermission.

When it was time for Mina's solo, Zack watched from the wings, almost lightheaded with anticipation. Walking onstage in her simple red dress and pointe shoes, her hair loose and makeup toned down, she took her mark and faced the curtain. Turning her face toward him, she met his eyes briefly, and he sensed her fear-laced excitement.

You've got this, he telepathed as the mirror mosaics descended all around her. *Just breathe.*

She did, two great big calming breaths, and then Chuck made the lighting calls. Overhead, the chandelier shimmered, and her skin sparkled like diamonds.

"House lights off," came the cue from Chuck.

A hush fell over the audience.

"Curtain…"

The curtain went up, and Harper's "Song for Camille" floated from the orchestra pit. Mina launched into her free-style with a painfully slow développé. Supporting herself on her right leg, she lifted her left leg and both arms until they were extended high above her head. She held her pose for several seconds in a gorgeous display of strength and control, then moved seamlessly into a promenade, lowering her leg to waist-level and turning a perfect circle on one foot.

She moved again, like water, and Zack felt the stage fall away…and the ceiling and the walls, and earth and matter. Only his soul was left, suspended in midair. Weightless. He sensed the thirteen hundred patrons of Tetley Theatre sharing the moment with him, witnessing France's Étoile become an American star.

At the end of the show on Saturday, the audience leapt to its feet, and Zack's heart left his chest to levitate somewhere over their heads. The sound of it beating seemed to drown out the crowd calls and mass of applause as the cast took their bows.

Lady in Red was locked and ready to face the press on Sunday.

❧

Hours before the final preview performance, Mina joined the company in the theater for Zack's champagne toast. Standing center stage and looking ten feet tall with obvious pride, he thanked the crew for bringing his dream to life, the cast for supplying bodies for the voices in his head, and the entire company for delivering a classical story with the vivacity it needed to feel accessible to anyone who saw it.

Enfin, he sounded a little…*touched*, but she knew he was having a vulnerable moment, and it made her sniffle.

"I think this is the part where I'm supposed to say, 'ignore the critics.'" He scratched his forehead. "Personally, I recommend pretending they're Statler and Waldorf from The Muppets, heckling us from their balcony seats. — They're gonna *hate* it, no matter what we do…" He cracked a crooked smile, waiting for the laughter to subside. "So let's have *fun* tonight." Lifting his glass, his eyes lingered for a split second on Mina's then moved over the rest of the group. "*Joie de vivre.*"

"*Joie de vivre!*" they shouted in unison, and Mina laugh-sobbed.

The noise outside her dressing room permeated the thin walls and the delicate layers of her skin, tightening into knots of nervous energy in her stomach. Inside, the room looked and smelled like *un fleuriste*, her own secret garden reflected in the vanity mirror. Her father's parents sent blue orchids in their stead, and a card expressing their excitement to see her on opening night. There was a bowl of pink water lilies from Sophie, and an arrangement of jasmine and lilies from her mother. *Mémé* and *pépé* had stopped by an hour earlier to gift her with chocolate, and Vera sent the entire cast white roses. But nothing yet from Zack…

Carefully, she put on her elaborate Victorian wig. Her own hair was blown straight, pin curled and tucked under a stocking for the first half of the show. Later, for her bedroom pas de deux with Zack, Amy would help remove the wig and pins, fluffing it out into soft waves. It had taken longer than usual to apply the heavy-handed makeup for Camille, but she managed not to look like a clown when she put the finishing touches on her deep red lip. In fact, she admitted, she looked *transformed*.

"*Merde!*" She jumped at the loud knock on her door, stabbing herself in the eye with false lashes.

Étienne popped his head in with a single rose between his teeth, a bottle of wine in hand. Instantly, his face fell, and he plucked the bud from his mouth. "Is it safe, *bichette*? Or am I in danger of falling victim to your homicidal pre-show jitters?"

"Don't tease me, I'm *terrified!*" she cried, furiously blinking away the sting in her eye. "We've been doing this for weeks! I wake myself talking in my sleep, running lines…I don't understand why I'm so nervous now."

"*Allez.*" He closed the door against the ruckus in the hall, then came over to kiss her cheek. Setting his spoils on the vanity, he leaned back against it in a suit tailored to him like a second skin. "Everything about you was made for high drama—your temper, your voice, your *excellente* genetics, even your little ogre feet…"

"*Ah!*"

He ducked the mascara she threw at him smoothly and laughed, which further irritated her, and his expression softened. "The stakes are higher tonight, but you've spent most of your life being judged by scarier people than the ones waiting out there. What's the worst that could happen?"

"Someone steps on my dress, and I'm naked in front of thousands of people?" Folding her arms across her silk-robed chest, she sighed. "Don't bother telling me to imagine them all naked. It won't work, and I can't see them anyway because of the stage lights."

"*Non*, you need something more pragmatic than that." He rubbed his smooth chin a moment, then lifted a dark brow. "Pragmatically speaking, your boobs are high and perky, and you've been waxed within an inch of your life. If you *do* end up teaching us all an anatomy lesson, this show's run will be solidified faster than you can pull your dress back up. So you see, it's win-win."

Laughing despite her nerves, she pinched his slim waist.

He caught her attacking hand in both of his. "You are living art, *bichette*. No one expects you to be perfect. It's more important that you—"

"Never be dishonest," they said at the same time.

"I…*merci, ma moitié*." She squeezed his hand, thanking her lucky stars again to see him alive and well. "You always know exactly what to say."

The thirty-minute call sounded, and after a quick knock, Amy slipped in. "Hope I'm not interrupting…"

"Of course not." Étienne pressed a kiss to the back of Mina's hand and released it, then paralyzed poor Amy with his magnetic smile on his way to the door. "Break a leg, as they say. It's an utterly ridiculous sentiment, but, *alors*, breaking a leg is worse than exposing yourself, is it not? And when in Rome…" With a wink, he left her to finish dressing.

❧

No one was more useless on press night than the director. The work was already done, and if Zack weren't in the show himself, he'd simply wish everyone well, humor Vera with some harmless flirting up in her balcony where she sat in her dress with the enormous train, then wring his hands for two hours and try not to sweat through his suit. He had Manny to thank for not letting the women in his life turn the backstage area into a block party. They'd visited him in his dressing room for five minutes, wished him luck, and gone to find their seats, leaving Zack with six shades of lipstick smudges on his face.

He washed it off and suited up as Armand, then went in search of Mina. Her dressing room was a bust, and shortly after the twenty-minute call, Jamal stopped him near the narrow iron steps to the fly tower.

"Ay, boss man…" Jamal leaned in conspiratorially. "Your girl's up there on the bridge psyching herself up. I can keep it clear for five minutes, tops."

"Ah, that'd be great. Thanks, man."

Zack took the steps two at a time, crossing two very narrow platforms to a wider one forty feet above the house and spanning the width of the theater. He found her at its center looking nineteenth-century regal, gripping the iron rail and looking over the edge. He knew she felt his approach, his steps shaking the catwalk. Turning in his direction, her eyes widened, and she offered him a tremulous little smile.

"There you are," he said. "Been looking all over for you." Tempted as he was to touch her, he didn't dare. He was sure Jamal was doing his due diligence, but there were just too many people seated below them and rushing all around. Instead, he stood about two feet away, admiring her transformation. "You look amazing, *petite*. Interesting place for a repose, though…"

"So do you." Her eyes flashed her appreciation, then she pressed a hand to her abdomen, her chest heaving with deep, measured breaths. "I needed a minute. It's just occurred to me how different this is than anything I've ever done. I was looking in the mirror and I couldn't see myself anymore. I couldn't think, and I…I…"

"There was a chink in your armor," he said softly. "You needed some air."

She gasped at the words, and he knew she was remembering the night they met, too.

"I want you to have something." He slipped his hand into the inside pocket of his tailcoat and removed a small wooden figurine. Allowing himself to touch her for just a second, he reached for her wrist, turning it palm-up, and settled the little swan into her hand. "I thought of a million things I could give you, but none of them felt big enough, important enough. Then I thought, maybe it's the smallest things that create the biggest memories."

Her fingers traced over the detailing on one of the swan's wings, then she turned it over, and her eyes filled with tears. Underneath, a single word was carved:

Petite.

"It's perfect," she whispered. "*Merci, mamour.* You're right—I won't forget this."

Staring at the stunning incarnation of his dream, his chest aching from wanting to hold her, and her artful stage makeup under threat of ruination, he couldn't think of a finer moment. The ten-minute call sounded, and Mina sniffed.

"I didn't get you anything," she said like an apology.

Shaking his head, he smiled. "You've already given me everything."

♥ FIN. ♥

Epilogue

Two years later

MINA WAITED IN the wings for her cue. Butterflies swarmed in her stomach, threatening to lift her from the floor and float her over the stage before it was time.

Non, not yet.

Closing her eyes, she shut out the commotion all around her backstage, focusing on her breathing. Slow and deep. In through her nose. Out through her mouth.

There, that was better.

Now she could open the origami swan Zack had given her without her hands shaking madly. Carefully, she undid the intricate folds, revealing his beautiful penmanship between college-ruled lines.

Oh mon Dieu. He'd written her a poem.

"Pour mon Cygne D'or"

Merde. The words were already beginning to blur…

The City of Light lent its brightest star

to the City that Never Sleeps;

to a theater well-known,

Pas De Deux

which rivaled its own,
and kept her beloveds close.
Thousands came to see her,
in the beating heart of winter,
braving Yuletide crowds and snow,
to witness History turn on her toes.

Beneath a crown of diamonds and feathers,
a bodice replete in plumes,
danced History's fine hue,
magnificent through
the stark white of her coveted costume.
An unlikely princess,
a stunning success,
she shattered the homologous spell
and led her bevy well.

Front-row and center sat the new master
of the eminent Great White Way.
In this hall of ornate gild,
he witnessed her dream fulfilled,
on a stage legends had danced upon.
He would never forget tonight,
the night his Lady in Red took flight

and skin of deep fawn

grew wings of a beautiful Queen Swan.

"*Merci*." Mina accepted a tissue from Amy with a tearful smile.

"Stoppit, you." Amy helped to tuck the awkwardly re-folded page into the sweetheart neckline of Mina's bodice. "You're in head-to-toe Christian LaCroix. *I* should be weeping."

With a wink, she performed her magic trick, disappearing backstage until Mina needed her again. Seconds later, a shimmering lake stretched across the stage beneath a moonlit sky, and Tchaikovsky called to her from the orchestra pit.

She took another deep breath.

Her eyes closed and opened once more.

And then, Odette flew.

Author's Note

As in his portrayal of Mr. Darcy in the 1995 adaptation of Pride & Prejudice (the best version in existence), Colin Firth is charismatic and dreamy as Armand Duval in the 1984 movie, Camille. That's all I really wanted to say, that the Colin Firth version of anything is the best version.

Acknowledgments

I want to thank my editors, Alex and Vicki for possessing hawk eyes and the patience of Job, and for seeing *me*. This book was a monster before you made it pretty. I owe so much to the incredible and incredibly astute beta, sensitivity and ESL readers: thanks to you, this story is rich and full-bodied. To the lovely Melanie, Mary, "Loops," Kimberly and Nina, without whom the incredible worlds of ballet and theater would not have come alive so vividly in this story, *thank you*! Many thanks to Caroline, my sweet French friend who taught me to curse properly. Thanks to The Mister, for being chauffeur to my womb fruit so I could finish this gem. Thank you, friends and family near and far, for believing in me, and showing me I am capable of so much more than I think. And to everyone who reads this story, I hope it touches you the way it's touched me.

ABOUT THE AUTHOR

Lynn Turner inherited her writing gene from her mother, who created fantastic tales about witches, invisible worlds and talking animals, and read them to her children at night. Lynn isn't as great with the voices as her mother, but Rome wasn't built in a day.

She discovered romance far too young, when a mission to find a young adult fantasy title led her to historical romance. She spent hours skimming those sumptuous pages, drinking in the vivid descriptions of settings and clothes, feisty heroines and looming lords, and poetic language. (She may or may not have enjoyed the PG-13 bits too, tucking a new title beneath her pillow at night).

She enjoys character-driven narratives most, and anything that transports her someplace else. Passionate about food and travel, she features healthy doses of both in the stories she crafts. Above all, she is dedicated to writing inclusive stories that explore what it means to be imperfectly human.

When she isn't writing, she's traveling, dreaming of traveling, or watching old Samantha Brown travelogue videos and wishing she had her job. She and her husband share their home in California with their two extraordinary children and sometimes cat, Bowie.

88447270R00253

Made in the USA
Middletown, DE
09 September 2018